THE LIGHT IN THE LABYRINTH

The light in the labyrinth

WENDY J. DUNN

METROPOLIS
INK

First edition 2014

Copyright © 2014 by Wendy J. Dunn

ISBN 978-0-9807219-2-8

The Light in the Labyrinth is a work of fiction inspired by the life and times of Anne Boleyn and her niece Katherine Carey. Names, characters, places, and incidents are products of the author's imagination or are used fictitiously.

A METROPOLIS INK BOOK

web www.metropolisink.com

email hello@metropolisink.com

Dedicated to my daughter, Elisabeth.
From little girl to adulthood, you have always
taught me the true meaning of courage.

Tudor, Boleyn and Howard family members pertinent to
The Light in the Labyrinth

m = married

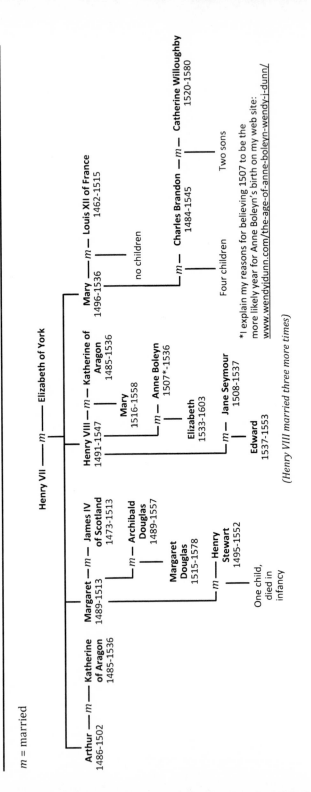

*I explain my reasons for believing 1507 to be the more likely year for Anne Boleyn's birth on my web site: www.wendyjdunn.com/the-age-of-anne-boleyn-wendy-j-dunn/

(Henry VIII married three more times)

The Howard Family Tree

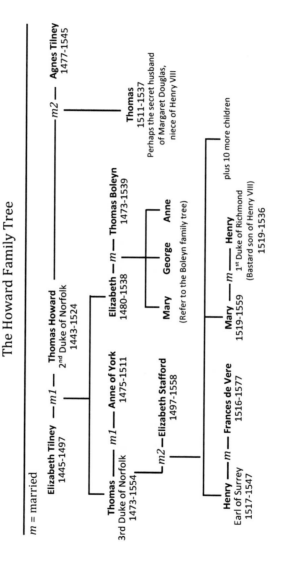

m = married

Elizabeth Tilney —m1— **Thomas Howard** —m2— **Agnes Tilney**
1445-1497   2nd Duke of Norfolk   1477-1545
                         1443-1524

Thomas —m1— **Anne of York**   **Elizabeth** —m— **Thomas Boleyn**
3rd Duke of Norfolk   1475-1511   1480-1538   1473-1539
1473-1554
        m2—**Elizabeth Stafford**   **Thomas**
            1497-1558   1511-1537
                                                                    Perhaps the secret husband
                                                                    of Margaret Douglas,
                                                                    niece of Henry VIII

Mary   George   Anne
(Refer to the Boleyn family tree)

Henry —m— **Frances de Vere**   **Mary** —m— **Henry**
Earl of Surrey   1516-1577   1519-1559   1st Duke of Richmond
1517-1547   (Bastard son of Henry VIII)
                                                  1519-1536

plus 10 more children

The Boleyn Family Tree

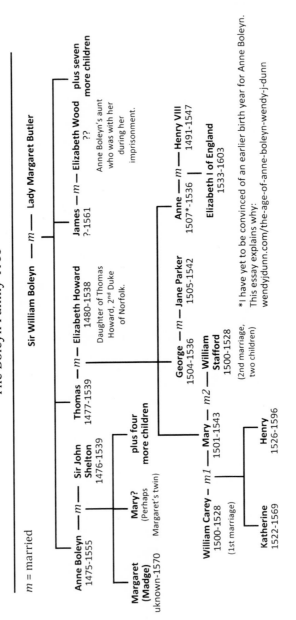

m = married

Sir William Boleyn — m — Lady Margaret Butler

Anne Boleyn
1475-1555

— m —

Sir John
Shelton
1476-1539

plus four
more children

Mary?
(Perhaps
Margaret's twin)

Margaret
(Madge)
uknown-1570

Thomas — m — Elizabeth Howard
1477-1539   1480-1538
                   Daughter of Thomas
                   Howard, 2ⁿᵈ Duke
                   of Norfolk.

James — m — Elizabeth Wood
?-1561   ??
                Anne Boleyn's aunt
                who was with her
                during her
                imprisonment.

plus seven
more children

George — m — Jane Parker
1504-1536   1505-1542

William
Stafford
1500-1528
(2nd marriage,
two children)

William Carey — m1 — Mary — m2 —
1500-1528   1501-1543

Katherine
1522-1569

Henry
1526-1596

(1st marriage)

Anne — m — Henry VIII
1507*-1536   1491-1547

Elizabeth I of England
1533-1603

*I have yet to be convinced of an earlier birth year for Anne Boleyn.
This essay explains why:
wendyjdunn.com/the-age-of-anne-boleyn-wendy-j-dunn

1

Rochford Hall, November 1535

"You were foolish to marry him," Kate said, perched on the edge of her mother's unmade bed. Her family had more troubles than most. They were of noble blood, yet poor. Kate balled her hands in anger, thinking, *'Tis my mother's fault. She's the one who has brought shame on us. A sister of the Queen of England should know better than to wed a commoner.*

She seethed in her black mood, the black mood that had brought her to her mother's chambers. Now she desired to annoy her mother by acting a child rather than a maid near to fourteen summers, and swung her legs, backward and forth. Her lady mother, as if aware of Kate's intent, did not look her way, but pulled the drawstrings of her red kirtle around her tiny waist. Nimble fingers knotted cords. Two months after the birth of her fourth child, she was as slender as a maiden—indeed, more slender than Kate.

Kate's heart burned with jealousy. Not only was her mother beautiful—more beautiful than she could ever hope to be—but since her churching, her mother's every waking hour was taken up with caring for her new baby son and infant daughter. It was time her mother remembered she also had another daughter.

Her mother shot her a look from underneath a shifting curtain of golden hair. "Remember to whom you speak," she snapped before snatching up the faded, patched bodice beside Kate and pulling it over her white shift.

"Pray, why should I remember?" Kate murmured under her breath. While her mother dressed, she crumpled her own skirts, pieced together from remnants found in the clothes coffers and made anew. Since the unwise marriage to Stafford, spending coin on material for a new gown or even a simple shift was out the question. Kate wanted to jump off the bed and stamp her foot. "Madam," she at last spat out, "'twas not me who dishonoured the family."

Straightening, Lady Mary stilled with widening eyes. Her mouth moved, but she made no sound; tears spilled down her pale, drawn face. Kate stood, and brought her hands up to her heating cheeks. She wished she could call the words back. For the past year, her anger had brewed, bubbled over, and scalded her too-tender mother. Confused, hating herself, she reached out her hand. "Mama, forgive me—"

Her mother waved her away. "How dare you!" She stared at Kate as if seeing a stranger. "Do not speak to me of honour or family. You understand nothing; nothing." The baby whimpered and she rocked the cradle. "Hush, poppet," she crooned, brushing away tears. She faced Kate again to speak in a quieter, firmer voice. "The only true honour I've known in my life has come from becoming the wife of William Stafford. Will loves me—despite the world and its opinion." A grimace distorted her beautiful face. "Why should I marry a man for his wealth or his bloodlines, when good fortune gave me the love of a true and honest man?"

Kate fidgeted under her mother's concern.

"I want the same for you. Why do you think I refuse to allow your grandfather to find you a husband? You will thank me for it; 'tis better to beg your bread with a man you love than end up simply as a man's property." Her mother firmed her mouth. "Can you not see how Will treats me? Can you not see his gentleness, his respect, his devotion? Believe me, I am richer than your aunt."

Lady Mary bent over the cradle and tucked the blanket around the tiny, swaddled infant, talking all the while. "I am a patient woman, Kate. I've excused your rudeness and closed my eyes and ears to your cruelty to my husband when he has only offered you kindness. Every night I've prayed—every night I've asked the good Lord God to help you see the error of your ways so again you would be my good and dutiful daughter. But no more. I vow to you, my child, I will use the rod. Aye, Katherine, I will use it if you continue down this road."

Half-covering her mouth in shock, Kate stared at her mother.

The baby bleated and filled up his lungs to ring out a loud cry. He kept crying until Kate clenched her fists at her sides. She wanted to block her ears. She wanted to hit something. She wanted to push over the cradle. To silence her brother forever. *Silence my brother forever?* Frightened by her thoughts, tears smarted her eyes. *Oh God! Dear God, I didn't mean it!*

Her mother gathered up the baby, blanket and all. Now she wanted to do the same, hug the child to her and beg for forgiveness. *I don't want you dead, but I wish both you and your sister had never been born. I will only share my mother with my brother Harry—not low-born, half-bloods like you.*

Sitting on the coffer at the end of the bed, Lady Mary loosened the drawstrings of her bodice and nursed the baby. Kate squirmed, discomforted by the sight of the white, swollen breast. Blue veins traced their way to her mother's heart. Reminded of life and mortality, she raised her eyes to

Lady Mary's taut, grim face. Feeling slapped, she dropped her gaze and stepped away.

"Do you want to know why I do not use the rod?" her mother asked. "Would you like to see the scars from my lord father's discipline?" Lady Mary laughed, gazing above her daughter's head.

Kate shook her head, taken aback by her mother's words and the sharp, bitter edge to her laughter. She had rarely seen her mother in this mood, with her temper so easily roused.

Watching her mother gaze down at the sucking baby before she stroked his fair head, Kate welcomed, after her sinful thoughts, an unexpected connection to her tiny brother. Despite their different fathers, he, too, was blonde like their mother, blonde like her and Harry. Kate drew out a tendril of her uncombed hair and studied its reddish tinge. *No. Close, but not completely alike.* For several heartbeats, she daydreamed of her tall father, the father she could barely remember. His face obscured, the sun shone down on his head and turned his hair aflame.

Lady Mary kept her eyes on her infant. Her low voice trembled. "The scars from his rod are still there for you to see."

Kate shuffled her feet. "What did you do?" she asked, not daring to pose the real question in her mind: *How could my kind, good-natured grandfather beat anyone?* She squirmed, putting aside the memory of his last visit. Nay—that day, and her mother's scars, must have been her mother's fault. *Everything was her fault.*

Eagle-proud that his second daughter was consort to the King, and proud, too, that he was now Earl of Wiltshire and Ormond, her grandfather shared that pride by his choice of costly gifts to Kate, his oldest granddaughter. "Ah," he would say, "the blessing of fine grandchildren. You and your brother are truly your father's children." He would laugh then and kiss her brow, ignoring the distress of her lady mother; it always upset her mother when she was reminded of Kate's father.

Kate bent her head to hide her smile. Her mother's eyes filled with tears whenever Kate mentioned her father, William Carey. It proved to Kate that her mother loved him more than she did Stafford. Happy in that knowledge, Kate remained content to keep her precious memories of her father to herself.

Her lord grandfather had visited them rarely at Rochford Hall. The last time was when he had come to express his anger at her mother's new marriage, his raised voice roaring in the solar so none could fail to hear him. "You not only unforgivably dishonoured the name of the family, but also the sire of your children," he shouted. After he rode away, her mother had hurried away to her room and locked the door. Despite its thick wood, Kate heard from within the sound of weeping. There had been no more visits or gifts since that awful day.

Lifting her gaze again, it seemed her mother, now focused utterly on her baby, didn't wish to look at her. *Is she still angry?* Kate pondered the threat. Her mother always disregarded their household priest when he warned her: "Spare the rod and spoil the child." Once, she only needed to narrow her eyes in Kate's direction for her to remember to behave. Now a devil had her in its grip. She struggled to control her rage, her jealousy, her smouldering resentment. Far too often, they devoured her.

"What did I do?" Lady Mary asked. She shifted the baby to her other breast. "I was unwise and spoke my mind about the offer of marriage to ... your father." She paused and stared at Kate. "As if I wished to marry a man I knew only by name. Daughter, I was not much older than you." Her lips formed an uneven gash in her unhappy face. "My harsh words angered my lord father. He called for his rod and broke me into submission. It was many days before I slept on my back again. I vowed then I would never use the rod on a child of mine." Lady Mary laughed. "But I had my revenge. The beating inconvenienced your grandfather, and he needed all his skills of diplomacy to smooth out matters before the wedding could take place. Your grandfather doesn't make a habit of damaging his property, but Anne and I had our ways to rile him."

Kate shrugged and stopped really listening. Basking in her own youth, Kate disregarded her mother's ancient history, thinking it no concern of hers. Mention of her aunt recalled to her the recent letter from court. She shuffled her feet for a second time. "I want to go to court."

Startled, her mother looked up, her quick movement dislodging the baby. Deprived of his milk, he yelled in protest. Murmuring, her mother resettled him and gazed again at her daughter. Had she mistaken her mother's fear? Now her stern expression made Kate blink.

"Why? For whatever reason would you want to go there?" her mother asked.

Kate hesitated over her answer, not brave enough to tell her mother how much she wanted to be with her aunt. From her first years, she had always idolised Aunt Nan, desiring to be just like her. She did not want to be weak like her own mother—a woman satisfied with so little. But a kernel of truth offered Kate an easy answer, one her mother would better understand. "I miss Harry. I haven't seen my brother for so long. Since—" She bit back the rest of the words, but her unsaid accusation thrummed between them.

Lady Mary did not move. Grief cut into her face: she no longer looked like a young woman. "I miss him, too." Holding the babe securely in the crook of her arm, she rubbed her eyes with her free hand. "I cannot understand my sister. Does she not realise how my heart aches for my son? Every day, I pray for my summons to court.... I beg her to send for me ... only to receive from my sister a gold cup and a bag of angels. She thinks coin and a costly cup, a reminder of the status I reject, recompenses me for Harry, for my son. Then she asks for you to come. Nay, commands you to come." The pain unhidden on her face, she blinked, her mouth moving silently, as if in prayer. She began to speak. "It was difficult enough before Will. Now I am punished and utterly robbed of Harry because I married for love." Lady Mary lowered her head, nestling the baby closer. "It seems she now wishes to rob me of you. Methinks Nan is jealous. Mayhap she has reason."

Kate almost laughed. "Jealous? Jealous of you?" She lifted her head in pride. "Aunt Nan is Queen of England."

Her mother raised her eyes, and a shutter fell down. "You're too young to understand."

Furious, Kate charged towards her mother, stopping but a step or two from her. "Always, you say that. I am near fourteen, Mother. Old enough to wed, old enough to leave this place."

Lady Mary's eyes flashed. "You are old enough when I say so and not before."

Before Kate could hurl back an answer, the door opened. Ducking his head under the low lintel, honey brown hair sweeping its curl against his shoulders, her stepfather entered the chamber. Seeing his wife nursing his son, he dimpled his boyish grin. Kate clicked her tongue in annoyance. When her stepfather noticed her, his wide smile all but disappeared. "Our Kate causing trouble again?"

Kate stiffened, and almost choked. It wasn't a question, rather a statement. She wanted to spit and snarl at him. *How dare you? How dare you?* He had no right, no right at all to lay claim to her. Since wedding her mother, he blithely purloined a father's role and showed his wide-eyed wonder when she took offence at his mummer's playacting. Was he such a fool, so blind, not to realise she detested him, that he could never replace her lord father?

Kate fought back her desire to shout, "He's not my father." Time after time, her lady mother forgot the man of true nobility who lay cold these last nine years in the grave. Kate did not forget. Her father lived in her memory bathed in golden light, a laughing, gentle giant who came home bearing gifts. He taught her to ride, to sing and make music. At night, he sat her on his lap, telling her stories about England's kings and queens. Sometimes he pretended Kate was a princess, making her giggle when he fell to his knees and begged for her boon, her mercy. Safe in his arms, she fell asleep listening to the croon of his lullaby. He still sang in her dreams— dreams in which she ran and ran towards the sound of his song, searching for him, calling for him, but never finding him. She awoke, weeping, her heart broken anew.

Even dead, her lord father, William Carey, was worth ten of Stafford—and more.

Bent over the baby, Lady Mary drew a deep breath. "She desires to go to court, Will."

Her stepfather frowned and looked towards Kate, then back at his wife. He smiled like a lovelorn country bumpkin and strode across the room, his stepdaughter all forgotten. He kissed her mother, next kissing the top of his son's head. Kate clutched the sides of her gown, once more wanting to hit something. Every day was the same, watching her mother and her husband at their love games. She might as well not exist; utterly engrossed in each other and their little daughter and baby son, their world left no room for her.

Her stepfather stirred. "Why not let her go?"

"You know why." Her mother spoke so quietly, so distressed, Kate stared at her, confused.

Her husband touched her cheek and dropped the hand to her shoulder. "You cannot protect Kate all her life."

Her mother shook her head and gazed at the sleeping baby before pulling firmer his swaddling cloth. His stomach full for a time and his mouth open, her half-brother reminded Kate of an ugly, dead fish.

"'Tis too soon," her mother said. "I do not forget what happened to me. I never will." Glancing Kate's way again, her stepfather kissed her mother. "Mary, tell her."

Kate's mother stared up, her face ashen and her eyes large and panicked. "I cannot. I vowed to William."

"Carey's long dead." He softened his tone and took her hand. "Sweetheart, no one expects you to keep a vow to a dead man. Think you. The vow was only important while he lived."

Lady Mary shook her head and lowered her face to smell the baby; she often did this since his birth. A faraway look transformed her face.

Where is this conversation leading? Sadder stories about Mother's youth? Kate wanted none of it. Her mother's past didn't concern her—even her lady mother's vow to her lord father. As long as it didn't prevent Kate from going to court, her mother was welcome to her secrets.

Audibly sighing, Mary Stafford dropped her husband's hand. "I swore to William, on my immortal soul, I would never speak of it. I cannot break a vow such as that. I will not." She turned. "Leave us, Kate."

"But—"

Her mother's eyes sparked in warning, her hand gesturing towards the door. "Leave us, I say."

"Do as your mother asks of you," her stepfather said. He touched his son's cheek, not even bothering to glance her way.

"You cannot tell me what to do," Kate snapped.

"Kate." Babe in arms, her mother rose, her eyes blue fire in a white, furious face. "Leave now, or I will find that rod and you'll rue the day you were born."

Kate opened her mouth, but her mother's burning gaze sizzled her protest into unspoken ash. She licked her dry lips. She had never seen her mother so angry, or so hard.

Her beloved lord Father had died from the Sweat when she was only five. One day laughing and singing, teaching her to play the lute, the next day, in the grave. William Carey was no more. She wished he had never died; that he was here to protect her, care for her. Guide her. Love her. Life would have been so different. She would have grown up with her brother, rather than grieve again two years later when her grandfather forced her mother to relinquish Harry. But her brother was the heir, the all-important male; he had to be raised at court to learn his proper position. From that time, Kate could wrap her lady mother around her little finger and get her own way. Her mother's unspoken terror that her daughter, too, could be stolen from her made Kate feel the most precious thing in the world.

She glared at her stepfather's lean, broad-shouldered back, wishing she could dagger him with a look. Taking the sleeping babe from her mother, he carefully and tenderly placed him back into his deep cradle, watched on by his wife with a beatific smile on her face. *Jesu', she looks like the chapel's holy Madonna.* Her mother was such a fool. Both of them, seemingly no longer aware of her, were fools. *Especially him.*

She blamed her mother for turning her life upside down, but shouldn't she lay the true blame at her stepfather's feet? Yes, all of it was his fault. Despite missing her brother, Harry, she and her mother were happy together. She had gloried in her mother's love and needed no one else but her.

She was ten when Stafford came to court her mother, and he had swept her away from Kate with his smiles, his sweet talk, his caresses.

Before her jealous eyes, her mother blossomed, became a young woman again. Marrying him she acted the bride, wed for the first time. Kate could not understand why her mother surrendered to him with joy and a bewildering relief. She could not understand her mother at all. Like a flower in full bloom these past years, her mother stood straight and tall, and astonishingly strong. A flower with petals opening to the sun; the sun of her husband's love. It was Kate who wilted now.

"Katherine Carey," said her mother, standing next to her husband. "Why are you still here?" She scowled at Kate, fisted a hand and enclosed it in the other.

Kate decided it was time to flee. About to shut the door,

she heard her stepfather say, "You've no choice; send the girl to court."

Astounded to hear him champion her, she paused outside the chamber. She cocked her head, full of disbelief as she listened to Stafford. Soft words, soothing voice and no doubt gentle hands—the thought flaming her anger again—at last coaxed from her mother the permission Kate needed. Kate shook her head in bemusement. He had patiently used the same tactics with her mother as he did with a nervous, man-shy horse.

My mother a horse? A ray of knowledge pierced the ugly laughter bubbling in her throat and prevented its escape. *Man-shy?* Her twice-wed, beautiful mother—*man-shy?* All Kate's life, her mother allowed few into her circle of trust and rarely ever a man. One year it took of Will's well planned wooing before her mother completely gave her heart to him. Most women, even her mother and sister, she viewed with suspicion; she put up a barrier of protection between her and the world. *Even with her mother and sister? Why?* Kate carefully shut the door. Something, or someone, must have hurt her. And not a little hurt. A hurt she could not forget. A hurt that still bled.

From the chamber came the sound of her mother weeping. Surely her going to court was no reason for her mother to sob like this, like her heart broke—or as if she had just learnt someone had died. Kate wiped her clammy hands on her gown and walked away, unable to shake away her sense of foreboding.

2

Outside the window, a lark broke into a ripple of morning song, joyfully adoring the new day. Finishing plaiting her hair, Kate fidgeted while her mother bolted down the lid of her clothes coffer.

"You truly wish this, Kate?" Mary Stafford half-sat on the coffer, hands planted on either side, her slim, long fingers curled over the carved wood's edge. "Am I wise to let you go...?"

Kate digested the question, and her mother's unfinished thought. She glanced at her again. Head bowed, strands of blond hair escaped from her untied linen cap and curled against her cheek. Despite her great age of two and thirty, her mother many times seemed to Kate younger than herself, untouched by time. Now she seemed a maid caught in transgression.

The drawstrings still undone, Kate's shift slipped off her shoulder. In the morning's cold breath, she shivered.

Her mother frowned and stepped towards Kate, pushing loose hair back underneath her cap. She tugged at Kate's shift, and tied and secured it. "Pray, child, remember your modesty."

Pacing to the bed, her mother, shoulders slumped, stroked the velvet of the new bodice waiting to be packed. She and two of her maids had spent weeks sewing, re-making old court gowns to fit Kate's measurements. In this instant, she seemed to be grieving. *Surely Mother isn't grieving for her old dresses?*

Kate's mouth trembled as she blinked away the memory of the once-beautiful gown she had worn for Aunt Nan's coronation two years ago. Now that she was taller and closer to womanhood, it no longer fitted her and her mother had cut the fabric to fashion two new bodices with matching sleeves. Kate punched her fists against her thighs, angry that not one garment in her clothes chest hadn't been made up from old gowns. Surely the niece of the Queen of England should go to court with at least one, new fashionable dress? It was hard enough to deal with her mother and stepfather's lack of wealth, but now she fretted that she would shame her aunt, the Queen.

Her mother held out her bodice and skirt. "You've sat in your small clothes long enough. Get dressed. Your father waits for you."

Kate bit back an angry retort. It made her sick to her stomach how besotted her lady mother was about her living husband, her sweet Will, her *Dearest Heart*. How she insisted that Kate honour him with a daughter's proper respect.

Even so, the last weeks gave Kate reason for thought. She could not forget that it was Stafford who convinced her mother to let her go. Her thoughts a jumble of confusion, she fumbled with her bodice's cords. Without a word, her mother took over and pulled until the bodice encased and supported her upper body; it took Kate's breath away.

Her mother hurried to the other side of the room to pack more clothes into her coffer. Almost dressed, Kate padded over to the unpacked gown, picking up from beside it a book, one of her most treasured possessions. A gift from her mother's brother and sister for her thirteenth birthday, not only had Aunt Nan painstakingly embroidered its deep red velvet covers with gold thread, but half its pages bore the handwriting of Uncle George. The letter accompanying the gift, written jointly by both her aunt and uncle, told Kate that he had translated from the Greek for her the words of a woman poet from ancient times. Sappho was her name, but little was known of her other than what her beautiful words conveyed.

In the letter, her uncle and aunt reminded Kate that poetry ran deeply in the blood of the Boleyns. They hoped their gift and Sappho's example would encourage Kate to write. Indeed, in twelve months they planned to ask to see if she had filled all the blank pages with scribblings and verse.

Kate sighed. She only learnt to write to please her mother. Now her mother's brother and sister expected her to write verse. Aunt Nan had written the request like a royal command, even saying she wanted to share Kate's poetry with her husband, the King. All of them were likely to be very disappointed with any of her efforts. But she liked to read the verses that her uncle had translated for her. She flicked open to the first page:

> *Six birthdays of mine had passed*
> *when the bones of my parent,*
> *gathered from the pyre,*
> *drank before their time my tears.*

She blinked away tears. Reading that brought to mind her dead father. Slipping the book into the deep pocket of her skirt, Kate turned to the window. Sighing, she wished the thick, crinkled glass allowed her more view of the countryside surrounding their manor house. She was always happiest when her mother allowed her to ride her horse or wander in freedom the meadows surrounding her home. On this grey, misty morning, the only thing she could really make out was the stately tower of Saint Andrews church. Built by her great-grandfather when he took possession of this estate, it had proclaimed to all his lordship of Rochford, a lordship that continued down to her grandfather. It reminded her that she had right to pride—and the right to claim her place with her royal aunt, rather than remain here, hidden away with her too often soft mother who lacked all trace of ambition.

Kate smiled. She was young—in the beginning of her spring, the golden, glorious time to plant the seeds for her own life. Her mother hurt easily, but her? She had the lion strength of her father's untainted nobility, his undoubted good blood.

She wanted to dance, to spin around and revel in the freedom that would soon be hers. The weather promised good travelling and a journey of no more than two days that would take her away from here, a home where she no longer belonged. London, the court and her Aunt Nan, England's Queen, beckoned.

A raven cawed and wheeled in the sky above Kate. Now almost at the end of her journey, she followed the raven's flight to the towering gateway of London Bridge. Along its ugly, overhanging spikes, more ravens returned to roost. Their wings fluttered and flapped in short bursts of flight, and opened the morning to horror. Black wings beat amongst white human skulls. Amongst death.

Silence fell, heavy like a shroud, before knifed open by a

new disharmony. One raven shrieked, its beak gaping wide apart. Bluish-black wings fluttered and opened wide, and thrashed the air with power.

The bird cawed again, its spread wings catching the wind in the dull sky, before swooping down to claim the fresh dead upon the long spikes. Trembling, Kate found herself unable to take her eyes away as the bird pecked and tugged, tearing at bloody flesh. Dark clots of blood oozed thick and worm-like from ripped skin.

Other scavengers alighted near the feasting bird. Crouched upon the bloody head, the raven screamed in warning, in possession. Its sharp beak scraped against bone and delved into grisly eyeholes. The bitter, cold wind brought down to Kate the smell of decaying flesh, fecund on this graveyard wall.

Kate swallowed down bile, tasting vomit in her mouth. Wherever Kate looked, right or left, black, empty eye sockets stared back at her. Eye sockets of the dead.

Kate shut her eyes briefly and prayed: *God in Heaven, forgive them the sins that brought them here. Keep safe their souls.*

She looked up again at the cast-off shells of these poor souls while, at the same time, the living eyes of the ravens glinted down to her with coldness, aggression, arrogance. Robins, doves and pigeons flocked beside the meat-eating birds. Their coos and chirps punctuated the harsh, punctuating caws of the ravens. But that didn't blunt the nightmare.

She tugged at the reins of Rachel, her mother's elderly palfrey, kneeing the horse's sides until she quickened into a trot. The entire journey from home, even when they broke for the night at Barking Abbey, Kate ensured she stayed a clear and careful distance away from her stepfather. Now her failing courage edged her closer to him. Reins held tight in leather-gloved hands, she steered Rachel beside his black stallion. Her stepfather grinned. "Keeping me company now, are you, lass?"

"I want to see Harry," Kate blustered and looked away from him. More mighty wings thrashed above her head, drawing her eyes back again to the ravens. Beside her, Kate's stepfather laughed grimly. "Aye, come to London and be greeted by the welcome of death. I hated it as a lad, and I hate it as much now."

Kate jerked around in her surprise. Resisting her stepfather's attempts at friendliness, his attempts to be her father, she had never heard him speak of his boyhood. And Kate had never cared or wanted to ask him. He cocked his head and smiled at her. "Do not be afraid. The dead cannot harm us—only the living."

Kate lifted her chin, tightened her mouth and stared ahead. *Why does he continue to smile and speak so gently to me?* She desired none of his friendship. Very soon, Kate would have no more need of him. Once he brought her to the court, she would bid him farewell and thank God for it. She hoped the farewell would be for good.

Beginning the journey over the bridge, Kate bent to soothe nervous Rachel, her thighs feeling the quiver of the horse's muscles. The horse snorted and neighed, her walk a jittery dance that tried to shy away from the press of women, men and children. Most of them made their way across the bridge by foot, but a few also rode like her and her stepfather.

With Rachel at last reassured and no longer threatening to balk at the crossing, London again captured Kate's attention. Over two years ago, she had come with her grandmother to London from Rochford inland by water for her aunt's summertime coronation. During the two weeks she stayed with her kin, she continued to travel by water in the Boleyn's stately barge, going up and down the river with her grandparents, from one destination to another.

This time her mother took it in mind to show that she, too, had the Boleyn pride, insisting that Kate journey to London through the only means that she and Stafford could afford: riding the horses they owned.

Now the city of London seemed to reveal itself to her for the first time. Their way to London Bridge had taken them through streets both wide and narrow, the narrower streets outnumbering the wide.

Travelling down the narrow streets, Kate had looked up to houses that jutted out and cast them into dark shadow and made the streets seem narrower still. Their occupants yelled to one another from their homes, tossing slops and the contents of their privy pots upon people rushing by.

Heady smells overcame and confused her senses, one moment vile, making her grab the pomander hanging on her girdle and bring it to her nose, the next appetising. The cries and songs of men and women selling their wares. So many people, young, old, rich, poor.

Kate's eyes darted everywhere as she rode across the bridge to the other side, passing under arched gateway after arched gateway. Tall shops of all descriptions mingled with four-storey houses that declared the wealth and status of those who lived within, preventing sight of the river. The outdoor, open privies occupied by poor men and women alike. Startled into staring, Kate's cheeks heated even more when a man caught her watching. Wiggling his bare backside in her direction, he gestured rudely, yelling, "Want to look, m'lady? Perchance you'd like to eye m'other side while you're at it?"

Her embarrassment was complete when her stepfather gazed over his shoulder and laughed at her.

The way at last open before her, Kate dug her heels into Rachel's sides, quickening her to a canter. *I must be close to reaching Greenwich Palace and the end of my journey.* So close to reaching an aunt who never laughed at her, or treated her like a foolish child.

Handed over to one servant and then another, Kate was brought with her clothes coffer to a chamber deep within the palace confines and handed over one more time to a young, pretty maid-servant.

When she heard Kate's name, the girl bobbed a curtsey. "Lady Margaret told me to expect you." She hung Kate's cloak on a wall hook over the place where they had put her coffer with two other coffers, and then came back. "I'm Alice, m'lady. I look after my Lady Margaret and her sister Mary. Expect now I look after you, too." Alice studied her. "First things first, if I do say, m'lady. How about you sit by the fire and take off that gown. I'll round up those squanderers outside to get the tub and hot water for you to have a proper wash before you go and greet the Queen."

Kate stared and the maidservant burst out laughing. "Well-a-day, m'lady, you do look like you've been journeying. The Queen, well, she's a good nose and likes us to keep our bodies clean, no matter our station. She is fastidious about that—more so than even the King. Don't you worry—I'll send one of the lads to let her know you're getting ready to see her."

Kate blushed and looked down at her dirty nails and grimy hands. Two full days of travel had left their mark on her. Obediently, she sat down a stool and began to pull at the cords of her bodice.

"That's right, m'lady. You do that while I go and get the lads organised to bring us the tub and good, hot water. Nothing better I say than a bath after a journey on horseback—you'll be back the pretty maid you are in no time."

Kate spent the next two hours washing and getting ready to meet her aunt. She luxuriated for a long time in a tub filled with water so warm it loosened her limbs and made her feel sleepy. Alice washed and combed her hair before helping her out of the tub and into a clean, fire-warmed shift. All the while, Alice chatted. She told Kate she was a daughter of a yeoman, a farmer who had fallen on hard times. For the last three years, the crops had failed. Alice had gone into service because there were too many at home; too many for the family to feed and care for.

"I'm not complaining, mind you," Alice said as she plaited Kate's hair. "There's famine everywhere—and we've still got a roof over our heads, while our neighbours were driven out of their homes like animals. At least my good father was able to place me here because he has served a lord or two in his day." Alice went over Kate's clothes chest and rampaged through its contents. Selecting the pieces that made up Kate's best court gown, she sang softly:

In every part
Dame Nature's art
Gives her the start:
With all my heart
I wish she could rule her tongue

Alice stilled into sudden silence and turned back to Kate, her eyes full of worry. "M'lady—I'm not one of those to blame all misfortune on Queen Anne."

"What do you mean?" Kate asked, taken aback.

"I am not like the others—I do not take it in mind that these bad times are brought about because of the King's marriage to your aunt. On my honour, I revere the Queen, as do many here who serve her. 'Tis the ignorant, who know no better, who say the dire things."

Kate blinked in her confusion. "What do the ignorant say of my aunt?

Alice, now lacing Kate's bodice, gazed up at her in alarm. "M'lady—I would rather repeat none of it." Alice bit her bottom lip. "And 'tis not my place to say, but I think you should know hard times are not simply for those of my station."

Kate tugged the cord of her skirt. Her tiredness opened up to anger. "If these hard times you speak of concern my aunt, pray spit it out and tell me all."

Seemingly not hearing her, Alice went over to Kate's clothes coffer and began to bring out her possessions. She turned with a tied bundle of white cloths in her hand. Kate blushed, and looked down at her feet.

"When it comes to your time, my Lady, do not be shy and think you cannot tell me. I'll find you a box for you to use for your bloodied rags, and then you just let me know when you need me take them down to the laundry maids for washing."

Alice returned to unpacking Kate's coffer, at last bringing out a small box. Opening it up, she took out a black gable-hood. While the headgear was plain and unadorned, it was clearly made with costly materials and once graced Kate's mother at court.

Her eyes resting on the gable, Kate fidgeted. Alice's avoidance of her question, and even the way she unpacked Kate's coffer, seemed a reminder that the servant held the upper hand within these walls, and anger was no way to win her acceptance. She swallowed. "Pray, Alice, could I not know of these matters that concern my aunt?"

Turning the gable-hood around and around in her hands, Alice bent her head. "You desire to know what the ignorant say, m'lady? They say that your aunt's marriage has displeased God and thus she is blessed with no son. They say it is her fault that famine curses the land, and blame her for all the blood that has flowed these past years. Aye—even when King Harry sent the good monks to their death last year, it was the Queen, your aunt, that people, low born and high born, spoke of with scorn and hate." Alice looked up. "But that is not what I say, m'lady. I've been at court for over one year now and have seen the Queen for what she is—a good, brave woman." She smiled, brought over the gable and carefully placed it on Kate's head. "Aye, the Queen has a temper that is wisest to stay clear of—but when she smiles it is like sunshine."

Alice stood back, and Kate squirmed under her close inspection.

"If I do say so myself, I think the Queen will be pleased with ye—a proper court lady, you are now." At a knock on the door, Alice rushed over and opened it. She spoke to someone and turned back to Kate. "Just in time, too. One of the Queen's grooms is here to escort you. Now—the other thing the Queen dislikes is waiting. You best be going."

All the way to her aunt's chamber Kate felt more and more a country lass, wide-eyed and astonished at what she saw. Along the long length of the galley Kate walked by groups of young men and women. Some danced together while one of their fellows played a lute, others sat on benches teaching one another to play their instruments, or just singing together. There was even a woman dwarf, dressed in unusual garb, juggling apples for a small audience of children. Music accompanied Kate all the way to the royal apartments as cold draughts escaped through cracks in the gallery's ill-fitting windows. Their uneven, dull glass could not hide the grey and weary yet rainless winter's day. Far below, the wind churned the Thames into frenzy, the froth of its water spilling over the steps to the river and the moorings of the royal barge.

Despite her thick clothes, Kate shivered, cursing herself for forgetting her mantle. Like her mother and aunt, she detested winter. Its slow, harsh, dark weeks, turning into slow, harsh, dark months, trapped her within walls and forbade her the outside world. She sighed, yearning for winter's end, yearning for spring. *Yearning for winter's end? Yearning for spring?* Her mother told her that everyone yearned for something; it was a song sung by all until death. She thought for a moment about her still unpacked journal. Might she try and write that first poem when she returned to her chamber?

At last, Kate's journey brought her to a place she

remembered from her last visit to court—when her grandmother had brought her to witness Aunt Nan's coronation. Lifting her heavy skirts, she gave an excited skip—very soon she would reach her destination and see her aunt again.

Kate turned into the final corridor. Startled that the door was open to her aunt's chamber, she came to a sudden halt and almost stumbled before remembering to walk forward again. During her past visits to her aunt, Aunt Nan's doors were not only always guarded but also closed. Now stock-still guards gave no inclination that they could hear what went on behind them. *Why this strange lack of privacy for the Queen?* Kate asked herself, bewildered. It was like Aunt Nan invited all to observe her chambers.

Halfway within, encircled within a diaphanous haze of winter light, Aunt Nan sat and sewed by a tall window. Lounging by his sister's side, leaning his shoulder against the wall, Uncle George read out aloud from a thin, leather-bound book. A beam of light gilded his fair hair gold and turned his blue eyes into iridescent gems. He recited in a strong, melodic voice:

> *All things obey their ancient law*
> *And all perform their proper tasks;*
> *All things thou holdest in strict bounds,*
> *To human acts alone denied*
> *Thy fit control as Lord of all.*
> *Why else does slippery Fortune change*
> *So much, and punishment more fit*
> *For crimes oppress the innocent?*
> *Corrupted men sit throned on high...*

Kate looked from behind the stocky groom. She caught sight of her aunt's hands, ever busy, as Kate had seen in times past, with embroidery hoop and thread. A length of material tumbled over her lap; its silken sheen shimmered against her black skirt. Head bent over her work, her aunt sewed quickly and with great skill. Curled up in a honeysuckle wicker basket at her feet lay a tiny white terrier, fast asleep.

With a low bow, the groom announced Kate as she entered the large chamber. He bowed again and backed out of the room. Kate gazed around the large chamber, taking in the stained-glass windows and the beautiful tapestries suspended on the long length of wall before and behind her, and their shimmer of gold, silver and silk threads.

Dropping into a deep curtsey, she rose to the welcoming smiles of her aunt and uncle. Uncle George was first to move. He put down his book, strode over and lifted her in his arms. Swinging her a little, side to side, he chuckled and bestowed a kiss. Kate giggled, rubbing her face from the tickle of his beard. "Dear girl. How dare you grow," Uncle George said, putting her down. He gripped her shoulders and studied her closely. "You make me feel old. A year ago you were a child, now look at you—you're a young woman."

Kate blushed and gazed at the floor. *Woman? My uncle called me a woman!* A shadow fell over her and she gazed up to the warmth of her aunt's smile. She blinked. Silver light outlined Aunt Nan's head and shoulders in a nimbus. Kate curtseyed again.

"Sweet niece." Aunt Nan laughed a little. "Your uncle is right. The child is gone and the pretty maid stands before us." Like her uncle but more closely, Aunt Nan considered her. "More and more, you remind me of your mother; aye, two peas in a pod." She pealed with laughter and said, "Well, not quite." She gestured to her small breasts. "My sister at your age drew a man's gaze. I see you're yet like me."

Kate blushed and circumspectly considered the toe of her green slipper peeking out from under her gown. Her mother told her once she flowered her breasts would come. Her flowers had started four months ago, but still Kate's chest remained as flat as a boy's.

Uncle George laughed. "Mary drew men's thoughts, but, unlike you, rarely to marriage."

Her thin brows brought together, Aunt Nan scowled at her brother. "Pray, George, speak not of our sister in such a fashion. She's Kate's mother, after all."

Kate shifted her feet and gazed uncertainly at her uncle and aunt. Aunt Nan smiled and took her hand, changing the subject. "Where have you been placed? I told my chamberlain to find you a room not far from my own."

Kate looked over her shoulder. The bold colours of the tapestries stilled time, and she was back in these same chambers over two years ago, the only time she remembered speaking privately with Aunt Nan during the days leading up to her coronation.

That bright afternoon, her grandmother had brought Kate to her aunt while she rested before the evening's banquet. With great delight, Aunt Nan had showed her a gift she had received from the King, a book from his own library. "*City of Ladies?*" Wasn't that what her Aunt called the book? Aunt Nan told her the illuminated manuscript was about a city of peace, built for women and by women out of books—the stones of learning. Carefully and slowly, she had turned the thick pages so Kate could see the exquisite depictions of women dressed in garb of one hundred or more years ago.

Her hand on the swell of her belly, Aunt Nan lingered over the illustration of the Virgin Mary. Crowned, she held proudly her son, leading the way for all the other women, entering the city to claim it for her own.

And what of the illustration of the woman who had written "City of Ladies," the one of her presenting her book to a queen in her chamber, where a strong gathering of her women attendants watched and talked? The same scene played out in her aunt's chambers on that sunlit day. Now these two images and four others took on another life, woven into huge panels of tapestry to adorn the walls.

"Kate?" Aunt Nan stirred impatiently, her grip tightening on her hand. "I asked, is your room close by?" Kate blinked away her memories and thought again about the distance from her aunt's chambers to the room allotted to her on arrival. It seemed to take forever to reach her aunt's rooms; it seemed forever since her stepfather had handed her over to another's care. Kate gnawed her bottom lip. "Everything is yet so new to me I cannot tell. I'm with Madge and Mary. I haven't seen them yet, only their maidservant."

Aunt Nan released Kate's hand. A look of meaning passed between her uncle and aunt. "You'll see Madge soon enough, but Mary's none too well and has gone home to be with her family for a time. No matter—you'll meet many more cousins. With all the young women at court, you won't lack for company—or kin. If I hadn't expected your arrival this morning, many of them would have filled this chamber with their idle chatter. Even your cousin Mary, our little Duchess, is here." Aunt Nan turned back to her brother. "She waits, like me, for her husband to return from hunting. For three days we have waited." She shrugged. "Your grandfather is hunting with the King, too. Still—their absence allows me more time for you, and gives you chance to draw your breath."

"Where's Harry? Where's my brother?" Kate asked. Ever since she had come into her aunt's chamber she had barely been able to restrain herself from bursting out with this question, heart-achingly aware of what lacked in this welcome. On her rare visits to court, Kate's brother Harry always greeted her with her aunt.

Aunt Nan screwed up her mouth and then sighed. "He wanted to be here. But he's twelve now and has other obligations. I'd fail my duty as his guardian if I granted him permission to escape his tutors." Her aunt gazed at Uncle George. "He's not like us, is he? Harry would rather hunt all day than spend time with his books."

Uncle George half closed his eyes and the suggestion of a smile disappeared from his face. Disquieted, Kate wondered what was wrong. "He's very alike to his father," her uncle said. He turned to his sister. "There's no question about his intelligence. Harry just has a common boyish desire to do other than read and write."

Aunt Nan's mouth tightened, her face becoming falcon sharp. "Boyish desire—fiddlesticks. As a girl I relished my hours of learning; everything my tutors put before me I lapped up. Can anyone deny the worth of the tutors I've chosen for Harry? Is the poet Bourbon to be scoffed at? A tutor fit for a prince—and one who honours his young scholars by dedicating to them his new book. Tell me, brother, is a work like Bourbon's *Paedagogion* to be quipped at? Our nephew but wastes his opportunities, and for what—boyish desires?" She sniffed in clear annoyance. "I relish the hunt, too, but I never allow my enjoyment of it to interfere with my duties."

Her uncle's hand rested on his sister's arm. "I remember well our childhood, if you do not. Mayhap the time you spent with our dogs and horses was the real cause for our lord father to send you abroad. You're too hard on the lad."

To Kate's bewilderment and embarrassment, her aunt's eyes shone with tears. For her mother, tears came easily, but never would have Kate said the same of her sister. The change seemed more than could be simply explained by the years since she was last at court; it seemed a change in her aunt herself. Something had shifted, and cracked apart. Her aunt seemed exposed—no longer the confident woman of the past.

Aunt Nan lowered her head, brushing her face. "Do you think I wish to be? What if I fail in my care of him?" Her aunt rubbed her temple with her palm and glanced Kate's way. "Kate will help me with her brother."

Uncle George shook his head. "I've told you before what troubles the boy. Harry wants his mother and not his aunt to worry over him. You could give him the world, Nan, but it would mean nothing as long as his heart's desire of seeing Mary is denied."

Kate stared from her uncle to her aunt. Wanting to go to court, she had never thought that her brother, perchance, wanted to come home. All his letters had spoken of his health and happiness; now she knew otherwise. Catching her aunt's eye, she was answered by a frown. "Do not concern yourself with this, Kate."

"But Mother desires to see Harry, too. Why can he not come home for a time? He would want to see our little sister and brother."

Aunt Nan, her eyes glittering, turned away. "My sister's other son, such is her good fortune. Mary does not know what trouble she causes me."

Uncle George put his arm around Nan's thin shoulders. His face serious, her uncle glanced at her. "Nor does Kate. None of this is her fault, or, if you but think of it, our sister's."

Turning a tremulous smile to her brother, Aunt Nan lifted her head, then turned to Kate again. "Forgive me. I am happy for your mother. She has the life she always wanted. But Mary must realise that it comes at a cost, and that the decision about Harry is not mine to make."

"Why?" Kate asked. More bewildered than ever before, Kate's eyes fell upon another nearby tapestry that told the story of the noble Queen Esther hearing of the plot to exterminate her people. The richly garbed figures seemed drawn from the men and women of court she had seen on the way to the Queen's chambers.

At a loss, Kate could not take her eyes from Esther. Praying to God for salvation, the woman in the tapestry looked lost, desperate—just like her aunt had looked a moment ago. *Just as lost as I feel now.* She stumbled as if blindly in a dark labyrinth. Unable to discover her way out, pit holes opened at her feet.

Kate's question ignored, her uncle and aunt spoke briefly to one another; their words seemed to twist and twirl, offering up very little meaning she could understand. Surely it would be a simple thing for her aunt, the Queen, to send her brother home? Even just a day would mean the world to her mother.

Her aunt and uncle considered her guardedly and met

each other's eyes. Aunt Nan tossed her head, and the tendons in her neck tightened. She muttered in an undertone, "Not yet." She threaded her arm underneath Kate's, then led her to a stool near the window. "Pray, child, sit," said her aunt. Picking up her embroidery hoop, she sat back on the chair she had vacated on Kate's arrival and studied her stitching. Vivid colours of silk threads depicted a spring knot garden hedged by purple lavender—a work of hours, days, weeks, months. Hollyhocks, daffodils, carnations, marigolds, every flower Kate could name, the garden burst into abundant, wild life. A threaded needle in her hand, Aunt Nan lifted her eyes. "Child, you do not understand, but I promise you will soon. Let's not talk more of this until then."

Uncle George joined them, putting his hand on Kate's shoulder. "One step at a time, sweetheart—first, settle in. Come tomorrow, I'll be on my way to your mother. I think when I return you'll find yourself less in the dark."

Aunt Nan lifted her eyebrows at her brother. "And Jane, George? Did you do as I asked and speak to her?" She poked the needle into her canvas as if in a gesture of impatience. "I do not wish to hear her protest in your absence that you neglect her."

He shrugged. "I have spoken to her, sister. I have explained the matter to her, but you know my wife. She thinks everything I do is forgetful of her presence. I am sick of her spite, and her jealousy. Believe me, I am happy to be away from her tongue for a time."

Aunt Nan gazed at him. "Be careful, George. I know you're not at fault, but Jane worries me. She can no longer hide her dislike or jealousy even from me." She turned back to Kate. "Pray, forgive us for speaking of family matters. But you, too, are family, and should know to be wary of your uncle's wife. She has little to recommend her. All she does is speak ill of your uncle." Aunt Nan glanced down and concentrated on threading a needle before smiling back at Kate. "While your uncle's gone to Rochford you'll find your place amongst us." Her eyes suddenly became serious. "You too are of the blood of the Boleyns; when we must, we adapt. And no matter what—we always make anew."

3

On the way back to her chamber, Kate thought about the behaviour of her aunt and uncle. They had looked at her so strangely, and now Uncle George rode to see her mother. *Why?* None of it made any sense to her.

Without taking in the return journey, or the departure of her escort, she stopped on the other side of the door of the antechamber of her bedchamber, rubbing at her cold arms. Winter and the nearness of night darkened the small room, while candlelight pulsed and flickered through the open door of the bedchamber as if a living thing.

"Kate? Is that you?"

The rush of slippered feet and flash of red silk announced the arrival of her cousin Madge, and she was gathered in her warm embrace.

"Welcome, coz," Madge said. She took Kate's hand and led her into the bedchamber.

A fire blazed in the hearth, adding to the light of many candles. But the dark spaces, where candle and firelight failed to reach, echoed Kate's confusion.

Madge's mother was her great-aunt, the sister of her grandfather. Madge and her twin sister, Mary, had attended Aunt Nan since their twelfth year. Despite their close kinship, Kate had only met her cousins once before, at Aunt Nan's coronation, over two years ago. Then, Madge and Mary were fifteen-year-olds and uninterested in paying any attention to their eleven-year-old cousin. Acting as experienced women, well-versed in court life, they had hurt Kate by shutting her out while they celebrated the Queen's coronation. Not just shutting her out; they had made her feel invisible.

Now Madge clasped her hand with a bright smile. Her chest tight with nerves, Kate tried to smile back at her, a smile she couldn't anchor. She felt reprieved when Madge let go of her hand to step ahead of her. They arrived at the table where platters and a simple meal of bread, cheese and cooked fowl had been set. Going to the other side of the table, Madge sat down to pick up a half-finished chicken leg. She gnawed at it as she pointed to the empty platter and goblet on the table.

"Sit, Kate. The fare is for you, too."

With another glance at Madge, Kate sat and reached for the other chicken leg before pouring ale into her goblet. The nearby night-candle lit the stream into liquid gold. Biting into the roasted, juicy flesh of the fowl, she closed her eyes, savouring the taste. At home, feasting on their young, egg-laying hens was out of the question. Only when hens stopped providing them with eggs did they have boiled fowl served as a meal. Not so at court.

Dabbing at her mouth, Kate cleared her throat and thought again about her cousin's greeting. She was older now. Perhaps that explained Madge's greeting. *Does Madge see the four years separating us as now bridged? Time to find out by tossing out a first rope.* "Thank you for sharing your chamber with me," she murmured.

Her cousin smiled. "The Queen asked me to help you settle in. Having you with me will make that easier." Madge's large, blue eyes twinkled with amusement. "You do not snore, do you? One thing I hate is a bed-companion who keeps me wide awake all night long with their trumpeting."

Kate shrugged. "I sleep alone most nights at home, but Grandmother has never complained when she has shared a bed with me." She laughed a little. "Although I could complain of her. Her snoring is like a blunt saw."

Chuckling, Madge washed her fingers in the provided water bowl, then pushed away from the table, wooden chair legs protesting against a rush mat. Madge pulled around a heavy plait of chestnut brown hair. Light from the tall candles close to them lit her plait with a shimmer of red and gold. She lowered her gaze and played distractedly with her hair.

Kate studied her cousin closely. Her skin was unblemished, her lips rosy and full. With a perfect oval face, she was truly beautiful, everything Kate wished for herself. She reached for the remains of the bread loaf and tore at it angrily. *I am plain compared to her. I am plain compared to most of my kin. 'Tis so unfair.*

Aware that Madge now scrutinised her, Kate straightened. She chewed fast and swallowed down her bread. *Does she know? Does she know why Uncle George rode out in winter to see my mother?* If she didn't know that, surely Madge could tell her why her aunt seemed so changed. Kate licked her lips, measuring her words before she spoke. "Madge," she said, "what is wrong with the Queen?"

Madge poured ale into her goblet and sipped. She wiped her mouth with the back of her hand. "I didn't think it would take you long before you asked me this question—although I'm surprised to hear it on your first day. Since the Queen asked me to share my chamber with you, I've thought hard on this. I cannot leave you in the dark, otherwise I leave you unwarned and unarmed, and likely to shame yourself, and your kin, too, in your ignorance. You must know what you'll find here."

Kate dipped her hands into the water bowl. Oil from the cooked fowl washed off her hands and turned into rainbow swirls. She dried her hands on a towel and looked across at her cousin. "You speak of the Queen?"

"Aye. I speak of the Queen. I do not know what news comes to you at home, but you must know this. The King and Queen are no longer content," Madge said.

Kate jerked back. "Oh—why?" She swallowed—remembering the triumph of her aunt's coronation. After witnessing that day, she held the story of her aunt's love affair close to her like treasure.

Slouching back, Madge played with her plait. "The King blames her for the loss of their last babe. He cannot see that none is to blame but fate. Since their marriage, he breaks her heart, time after time, with his cruel and thoughtless dalliances—even while she recovered from losing their child. If she protests, the King tells her to do as her betters have done: endure."

Madge's mouth tightened before she spoke again, reaching for her goblet. "He is kinder now, showing her affection at times. Strange to think it is because of another woman."

Kate looked at her cousin, more and more disbelieving her ears. *The King unfaithful to my aunt? Breaking her heart? Telling her to do as her betters had done before her. Her betters? There are none better than my aunt.*

"'Another woman'?" Kate echoed, treading on shifting sands, all her illusions about her aunt's life at court under threat.

Madge shrugged and then wiped her mouth. "During the court's summer progress we stopped for a time at the Seymours' Wolf Hall. Our Lord Seymour had already placed his daughter, Jane, under the King's nose. Now he made certain wherever the King was, so was she. Coming back from the hunt one day, the Queen found him with Jane." Madge met Kate's gaze. "You understand my meaning?"

Her cheeks heating, Kate nodded.

Madge continued her story. "Only by good fortune did the wet weather bring the Queen back earlier than expected, otherwise Jane might have consummated her desire to snare the King. This time, having disturbed the King at his play, the Queen reined in her temper. She reined it in so well that he reconsidered his liking for one who acts with him like a timid, dull-witted white mouse. He returned to the Queen's bed, thank God."

The nearby night candle sputtered and sizzled, its light flickering furiously before going out. Madge's face dimmed. Kate leaned closer to her cousin and listened.

"But you must understand that their lack of a son builds a wall between them—a wall that daily becomes higher and harder to climb because there is no prince."

Aunt Nan had given King Harry only one living child, a daughter, Elizabeth, little Bess—not the wanted prince that would safeguard England from civil war. Since Aunt Nan's marriage to the King, crops had failed, bringing famine to the land, and good men had gone to their deaths. When Kate's mother heard of the recent executions of Bishop Fisher and Sir Thomas More, she had railed and wept. They died rather than agree to the supremacy of the King, that he had the right to do what he willed. Yet it was the Queen, and not the King, who was hated.

Madge talked and talked. More candles had guttered to congealing masses of wax, their light flicking and sputtering, by the time Madge arrived at the most important news of all: The King's return to his wife's bed had achieved its purpose. Aunt Nan was with child.

Aunt Nan emerged from her litter at Westminster, a picture of grace, in her coronation robes. Her ladies rushed around to help with the long trail while she gazed at the abbey. Sunlight struck and glittered the rubies of the golden chaplet encircling her brow.

Darkness fell, a backdrop for hostile faces. Too many hostile faces. They jutted at Kate and sneered, surrounding her until fear tightened around her throat.

Kate fought her way through the men and women, while Aunt Nan lifted her head and laughed. She seemed unaware of any hostility. Without faltering, she strode towards the abbey.

One, two, three voices called out, "God save the Queen!" At the door of Westminster, looking over her shoulder, Aunt Nan waved in greeting and turned aside to joke with her ladies.

A man's voice shouted, "God save Queen Katherine!" The floodgates opened to voices of hate, a torrent of execration: "HA! HA! Henry and Anne!" "Witch! Goggle-eyed whore!" Soldiers pushed and beat back the rowdy crowd. More cries of protest rang out followed by another roar of hate, and yet another, and another. "God save Queen Katherine!" men and women yelled in unison.

Aunt Nan's hand protected the pronounced swell of her belly. She straightened her shoulders, adjusted her purple mantle to a better position on one side. Again, rubies, sapphires and diamonds twinkled in her chaplet, dazzling the eye like fire.

Now, all the hostile faces disappeared, replaced by only her aunt's: ashen, all joy cast down, large, dark eyes even larger, unfathomable, deep as the ocean itself. She was the first woman—Eve who looked back at Eden, forbidden to her for eternity. Aunt Nan laughed a pealing laugh of defiance, her hand on her belly again. She entered the candle-lit darkness of Westminster.

Kate awoke in the bed she now shared with Madge. Tears trickled down her face and her heart beat fast with terror. A rooster crowed, its full voice chasing her dream away until all that remained was the memory of hatred—hatred that threatened her aunt.

Drying her eyes, she looked through an opening in the drawn bed hangings. Despite the darkness, a narrow strip of morning light escaped from a gap in the closed window curtains and seemed to spearhead towards her.

Kate listened to the waking songs of birds and glanced aside at Madge. Lying back, an arm flung over her head, she breathed softly, undisturbed. Her hair coiled charmingly on her pillow and a loose shift revealed a naked, well-shaped shoulder.

When the rooster crowed again, Kate swung out of bed, grabbed her fur mantle and tossed it over her shoulders. The cold floor made her gasp. Her bare toes curling up in protest, she jigged a strange, disjointed dance to the fireplace. Fire had turned most of the night's huge log into a crumbling city of red embers and winding grey ash roads.

Stirring the fire back into life, she held out her hands to the heat. The fire licked at the remains of the log as she struggled to understand the rest of what Madge had told her.

Now that Aunt Nan was with child, the King pursued and bedded other women, using as justification the physicians' advice that he no longer bed her for the sake of the child. Kate remembered her mother's two recent pregnancies. All through the long months leading to childbed, her mother and stepfather did not sleep apart, or change their loving ways towards one another during the day. If anything, they were more loving than ever. Not so the King. The King took mistresses.

Why had her cousin fidgeted in discomfort when she said this? Averting her face into the darkness, Madge mumbled that they should talk of other matters—ones more suitable for a maid of Kate's years.

When Madge cut off her conversation about the King, it hurt. She wasn't a child, even if Madge thought her one. Yes, she was a maid, but that did not mean she lacked the ability to understand.

Flickering flames reflected on Kate's pale hands. She stared at them. No wonder everyone thought her a child; her body resembled a child's—she even had small hands with short, nondescript, stubby fingers, broken nails. They looked like they belonged to a ten-year-old. An image of Aunt Nan flashed into her mind. Kate would have given anything for a morsel of her grace and charm, to possess fingers such as hers, long and tapering, fingers that needed no jewellery to draw eyes their way.

She picked up her comb, grabbed tresses of her hair and began combing. Soon Kate would need to call in Alice, who slept in the antechamber, to plait her hair for the day. She stilled, hair in her free hand, studying its colour. The strands sparkled with red lights in the fire's glow. Thank God she was blonde like her mother. The enemies of her aunt ridiculed her dark hair. *Night Crow*, they called her.

Close to Kate, a silver goblet mirrored back her distorted reflection. She stuck out her tongue, hating how she looked. Did her lady mother lie? She said she was pretty, blessed with a prettiness that did not threaten, but beckoned to friends. She said her mouth was meant to smile. Uncertain, an outsider, Kate did not feel like smiling. *Perhaps Mother was right. Perhaps I should not have come to court.* Kate sighed before hurrying to the clothes chest to start dressing.

4

After breakfast, Madge accompanied Kate to the Queen's chambers. Yesterday, the unfamiliar journey from one side of the palace to the royal apartments seemed to take forever. Now Kate arrived at Aunt Nan's closed door in no time at all. *Closed door?* Getting accustomed to her new surroundings, she discovered another reason for confusion. Opened one day and closed on another? *Why?*

Coming nearer, there was the unmistakable, albeit muted, sound of Aunt Nan's laughter; an accomplished singer sang to the accompaniment of a lute. Gently, Madge elbowed Kate in her side and grinned. "The Queen's merry today. Be of good cheer, coz, and be merry, too."

Kate gazed at her, surprised. Did she look glum? Straightening her shoulders, she forced herself to smile. Side-by-side with her cousin, Kate entered the Queen's apartments. They curtseyed together just inside the door. Aunt Nan danced in the centre of the room, threading in and out amongst a small group of dancers. Catching sight of Kate, she waved in greeting, gesturing to her to come deeper into the room. Kate watched the dancers closely, her feet soon tapping in time to the beat. As if sewing threads to an unseen tapestry, they wove their way until couples regrouped again into two lines.

A young man sat to the side, strumming his lute and singing in a pure, golden voice. Kate stood for a moment, listening, a shiver going up and down her backbone, her body responding to his voice like the lute in his hands responded to his touch.

"That's Smeaton," Madge whispered. "Isn't he the pretty one?" She giggled. "While he is the King's lute player, he often makes music for the Queen."

Gazing back his way, Kate found herself transfixed. Her cheeks warming, she finger-counted all that made him comely: blonde hair; unblemished, youthful skin; deep cleft in his beardless chin; and eyes any maid would envy. There was nothing maid-like about the way he gazed at Aunt Nan.

"Mark Smeaton's a son of a carpenter," Madge continued. "In spite of his low birth, he has served the King since before the Queen's coronation and often plays for her. Smeaton plays like an angel—wait until you hear him on the virginal." She sighed. "Doesn't he sing like an angel, too?"

Madge didn't need her answer for the obvious. Kate grinned at her while joining the loud applause at the end of Smeaton's song. The dancers bowed and curtseyed to one another before clapping, too.

"You did well, Mark," Aunt Nan said, a little out of breath, hand held protectively over her belly. As yet, there was no sign of a baby. She headed towards the high-back, intricately carved chair not too far from the huge fireplace. By the chair, a tall man bowed with a flourish of his cap, then rubbed his well-shaped beard as Aunt Nan neared. Reaching his side, she laughed, tapping his arm. "What say you to Smeaton's arrangement, Tom?"

He frowned, running a knuckle back and forth across his forehead. "I did not think my poem one to make a song and dance of, but he surprised me." With a grin, he bowed again. "But then again, the sight of grace dancing, personified in the form of my Queen, left me unable to listen too closely to the music, even if written to my words."

Her eyes sparkling, Aunt Nan pealed with laughter and then gestured to Kate. Madge grinned in reassurance before joining the knot of chattering females by the window.

Kate turned to her aunt's proud smile meant just for her. Now standing alone, she stepped closer and made her deep reverence. Aunt Nan brought her closer. "I believe you two have yet to meet. Tom, this is Mary's daughter Kate." She beamed at him, a genuine smile that spoke of her affection, before taking Kate's arm again. "Sir Thomas Wyatt is kin to us, as is his sister and my other good friend Meg Lee.

"We are fortunate to have Tom home for a time. The King's need for his skilled diplomacy often keeps him on the continent. We were children together at Hever with your uncle George."

Curious, Kate looked up to his bright blue eyes. "Mother, too?"

He hooted a barrel-chested laugh, glancing aside at Aunt Nan. "Verily, aye, your mother, too."

Kate tried to imagine her lady mother and this ageing man as children. "Mother never speaks of her childhood," she said slowly.

No longer merry, he glanced again at her aunt. "Your lady mother was often unhappy at Hever."

Aunt Nan tended to a loose thread on her bodice. Thoughtfully, she twirled the thread around her fingertip. "You're right. Now I think of it, she was much alone then, as she is now."

Taken aback, Kate blustered, "Mother's not alone, or unhappy."

Aunt Nan's thin brows came together and deep lines furrowed her high brow. "I am glad to hear it." She lowered her head, and spoke in an undertone. "Then 'tis I who is alone and unhappy."

Looking furtively around at the people in the room, Sir Thomas touched her arm with concern. "Why say that? While you have me and George, you will never be alone, Anna."

Anna? As if in answer, Aunt Nan smiled tenderly at him. Kate stared at them, astonished at their familiarity, before remembering they had been children together. Those kinds of bonds, her lady mother had said, could last forever. Kate squirmed. She had grown up with no true childhood friends, thanks to her mother's desire to keep her at Rochford Hall. She then remembered where she had seen him before: at Aunt Nan's coronation. He had acted as the Queen's chief ewer, pouring scented water over her hands whenever needed. How long ago that now seemed.

Threading her arm underneath Kate's, her aunt walked her to the window. "Time for more introductions. Come, niece, come and meet more of my good friends."

First, Aunt Nan introduced her to Sir Thomas's sister, Lady Meg Lee, round of face and plump of body. Giving a quick smile to Kate in greeting, Lady Lee then whispered something to her aunt, gesturing towards Smeaton. Red faced with embarrassment, he was surrounded by a group of chattering girls. One teasingly took his lute out of his hands while another closed in on him like quarry. A little distance from them, Kate recognised the woman who had entertained the children by juggling apples in the gallery yesterday. The back of her hand held against her forehead, she pointed to Smeaton and pretended to swoon. Lady Meg laughed a deep belly laugh. When Aunt Nan joined in, Kate forced out a laugh, too. Out of step with the other women, her laughter rang loud in her ears. She raised her hands to her hot face.

"See you my good fool, Kate?" Without waiting for an answer, Aunt Nan took her hand and led her deeper into the room.

Not even glancing towards Lady Meg, let alone the carefree young women near her, a heart-faced girl with large, dark eyes, thin, arched eyebrows and full lips chattered animatedly to an elderly, solemn man robed as a man of God. Her dark eyebrows suggested she would be dark headed under the confining headgear that proclaimed her a matron. Still, she seemed not much older than Kate and a strange partner for the old man beside her. Kate had never seen a man with a swan-white beard as long as his; the sight of it almost made her giggle.

"Another Catherine, Kate," said Aunt Nan. "The Duchess of Suffolk."

Hearing her title, the girl looked towards the Queen. Kate dropped a deeper curtsey than she had just given Lady Lee, and then rose to the Duchess's smile. The girl opened her eyes wide and blinked, sweeping shadows of long, thick lashes upon her rosy cheeks. "What to do?" she laughed. "I've lost count of the Catherines at court." Her eyes travelled to Aunt Nan and then back to Kate. "No matter; the Annes outscore us all, and the Queen reigns over them, as she does us all. Do you mind if I call you Kat while I keep the Kate, or Catherine?"

Liking her, Kate smiled in return. "I care not. A name is but a name; it's for us to make it our own."

Aunt Nan beamed with approval, took her arm again, and turned her to a woman who looked about the same age as Aunt Nan, and, despite a pregnant belly, just as slender. Dressed in black and silver like the Queen, she seemed competing with her in elegance. "And this is another of my friends, Elizabeth, Lady Worcester."

Kate smiled, bobbed another curtsey as the silent Lady Worcester bent her head. Her stern eyes glimmered, assessing Kate before looking away in dismissal. Taken aback, Kate stared at the woman, and then down at her feet. *She judges me? She dismisses me? What right has she? I am the niece of the Queen!*

Aunt Nan brought her to one of the few men in the chamber. "And I cannot forget my good Latimer, Bishop of Worcester. You'll find he watches vigilantly after the souls that come under his care. Catherine here"—her aunt smiled at the Duchess of Suffolk—"has elected herself his devoted follower."

The old man bowed to the Duchess, his bright eyes crinkling. "And honours me by it."

Flushing, the Duchess dropped her gaze before meeting his again. "You're the one who honours me, good Father, granting your valuable time for my comfort and betterment. I remember your sermons by heart." She closed her eyes and recited, "The saints are not saints by praying to them, but by believing in Him who makes them saints, and as they are saints, so may we be."

Latimer grinned and stroked his beard as if in thought. "We're all followers of the One who first led twelve men to speak and spread the gospel. For myself, I am Our Lord Jesus' humble servant, who prays daily to God to be a good shepherd to his flock."

"That you are, good sir," Aunt Nan said with a brisk nod. "Catherine knows, as I do, what a good shepherd we have in you. I thank God every day for the guidance of you and Cranmer. More now than ever before."

Latimer smiled again. "I am only a spokesman of the good, merciful God, my Queen. Only He knows our hearts and hears our prayers, as He did when I prayed for release from imprisonment and found He had not forsaken me. He spoke to your good heart, and I am here now, doing again His work in my poor way."

Aunt Nan met his eyes. "Never a poor way, my good Father. Never that."

Kate listened to the conversation, feeling prouder and prouder. This was the aunt she well remembered from the days celebrating her coronation—confident and self assured, her sharp intelligence alight in her eyes. All around, people listened to her, their respect clearly apparent. This was what Kate had come to court to see—her very own aunt, ruling her court as queen.

Turning, she took Kate's arm again. "Come, child, there's someone else I wish you to greet."

They walked to the other side of the fireplace. Speaking in a low undertone to Madge and another young woman, more richly dressed and jewelled than either of them, a tall, slender woman leaned against the wall, her hazel eyes watching the approach of Aunt Nan. Not as young as the Duchess of Suffolk, yet she seemed no more than twenty. Not in question was her beauty—she was even more beautiful than the younger Madge. Yet, like Madge, under a French hood that shimmered with pearls, she wore her hair long and decoratively plaited, declaring her maiden status. Nearing her, Kate could not help but stare. Her heavy-lidded eyes looked familiar. *I know her. I don't know from where, but I know her.*

"The King's niece, the Lady Margaret Douglas, and your cousin Mary, Duchess of Richmond, wife to the King's son," Aunt Nan whispered.

"Your Grace—Lady Margaret." Kate clutched the sides of her gown and dipped a low curtsey. With a glance at the shorter Duchess, Lady Margaret looked Kate up and down. Annoyed at the rising heat in her cheeks, Kate steeled herself to meet her eyes without flinching. Not only did the Lady Margaret study her with great interest, but also, her sandy brows puckering in concentration, the deep blue eyes of the Duchess remained fixated on her. It made her want to run away.

Lady Margaret spoke, her deep voice a whip of command. "Raise up, cousin. The Queen desires informality in her chambers. Or, should I say the Queen commands?"

Tapping Lady Margaret's arm, Aunt Nan laughed. "In privacy, bowing and curtseying become tiresome after awhile, don't you think, Meg?"

The young woman lifted her chin and looked down her exquisite nose. "If you say so, Your Grace."

Amused, Aunt Nan wagged her finger at Lady Margaret. "You don't agree with informality?"

"I believe in showing the respect due at all times, Your Grace. If we don't hold to that, commoners will take the opportunity to step beyond their station. Nobility is a sacred estate and protects us from anarchy."

"I know that well." Aunt Nan shrugged. "Methinks the

world grumbles no matter what we do. In my own chambers, I like people to be themselves and not hide behind titles and bloodlines. Let there be at least one place at court to be ourselves."

Aunt Nan glanced towards Madge. Now a little distance away, she spoke earnestly to a young man. About his square, strong face, a sudden ray of sunlight lit his hair to bright silver. Aunt Nan grinned at Lady Margaret. "If I'm not mistaken, you've enjoyed your time in these chambers."

Lady Margaret gazed at the man. She seemed to Kate a different woman, with all her frightening hardness gone. She just stood there, her mouth slightly open, her eyes shining and her vulnerability almost tangible.

Kate looked from Margaret to the man. As if tugged, he gazed at Margaret and smiled. His expression called out to her like a hunting horn. Close to her side, the Duchess, her ink-stained fingers at odds with her rich robes, toyed with her girdle and seemed not to notice. But an indulgent smile played at her lips.

Playing nervously with her hair, Lady Margaret lowered her gaze. "I suppose I have." She looked at the Queen before speaking in a rush. "Your Grace, I am in agony. I beg you, pray speak to the King, my uncle. I don't know how much longer I can bear this."

Aunt Nan frowned. "Be patient, Meg. I promised to do what I can, but I must wait for the right time." She looked one way and then another before speaking softly. "You have my sympathy, but you know your royal blood makes what you ask hard, if not impossible. You must realise you may yet pay for your recklessness." Cutting off the conversation, Aunt Nan searched the room before looking at Kate.

"Welladay, there's one left to greet who needs no introduction. Come, he's waited long enough."

Kate's heart fluttered with excitement. Behind her royal aunt, she threaded through the people as they offered their reverence to the passing Queen. Aunt Nan stopped at the door of her bedchamber and smiled. "I shall stay here. Go, Kate, and see your brother."

Without further ado, Kate entered and shut the door behind her. Harry sat on the Queen's great bed, swinging his long, slender legs. His hand held on to the peculiarly carved bedpost, on which Kate recognized the symbols of her aunt's heraldry.

The green bed hangings and gold and silver bed cover edged with crimson satin, too, had more of her aunt's emblems, embroidered in bright colours and gold thread, with a large number of honeysuckle and acorns; Kate grinned, knowing they were the private love tokens of the Queen and King.

Dappled by shadows of the gold tassels hanging over him, Harry tossed back his reddish-gold hair and grinned. "You took your time."

Kate smiled, a little uncertain. He had changed in the twelve months since she last saw him. He had been still a small boy; now he looked a youth.

He jumped from the bed, and Kate gasped. "Good God, Harry, you're taller than me."

Ruffling up his own hair, he laughed with pride. "I am taller than our aunt; that must mean Mother, too."

Kate stood on tiptoes and kissed his cheek. "You'll always be two years younger than me. I've missed you, brother."

Harry's grin revealed white, straight teeth. "Even after

Mother giving you a new one?"

Kate screwed up her nose. "That brother cries, pukes and smells. I cannot understand why she dotes on him as she does; it turns my stomach."

Suddenly serious, Harry cocked his head, chewing at his bottom lip. "How is she?"

"Happy and content, until she thinks of you. She yearns to see you, Harry."

Her brother stared at his feet. "She writes often. I am no penman, but for her I write." He glared, as if she was the one at fault. "Why did she marry that lowborn rogue? She was allowed to see me before then."

"She was lovesick." Kate shifted in her discomfort. "I don't think she could help herself." To Kate's confusion, hearing Harry call their stepfather a rogue made her want to defend him. "He loves her—truly loves her. He's kind to me, but I don't want another father. The memory of our good father is enough for me."

Harry's startled look puzzled Kate. He reddened and averted his face towards the window. Outside, peacocks screamed, piercing any semblance of peace. Their strident cries, as if panicked calls for help, only added to her apprehension.

Still looking at the window, her brother frowned. "My faith! Why are the peacocks back? The Queen, our aunt, had them banished from the gardens long ago."

Kate squirmed under his sudden perusal. She was the elder, yet he looked at her differently to what he had in the past, like she was the child, not him. "Why are you acting strange? Everybody is."

He hunched his shoulders and refused to meet her eyes.

"Poor Katie," he murmured. He glanced at her, then away again. "I cannot tell you."

One day, only one day at court and secrets seemed everywhere. Secrets kept from her, secrets about the Queen and King. Now the secrets involved her. She glared at Harry. "God's oath, why? Am I not your sister?"

"Aye, of course, but this first concerns our mother. Uncle and Aunt do not want her any more heartsore than necessary."

"Heartsore? Why do you think that?"

He shrugged. "Believe me, she would be heartsore if they spoke to you without her permission. That's why Uncle George has gone to her."

Kate clutched her aching head and tried to loosen her gable hood. She sat on the bed and glowered at her brother. "Harry, this is not fair. I don't understand why I must wait. Especially if this secret touches on me."

He sat beside her and held her hand. "Life's hurt our mother far too often. I beg you, sister, be patient for her."

Kate tightened her mouth. "What happens if Mother does not wish to give her permission to our uncle?"

Lowering his head, Harry inspected a stain on his doublet. Kate tugged his hand. "Harry, answer me."

He combed his fingers through his hair and looked at her with sober eyes. "Whether Mother says yea or nay, Aunt Nan just waits for our uncle to return. Then, I promise, you'll know."

5

Kate bit her bottom lip, frowned in concentration, and wrote on the first blank page in her journal:

I stand on a sacred threshold—a bridge between reality and dream. Time there has no meaning.

She frowned again, recalling the poem that had brought these words to mind. Her stepfather had recited it, just days before she left her home for court.

This never-lingering Time, who all day long
Is going on and never will return,
Resembles water that forever flows
But ne'er a drop comes back.
There is no thing
So durable, not even iron itself,
That it can time survive...

She saw him so vividly in her memory—smiling and looking at her mother, his eyes humorous, trying to lift her spirits. Trying to tell her that nothing ever stays the same. Kate blotched the parchment, annoyed to be even thinking about her stepfather. She sat straighter and returned her quill to the parchment.

Surely I possess eternity, the now, the past, the future, forever one.

Kate sighed. Would Uncle George or Aunt Nan think this a poem? *But what is poetry?* Kate stared at the words she had written and put down her quill. Should she scrape the words away and deny them the right to make such a claim?

For days now, she had tried to find her place at court. She felt an incongruous creature—bound through blood to the Queen, yet low in her service. Her new world was so strange. There was an air of expectancy—and of an even greater malaise. The chill of winter seemed to have seeped into the very spirits of those at court. She could make no sense of it. The court was like a dead hearth that waited for fire and life.

On her third day at court, early in the morning, Kate hurried to her brother's chambers. Uncle George, given good weather, would now have reached her mother. Unhappy with this forced wait for his return, she planned to make Harry reconsider and tell her the reason for all this foolish secrecy.

She badgered him with questions, but discovered Harry had learnt too well the ways of the court and its skills of dissembling. He shrugged at her interrogation and then made her laugh with his telling of how he had put a purge into the drink of one his fellow scholars, a boy who too many times broke wind without apology. When Harry shared the punishment he received from his tutor, she laughed even more heartily. On a parchment, he had translated from Latin to English Erasmus's "On Good Manners for Boys."

*There are some who lay down the rule that a
boy should refrain from breaking wind by*

constricting his buttocks. But it is no part of
good manners to bring illness upon yourself
while striving to appear polite. If you may
withdraw, do it in private. But if not, then in
the words of an old adage, cover the sound
with a cough. Besides, why do they not rule
in the same way that boys should not purge
their bowels, since it is more dangerous to
refrain from breaking wind than it is to
constrict the bowels.

Harry next invited her to explore his small library. Drawn to the shelves laid out with valuable books, Kate forgot her questions and became lost in opening covers, seeking the treasure hidden inside. When it came time for him to go to his tutors, he gathered together five of his discarded books, some loaned to him by the Queen, and told Kate to take them. She could hardly believe her good fortune that her brother would allow these valuable books to be in her possession.

Taking the books and more gifts, she looped her heavy skirts into her girdle so she could walk more freely. He opened his chamber door and waited until she was in the outside gallery. He then forgot her as he strode to join his fellow scholars.

She turned in the opposite direction to begin the journey back to the chambers she shared with Madge. With each step the weight in her arms grew heavier. By the time she reached the antechamber that led to her bedchamber, she struggled to regain her breath. The oak door looked closed, but a firm swing of her hip proved otherwise. She entered the room with relief.

Her good fortune continued. The bedroom door was ajar. Once more, she swung her hip, only to discover she had used the last vestiges of her strength. Her swing lacking any true power, the second door only opened a little more. Just enough for her to see inside the darkened room. Just enough to startle her. She made a sudden movement of fright that almost toppled Plato's *Phaedo* and *The Republic* from the bundle in her arms. Kate leaned against the wall beside the door to regain a firmer hold. She peered into the chamber again. Her eyes—nor the thin winter light—hadn't misled her. Seated on the window-seat, her aunt embraced the weeping Madge. Her face white and drawn, Aunt Nan looked ready to cry herself.

"Bow out," Aunt Nan said to Madge, her voice bell clear and distinct despite the distance. "You've a lion's heart, but believe me, you play with fire. 'Tis too dangerous. Let it be."

Madge rubbed her face before looking up again. "And open the field for the little white mouse to gnaw deeper into the King's heart? My Queen, how can you say, 'Let it be'?"

Long, thick lashes swept a fan-like shadow beneath Aunt Nan's eyes. Resting her head against Madge's, she placed her hand on her flat belly. "My best weapon I hold here. Our hungry mouse cannot win if I give the King his son."

Madge spoke almost peevishly. "'Tis not fair the King distresses you at such at time!"

Aunt Nan nestled closer and drew a sharp breath. "Life is not about fairness, especially for those who wear crowns. That's a luxury I cannot ask for. How can I when I cannot afford to give it to others?" She shrugged. "The King's back at the hunt because I am breeding. He says he does so because of his care; he cannot bed with me, not while I carry his son. He refuses to see how his dalliances degrade our love." Her sigh seemed to skate close to tears. "I'll not give up my husband without a fight. All I can do to keep his love I will do, but it must be in truth and honesty. Do any other, I lose everything that made this road worth all the battles— all the bloodshed. I cannot lose his love utterly. I would sooner die than for that to happen." She touched Madge's cheek. "Sweet Madge, I ask for your forgiveness. I should never have agreed to you distracting the King from Jane. This is not your fight. I do not want you to dance a dance that fails even me now. I know my husband too well. Sooner or later, the King will demand payment for his songs and smiles. I'm no Wolsey or Cromwell that I can be content to see you, my young kin, be the payment for distracting my husband from his mouse. I love you too much for that."

Kate could no longer ignore her heavy load. Once more, she tightened her hold and, as quietly as possible, backed away from the door. Whatever did this mean? Their conversation spoke a language beyond her comprehension.

She left the chamber and wandered some distance away, searching for a place to sit. At last, in the long gallery, she found a bench backing the wall's high, wide windows and put down her bundles. Sitting beside them, she rubbed her aching arms and pondered the conversation she had overheard, but her fear and bewilderment only deepened.

One by one, she looked at the five books. Which should she read first? The third book, impressed not only with a gold border but also gold letters, was a thin, beautifully bound volume titled *Le Pasteur Evangelique*. She opened it. Unlike her aunt and mother, who spoke French fluently after spending years of their youth in France, hers was slow and sometimes clumsy. Now with time on her hands and desirous to better herself, she managed to translate the dedication to her royal aunt:

Oh Anne, my lady, Oh incomparable Queen,
This good shepherd who favours you...

Reading on, she arrived at the poem's prophecy. Her eyes filled with tears. Kate rechecked the words and made certain she had made no mistake. The verse sang out the prophecy that her aunt would watch her son grow to manhood. How Kate prayed and hoped for that.

"Katherine Carey!"

Kate looked up to the mischievous grin of the Duchess of Suffolk. A little distance behind the girl stood a solid, middle-aged woman, dressed in Suffolk livery. Blushing, Kate dropped the book back on the short pile, bounded up, and curtseyed.

The young Duchess gestured to the seat, and then laughed. "Sit down. Sit down. Pray, give me one moment of informality this morning." She addressed her servants. "Patrick, go to the Duke, my husband. Tell him I crave forgiveness for my delay, but I wish to speak to the Queen's niece, Lady Katherine, alone. Come back when the bells ring out the next hour. Mayhap, by then, we can escort this maid to a safer place than this.

Sitting beside Kate, the Duchess tidied her skirts and then picked up the book with the dedication to the Queen. "'Tis the Queen's," she said in surprise.

Hearing the unspoken question, Kate smiled. "From my brother's chamber." She gestured to the other books. "With great generosity, he has allowed me to take these books into my care."

The Duchess grinned, dimpling. She seemed younger than ever. She picked up another book and frowned. "Great generosity, indeed. These are costly books, no doubt loaned by the Queen in hope he would actually read them. Young lord Harry may soon find himself confronting a very unhappy aunt when she discovers these books not in his chambers. When that happens, I would not wish to be in his shoes."

Kate raised her hand to her heating cheeks. "Your Grace, I don't believe my aunt would mind if I read them before Harry. It may encourage him to read them, too."

Shrugging, the Duchess placed the book back with the others. "You could be right." She dimpled once more. "How many years have you, my namesake?"

"I will be soon fourteen, Your Grace." Kate stared down at her clenched hands. *Fourteen.* An age just as meaningless as thirteen, still stuck in limbo between childhood and adulthood.

"Near to fourteen," the Duchess said thoughtfully. "I'm sixteen, not much older than you. Lady Katherine Carey, you're niece to the Queen of England. Pray, can you not call me Kate, or at least Catherine?"

Something unfroze inside Kate. For most of her life, her mother's few servants had been her only company. She often starved for friendship of maids her own age. Now one offered what she yearned for. Kate wiggled with delight. "I would like that, Your ... Catherine."

Catherine smiled and laid her hand on Kate's arm for a moment. "Now that we're good and true friends, pray may I offer you counsel?"

Alarmed, Kate jerked around. "Counsel?"

"Aye, Kat, counsel." There was a noise like a muffled,

faraway cough. Warily, Catherine lifted her head and looked down the empty gallery. Some distance away, the steady rhythm of footfalls faded and silence fell again. She inhaled and exhaled deeply, visibly relaxing. "This court's not a place for a well-born maid to wander alone. Surely, the Queen told you this?"

Kate firmed her lips. "I don't need servants to be always at my beckoning." Breaking eye contact with Catherine, Kate again studied her hands, wishing she could stop chewing her nails. Like her aunt, her apprehensions often got the better of her. "I hate being shadowed. I like being alone." She swung out her foot, rotated her toe, and moved out her other foot, staring at the new slippers Aunt Nan had given to her only yesterday. She looked again at Catherine. "I'm used to it."

Seemingly with great concern, her new friend clasped her hand. "Pray, don't be a fool. Very few of us have that luxury, and you're too close to the Queen to ever walk alone in these galleries, or any other place for that matter. I would be failing as your friend not to tell you this. You need a servant, one like my good Betty." She smiled at the silent woman. "Between Betty and myself, only a foolish man would take it in mind to accost us."

The servant grinned, showing a missing eye tooth. She pulled a dagger from a pocket in her dress. "Aye, m'am. You need not fear if old Betty's with you. I like my needle, and none yet have complained about my skill with it." The woman cackled. "Welladay, maybe those who find themselves on its wrong end." She cackled louder. "Its sharp end soon sorts out any quarrels."

Catherine laughed. "That I don't doubt!" She turned back to Kate. "My lady mother placed Betty in my service when I wed. She wants me safe at court. I want you safe, too."

"Why should I not be safe?" Kate asked.

Catherine leaned closer. "What an innocent you are. My lady mother came with Queen Katherine..." Looking one way and then the other, Catherine flushed. "My tongue slipped. Pray, forgive and forget it. I am named for Katherine of Aragon, and my mother remains one of her closest friends. But believe me, I'm loyal to your aunt."

With a smile, Kate sought to reassure her friend. "My own mother, my royal aunt's sister, at times suffers from the same slip of the tongue. Katherine, Dowager Princess of Wales, was known as the Queen of England longer than we both have lived. Mama told me she was a very loved Queen and, for many, there is none other."

Catherine nodded. "Aye, it is safest for us to say no more. Euripides tells us the wise man's answer is silence, and silence is often the only and best armour we possess. Alas, even that is not enough to give us the protection we need." Her face flushing, she halted and sucked in her top lip. "My mother hates it here. The court of the old King shocked her, after her early life with Queen Isabel of Castilla. The court may be now refined and civilised, but Mother still keeps to her house in London rather than seek out company here. She worries about me—even knowing Betty's skills.

"But let's return to you. Surely your mother didn't send you to attend Queen Anne by yourself?"

Kate shifted in discomfort and gazed at her shoes again. "We're not wealthy. With caring for my new brother and little sister, there were no servants to spare when my stepfather brought me here. Mother said the Queen would see me attended properly." She looked at Catherine. "I beg you, do not speak to my aunt about this matter. The Queen has troubles enough without concerning herself about me."

"Troubles enough." Catherine pulled at her skirt, straightening a fold. She met Kate's gaze. "You're right, she has more than her share of them. But you don't want to add to her woes by putting yourself in a situation that would only distress her—not at this time. Likely Queen Anne assumed your mother sent you to court with a woman to care for your needs. 'Tis not something the Queen would think to ask you."

Kate felt suddenly strange sitting there, looking at this girl who had already experienced so much more of life than her. Curious, Kate asked, "Have you been at court long?"

Tears brimmed in Catherine's eyes and then, as quickly, were shuttered away. She lifted her chin and smiled. "It feels like a long time, but it's only the last two years or so. I grew up at the Duke's, my lord husband's estate. With two infant sons, I still spend a goodly portion of my days there."

Kate lifted her eyebrows, surprised. "You have children?"

Catherine laughed. "I have been wed for over two years, and my lord husband is not one to wait to bed his wife. My firstborn was born ten months after our marriage, and I am not long from my churching of my second."

Something niggled at Kate. "Did you say you were raised by the Duke, your husband? What about your mother?"

Catherine shrugged. "My father died when I was but a babe. As I was his heir, for my best interests, my lady mother agreed to allow the Duke and his wife—the King's sister, Mary, the White Queen—to take me as their ward. My mother was good friends with Queen Mary, God bless her soul, and saw me often." Silent, she lifted a hand to her pensive face, tilting her head. Her long fingers rubbed close to her ear.

"What is it?" Kate asked, seeing Catherine brush away her tears.

"'Tis no matter."

"Then why do you weep?"

Catherine shrugged again. "At the whims of fate? A silly thing, surely, to cry for. What one cannot change, one must learn to accept and make best of." Sighing, she took up one book and flicked through its pages. "Boethius's *The Consolation of Philosophy*..." She glanced at Kate. "Have you read this?"

Confronted by the Latin text, Kate grimaced "No, my mother possesses few books. I never knew there were so many until seeing my aunt's library."

"Aye, the Queen has a great passion for books. Her chaplain, William Latimer, often purchases them to help increase her collection. He gave me the gift of this book when I first came to court two years ago, just wed." She closed her eyes. "'Why then do you mortal men seek after happiness outside yourself when it lies within you?'" Catherine turned a smile to Kate. "I have read it often since my marriage. Would my new friend like to read it first, so we may discuss Boethius together? I know the Queen, your aunt, would approve. She holds Boethius in great regard."

Kate smiled. "If you recommend it, then of course, I'll read it before I start on the others." She gazed at the pile of books. "Mother did not tell me how long I am allowed to stay from home, but I desire to remain here as long as possible. And while I am here, I want to learn as much as I can."

A hunting horn sounded, answered by another—the gay sound of triumph and homecoming. Kate turned with

Catherine to the window and peered into the courtyard. Through the gateway, a party of men rode in, flicking up white snow in their path. Gold and silver glinted from buckles and swords. Under fur mantles hinted rich colours: purple, blue, crimson, and green.

Horses wheeled around, tossed heads, and lifted forelegs in protest as riders shortened reins and pulled their mounts to a halt. Servants rushed around, taking hold.

Catherine sighed. "So ... it starts again."

Kate blinked. "What?"

"Silly goose, do you not see? The King returns."

6

Nervously, Kate approached the open doorway of the throne room. Looking straight ahead, pike-bearing guards stood to attention on either side of heavy oak doors, swung outward to reveal the milling crowd within.

"Time for you to meet the King." Aunt Nan glanced over her shoulder at her. "Come, follow me." She smiled in reassurance.

Aunt Nan's other attendants mingled with the rest of the court, while her chamberlain walked before her. In a ringing tone, he announced to all, "The Queen. Make way for the Queen. Make way for Queen Anne."

A path opened wide for Aunt Nan. On either side, the men bowed and women curtseyed.

Her heart beating fast with fear, Kate trailed close behind her, aware of the King observing his wife's approach. Kate caught the assessing eye of her grandfather. Standing beside another man, he nodded before murmuring something to him. *Why hasn't he come to see me since his return from the hunt?*

The King sat on a high-back throne, on the dais, all alone. Long, muscular legs spread apart, knees bent, feet slippered, his repose was that of an active man, a man of power, one restless with inaction. Upon his head was a flat, circular hat, trimmed with the down of white feathers. What was seen of his hair was reddish, thin, threaded with white.

The Queen's empty throne was next to him. Padded with

green and gold velvet, emblazoned with the Tudor rose, its dark wood gleamed as if newly polished. Now and then, the King glanced at it.

Kate looked around, aware of the almost palpable fear of many in this chamber, fear that enclosed her own heart in its vise. *No wonder.* The King gazed around his court with hard, fierce, frightening blue eyes. She blinked. In the next second, he looked bitter; suffering; suspicious.

Men and the few women stood at a safe distance from him. They all watched him; waiting for him to speak; waiting for his command.

The King impatiently drummed his jewelled fingers upon the arm of his throne, or the thigh of his leg, waiting for the Queen to reach him. His rubies flashed and sparkled red droplets of light that danced upon the whitewashed wall.

Besides the cloth of estate erected over his head, tapestries, hanging on the walls nearby, also decorated the room with bright colours. Rich, gold-threaded depictions of two Biblical kings: Solomon in all his glory and his father, David. King David played his harp while, in the background, Bathsheba wept. Kate shivered, recognising that both kings had been modelled on the Tudor king before her.

Now slouched on the throne, he toyed with his thumb ring, straightening as his wife and Kate neared the dais. A ray of light glinted on the death's head of the gold ring on his little finger. Aunt Nan, followed by Kate, dropped into a low courtesy. The King came down from the dais, reached out a hand to his Queen, and helped her up, while Kate stayed on her knees.

"You look well, Nan." He positioned her body in profile for the court, rested a hand on her stomacher and grinned.

"And how is our son?"

Lowering her eyelids, she smiled warily, wanly. "Giving me a taste for apples, my lord husband, and making me regret it afterwards. But I am not sickening with this babe as much as I have before. All is well." She smiled again—a brighter smile, yet also brittle. "How was the hunt?"

With a laugh and smile, his arms stretched out wide in mime. "My arrows brought down my targets at over two hundred yards. I killed three bucks. We shall have fresh venison tonight."

He looked behind his wife and seemed to notice Kate for the first time. Remaining on her knees, she stayed silent and still, waiting for permission to rise, for once wishing she could make herself invisible. All last night, she had tossed and turned knowing today she would meet the King. Likewise, Madge had been restless from the moment she came to bed.

"Who is this girl?" the King asked.

Aunt Nan glanced at her with encouragement and gestured for her to stand. "Come, sweetheart. Come and give your greeting to the King."

Kate's knees almost buckled as she stood upright. Annoyed at her lack of grace, she walked forward a few steps. Aunt Nan took her hand and turned back to her husband. "Surely you remember her from my coronation? This is Katherine Carey, sire."

"Katherine Carey," the King repeated, regarding her with new attention "Katherine Carey."

He looked her up and down, from head to toes. So like his niece, the Lady Margaret, the King's penetrating gaze disturbed Kate—she felt like goods brought out for bartering.

Her hand clammy, she curbed the urge to wipe it on her skirt. The king exchanged a strange look with Aunt Nan.

"Why is she here?" he asked.

"I thought it time. My niece is well overdue to learn the ways of the court."

"Katherine Carey," he said again.

Kate blushed. Unused to being the centre of attention—now a King had named her three times and would not stop staring at her—she squirmed, just wanting for this audience to come to an end.

The chamberlain banged his staff on the floor two times and announced, "Lord Cromwell!"

A short, solid man entered the chamber. Her aunt made a sudden movement closer to the King. The graceless man took off his cap to reveal closed-cropped, coal-black hair underneath. He made an awkward, deep bow and then approached. His graceless gait was so different from the many at court who moved with measured, carefully considered steps.

"Tom!" the King said. "What brings you here?"

The man bowed. "Your Grace, we are glad to see you back at Greenwich." He bowed to Aunt Nan. "We have all missed the King's presence for this last week and more, have we not, my Queen?" His small, hard mouth twisted into what seemed to be his attempt at a smile.

Aunt Nan took the King's arm and smiled up at her husband. He didn't seem to notice. "Aye, my lord Chancellor. I am glad to have my husband home again."

"What do you here, Tom?" the King said again. "Have you come to claim the coin I lost to you at cards before I went away?"

Cromwell's double chin wobbled and wobbled with his laugh. His face lit up with animation and amusement. "It is I who usually loses at cards and dice, my liege. I am happy to be the King's moneylender for once."

His hand on his hip, the King hooted out a loud belly laugh. "Sometimes I wonder who is richer—you or I."

Those around the court who were not listening before now listened in earnest. Kate noticed her grandfather murmur once more to the man next to him.

Cromwell barked another wobbly-chin laugh, and scratched his head. "Marry! My Grace, I know my place. All I have is yours. I am your servant who willingly places his fortune in the service of my King."

Aunt Nan's half-hooded eyes opened wide. She remained oddly silent and moved restlessly beside her husband. She seemed to challenge Cromwell before lowering her eyes. Cromwell ignored her. It was all very strange.

Kate found the King watching her. "Tom, I do not believe you would know this girl," he said. "'Tis Mary Carey's daughter."

Cromwell cocked his head, while furrowing his brow. "What is your name, child?"

Kate curtseyed and murmured, "Katherine, my lord."

"Hmmm. Sister to young Henry, is that not right? I know your lady mother—you're very alike." He spoke to the King. "And she has a strong look of her father, too."

The King's face flushed and seemed to swell. But then he suddenly boomed out a laugh. "Aye. I see what you mean."

Flushed, Aunt Nan shook his arm. "My Lord, may I have permission to take my niece back to my chambers? She is new to court and has had enough taste of it this morning. I also must rest. I have not slept well while you were away from me."

He frowned. "What I do should not concern you, Nan. I have told you this before."

Their eyes locked and seemed to war against the other, with Aunt Nan surrendering first, but not before a weary look settled upon her face. Close by, Cromwell stood there, eyes lowered, hands together, a smile hinting at his lips.

Going back to Aunt Nan's chambers, Kate tried to make sense of the puzzle. Why had her aunt seemed so worried, almost scared, when the conversation turned to Kate's father? Kate had discovered his portrait, a miniature kept by her mother, in a coffer of garments earmarked for making anew. Her mother must have placed it there in mistake. Despite losing him at only five, her handsome father remained clear in her memory: a rather square face on a long neck, eyes set wide apart, thin, well-shaped mouth. The only flaw was a narrow, yet somewhat bulbous nose. She had not thought she looked like him, but rather her mother. Since she had brought the miniature with her, she could barely wait to dig it out again from underneath her gowns and shifts and search for the similarity she must have missed before.

Aunt Nan arrived back at her chambers and reached for Kate's hand. Dismissing her attendants, she led Kate deeper into the antechamber before releasing her. She sat on the chair by the window and kicked off her shoes.

"That's better." She flexed her long, shapely toes. "My new shoes were pinching me all the time I was with the King." She gestured to her footstool. "Come, sit next to me."

Thankfully sitting down, Kate gazed out at the day. The morning sun shone weakly, snow lay on the ground, thick and white, and otherworldly. She blinked. For a moment, the wind lifted a flurry of snow. It seemed to take the shape of angel's wings.

Within the room, someone had built up the fire in the huge fireplace while they had been away and lit the braziers around the room. Kate closed her eyes, letting the welcomed warmth seep back into her bones.

Aunt Nan laughed and laid a hand on her shoulder. "Who gave you permission to sleep?"

Kate smiled at her aunt. The love in her eyes made Kate brave enough to do as she did with her mother. She leant on her aunt's knee and rested her head.

Aunt Nan laughed again. "If you want, you can remove your hood. I remember how I hated them at your age."

Kate yanked off her new hood. Her long, unbound hair, now free from its confinement, cascaded to curl upon itself on the floor.

Her aunt stroked her head. "A very pretty colour, Kate, not blonde, nor red, but something in betwixt."

She stopped speaking, and silence reigned for a time. Kate thought about the King and the way he looked at her, how he studied her. Not lust, no, not lust, but it still frightened her.

Her mother had warned her of the men she would meet at court. "Guard your maidenhead as you would your life," she had said. "Don't ever let men get you alone. If you do, you might find yourself wishing for death."

Raised in the country, the sight of animals mating was a common occurrence. She had seen servants dally with one another before she had to endure the sight her mother and her new husband kissing and caressing. Kate believed she knew what happened when they locked the bedchamber door after them. Sometimes they forgot to close it completely. Before her mother became big bellied with her sister and brother, Kate would pass their chamber to hear the bed creak and creak and their raised voices joined in unintelligible moans. Sometimes her mother cried out, "Will!" over and over, as if somehow she was lost and wished to be found again. Discomforted at where her thoughts had taken her, Kate sat up.

Her aunt smiled. "I thought you had really gone to sleep this time."

With a shrug, Kate put fingers at her mouth and pulled her lower lip.

Aunt Nan cocked her head. "Welladay, child. Methinks you have questions. Do you wish to ask them?"

Kate took a deep breath. Her smile seemed to invite confidences. "The King. Why did he keep saying my name?"

"Did he?"

"Aye, three times he said it."

Sitting back in her chair, Aunt Nan smoothed down her dress and then stroked her slim belly. She left her hand there as if shielding a vulnerable treasure. "I suppose three times is curious." She let out a long sigh. "I wish your uncle was returned from seeing your mother. The King came back sooner than I expected."

Perplexed, Kate frowned. "My uncle? Pray, what has Uncle George got to do with the King's interest in my name?"

"Your uncle? Nothing, really." Aunt Nan put her elbow on her chair's armrest and cradled the side of her face with her hand. She screwed her mouth to the side and clicked her tongue. "I don't know what to do. If I leave you in the dark, someone might blurt it out in any case." She sniffed with annoyance. "Your mother should have told you sooner than this."

Moving closer to her aunt, Kate blurted out, "Told me what?"

Aunt Nan studied her for a long moment, then leaned forward. "Give me your hands."

Kate placed her hands into Aunt Nan's. "Aunt, you're frightening me."

"Frightened? My niece, the daughter of your mother, frightened? You do not know yet the bravery of the women in our family. Niece, my Kate, believe me, you're brave and strong enough to hear what I am about to tell you. Child, there is no easy way to tell you this." Aunt Nan lifted her chin. "William Carey was not your father."

Kate snatched away her hands and bolted up. "Not my father? What do you mean? He *is* my father."

Aunt Nan shook her head. Pity shone in her eyes. "I wish I could tell you otherwise, but 'tis the truth. William Carey gave you and your brother his name, nothing more."

As if from a long distance, his voice sang the lullaby that had sent her to sleep whenever he was home: *"Lullay, thou little tiny child, lullay; bye bye, lully, lullay,"* her father sang. Her father.

The times she rode before him on his horse while he told her yet another story or taught her another song. He gave her nothing but his name? She clapped her hands over her ears and shook her head with violence. "You lie! He is my father! He is!"

Aunt Nan took Kate's hands and held them in her firm grip. Her eyes shone with tears. "No, child. The King is your father."

She stared at her aunt, her heart pounding. In her mind,

she heard her mother's voice reciting one of her favourite Bible verses: *For now we see through a glass, darkly, but then face to face: now I know in part; but then shall I know even as also I am known.*

Slapped with horror, she picked up her skirts and ran all the way back to her chamber. Once there, she flung herself on the empty bed, and sobbed and sobbed.

7

The tears falling down her face, Kate flipped the pages of her journal. She came to the one she sought, where Uncle George had written the words of Sappho:

Day in, day out
I hunger and I struggle.

Hunger. Struggle. Was that all she had to look forward to in life—the hunger of body, the hunger of soul? The struggle to simply to live? More tears dripped down her cheeks, dropping like raindrops on the parchment of the book, spattering and smudging Uncle George's perfect calligraphy.

She shut the book, thinking of all the lies. What if they lied out of love? That did not make it right. Feeling so betrayed, she returned to the bed, rolling over to her stomach.

A soft knock followed one harder on the door.

"Go away," Kate said through her tears, her voice muffled and hoarse, as she remained face down on the bolster.

The door opened and light footsteps padded to the bed.

"Go away," Kate said again, but lifted her head to see her brother standing at her side. She sniffed, wiped her runny nose on her sleeve, and rolled onto her side. "Why are you here?"

Harry sat on the edge of the bed and picked up a lock of her hair. "Not as red as mine; methinks more like Mother's. Why am I here? Why do you think?" He released her hair from his fingers. "Our aunt sent me. She tells me you know now."

Kate sniffed again. "I do not believe it. 'Tis a lie, an evil,

evil lie!"

Harry clambered onto the bed beside her, his back against the headboard. "Would our aunt tell such a falsehood?" He drew up his knees, his arms encircling them. He possessed an air that combined youth and maturity. "I found out years ago. It is why our aunt makes such great efforts to turn me into a great lord. I hate that more than knowing I bear the name of a man who is not my father. But I was only three when William Carey died. I do not remember him like you."

The bolster's pattern work of thick embroidery imprinted on her face, and her brother's hand rested on her shoulder.

"Don't take it so to heart," he said. "I am twelve and no longer care. Our aunt and uncle have long explained it to me."

Unable to fight her curiosity, Kate wiped away tears and looked up at him. "What did they explain?"

Harry gave her a preoccupied smile and scratched the side of his face, reddening his pale skin. "How it was with our lady mother—could she say nay when the King wanted her? Of course not. Aunt Nan says the world is not like that, especially at court. She wants me to remember how it was for Mother."

"You, Brother? Why should you have to remember?"

"Because she wants me a good man, like Uncle George, who treats women with the respect due to them. He does not regard them simply as the property of men."

"And what did the King"—Kate could not name him father—"tell you?"

Henry settled back, his gaze travelling to the ceiling. "He has not told me anything. He does not call me son or deal with me thus." He shrugged. "Sister, he does not claim us as his. He cannot. Aunt Nan is our mother's sister after all.

Uncle George explained about the King ridding himself of Katherine of Aragon because his brother bedded her first. He didn't want to give reason for those at court to think he had done something likewise in his dealings with our mother and aunt." Harry paused for a moment. "Uncle George has been like a father since I came to court. The King rarely acknowledges I am here."

Her brother looked at her with adult eyes. "We have one father who gave us our name, another father who won't own us, other than as the niece and nephew of his wife."

Their positions seemed changed from days ago. Now there was no doubt in her mind; he treated her like a child. But perhaps she deserved that. While her brother possessed a pragmatism beyond his years, she struggled to understand.

"So—" Kate swallowed and sniffed again. "So—I have no father now. This morning I was Katherine Carey. Now, my whole world is taken from me. I am nobody. Nobody, Brother."

With a brisk, sharp rap, Madge came into the chamber and strode towards the bed. She held to her chest a small, thin manuscript. Its brown leather cover bore the initials M. F. and S. E.

"How much longer are you going to stay here?" she demanded. "Are you not hungry?" Without waiting for an answer, she dragged a stool over to Kate's side and sat there, thumbing through the loose pages of the book. Sometimes she would smile at what caught her eye. Several moments passed before she looked back at Kate. "Your melancholy will not help."

"What business is it of yours?" she snapped.

Madge cocked her head. "One thing. I have no desire to see you so unhappy, even if just because I share this room and bed with you, and have no wish for a doleful companion. Second, I know more of the world than you. We cannot change the past, but the future? Who knows what that will be if we are willing to make the best of today. That is what matters, not the past."

Kate turned on her side and pounded her pillow. She wanted to be left alone; she wanted to curl up and die. "You know, too? Tell me, am I the only person at court who did not?"

Her cousin shrugged. "The court is no place for secrets. No one blabs it in public places that your brother, Harry, is the King's son, but people speak about it behind closed doors." Madge rested a hand on her shoulder. "And that his sister, too, shares the same father. You both couldn't hide it if you wished. You and Harry have the look of the King."

"I have the look of the King." Kate hiccupped, remembering how Lady Margaret, the King's niece, had looked familiar to her. Now it made sense to her; they were close kin. "Everyone has lied to me. Everyone!" Kate angrily rubbed at her tear-wet face. "Why did my mother never tell me? Why did she let me go to court believing her lies? Is she such a fool that she did not realise I would find out?"

Her head bent, Madge turned the pages before looking up again. "Kate, I cannot speak of your mother's reasons. If you wish to know more, the Queen has told me she will speak to you. Will you not come with me now? She worries about you and she should not be worried. If you bear your aunt any love at all, come and hear her out."

Kate tried to comb her fingers through the knots of her tangled hair. "Very well," she said at last. "I'll come."

She swung her legs around and got gingerly off the bed. She caught sight of herself in the burnished mirror hanging on the dark panelled wall. Her uncombed hair was a mess and her face red and botchy, unrecognisable from the girl made ready to see the King that same morning. "First, let me wash my face."

Madge's book still open on her lap, a few words caught Kate's attention. Going past to grab her comb, she asked, "What have you there?"

"My sister Mary has come back with our book." Madge smiled.

"Mary?" Kate stopped mid stride.

"Don't worry, the Queen has found another chamber for her. Nine months together in our mother's womb was more than enough for us. We spend so much time with each other in the day, we'd rather sleep apart.

"But back to the book—a group of us pass it amongst ourselves and write down our thoughts, or perchance a poem. I thought you might like to join our number."

Kate stood in front of the mirror, straightened her hood, and spoke distractedly. "Write poetry?" She remembered her recent effort in her journal, now hidden away in her coffers. "I do not know if I can."

"That is easily rectified by practice. None of us write well. My penmanship is blotch after blotch, but using this book has shown me there is more to writing than pen and ink. Who knows, it might help you over your troubles."

Kate turned to her cousin and scowled. "You must think

me a fool if you believe I can be so easily diverted after this."

Madge shrugged, closed the manuscript and placed it on the bed. "Read it later. You might be surprised at what you find. As for being a fool, it was you that used the word, not I. I am waiting to see what you prove yourself to be." She stood. "Are you ready to go and see the Queen?"

My dearly beloved daughter,
I send this missive in the hand of my brother George, for your eyes only. Pray, once you read these words, burn my letter, and find it in your heart to forgive me. I did not want you to go to court; I never hid that from you. But I never told you why. My good husband told me I was wrong to send you without first telling you what I write now. Believe me, I break a long held vow by this letter, and pray to God for forgiveness. Methinks, though, the vow I made so many years ago was to a living man, who saw his life stretch out long before him. His death left me tied to my vow to him. But I do not speak of it; I will never say out loud what I must write now, in this letter you will burn—nay, must burn. Let me write it quickly: William Carey is not your father. Kate, my beloved Kate, your father is the King, the husband of my sister. It is a cesspool, I know. How can I expect you to understand?
William Carey loved you, my Kate. He loved you like a true father—far truer than our good King, who sired you. William never wanted you

*to know you were not his. Your brother, he was
a different case. He was a son. William always
knew he would lose him to the King. But you,
Kate? The King was always happy enough to let
poor Will make-believe about you. William was
not a man like other men; he had no other
children but you and Harry who bore his name,
but not his blood.*

*Aye, Kate. You and your brother both share
the same sire. I know you will be heartsore
learning this. I am heartsore that I cannot tell
you otherwise. William Carey was a good man. I
could not have wished for a better father for you.
I would have been happy to remain his wife, even
though it would have been in name only, to see
you grow up content in his love. I would have
gone to my grave denying what I know true, that
you and Harry were of the King's blood. I would
have done it for you. What does it matter in any
case? William deserved the name of "father." The
King? Once he became enamoured of my sister,
he forgot me, he forgot you. I hoped he had
forgotten about Harry, too, but discovered to my
grief that a son is harder to forget, especially for
him—a king so desirous, nay, desperate, for sons.*

*I know you have many, many questions.
Forgive me if I do not speak too much about the
past. I thank God every day I have you and
Harry, but I'd rather not remember how it all
came to be. Just let me say I was very young,
and had no choice in the matter. But let me also
say this: I told you how my father whipped me.
That was when the King desired me and*

arranged my marriage to William. I pray to God
you never have to live through something like
that.

Also know that I would suffer those years
again for you and Harry. Believe me, Kate, I,
too, wanted to believe Will was your father. The
truth is overlaid with painful memories. The
only joy and love I had in that time was what
you and your brother gave to me. Tell my sister
she has my permission to speak more of this
matter; she knows just as I do that the world
often makes us dance a dance not of our own
choosing.

Your loving and devoted mother.

Pray kiss your brother for me.

Burn this letter, I beg you.
Nay—I command you.

Kate lifted her tear-glazed eyes to her uncle and aunt.
"This is what you went home for, to bring back the soiled
tapestry of my mother's lies? She tells me to burn it. Here,
take it now, and toss it in the fire!"

Her uncle frowned and reached for the parchment. He
closed it up, then glanced at his still and silent sister before
looking back to Kate. "Aye. It needs to burn, child, but not
with anger—with understanding." He put a hand on her arm.
"Your mother asked you to forgive her. She begged me to ride
like the wind so I could give you her letter. She loves you, Kate,
more than life itself. She never wanted to see you hurt."

Kate yanked her arm free. "Then she is fool and more!
How could I not be hurt after living with her lies only to come
here to discover the truth?"

Aunt Nan leaned forward and gazed at her with compassionate eyes. "You have a right to be angry, Kate. But if you knew how badly our sister has been hurt by life, you might understand better why she found it too difficult to hurt you." Aunt Nan glanced at her brother. "Mary was never the strong one. She is sweet, gentle and humble. She never had the armour needed to live long at court. Her beauty drew men like honey, but only to her great injury. They called her a whore, but she was not much older than you when the French King François seduced her with his talk of love, and then she came home to find another king eager to take his place, and our father more than eager to see it happen.

"François thought it amusing, but it was I who comforted your mother when it came to her ears that he called her his mule, there for all to ride. Your grandfather did not care. Neither she nor I had a way out, other than to make the best of the bad goods life offered to us."

Surprised, Kate shook her aching head "But at least the King married you and made you his consort. My lady mother?" She sputtered out the words. "She was the bad goods, the whore! The one who made her children bastards!"

With a sobbing cry, Aunt Nan slapped her face, before gathering Kate into her arms. Her aunt's tears fell and wet Kate's face, too. "Don't! I know you are angry, but your mother does not deserve that. I said before she was never the strong one. That is not true. George and I discovered long ago that Mary has different type of strength—one able to untangle itself from the web found here. She has been able to make a life of her own. No one owns her now. More and more I envy her."

Kate pulled away, confused. Her head hurt even more.

"But you are the Queen!"

"Aye, the Queen. Kate, if you chose to remain with me, you must know that my enemies wish otherwise." Aunt Nan smiled sadly. "Aye, niece, just because I am the Queen doesn't mean my enemies do not have the power to hurt me."

Peacocks screamed. Aunt Nan grimaced and whirled towards the sound. "Even our uncle of Norfolk hates me. He calls me the great whore," she said slowly. She turned to Kate, her face solemn and stern. "The new peacocks disturbing my nights are his recent gift to the King. He is pleased and smug to see the King put me in my place with his acceptance of those cursed birds." She rolled her shoulders, moving her head from side to side, as if releasing tension. "Much of this is my own fault. I lack a woman's proper humility and have a temper difficult to rein in at times." Aunt Nan's smile was both wry and resentful. "I speak my mind, niece. For years, the King valued and sought my counsel, but no more. He desires my silence, but how can I be so when I have spent years being otherwise? Once abandoned, silence is a difficult art to relearn. Every step I take is fraught with danger, and if I stumble, there are many who would soon bring me down. Master Cromwell just waits for the opportunity."

"Bring you down?" Her mouth suddenly dry, Kate tried to swallow, her mind filling with the hostile faces from her dream of her aunt's coronation. But she also remembered something important. "How can anyone do that? You're the Queen of England."

"Queen of England." Aunt Nan turned to her brother before speaking to Kate. "I tell you again there are many who would deny me that title. I am unlike my sister. I cannot risk avoiding the truth, even if it makes for my own unhappiness."

She sniffed, lifted her chin, her eyes alight with what seemed amusement, but one her words did not echo. "As my sister has found again to her hurt, cards of make-believe sooner or later get tossed to the ground." Uncle George took her hand. "Only here, in my chamber, am I really safe, with the few I can trust."

Aunt Nan's solemn eyes made Kate squirm and lower her head.

"Can I trust you, niece? You look so much like your mother that I think I can. But, speak you, are you strong enough to withstand the storms, if they come, and stay true to me? Or are you your father's daughter, who is no longer steadfast, but inconstant and changes with the wind."

Kate lifted her chin. "I do not know the King. I have always loved you, admired you, been proud of you, my aunt. I would never betray you." Kate stared at the folded letter in her uncle's hands. "I know how betrayal feels. I pray to God that I will die before doing it to another."

"Oh, Kate, I beg you: forgive your mother."

In answer, Kate snatched the parchment from Uncle George and tossed it into the fire. As the flames took hold, the words seemed lit with gold before they crumbled into ash. The blackening parchment became one with the fire, and Kate blinked away tears. "I vow to you, my aunt, you will never find me breaking your trust. As for offering my mother forgiveness, I have none."

8

Later that afternoon, back in her bedchamber, Kate had another visitor. Ignoring a knock on the door, she curled up on her bed, but Catherine, the young Duchess, closed the door and stood against it, gazing at Kate with serious eyes.

"Has the Queen sent you?" Kate asked.

Catherine shook her head. "Nay, I wanted to see you. To speak to you." She paused, looked at her feet before considering Kate again. "Believe me, I come in friendship."

Kate sat up and swung around to glower at Catherine. "You are the Duchess of Suffolk. Why would you want to be friends with me, the unwanted bastard of the King?"

The older girl sighed. "I know this is not an easy time for you. I, too, am fatherless." She padded closer and sat. "Time will help lessen the hurt and make you see that to be an unclaimed daughter of a king is better than one who is claimed. At least you have some hope of freedom and choice denied to us poor pawns who are moved where the King wills. And there is no chance the King will decide he wants you for his bedmate, as he did with your mother, as he did with mine. He is a great sinner, but not one who would ever bed his own daughter."

Kate bounded up in shock and crossed herself. "Bed with me? Don't speak such vile words, even in jest!" She swallowed hard and gazed at the Duchess. "*Your* mother, too?"

Catherine nodded. "Pray, this is betwixt just us, and must remain unsaid afterwards. My mother told me to beware of the King and why. She believed he offered her friendship, but found his kindnesses came at a hefty price." She shrugged. "'Twas just one night, years before my birth, but my lady mother still wears a sackcloth in penance. Queen Katherine is her lifelong friend, and my mother carries the heavy burden of her betrayal to this day." With a sigh, she shrugged. "Too many men think women whores—starting from the King. He thinks all women are at his service, to do what he wills. Queen Anne taught him different for a time, but no more."

Kate crushed the sides of her gown in her hands. "I cannot bear to think of him as my father."

"Do not then," Catherine said quietly.

Lowering her head, Kate shifted from foot to foot. "You speak as if this is easy; what would you know? No one could understand how my heart breaks." Kate looked desperately at Catherine. "All my life I believed William Carey my father, called him Father. My heart and soul believed him thus."

Catherine took her hand. "I think I do understand." Her lips tightened. "Once I called my lord husband *Father*."

Kate rounded on Catherine. "What?"

Her expression slack, Catherine spoke flatly. "I lived in the home of the Duke as a small child, betrothed to the Lord Harry, his son. What else was I to call the Duke? Or think of him? I had no father of my own, so my heart easily claimed him as mine, with pride. His wife, the White Queen, the King's sister, Mary, whom I also loved, encouraged it. None of us knew the tragedy that would befall us." She paused and toyed with the rings on her left hand. "But when the White Queen died, Harry, never strong, sickened with grief. I married his father instead."

Why did Catherine tell her all this? She rubbed her aching head. "Did you have to?"

"Have to?" Catherine's eyes widened. "I was little more than your age. Harry was heartsore over his mother's death, and very, very ill. His father married me three weeks after the death of the White Queen. I was grieving for my beloved adopted mother, and for Harry, who was dying day by day." She gathered herself up, her hand at her throat. "Pray, I have said enough."

"But why did you have to marry him?" Kate winced to hear the harsh tone in her voice.

"Kate, are you listening at all? I had no choice. I had just watched the White Queen die a hard, dreadful death and now watched her son fight for his life, coughing his heart out. The physicians told us he sickened with consumption and gave us no hope he would live. I was alone. The boy I loved too weak to leave his bed. What I wanted meant nought. The Duke was all the security life left to me. At first, the thought of marrying the man I saw as my father.... Kate, I thought I would rather die. I wished for death. I prayed for it, too, but when the day came for my marriage, I found I wanted to live. With Harry dying and so much in my life already changed, it was easier to let the current take me than fight against it. Mayhap I was a piece on the chessboard that required moving into another position, but at least I knew what to expect—well, a goodly part of it, even if the rest of my world was in ruins."

Despite herself, Kate felt drawn to the other girl's story. "How mean you?"

"I was raised to be Duchess of Suffolk. My Lady Mary, the White Queen, brought me up as a princess, preparing me to take my place as one of the foremost women in the realm. Harry was his father's only male heir. With him close to death, my husband needed a wife to give him another one—a son likely to live. Who else should he choose to take his wife's place but one he knew healthy, of childbearing age and already trained to be the Duchess of Suffolk?"

Kate gazed at her in wonder. Catherine had grown up looking to the Duke as a father and never as a husband. But did she not say she loved her betrothed? Kate could not resist and asked, "And the Lord Harry, the Duke's son?"

Catherine wrapped her arms around her body. "Harry?" She said it like a sob. "He was my dearest friend—the boy I rode alongside from the time I learnt to ride. We shared the same schoolmaster. He knew all my secrets, every one of them, big or small. We shared everything—everything except the marriage bed. How I wish it could have been otherwise, but it was not to be." Her eyes swam with tears. "Pray, I beg you, no more questions. Not about my sweet, sweet Harry." She clasped Kate's hand. "But you can see, can't you, that you are not alone? All of us carry crosses of some kind. We are women, Kate. Whatever power we have is only what men give us. It can be taken from us with a snap of a man's fingers. Do not blame your mother. What choice had she other than what the King or her father wanted?" Hunched over like one cold, Catherine crossed her arms over her chest, her hands holding on to her shoulders. "Sometimes, we take what we must to live."

The next morning, a servant came from Aunt Nan summoning Kate to the Queen's privy chamber. The servant refused to listen when Kate gave her apology of ill health, expressing her desire to stay the morning abed, and waited until she dressed, before escorting her without further ado to Aunt Nan's rooms.

Kate entered with a curtsey, finding not only her aunt seated by the fire, but also her grandfather. With his silver grey hair covered by a flat, black velvet hat, he was garbed in what looked like travelling clothes: black, woollen hose and unadorned black doublet with straight sleeves on the lower arms and only a slight puffing from elbows tapering into shoulders. Costly, well-cut clothes, but far less elaborate than the garb he had worn on the day Kate was presented to the King. A man's three-quarter cloak slung over a chair next to the chamber door confirmed her suspicions: her grandfather was going on a journey.

Thomas Boleyn looked at her with stern eyes that seemed to calculate her worth. They were not the eyes of the loving grandfather she knew as a little girl, but the eyes of the man who had chilled her to her marrow on his last visit home. With a glance at her aunt, Kate fell to her knees before him and bent her head.

"Pray, your blessing, sir," she said.

The Earl got up then. Despite his great age of nearly sixty, he was still straight, trim and agile. He rested his hand on her head for a moment, before taking her shoulders to raise her up, kissing her briskly on the cheek. He peered at her closely and nodded.

"You look well and hearty, Kate. I'm glad to see you at court. 'Twas time your mother stopped her foolishness and let you join your brother."

She blushed, uncertain how to reply.

He pointed to an empty chair by the fire, turned toward his. "Sit down, child. I wish to speak to you before I leave for Hever. I'll not likely see you for some time, not until I return from the King's business."

Gingerly, Kate sat on the edge of the seat. Her hands clasped in her lap, she regarded her grandfather and strangely subdued aunt. *Why is Aunt Nan not looking at me?*

Her grandfather returned to his seat and rested a hand on the arm's rest. "So, you know now that you are the King's daughter."

Kate swallowed and lowered her head. It wasn't a question, but still she answered, "Aye, Grandfather."

"God's oath, child." He clicked his tongue. "No need to take on so. There's no shame in it. If I had my way, it would be out in the open for all to acknowledge."

She jerked back and stared at him.

He grunted and shifted. "God's teeth! I but speak the truth, and you sit there with the eyes of a kicked dog. Aye, just like your mother has looked at me, time after time. If she had listened to me, she would have done better for herself than two unclaimed bastards and a purse now left short of coin." He glanced at Aunt Nan. "Your aunt listened to me, and look where it has led her."

Aunt Nan started. She turned a look of sympathy to Kate before hooding her eyes and hiding away her thoughts once more. Not appearing to notice, Kate's grandfather moved forward in his chair.

"Now that you are at court, we will find you a match worthy of one who has the King's blood flowing in her veins."

Kate opened her mouth, but no words came out. Aunt Nan rose to her full height from the chair. With unstudied grace and a lift of her chin, she stepped towards her father. "Remember your promise, Father. Kate's husband is for me to decide. I wish my niece matched well—not only for the family, but for herself."

Scowling, he waved a hand. "Pray, do not concern yourself and return to your seat. You must keep quiet, Anne. You bear the King's child."

Aunt Nan met his eyes for a heartbeat, then did as she was bid. "But your promise, Father," she murmured.

He shook his head. "I am not so old that I need reminding, daughter—although 'tis in my mind you grow soft, Anne. The girl's well matched as long as it bodes well for our family. You would be wise to marry her quickly to someone who may strengthen your hand."

Kate, feeling ill, turned in panic to her aunt. Now she began to understand more fully what Catherine had tried to say to her.

With a worried glance, Aunt Nan shook her head imperceptibly. "With respect, Father, I do not believe Kate's marriage is likely to help my own. And my husband is not a fool. If I put forward a candidate for her hand, one who would support me, he would look at the match with suspicion. He would look at me with suspicion. Methinks it's wisest to leave Kate off this chessboard." Aunt Nan sat up straighter. Her hands gripped the armrests, her knuckles white. "Your granddaughter is not fourteen until early next year. I desire my niece has a few months to learn the court ways before we seek a good match for her."

"Soft. Aye, you grow soft, my girl," grandfather Boleyn

scoffed, his blue eyes like flint. "I have told you before—to win this game, you must keep your heart hard. You're the Queen—act it."

Aunt Nan bent her head and clasped her hands. "If you do not think I act the Queen, then your understanding of queenship is different to mine." She drummed her fingers on her stomacher. "If we do not learn from the lessons given us by life, then we learn nothing. These last years have been a hard school, but I walk now on the road I must if I'm not to lose my honour."

She lifted her chin and straightened her back. Aunt Nan appeared a queen ready to go to war. "For many years, Mary and I willingly allowed you to sacrifice us for the good of the family. I—to my great shame—even allowed you to persuade me to convince Madge to do likewise. But I am the Queen of England, Father. If others wish to take that from me, it will no longer be because I fail to keep in mind what that means—or let others persuade me to disregard it. I will no longer sacrifice Madge, or ask that of Kate. If anyone is to sacrifice, it must be me, and it must be for the good of all, not just for the Boleyns." She shook her head. "I choose now to no longer sacrifice others on an altar that I vowed to give my blood, my life. I am God's servant first, Father, and then England's. I no longer serve you."

His eyes furious, the Earl slapped his hand against the armrest and inhaled a deep breath. His jaw tightened. He drew in slow, steady breaths. He eased back in his chair, taking in his daughter's measure. "I never thought I'd hear from you the echo of Thomas More. What would the King, your husband, say to that, I wonder?"

Aunt Nan toyed with a ring on her hand, twisting it

around her finger. "I told you, the last few years have been a hard school. There have been too many deaths. And too many ghosts who walk around my bed at night when my husband leaves me lonely for his company. I pray much on those nights and reflect on the road that brought me to an empty bed and an aching heart." Her eyes hardened. "I cannot say if Thomas More deserved his death, but he died with a good heart and conscience." She shifted in her seat, clasping her hands in her lap again. "I only want that for myself." For a long moment, she rested back her head and half closed her eyes.

"When my husband told Katherine of Aragon that he would marry me, no matter what, she spoke of an old proverb of her country: 'Take what you want, said God. Take it and pay for it.' I took what I wanted and have paid for it, with more sorrow and suffering than joy. Now, I feel I have been offered a choice. I can continue to take, or I look for what I can give." She sighed. "I no longer hope England will ever love me as it loved Katherine. The hatred of many is something I must bear as the price for taking what I wanted. But mayhap there is hope that England will one day see that what I do, I do for England. That must be my Magna Carta, Father."

With a shake of his head, the Earl stood up and bowed. His cold eyes glittered like sapphires. "With your Grace's permission, I must be on my way."

She gestured wearily. "Go then, and Godspeed. Pray do not forget to tell Mother I miss her and impatiently wait for her company."

With a nod to Kate, he bowed again and strode towards the door.

"Father!" Aunt Nan called. "Do you not wish to kiss me

and give me your blessing before you go?"

He turned about on his heel and glared at her. "Blessings are for daughters who listen to their fathers—and who do not take it in their foolish heads to go their own way."

When his eyes fell upon her, Kate squirmed.

"Clearly, you do not wish to listen to my advice about marrying Kate to someone who will make Cromwell think again before crossing you. You say you think of England. I say you are soft and will regret of it one day." He bowed again. "I bid you good day, Daughter."

Grabbing his cloak from the chair, he left. Kate stared at the closed door before turning to her aunt. Fixated on the fire, hands over her belly, she was a picture of despondency.

"Aunt Nan." Kate swallowed, frightened. "My Queen, if you wish me to wed—"

Aunt Nan swung around. "I do not. Not for that reason. If my father thinks me soft, so be it. But I no longer will pay for my actions with my conscience. I spoke the truth. I have enough ghosts disturbing my nights. 'Tis time to do what my heart tells me is right. Life teaches us lessons, child. 'Tis only too late if we never take heed of them."

Kate attended on the Queen that night, sleeping on a trundle bed in her room. Her aunt did not sleep in the costly state bed. Kate had already discovered that its padded brocade and bed-hangings, embroidered with real gold thread, were only for show. Rather, there was door in that chamber—a door that did not call attention to itself, a door that took her to a smaller room, with an oriel window overlooking the garden. In it, the Queen's bed was smaller and simpler, too, the hangings made to protect the inhabitants on the coldest night, just as the smaller room was easier to keep warm in the cold months of winter than the draughtier room before it.

For hours, Kate struggled to sleep. Every time she thought about her grandfather, she wanted to cry. A hole had opened in her heart that once had been filled with love, leaving her wounded and bruised.

But if she felt bruised and bloody, it soon became clear one other was more so. In the darkness of the night, her aunt wept—muffled, yet heart-rending sobs. Kate rose from her trundle and stood at the side of Aunt Nan's bed.

"Can I come in with you?" she asked quietly.

The nearby night candle revealed her aunt's worn face and glittering eyes. The fire, burnt low, crackled and snapped, glowing with red heat. Nodding, Aunt Nan wiped her face, then pulled open the bed covering for Kate to clamber in beside her.

With her head close to her aunt, Kate asked, "What's troubling you? Is it Grandfather?"

Aunt Nan shrugged. "That is but one thing." She stirred as if in discomfort.

"You're not feeling unwell, are you?"

Aunt Nan wiped at her face again. "Well enough. I have to be"

Kate clasped her hand. "I am here if you wish to talk."

Candlelight gleamed on her aunt's teeth when she smiled. "I know. I am beginning to think God sent you to me. My own, sweet angel. There are few who I can really trust. I'm so lonely, Kate."

She gazed at her aunt, bewildered. Every day, Aunt Nan lived her life surrounded by people. How could she be lonely? As if she heard Kate's unasked question, Aunt Nan continued to speak.

"So many nights I lie here awake, listening to the breathing of my attendant. It's my only human comfort. But it doesn't prevent me from thinking of dark things, Kate. I think of endings, wondering if this is the end."

Kate blinked. "Why think that when you're with child?"

Aunt Nan gulped back a sob and spoke hoarsely. "Aye, I bear a child. I want this child, desperately I want this child, but I am so weary. My husband, the King, has put me aside in his heart. Sometimes I think death would be easier to bear. Sometimes I wish for it."

Clasping her aunt's hand tighter, Kate nestled closer to her. "Don't wish that. Don't say it. I vow to you I will never desert you. I am yours."

Her aunt sighed. "My husband once said that to me. 'Tis easy to speak the words, but far harder to live them."

9

The days sped by and Kate returned fully to learning her duties as one of the Queen's maids. No one spoke of the reason for her absence, but far too many eyes followed her—some with compassion; some with curiosity; some with smug, wilful spite. Some even with jealousy. But more certain of her true friends now, she welcomed the daily proof of the love held for her by her aunt, uncle and brother.

Soon she began to feel certain of another kind of love, one she hugged to herself in secret during the cold, wearisome, winter months. Trailing some distance behind Madge, she saw him for the first time in the gallery. A very tall, very handsome young man. He held two dog leashes, while two regal Irish wolfhounds pranced beside him. He concentrated only on the dogs, keeping their leashes short and the huge dogs under firm control, not even glancing towards the girls as they passed him by. Kate caught the smell of him—a strong whiff of musk, leather, dogs, horses and a hint of manly sweat. Suddenly, her insides felt like a bottomless pit, with her heart and stomach drawn into a spinning vortex.

One of the dogs raised its head, caught sight of a cat, and bounded in its direction. Next thing, the man swore as both dogs pulled him along in their swift pursuit, his dark, longish hair lifting as if in the wind's grasp. The young man laughed as he ran to keep up with the dogs. His agile, lean body spoke of grace, of dance and of the music that belonged to Kate's beating heart.

She paused to watch; her knees wobbled. About to turn a corner, Madge looked over her shoulder and grinned. "The Queen is waiting. Tarry not, Kate.

"Saw you Francis?" she asked, lifting an eyebrow, when Kate caught up with her.

"Francis?" Kate almost tripped over her feet before facing her cousin.

"Francis Knollys, the man exercising the Queen's wolfhounds. Do you wish for an introduction?"

She cleared her throat. "Introduction? Why—what for?"

Madge laughed. "For the usual reason. God's oath, Kate, for a maid close to fourteen, you're a green girl." Madge considered her gravely. "An innocent. Methinks, too innocent." Turning from her, she spoke as if to herself. "One of the reasons the Queen likely wanted you at court is to match you with someone suitable."

Kate halted. Madge kept walking as if she did not realise Kate was no longer beside her. Kate stood alone with her bearings stripped from her. Once again, the subject of her marriage left her cold.

"Match me?" Kate croaked. "But my aunt said otherwise." Her voice echoing in the gallery, she raised her hands to her hot cheeks.

Madge looked over her shoulder. "Don't take on—surely you must know the time has come for your betrothal? You are no longer a child." Her face puckered in thought, her head turning to the bark of a dog. "Francis Knollys is handsome and well placed," she said slowly. "You seem interested in him; why not let me introduce you? If you like him, your aunt could possibly arrange the matter for you, rather than select someone less to your taste."

Kate continued to stare at Madge, too confounded to move. Bells rang out the hour and singing voices drifted from the nearby chapel. Kate turned her head to listen more closely. Her heart drummed so loudly in her ears she seemed deafened.

Madge grabbed her arm. "Come you. The Queen does not like it if we are late."

Kate didn't need Madge's introduction after all, not when she was helped by one of the Queen's wolfhounds. She read alone in the Queen's library, when a young dog burst into the room. Tongue lolling, it scampered this way, and then the other, as if searching for another exit. Seeing her, the dog shook its head and barked in greeting, its friendly, amber eyes full of trust and attention.

Gracefully prancing over to her, it sat, scratched at its hindquarters and turned towards the door in expectation. The dog barked once more, and Francis Knollys entered, a leash in his hand. "There you are!" He then noticed Kate, and bowed. "Pray forgive the interruption, Lady. I made the mistake of letting him loose, and he was away before I could grab him." He kneeled beside the sitting dog and put the leash back on his leather collar. "He's a puppy, really; he's just so big I sometimes forget all the training he still needs."

She smiled. "Are you his trainer?"

He looked up, amused. "If I was, I would soon be asked to look for other employment. This wolfhound and another were a gift from my family to the Queen. They still know me best, and she requested that I get them used to their new home before I take them to meet with Urian, the Queen's older wolfhound."

"Why is that?"

"The Queen worries that Urian will be jealous. She thinks if they have the smell of the court and their new mistress, he'll accept them with greater grace." Knollys stood, and then turned as if he remembered something. "Forgive me, I have not told you my name." He bowed again to her. "I am Francis Knollys, knight. And who may you be, my lady?"

She lowered her eyes, her cheeks warming. "I am Katherine Carey, the daughter of Mary Stafford, she who once was Mary Carey and before that Mary Boleyn." She studied him and chewed her lip. Was he yet another who knew she was the daughter of the King? "My friends call me Kate or Kat, it matters not."

He smiled. "I choose Kat, if you will honour me by calling me friend." He examined her closely. "I have not seen you before. You must be new to court."

"Aye, new to court." Kate turned her head away from him, brushing away her tears that blurred the frieze of plump putti decorating the length of the wall. As if disputing their grotesque, oversized figures, they tumbled and played in blithe innocence.

"Pray, may I sit down?" Knollys asked, stepping towards her.

Her cheeks burning, she nodded and bent her head.

Sitting on the stool beside her, he began talking to her, asking questions about her life at home, and telling her about his. He was the eldest son of a family that spent more months at court than at their family estate while in service to the

King. Coming to the end of explaining his duties at court, Francis studied her.

"You say you're the daughter of Mary Boleyn? Forgive me, I have just realised you're the niece of the Queen." Again, tears blurred her eyesight. She could no longer read the poetry in the book on her lap. *Does he know I am the bastard daughter of the King?*

"This is not a happy time?" he asked.

She cradled the side of her face and shook her head. He frowned at the open door. He leaned closer and quietly said, "This is not a happy time for many at court. I have lived here since a small lad, long enough to recognise the cesspit smell of plots. Believe me, I know the Queen concerns herself to ensure a better and more just England. For that, she has my loyalty."

Realising he thought she wept because of her aunt, Kate forgot her own worries. "Is it as bad as that?"

"It depends on the Queen giving the King a son." Francis swung his full attention to the open door. "Come, boy. Come, Brutus," he said to the dog, tugging on its leash. He hurried to the door and securely tied the dog to another chair, one placed on the other side of the door. When he came back to Kate, he moved his stool even closer to her. "If I shut the door, it would look suspicious, and not only for your good reputation. Young Brutus will warn us if anyone approaches. Now, we can speak freely. But softly, lady. Softly."

In answer, she leaned towards him. "You spoke about the Queen giving the King a son."

His blue eyes narrowed. "Aye, it all hinges on that. If she fails, the plots will begin again in earnest. I tell you this because you are her niece and should be on your guard.

There are many you should be careful of—Cromwell, for one. He is a skilled hunter who sets up his traps with great care."

"My aunt mentioned him." Kate remembered the strange tension between her aunt and Cromwell when she had met him in the King's throne room. The puzzle falling into place, she moved suddenly, almost dropping her book. "My lady mother told me he is one of the Queen's men." She spoke more to herself, than to Francis.

"I mean no disrespect to your lady mother, but she has been away from the court long if she thinks that. Allegiances change quickly when power is involved. Did you not know that the Queen once threatened to behead him? He hates her and plays a heady game of politics against her."

"But what of the King? Surely he protects my aunt?"

Something shifting interrupted them. Knollys turned to the dog and Kate turned too. Brutus had dropped to the ground, laying his head on his front paws, his eyes shining in a stream of light from the window. He appeared relaxed and ready to go to sleep. Knollys spoke. "We have only met today, yet I feel I can trust you. Tell me, am I a fool to do so? Can I speak the truth to you?"

Kate lifted her chin. "I am the Queen's niece. I would rather die than betray her."

"Very well, but pray remember that these confidences I tell you now put us both in danger. As for your question about the King, Cromwell has his ear. Already, he seizes on the King's discontent with his marriage and plants seeds of doubt about his wife, or whether God blesses their marriage." Knollys stood before going to the door to undo the dog's lead. "The King no longer protects the Queen, only the son he hopes to see born next year." He bowed. "Lady Kat, I hope to see you again, and soon."

Kate stared long at the empty doorway. For a while, she sat there, smelling dog and stables, and a scent belonging to Francis alone.

Swimming in waters too deep for her, she thought about everything that had happened since her arrival at court—everything that had turned her life upside down. Furious with her mother, grappling with her new identity as the King's daughter, surrounded by who knew what, now it seemed coming to court also did strange things to her heart. She could not get back to reading, no matter how hard she tried.

Wanting time alone to think, Kate slipped back unnoticed to her chamber. Inside a woman sat at the writing table. A quill in her hand, she wrote in the same book Madge had recently shown Kate. *Madge's back from attending the Queen?* But then the woman looked over her shoulder. Prematurely aged, the face of Madge's twin hinted only a pale echo of her sister's healthy beauty.

"Mary!" Kate said in surprise.

"Good morrow, coz." Mary, as if waking from a dream, seemed to take in Kate's disorientation. "I did not mean to startle you, but Madge told me she had our book. I thought to use these few moments while the Queen has no need of me to come here and write a verse or two." She placed the quill carefully in the inkpot and inspected her ink-stained fingers, sighing. "I do not know how this happens. I try to be careful, but still I soil myself. No matter how hard I wash, I cannot get off all the ink." Going to the washbasin, she grinned and youth returned to her face. "The Queen will tease again, but perchance her smiles will make my black nails worth it."

Kate approached the table. Still wet, the newly written text stood out on the page of the open book. "May I read what you have written, coz?"

Mary grinned, scrubbing her hands. "You can but try! My handwriting is as bad as Madge's, but at least we can decipher each other's."

Kate sat, pulled the book towards her and slowly made sense of the words. She laughed. "Oh, this is good. And amusing. You are so clever to write such verse."

Her cousin reached for a towel and dried her hands. "I am glad you found it to your liking. I have mulled over the verse all this morning. I think if the Queen hadn't freed me from her service until this afternoon, it would have driven me mad."

"But how do you do it? How do know what words to write? And write in verse! What a gift you have!"

"As for words, that's easy. All you need do is listen. Sometimes I feel like a magpie, gathering bits from here and there to build a nest for my eggs. Verse? Have you not tried it? All of us can do it, if we put our mind and heart to it. I think verse is part of us, just as much as the songs we hear from birds are part of them."

Kate hid a smile at Mary's seriousness and studied the book. "I am trying to write poetry, but I don't think I am very good at it."

Mary came over to her. "Then you must keep trying. 'Tis time for me to go back to the Queen. If you don't have anything else to do, why don't you look through our book and see what you can add to it."

Kate almost bolted up from the chair. "I can't do that!"

Mary laughed. "I always say to Madge that 'can't' and 'do' marry not; but do, and you will find you can. If you cannot think of your own, why not write the words of a poem or song you know and would like to share with us. Many poems in this book are copied from other books." Nearby bells rang out the new hour. Her cousin grabbed the cloak tossed over the back of a chair. "I must be away. You are fortunate, Kate; the Queen has not asked you to do any more than attend her for a short time each day and be a companion to your brother. Why not use this free time to your advantage? Madge tells me you love to read. Writing is the other side of the coin. You might discover you enjoy it."

She padded to the door and quietly shut it behind her. Alone again, Kate sprinkled sand to dry Mary's verse and then flipped the pages. There were short verses, long verses, riddles, and bits and pieces of Latin with their English translations beside them. Some pages of the book were in Madge's or Mary's writing, but there was also writing that came from different hands. Finding a love poem, Kate read it out loud. The yearning, the desire, the grief of love unreturned almost made her weep.

The poem brought to mind Francis Knollys. He was so handsome, years older than she. Her cheeks warmed to her memory of almost crying in front of him. He probably thought her a silly, ignorant girl, one in need of his greater wisdom. Yet did she do him justice? His concern for her aunt had embraced her as well. *Embraced me?* Holding her hand over her heart, her emotions twirled around and made her dizzy, almost ill. Words popped unbidden in her mind, and she could not rid herself of them—or of the image of Francis taking her into his arms. Her insides felt just as peculiar as the day he had strode by her in the gallery, unaware of nothing else but keeping those two wolfhounds under tight restraint.

Now she had spoken to him and sat close enough to see the black, thick eyelashes framing his dark blue eyes. And his lips! Wide and generous, with a smile that gleamed with white, straight teeth. She shivered, remembering his sweet breath so near to her. Kate turned to a blank page in the book and reached for the quill, writing:

> *My love,*
> *Dark and gentle*
> *My heart is his.*
> *Forever.*

Forgetting to lift the quill from the paper, she stared at the words. *My heart is his? Forever?* Black ink blotched beside the splotches of her tears.

10

A slim book in her hand, Kate opened the door to the Queen's dim bedchamber. The sight before her shocked her into stillness and silence. Unaware of her, seated on a bench and locked in a tight embrace, a man and woman kissed. Ghostly winter light shrouded them and dulled the colours of their rich robes into almost tones of greys. Only the human sounds they made and the increasing passion of their kiss showed that the man and woman belonged to life and were not ghosts themselves. Kate almost cried in fright when someone put a hand over her mouth and grabbed her arm, pulling her back into the Queen's privy chamber.

Rubbing her sore arm, Kate waited in mute, smouldering anger as Madge closed the door, cutting off the weak light escaping from the room. Winter's gloom enclosed her until she adjusted to the change of light. It did not stop Kate from glaring at her cousin's back. "God's teeth! Why do that?" When Madge gave her no answer, not even apology for hurting her, Kate snapped at her. "Why are you here?"

Madge spun around and faced her with fury. "Fool!"

Kate stepped back, her growing anger crumbling under Madge's far more heated assault. "Would I be here without the Queen's knowledge?" Madge's gaze returned to the shut door. "And you? Are you in habit of going into rooms without knocking first?"

Kate glanced down at the book in her hand before braving her cousin once more. "I wanted to return the Queen's book.

She asked my brother for it this morning, but it was I who had it." She tightened her mouth and, like Madge, checked the door of the bedchamber. "I didn't want Harry to get into trouble." She studied the floor. "The guards let me in. How was I to know that I would find Lady Margaret with a man in the Queen's bedchamber?" She turned to her cousin. "Is it Lord Howard?" Time after time in her aunt's chambers, Kate had observed how the King's niece used any excuse to go near him. How he also came close to her. It was like they danced without music, without steps other than dictated by a force that throbbed between them, and that few could mistake. "Why are they there? What's going on?"

Madge led Kate to another window-seat embrasure on the far end of the narrow room, where windows overlooked the Thames. Candles in wall sconces lit their way. She gestured. "Sit down."

Feeling once more out of her depth, Kate set her aunt's book on the table next to the window and did as she was told. Attending first to the door that led to the gallery, Madge sat beside her. "Give me your vow that you will not say a word to anyone about this."

Kate jerked around. "How can I vow without knowing if it touches my loyalty to the Queen."

Madge straightened and crossed her arms. "As if I would ever be disloyal! Never! Believe me, this matter is known to her, and I am here in her service."

Kate relaxed, knowing Madge was one of her aunt's few close confidants. "Very well, you have my vow. I swear on my immortal soul that I will hold my tongue."

"Good." Madge leaned against the cushions of the window-seat. "I am here on guard, for them." She waved a hand at the door and gave a tight smile. "If I hadn't gone to the privy, I would have caught you in time."

Bewildered, Kate frowned. "Guarding them? Jesu', why?"

Madge tilted her head and cupped a cheek with her hand. Kate stirred in discomfort as her cousin fixed her attention on her. Madge sighed. "This is what you must never tell. Poor Margaret. Poor cousin Tom. They wed in secret last November. Margaret confessed to Queen Anne and begged for her help. The Queen desires to do what she can, but there is too much at stake." Madge paused as if in thought. "It is doubtful the King will take kindly to his royal niece presuming her own choice of husband. Heads have rolled for less cause. All the Queen can do is to let them come to her bedchamber when she is with the King—and wait for a time when his black humours give her less reason for grief. While she waits, I keep watch."

Pondering her cousin's words, Kate turned to the window. Driven by the wind, the tidal Thames frothed and tossed around the royal barges. The wind, a raging giant, buffeted its fury upon the palace's walls, holding them at siege. How it howled with frustration, beating all its power on stone walls that kept them safe.

She turned back to Madge. "They come here? In the Queen's own chambers? It is that wise? Surely the Queen risks bringing upon herself the King's anger?"

"Mayhap." Madge reached for the tiny jewelled book hanging from her girdle, snapping it open and close. Madge smiled at her reflection in the gold of its cover. "See you the gift of the Queen? 'Tis a psalm from the Bible. She gave me the girdle book when she thought I needed to think about more serious matters than the posies I read and write."

Guessing her cousin desired to change the subject, Kate shook her arm. "But what of the King? Won't he be angry with my aunt?"

Madge spoke slowly as if thinking out loud. "Mayhap. Even more considering that Tom is a Howard and thus her own kin. Believe me, she was not pleased to be embroiled in Lady Margaret's schemes, but the deed was done and the marriage consummated. Only a trusted few know about Meg and Tom, and we all protect them. With the same arrow leaving them love-struck, the Queen could not help but pity them. She allows them the privacy of her chamber, as does our cousin, Mary, wife to the King's bastard son." Madge reached into the deep, secret pocket of her gown and brought out the manuscript of shared poetry. "Look at what Lady Margaret writes to her Tom." She turned to a page and gave the book to Kate.

My heart is set not to remove
For where as I love faithfully...

Kate read on, touched by the heartfelt words.

"There's more," said Madge.

Despite her thick layers of clothes, Kate shivered. Her fingers, numbed by the cold, clumsily turned the page to read on.

Wind rattled the window behind her. The rain hit the glass like small stones, the large droplets bursting and forming into tiny rivulets that raced down the glass. Something moved in the upper corner of the window. A cobweb, broken into parts, swayed in the current of air from the crack between window and stone. Another darting movement drew Kate's attention. Locked together on the cobweb's edge, two spiders tumbled, one big and black and the second, a paler spider, half the size of the other. Their legs a mass of confusion, the two spiders twisted and fought, going one way and then another. The colour of the smaller spider reminded Kate of her fingertip held out to candlelight.

Madge moved restively beside her. Turning away from the spiders' ferocious battle, Kate returned the book to her cousin. "Why should the King mind that they're wed? Thomas Howard is noble and a lord." Her stepfather popped into her thoughts. "It is not that he is low born."

"He may not be low born, but he is not of the same station as Lady Margaret. You know her lineage?"

Kate thought for a moment, her concentration captured again by the spiders. There was no doubt that theirs was a fight to the death. Black and pale legs entangled together, making it difficult to see where one spider started and the other ended. Venom dewed a cobweb as if mimicking the raindrops falling on the outside of the glass.

Sensing Madge's growing irritation, she turned to her cousin and shook her head. "Forgive me. I do not."

"Fie! For shame, Kate, you should know this. If Lady Margaret Douglas is the King's niece, then it should be easy to determine that she must be the daughter of one of the King's two sisters. She is not a Brandon, so she has not sprouted from Mary Tudor's marriage to the Duke of Suffolk. That leaves the King's elder sister, Margaret, she who wed James, the Scottish king. After his death, she married Margaret's father in lustful haste and soon regretted it. Margaret was their only child. I was here at court when her father brought her to the King, after he stole her away from her mother. It mattered little that the King's sister begged her brother to send her daughter back to her. By that time, the King had decided to keep his niece as a chess piece to put forward for consideration in the marriage games played by the royal houses. He has only a few marriageable-aged women close enough in blood, and to the crown, to barter over with his fellow kings. Now Lady Margaret is damaged goods, and with a husband to boot. Do you understand now why the Queen waits for the right time to break the news to the King about Margaret's marriage?"

Kate nodded and lowered her head. She seized yet another reason to give thanks that the King did not recognise her as his daughter. Her world constricted to just her thoughts. She had only been a court for a short time, but already the stories about how so many marriages came about threatened her. Two years ago, Catherine, the Duchess of Suffolk, wed a man more than four times her age, a man she once called *Father*. Now Madge talked of bartering and chessboards. There was no talk of hearts, rather the games of kings and the marketing of human flesh. It made her feel uneasy. More than that, it stirred within her feelings of disgust and horror.

Her mother had married for love and wanted the same for her. Mary Stafford had defied her father when he put forward his candidates for Kate's hand. "She is my daughter," she had said. "This time, 'tis for me to say when and to whom Kate weds. When the right time comes, I will talk to her and see what is in her heart before deciding on her husband."

"Mary, you're a fool," her grandfather had shouted. Bucking at having to adapt to her mother's new marriage, Kate had felt her mother deserved that and her grandfather's fury. When he rode away without giving his blessing, or even bidding her farewell, Kate blamed her mother. Remembering that day, she recalled how he had glared at her, in passing, with stern coldness. She shivered now for another reason than this winter morn. She had taken the hurt, and then waited to hurt her mother—the first of many times.

Bowing her head, Kate steepled her fingers together and thought. Her mother had always tried to do the best for her, tried to protect and keep her safe from this heartless world she found herself in. Now Kate realised her mother had also let her be herself.

The anger towards her mother swayed like the broken cobweb above her head. Only a few sections of threads kept it secured to stone. Life was not black or white. It had rarely easy answers, and was hard to fight when one stood against many. Almost impossible, if you were a woman.

But the lies. All the lies. How could her mother let her believe she was the daughter of one man when she really was the daughter of another?

The smaller spider broke away, retreating under the shadow of the stone overhanging the window. The black one weakly stretched out its legs, tried to move, its efforts to escape entangling it more and more in the remains of the cobweb, while the other spider relaxed and waited. Waited for the larger one to wind its own winding cloth as it succumbed to poison.

What if her mother spoke the truth in her letter? She hadn't wanted to lie. But the lie gave her the only means to seize power over her life. But, surely, it was wrong to lie. Kate blinked away tears. What right had she to judge her mother? Aunt Nan had said her mother had the strength to untangle herself from the web of court. Aunt Nan's voice echoed in her thoughts. *No one owns her now.* Her aunt's heartache and envy had been palpable.

Already the time with her aunt had shown that women must fight for power to live, to love where their hearts desired—using whatever weapons they could to surmount an unequal battle.

Had the black spider believed the smaller one an easy target? The pale, victorious spider latched itself upon the bigger one and began to feast.

Kate remained silent and thoughtful as Madge chattered about the two lovers and love in general. The poetry manuscript lay between them. Kate flicked through its pages. She did not hear someone approach until a voice made her almost jump out of her skin. Recognising the voice, she stood, and Madge stood, too, both girls bobbing a curtsey to Mary Howard, the young Duchess of Richmond.

Mary grinned. "Welladay, I thought to give Madge the charity of my company. I did not think to find you also here, coz."

Kate's cheeks heated. Uncertain on how to reply, she shrugged.

Mary turned to Madge and lifted an eyebrow in question. She bowed her head to the Duchess. "Aye, she knows what we do here. Pray, your leave to sit?" Without waiting for an answer, she took Kate's arm and they sat again. Madge gestured to the spot next to her. "Your Grace, why don't you join us?

Mary lifted her chin askance to Madge. Then she looked

over her shoulder and around the room. With an amused twist of her mouth, she nodded and sat. "Aye, why not?" Her deep, blue eyes widened at the manuscript in Kate's hands. "Who gave you that?"

Kate flinched, but this time found her tongue. "Madge, your Grace. She was showing me the poems."

Her cousin grinned. "I have invited Kate to join our scribblings." She took the book from Kate and turned a page. "See, she has already left her mark."

"Oh!" Kate cried, her hands going to her cheeks. "Pray—don't—"

The two older girls laughed.

"I told you she is a green maid," Madge said aside to Mary.

Scowling, Kate jumped up, her hands on her hips. "Stop calling me that! I am not a green maid." She swallowed. Even the verse she had written only days ago seemed to mock her. "I'm *not* a green maid."

Madge pursed her mouth and shook her head. She waved her hand at the place by her side. "Sit down and listen."

Hunched over, Kate sat on the edge of the seat. If only she could disappear.

"I told you we share this book. If you write something, it is for us all to read." Madge sniffed. "You have read what our Lady Margaret and others have written. Why be all out of humour when you only did what all us have done—and spoke from your heart?"

The pretty Duchess took the book from Madge and read out loud Kate's verse. She smiled gently at Kate. "A good start. What name has he, the dark, gentle one?"

Kate stood, clasping her hands before her. "Francis Knollys," she whispered. "Pray, I beg, do not tell him. I would die."

Mary and Madge laughed. Nervously toying with her hair, Kate felt younger than ever. She wished she could think of a retort that would make the other girls take her seriously. But the longer she stood before them, the more it seemed Madge was right. She was a green, foolish maid. *Francis Knollys? He will never look my way. Never. Never. Never.*

The door to the gallery creaked and swung open. Alert for another cause, Madge stood, all her attention going to the door. Lady Worcester entered, carrying the struggling Purkoy. Her lips curling, she held the dog away from her as if worrying about getting its white fur on her black gown. Madge paled and lost her animation. She shared her panic with the equally ashen Duchess.

Lady Worcester curtseyed. She walked towards them and curtseyed once more. "Your Grace. Welladay, this is an unexpected meeting." She smiled at the door of the bedchamber. "Are you attending the Queen?" She grimaced as the dog wriggled in her arms. "I found this cod's-head alone outside. No doubt he escaped whoever had him in their care. I'll never understand why he cannot be placed in the kennel with the rest of the Queen's dogs."

Madge glanced at Mary Howard with meaning. The Duchess walked over to Lady Worcester. "Shall I take him?"

Lady Worcester passed over the dog with visible relief. "The Queen can have him with my blessing. He is better behaved with her." She scrutinized the door again. "She is resting no doubt." Lady Worcester put a hand on her pronounced belly. "I will do the same—unless you think there is call for me to stay?"

The Duchess smiled. "Nay. Pray, go and rest."

Lady Worcester returned the grin. "When the young

Duke, your husband, does his duty and gets you with child, your Grace, I will delight in telling you the same." Just as she opened the door, laughter—a man's echoed by a woman's—came from the bedchamber. She stopped and turned to them a face that spoke of confusion. "Who is that?"

The Duchess started. "Oh," she said slowly, "just the Queen's brother."

Lady Worcester appeared taken aback. "Lord George? I thought he rode out this morning. His wife said he would be gone all day." Her frown deepening, she left the room.

Kate's cousins returned to the window-seat. Both girls silent, Mary patted the little dog while Madge, staring ahead, twirled a loose tress of her hair around a finger. The dog, as if wanting to get away from their unhidden distress, jumped off Mary's lap to go to Kate.

"She's friends with the Queen. It will be alright," said Madge.

Kate picked up the dog, wanting to hold him close for comfort. Her body trembled, but not from the cold.

11

Daily at court, Kate struggled with the knowledge of her true parentage. What made it worse was that when she was with her aunt and the King came near, he never once looked her way. Even weeks after their first meeting, it was the same and, coming from his throne room with her aunt, she had to beg permission to go back to her chamber, alone. That she seemed so invisible to him left her ill—ill in heart and spirit.

Seated by the hearth, her journal in her hand, Kate watched the fire as if the burning flames could reveal answers that so far eluded her. She wanted to weep, but detested this forever-weeping girl that she had become. She had never cried at home. Now she fidgeted in her seat, regretting the contempt she had offered her mother, thinking her weak for her tears.

Everything seemed to crumble around Kate. She had believed coming to court would give her happiness, only to discover sorrow in its stead. At home, the life of her aunt held true to her motto of "Most happy." She faced the lie of that now. Aunt Nan was a woman whose laughter grew increasingly brittle with each new day. Kate sighed. At home, she had worshipped her aunt and seethed with shame for a mother who wanted no more than to see her family safe and happy. Now, close familiarity to her aunt had revealed that her idol was truly a woman of flesh and blood—a woman who did not feel safe or happy. Her aunt's misery added to Kate's desire to see

Francis, even if but from a distance, and kept her from asking to be sent back home. *But do I stay here only for them?*

If her aunt acted like one who walked on shifting sands, Kate simply fell and fell, unable to find a handhold in her confusion about the King. He was her father, but did not own her as his daughter. Despite her being not of his blood, William Carey owned her as such. Since his death, she had yearned for a father's love, prayed for a father's love—a love to embrace her through her whole life. She had searched for what seemed an eternity, but now, more than ever, it seemed the unattainable grail of her existence. She blinked away tears.

She once had a father who loved her, and now had a father who rarely glanced her way. She meant nothing to him. Less than nothing. Unchecked, her tears fell down her cheeks. Did she want his love? Could she ask for his love? Perhaps it was true—*I am less than nothing.*

The fire crackled and burst into new life. In her mind, her mother read from the work of Seneca: *If you wish to be loved, love.*

Love the King? It seemed an impossible task. Impossible, because Kate hated him.

At the writing desk, she opened to a blank page of her journal and dipped her quill into the inkpot. She scored deep upon the vellum parchment, the quill scratching it like a sharp fingernail seeking blood.

> There's hatred in my heart
> Hatred I want not
> Anger closes my throat
> And seeks to burst forth
> My soul is black with sin

My thoughts are dark
And evil
I desire to kill
See a man bleed before me
Make him hurt
For all the hurt
He gives to me.

Called back to her chamber later that day, she found Will Stafford seated near the fire. Her stepfather's hair uncombed, Stafford looked weary, unwashed and saddle-sore. A three-day beard darkened his cheeks and chin. Beside him was a low table, and on it a wooden trencher with the remains of a small loaf of bread and a chicken carcass. To one side, yellow cheese crumbs formed lace-like patterns on the trencher. Tossing a half-eaten fowl leg back, he got to his feet and smiled.

"Look at you, Kate! Aren't you the lady!" He flourished a bow. "Young madam, I greet ye."

"Why are you here?" She tugged at the girdle of her new velvet gown. "Should you not be with Mother?"

Speaking out of habit, out of hurt, the words had rung out short and rude. She flinched. Her weeks away from home had taught her shame. Her mother wasn't the only person who had cosseted and protected her. When her stepfather's smile disappeared, she flinched again.

Stafford sat back on his seat with an audible groan.

"Must it start again, Kate? You ask why I am here. If you were any kind of daughter, you would know it has to do with your mother."

Fear seized her heart. "Mother? Is she ill?"

Her stepfather considered her. "So," he said slowly, "you do have feelings for your good mother. *Ill?* Kate, it has been weeks since my Mary wrote to you. She bled her heart out in that letter. And for what? Her daughter's silence. Of course your mother is sickening—and you're the cause of it."

Kate shifted angrily. "Do not blame me for my mother's sins. What was she expecting? My forgiveness?" The raw hurt within her bled again. "She made me a bastard. A bastard!"

His mouth grim, he shook his head. "Bridle your tongue, maid. Of course your mother wants your forgiveness. As for expecting it, my Mary is too gentle and good for that. Don't you know her children are the sun and the moon to her? 'Tis breaking my heart to see her become more despondent as each day passes without a letter from you. 'Tis time you remembered you are no longer a child and count your good fortune you have such a mother. Don't you know how much she sacrificed to keep you safe at her side?"

Cosseted. Protected. Loved. Yes, that had been her life growing up with her mother. Homesick, Kate blinked at the smart of tears. Her mother toiled with hands as beautiful as her sister's, only hers were reddened and broken-nailed with menial work, and matched her threadbare work day clothes, even if carefully patched. A large estate took much hard work to run and there never was enough coin to pay their few loyal servants. Yet her mother made their home a happy place.

Kate considered her stepfather. Life had become easier for her mother since her marriage. She no longer worked so hard, and their home was filled with the joy that only came when a woman loved her man. Throughout the day and night, apart or together, Will and her mother sang. This time, joy was mutually given and shared, and no longer dependant on just one. Kate bent her head and swallowed, ashamed once more. Surely it was time to own her stepfather as a good man. But her mother? Kate's eyes filled with tears. How could she forgive her mother?

She turned to her stepfather in desperation. "I don't know what to do."

He came to her and rested his hands on her shoulders.

"Aye, you do, child. If you love your mother, you do."

Kate broke down then, her sobs muffled in his doublet. He patted her back. "There, girl, those tears will do you good." He laughed softly. "Boleyn women may not like to weep, but for certes it helps their menfolk when they do."

Later, they sat by the fire and spoke quietly together, as if getting to know each other for the first time.

"Do you want to come home?" he asked. "You can, you know. You can sit behind me, and we will ride like the wind to your sweet mother. It would be good to have you back for Christmas. Your little brother has changed so much in the weeks you have been away. Little Nan misses you, too."

Kate thought hard. *What of Catherine and Madge? What of Francis? What of my aunt? What of the man who is my father?* If she returned home now, she would likely hate him all the days of her life. *Do I really want to hate him?* The poem she had written had shocked her. She had never wanted to kill anything in her life. She started, remembering her evil, jealous thoughts about her little brother. *Is something evil deep inside me? Something evil and murderous? Am I truly a fiend?* Whatever the evil was, she recoiled from it with horror.

Nay, she did not want to hate the King. Even for the hurt he gave to her, and the hurt he gave to her aunt. Perhaps if she stayed, he might recognise her as his daughter, and she could feel something for him other than hatred. Perhaps, if he saw her—really saw her—she could speak to him about her aunt. Make him realise he did wrong by her. Surely there was hope of that? Life always gave reason for hope. Her mother had told her that.

The terrible heaviness of spirit at last lifted from her. No, she did not hate her mother, but still she shook her head. "It is not that I don't want come home, but I have a place here, too. This seems where I must make my real life." She clenched her hands before her. "And Aunt Nan needs me more than Mother. She has so few she can really trust, so few who really love her or protect her. Mother has you, Father."

The word was out. Kate lifted her gaze to his beaming face, and they both burst out laughing. He took her hand. "I have waited a long time for that, my maid. If your time at court has brought you to name me Father, I think these days have brought us an unexpected blessing. One that will bring great joy to your mother." He bent and kissed her cheek. "Aye, and a promise of a true homecoming at last—one that comes from the heart. But if you change your mind, all you need do is send me a message, and I'll ride through summer storm or winter snow to bring you home again."

He checked the undraped window. In the time they had talked together, the light had edged closer to darkness.

"My girl, I must be on my way while there are a few hours of daylight left. I do not want to be away from my Mary any longer than need be." Stafford gestured over to the table with the inkstand. "Isn't there something you should do before I leave?"

Kate smiled, really smiled, at him, and then hurried over to the table. She picked up the quill and studied the blank parchment. She wrote five lines:

You have my heart.
I miss you more with each passing day.
I forgive you.
I begin to understand.
I am your daughter always.

Then she signed "Kate." Nothing more. But at least that name no one could take away.

12

While he did not request it of her, Kate accompanied her stepfather back some of the way towards the royal stables. They talked softly all the while—of homely things mostly, although when it came time to bid her stepfather farewell at the back entrance of the palace, he faced her with worried eyes. "Remember," he said, taking her hand, "you must be careful to whom you speak, child, and be careful of what you say. Your mother and I want you to keep out of harm's way."

She attempted a smile of reassurance. "You said the same when you first brought me here. I shrugged off your words then, but no more. These weeks at court have taught me caution."

He nodded and gazed down the long corridor they had just walked. Servants scurried around lighting the sconces along the walls. "Yet, methinks if I hadn't stopped at this place to say farewell, you would likely have walked all the way with me to the stable." He took her hand. "This is not home, Kate. The freedom you had there is not what you can here. Only walk in public places with those you trust, and never alone. Promise me you will remember this."

She enclosed his hand in both of hers. "I promise." This time she widened her smile. "Father."

He laughed and embraced her. "All right, lass. You go back now while there's still daylight. I'll be on my way."

Thoughtful, Kate made her slow way back to her chamber,

ignoring the cold drafts that accompanied her every step along the corridor. She sniffed and paused. A lit torch in a high sconce wisped with grey smoke as it crackled, the flame fighting to gain ground. Sizzling, the flame increased before it crackled and smoked again. One last struggle and it died. In the sudden fall of darkness, she coughed, her lungs tickling from the acid smoke. She averted her face, her attention caught by the pooling golden light coming from a deep embrasure where an oriel window overlooked the Queen's garden. Kate wandered over to it and sat in the amber haze.

Deep snow covered the garden. After a day of continual flurries and strong winds, all was still and calm. Broken islands of grey clouds and ribbons of pink and purple glided across a pale, azure sky. The lowering sun shone upon the garden a gloaming that painted everything with magic. Even the white-speckled trees shimmered with mauve, gold and glassy greens of melting snow.

Kate drew up her legs, hugged them to her, bracing her back against the stone of the corner of the window-seat. She pushed from her mind her stepfather's worry. Surely no danger could come to her so close to her chambers? Watching the ebb and flow of the final moments of day, it seemed eternity weaved all around her. She became aware of her breathing—inhaling, exhaling, inhaling, exhaling—that drank deep from the sweetness of life. *My life.*

Enwrapped by the gloaming light, she put a hand over her heart and gloried in her warm, young, healthy body. She owned the world, and everything was possible, there for her to take. Life held her in its wonder, its beauty. She was part of a fabric that went on and on without end. She thanked

God for it.

She shivered. Now sitting in the dark and very cold, she stirred as if from a deep dream, realising she could no longer see the garden. Night had fallen. She drew her mantle closer around her and shifted in the window-seat, preparing to leave and head back to the warmth of her chamber. But then quiet voices spoke close by—one belonged to Cromwell. She jerked back and flattened herself against the stone of the embrasure. *Dear God, let me be out sight. Pray, don't let them hear me.*

"Are you certain this place is safe?" he asked.

"Is any place safe, Master Cromwell? But, look around. None can approach us without our knowledge."

Heavy feet shuffled, then Cromwell spoke again. "Aye, all is clear. I have my man on guard to ensure we are undisturbed."

"Very well, my Lord. Let us come to it. Why did you ask for this meeting?"

"A bird came and told me certain things."

Another pause.

"What things, my Lord?"

"Oh, a certain matter of treason. One that could see a man boil in oil. A waste of both good man and oil, I'd say."

Kate's heart drummed hard as if counting out the seconds until the voices spoke again.

"Treason, my Lord?" the other man said slowly. "I am a loyal servant to the crown."

"And what crown is that?" Cromwell laughed softly. "I believe you desire a change of crown—to that of an untried, stubborn and vengeful girl. What would the King do, I wonder, if I passed on to him what this little bird said to me?

War or poison—such are your remedies to the ills of the land."

Feet shifted. "Your bird sang the wrong tune, my Lord."

"I do not think so."

The man's breathing quickened.

"If you don't think so, why not tell the King and have me arrested?"

"Because I might use you better if you remain with the King. A bird placed there could tell me things that would only strengthen my hand."

Silence fell, heavy with menace and fear.

"Why should I sing to you?"

"You're not a fool. You know as I do that change is in the wind. You dislike Queen Anne almost as much as I do. If she gives the King a son, we are both doomed men. Perchance you, good sir, are doomed no matter what."

One heartbeat. Two. Three. Four. Five.

Cromwell laughed. "I can guess your thoughts. You, my good man, are only one of many who plot her demise. My little bird told me of your talks with the group of churchmen who just wait for the King's concubine to fail once more in the birthing chamber. Not that I agree with their conspiracy. I have no use for the papacy. Queen Anne and I once agreed about the religious path for England. Now she has got in her head that she knows better than me as to what should happen to the monasteries, and desires for all English men an English Bible and the Gospel open to interpretation by all. She is a fool. A fool who does not care where this but leads: aye, anarchy and sedition.

"What does it matter if monasteries are sold off as long as gold comes back to the King's coffers? She will not leave him alone in this matter. She is a fool, and he has lost patience with a wife who thinks she knows better than he and tells him so."

Impatient, angry feet stamped. "I do not want to see the monasteries disbanded either, Cromwell. The King goes too far. Soon, it will be too late for England to return to the True Faith."

There was hush for a moment before Cromwell spoke again. "And you may go too far, sir. I don't think I need to tell you the agony of a man who is boiled in oil. The King would take your betrayal very hard. So hard, I doubt not the hardness of your death."

Boots scraped the brick floor. "My lord, I am a physician. Do you not think I carry a gentler means of death always on my person?"

Cromwell laughed. "You should not have told me that. If you refuse to be my man, I will call my men now. We will strip you down to your skin before we take you before the King. There'll be no gentle means of death for you."

One man coughed then swallowed. "My Lord, what do you want of me?"

"Oh, nothing more than to be another of my birds who sings to me of what goes on between the King and Queen Anne. Doesn't that make you feel better, my good man, to know you work with me to bring the bitch down? And you get what you want, too. Once she is gone, it won't be long before the King's daughter resumes her rightful place."

A long moment passed. "So I give my soul to the devil."

Cromwell laughed. "Say you the devil? You flatter me." Feet moved. "It is time for us to return before we are missed. On Friday say, you will sup with me, and every Friday after that until we achieve our goal."

The heavy pad of feet receded. For a long time, Kate was too frightened to move. At last, reassured by the silence, she slipped from the embrasure and went in the opposite direction of the men, heading swiftly along the torch-lit corridors to her aunt's chambers.

Madge and Mary emerged from the Queen's chamber. Madge frowned at Kate. "What to do? Why come you here? And alone? Kate, I'll not be answerable to your fate if you continue in this fashion."

"Who attends the Queen?" Kate asked.

"Why us, of course—and the Duchess of Richmond. But the Queen asked us to leave while she rests for a time."

"I must see her!"

Without waiting for yea or nay, and ignoring the startled look of the Queen's usual guard as she boldly passed him, Kate entered her aunt's antechamber. The Duchess sewed by the fire. Her eyes narrowed at Kate. "The Queen has not called for you."

Kate lifted her skirts and ran through the open doorway of the bedchamber. Aunt Nan stirred.

"What is it?" she said sleepily.

Kate fell to her knees beside the bed and took her hand. "Aunt Nan, wake up, pray wake up."

Her aunt moved her on her side and her eyes opened. Leaning on her arm, she half sat up. "Kate?" She straightened up, sitting against the pillows. "I hope you have good reason to disturb my slumber."

"Forgive me, Aunt. I do have good reason." Kate dropped her head in her hands. "Oh, Aunt, I am frightened for you."

"Frightened? For me?" She tightened her grip on Kate's hand. "Tell me, child."

"I heard Cromwell, my Queen. He and one other. They spoke of bringing you down."

"Cromwell?" Aunt Nan paled and swallowed. "You heard him? In God's good name, where were you that Cromwell spoke so freely?"

Kate's cheeks heated. "In the window-seat at the far end of the gallery—the one that overlooks your garden." She shrugged. "I lingered overlong to watch the setting of the sun. I was readying myself to return to my chamber when I heard Cromwell's voice. I hid until it was safe to come here."

The Queen's brow drew into a worry knot. "Kate, you must vow to me that you will no longer be so foolish as to wander about the court without an attendant." She shook her head. "I almost lost my maidenhood because I once was a young fool like you. I beg you, take heed of the mistakes of your elders and desist. Nay, I do not beg, but command. If I hear you disregard my warning, I will send you home straight to your mother." She shook her head. "I cannot believe you placed yourself in such danger, eavesdropping on Cromwell—Cromwell of all men."

Kate bowed her head in submission before she spoke again. "But Cromwell, Aunt?"

Aunt Nan inhaled a deep, sharp breath. "Tell me then. What did you hear?"

Kate thought for moment, trying to get the story straight in her head.

"There is a man, close to the King, who is treacherous. Cromwell told him he would tell the King if the man didn't do what he said. Cromwell told him the King would boil him in oil."

Shifting against the pillows, Aunt Nan frowned, then

murmured, "That's the punishment for poison. It must be that, then. Good thing then that the King and I have food tasters. And the punishment for the crime is such to make it unlikely that any would-be poisoner would proceed to put their plan in action." She faced Kate again. "Do you know this man?"

Kate shook her head. "No, I cannot name him."

Aunt Nan sighed. "You may not be able to give him a name, but I have my suspicions. There was a time when I could have gone to the King, and he would have listened to me. Now, unless I have real proof, I cannot do that." She pursed her lips. "Even to send you would be a mistake. The King would hear you out and then decide you are my creature. He knows I hate Cromwell and would like to see his head off his shoulders. In less than three years, he has become my greatest enemy. He has destroyed the King's trust in me." She placed her hand protectively over her belly. "Once I have my son, my husband will come back to me. I must wait until then—and then Cromwell is a dead man."

Kate listened to the chorus singing in her head the same tune, over and over: *You must not walk alone.* Now her aunt's command slammed the final door to her freedom. Disturbed by the night's events, Kate was pleased when Madge and Mary offered to take her back to her chamber. Kate soon discovered why, with both girls demanding to know the story behind her panicked night visit to the Queen. But her aunt had issued another command before ending their conversation. Kate was to remain silent about what she had overheard. Her aunt warned her to do any other would put in risk both their safeties.

Once she told them she obeyed the Queen's command in not telling them, Madge and Mary left her to return to their post, leaving her in the bedchamber to her own devices. She shivered, her bones hurting with the cold. The fire was out, the chamber icy and Alice, their maidservant, was nowhere in sight to restore the hearth to its proper state and purpose.

My mantle? Where is it? Kate remembered pulling it around her while seated in the window-seat. The cheap clasp from home must have broken again and caused it to fall from her shoulders when she had raced to her aunt's chamber. Her heart missed a beat. *What if Cromwell finds it?*

Aunt Nan had only recently given her the mantle as a gift. Cromwell had remarked on it only two days ago— commending the embroidery of falcons, the crest of the Boleyn family. He would know it belonged to her.

The embrasure was only a short distance away. She could get there and back in minutes. She had to retrieve her mantle, even if it meant disobeying the Queen. But wouldn't she understand why?

Holding up her skirts to keep her feet free, Kate rushed out her chamber, going back down the long corridor and around the corner that took her back to the window-seat that overlooked the garden. To her relief, her mantle was on the floor in front of it, seemingly untouched and undisturbed.

She flung it over her shoulders, raced back the other way and straight into Cromwell's arms. She cried out in fright and he laughed.

"Why in such a hurry?" He laughed again. "You look like you've seen a ghost."

Gathering back her wits, she curtseyed. "I beg your pardon, my Lord, but I return to my chamber. It is night, and I should be there, not here. My cousin will scold if she knows I left it.'

Cromwell crossed his arms "So what do you do here?" He winked. "Have you already a lover, young Katherine Carey?"

She swallowed but thanked God he gave her this opening. It was far better for him to think she returned from a dalliance than begin wondering why he found her alone. She attempted a smile. "Master Cromwell, I beg you, do not tell of this to my aunt."

He smiled. "Let none say that I put anything in the way of young love." He studied her. "But service for service, I say."

Kate frowned. "What mean you, sir?"

"Let's be clear. If I do not tell your aunt, what will you do for me?"

"I do not understand."

"Don't you, girl? Let me spell it out for you then. You attend the Queen, and I would like to hear more about what goes on in her chambers."

Kate stared in disbelief. "Sir, are you asking me to spy on my aunt?"

"Spy? Did I say that? I ask you to talk to me, no more, no less."

"You ask me to speak about the Queen? I cannot do that."

His thick brows came together, and he scowled. All at once, he appeared to threaten her. "So you are happy that I tell your aunt about our meeting?"

Kate swallowed. "She will be angry, but that is better than what you propose."

Cromwell grabbed her arm and thrust his face at her.

"Foolish girl. Be careful. Very careful. Take it from me, child, if you choose the wrong side, you will be pulled under, too." He pushed her away from him, almost causing her to lose her balance. "And don't think the King will care to hear about this conversation. Believe me, in all things, I act for the King. What he wishes, I do."

13

Green groweth the holly, so doth the ivy.
Though winter blasts blow never so high,
Green groweth the holly.
As the holly groweth green
And never changeth hue
So I am, and ever hath been,
Unto my lady true.
Green groweth.
Unto my lady true.

It was Christmas. On Kate's way to the chapel for evening prayers, voices sang the King's song once more. She stood still, listening to the refrain: "Unto my lady true."

Did the King believe those words when he wrote them? Did he believe he gave his heart and that life promised him rebirth, a new beginning? That he would never forsake the woman he loved? Now it seemed that the winter blasts of disappointment, disillusionment and despair froze him, heart and soul.

"Adieu his lady," the singers sang. "Adieu."

Kate trembled. *Stop it! All is well.* Once her aunt gave the King his desired son, all would be more than well. But Kate could not shake away her sense of apprehension.

Holly, ivy and winter flowers garlanded the doorways and walls at Greenwich. Verdant green contrasted vividly with bright red—red holly berries, red flowers, red glass, red ribbons—used to tie up the Christmas trappings and hang them in every possible place, even around the window-seats overlooking the Thames. The trappings became arches then, partially hiding the people who sat there taking rest from the many games, or those who dallied in games of love.

On the fourth day of Christmas, Kate rested in one of these window-seats. Christmas at court was a busy time, even if normal duties were on hold for the while. Days and nights of merriment took their toll.

Her brother played Blind Man Bluff. Kate grinned. The melee of young people darted in and out all around him. His laughter was carefree, so unlike the increasingly circumspect boy who considered his every move with caution.

Only a little time before, she, too, had been blindfolded, her hands outstretched, forced to search for her fellows by hearing and touch, going one way and another. A little scared by her blindness, it didn't stop her laughing until her stomach hurt. For a short time, she even forgot the absence of her best friend at court. Almost a week ago, Catherine, the Duchess of Suffolk, had left the court to go home to attend her ailing son.

Resting her cheek against the cold stone of the embrasure, Kate tried to ignore the icy fingers that seeped through her gown, draughts let in by the badly sealed window behind her. She struggled to keep her eyelids open—the desire to sleep began to steal upon her.

With a shake, she sat straighter and gave herself a shake. *You are young, a maid, not a grey-head crone!* Had she fasted overmuch on the days leading up to Christmas, wanting her aunt to be proud of her? How she suffered for it now. Even her aunt did not wilt like this despite her daily struggle to keep down her food. Since the start of the festivities, she had made merry with the King, partnering him in dances, singing with him, talking long with him. Her happiness was contagious and spread to the court. Kate sighed. Aunt Nan had a steel will; she was not likely to seek out her bed as Kate wished to do.

Giving in to her tiredness, she leaned against the stone again, and drifted into a daydream about the Christmas masses four days before. That night she had held a taper in her hand, adding to the light of many borne likewise. The candles lit blue lights in Aunt Nan's unbound hair and glittered her jewels, casting upon her the gauze of beauty. Side by side, hand clasped in hand, the King and Queen had taken their places to hear the three masses. As the priest told the lineage of Christ, the King bent to whisper something to Aunt Nan, his hand going to her belly. She met his eyes and smiled. Putting her hand over his, she lowered her head to pray. Joy seemed theirs that night, as on the first Christmas when the Son of God came to live among men. The joy of the first Christmas too, concerned a child. As from the beginning, a child is always hope.

Kate had started then, knowing her thoughts influenced by her mother. She had been so angry the day of her mother's churching. The first moment she found herself alone with her, she had snarled, "Why have more children? Why bring us in the world when it is only pain?" Her mother's smile had maddened her, but her answer made her cry. "Not only pain, Kate, not when a child's loved like all my children are loved.

All my children have been born in faith. Hope and faith in life." That Christmas, Kate had no doubt her aunt believed the same.

Leaving the chapel with Madge, Kate's happiness for her aunt kept her smiling. A smile she found answered in a slight, amused smile of an aged man who stood alone in the gallery, leaning on a walking stick. The light of one torch shone not only on the weave of holly decorations, but also his amicable, angular face framed by longish, greying hair. Despite his amused smile, Kate detected an unmistakable air of sadness around him.

Taking off his black cap, he half bowed to them. Madge bobbed a brief curtsey, and Kate did the same.

Madge approached cautiously. "Greetings, Master Chapuys. Were you in the chapel with us? I did not see you."

The sadness around him now told its story on his face. He adjusted his black cap back on his head. "Nay, Mistress Shelton." The voice was accented—the words slowly drawn out as if ensuring their correctness. "I am here to see the King."

Madge glanced at Kate with a lift of an eyebrow before turning back to Chapuys. "The King? I do not envy you. Ambassador or not, I do not think he will welcome you tonight. He goes with the Queen to her chambers for supper."

"The *Queen*." Chapuys spoke even slower. His mouth pursing, he scraped his walking stick on the ground.

Why did he linger over *Queen*?

Changing position, he shifted his walking stick again. "Welcome or not, I will see the King tonight. Master Cromwell has gone with my message. The King will come."

Now, four days later, Kate understood better that strange meeting. She knew from Aunt Nan that the King had seen

Chapuys. The King had returned to her chamber furious and difficult to soothe. That same night Chapuys had rode with the King's permission, permission that had cost him the King's anger and was only obtained under duress, to be by the side of Katherine of Aragon.

Was his news true? Was the old woman really dying?

"Why alone, Lady Kat? May I sit beside you?"

Kate straightened at Francis's voice.

"Good sir, pray do," she said. "How does Brutus?" Inwardly cursing her foolish question, she dared not say one more word in fear of her tongue stumbling again.

Amused, Francis sat close to her. "'Tis my hope he is sleeping in his kennel." He inspected the window. "But more likely baying at the moon tonight. I'm thankful I am no longer on duty as his nursemaid. Brutus and Persephone have had their introductions to Urian. He told them their place, and they accepted it well. The rest of their training is in the hands of the Queen's kennel keeper."

Half-turning to the dull window, Kate sighed. "I wish I could see the moon."

Francis bounded up and held out a hand. "Why not come and get some air with me? The snow has stopped for a time, and the night is crisp and clean."

Kate stared at his hand and then at him. She didn't know what to do or say.

"You can trust me." Francis laughed. "The Queen's temper is not something I am likely to risk even for a pretty girl like you."

Kate trembled, but this time she took his hand and grabbed her cloak. *Pretty? He thinks me pretty?* She wanted to skip in her delight.

Hand in hand they weaved through the revellers until they reached one of the courtyards that looked over the river. The snow crunched underneath their feet. She sniffed the salt in the air from the nearby sea. Above, a full, huge moon sailed in a clear night sky, a shiny disk of silver against black velvet. Despite her thick cloak, she shivered.

"Are you cold?" Francis clasped her hand tighter.

The warmth of his hand edged her away from him in her greenness. She was both scared and excited, her blood turning to honey in her veins, her knees weak, her woman parts tingling, demanding she go closer to him.

"Your hand is like ice," he said.

She smiled. Removing her hand from his, she walked a few steps away. "'Tis of no concern." She inhaled a deep breath, hoping it would release her from this feeling that tightened around her its spell. He was still too close. Her heart thumped so hard in her chest she thought he would hear it. She gazed at the sky. Stars pinpricked the heavens.

Francis came to stand beside her and pointed. "There's the Hunter—and see there the Crab?"

She scanned the night sky.

"Nay." He took her arm, turning her a little. "That group of stars."

Despite the freezing night, his hand lit a fire in her blood. She no longer cared about the stars. The nearby torchlight lit up his teeth and the beauty of his heaven-drawn face. His attention returned to her. They stood there silently for a moment. He touched her cheek, bent down, kissed her lightly. His mouth was so warm, so gentle. She shivered again, but this time not with cold.

"I best take you in," he said, his voice hoarse. His hands

were on her shoulders now.

She leant on him and raised her face. "Kiss me again."

This time his kiss was deep and long. Her limbs became loose, her body melding into his. Francis groaned, and pushed her away.

"Little minx," he said. "I cannot answer for your maidenhead if we stay out here any longer."

"Francis," Kate said, cresting on the swirl of her emotions, "I care not. I love you." She lifted her face once more. "Pray, kiss me."

He shook his head and took her hand. "Little minx," he repeated. "My faith, you're a temptress. Thank God, I have more years than you, and know we would win nothing if we stay out here much longer. As for love, you are very young. Take my advice—be young for a little while longer. There will be time for dalliances in the future." Still holding her hand, he led her back towards the music and laughter of the court. "Let's return before we are missed."

She swallowed her urge to cry. Feeling slapped and rejected, she swivelled her head a little towards Francis. Despite clasping her hand, he no longer seemed to notice her. Her free hand went to her mouth, and she blinked away tears. Only moments ago they had kissed, really kissed. Now he acted as if it hadn't happened—as if she meant nothing to him. *Nothing?* She floundered in deep misery. *Aye, all the world thinks me nothing.*

Back inside with the revellers, Francis released Kate as soon as he found Madge. He bid them both farewell and disappeared into the crowd of courtiers that edged one side of the room, leaving the floor to the dancers. Kate shuddered.

"What is it?" Madge asked.

Kate remembered her aunt's command. "Would you care if we go back to our chamber now?"

Madge lifted her eyebrows before searching the direction that Francis had gone. "It matters not to me if we leave now, but you have some explaining to do when we get there."

Kate turned to Madge in anger, but her defeat won out. Her shoulders slumped. Not waiting for Madge, she strode fast towards the gallery that led to their rooms. Madge caught up, took her arm, walking with her in silence until they reached their destination. Opening the door, Madge cocked her head. "Are you all right, little coz?"

Kate bit down so hard on her bottom lip she tasted blood. She shook her head, rushing ahead to the bedchamber. Kicking off her slippers, she threw herself on the bed, then pushed her face against the pillow. Uncontrollably, her body shook and shook.

Madge's hand touched her shoulder. "Is it Francis?"

Kate gazed aside at her. "Pray..." Kate's voice quivered like her body. She swallowed to gain control. "Do not speak of it."

Madge sighed. Sitting on the edge of the bed, she removed her slippers before turning back to Kate. Her grave expression spoke of concern. "He didn't hurt you, did he?"

Hiding her face again in the pillow, Kate shook her head from side to side. The bed creaked and adjusted to Madge's weight as she swung around to lean against the bed-head. "I cannot help unless you tell me what has upset you so."

Kate hiccupped and lifted her head. "He kissed me."

Madge gaped at her. "Kissed you?" Her cousin smiled. "Is that any cause for all this carry on?"

Kate drew a ragged breath and rested her cheek against the pillow. Thinking back to what happened made her body tremble again. "I told him I loved him."

"You did? God's teeth, Kate, one kiss and you tell a man you love him?"

Kate bolted up beside her cousin. "But I do love Francis!"

Madge raised her eyes to the ceiling. "God and all his angels help me." She pursed her lips before letting out a loud sigh. "Must I be forever in service as your nursemaid? Do you not know you cannot profess love for any man?"

Kate raised her hands to her face. "I cannot tell Francis I love him?"

Madge shook her head. "Silly goose. You are the niece of the Queen, and while the King doesn't claim you, there are few who don't know you are his daughter. It is not for you to pick your own match. Consider Lady Margaret. She took it into her mind to marry for love, and all us in her confidence now fear what will happen when the King finds out. I tell you what I think will happen. Lady Margaret and Lord Tom are likely to find themselves cooling their passions in the Tower. Tom may lose his head over this."

"Lose his head? Surely you're wrong? My mother married for love—"

"Aye, she married for love and has suffered since. She will never again be allowed openly at court."

Head bent, Kate mulled over her cousin's words. "It doesn't matter," she said at last, shrugging. "Francis doesn't love me."

"Why say you that?"

Kate half covered her mouth and trembling chin. "I told him I loved him. I asked him to kiss me again. He took me back inside."

Madge groaned. "Oh, for God's sake, Katherine. What else could the poor man do? Do you think he would want his head struck from his shoulders because he deflowered the niece of the Queen?" She shook her head. "I only hope for your sake that he doesn't think you a maid with little regard for her reputation."

Already reeling from the night events, Kate seemed to walk on quicksand, sinking deeper with every new step. "Do you think he would?"

Madge shrugged and untied the side cords of her bodice. "How would I know?" She pulled the bodice over her head, heaving a sigh of relief. "Just remember this in future; you are not free to do as you please, Kate. One false move could not only destroy your life, but lead to the deaths of others." She sighed. "Fools do not last long at court."

Kate studied her and gathered the courage to ask her the question she'd kept silent about for weeks. "What of you and the King?"

It was Madge's turn to stare. She swallowed. "As I've told you, the court is no place for secrets. I do not wish to speak about the King, now or ever, other than to say, thank God, that he hunts other quarry now. But as for you, no more assignations, I beg you, unless I am with you to act as witness."

14

Alone for a time in her chamber, Kate took the opportunity to write in her journal. Placing her quill back in its inkpot, she studied the parchment.

Here I am, love me.

Her mouth trembled, and she struggled against tears. How she wished she had the courage to speak those words to Francis. But what if she said them and he laughed at her? Told her he did not have any true feeling for her?

Already, life had broken apart her world. She did not want that to happen again. Her time at court had cast her into a mire of self-doubt. Was she strong enough to withstand any more rejection?

Life left her naked, so broken hearted and vulnerable in her misery. Life stripped her of her identity.

Who am I?

she wrote in her journal.

Katherine. Kate. Bastard.

Francis was right not to have further dealings with her. She picked up her quill again.

I love and am trapped
In a world full of woe
I love, yet he loves me not.

Dear God,
Let his heart turn to mine
For I am his
Forevermore.

For days afterward Kate did not see Francis other than in passing or from a distance. Despite Madge's efforts to explain the implications of courtly romances for one of their station, Kate walked on dark, unmarked paths charted by confusion. Day after day she relived their kiss. She could not believe Francis was false, that he felt nothing for her.

Miserable, Kate busied herself with finishing the gift she was making for her aunt for the Feast of Epiphany. She hadn't at first known what to give Aunt Nan, but the tapestries telling the story of Esther and the beautiful English Bible—a treasured gift to Aunt Nan and generously shared with all those who served her—gave Kate the idea of translating the conclusion of the Jewish Queen's story into French and decorating the pages with drawings of honeysuckle and other of Aunt Nan's favourite flowers.

First, she laboriously copied Esther's triumphal end from the Bible. Completing the first part was difficult enough, but translating it into French intensified the labour, so much so Kate feared she would not finish in time for the gift giving. But it gave her a good reason to escape Madge's supervision and go to her brother's chamber. Since he shared his chamber with no one else, it was a far quieter and more private place to work. Harry had also kindly arranged for all the writing and drawing tools necessary for her to complete her gift as well as staying for awhile to help her with the French. Day by day, she had less need to call on him in her struggle to find the right word for the translation.

Harry told his French tutor and Uncle George about what Kate was doing. After Harry's lessons, his tutor accompanied his young scholar back to his chambers and cast an interested eye on Kate's progress, offering suggestions. Uncle George often joined them as well. She discovered then that the poems he had translated in her journal were just a small part of a long line of work he had completed over the years. "I like how it challenges me," he said. "And your aunt likes it when I give her a translation as a gift." He laughed. "The skill of translation comes from our father, your grandfather. That you do it too just proves that it is in the blood."

Kate took all the help offered with gratitude. She dared not write on the costly parchment until she was confident that the translation etched on her brother's hornbook was as perfect as she could make it.

The mornings spent working diligently and carefully on her aunt's gift were the only time she put aside her broken heart and was assured of a few hours when she could distract herself from thinking about Francis. But it was hard. So very hard.

Working through Esther's story did not prevent her from wondering why he didn't come to speak to her—or wondering if Madge was right. Did he think less of her because she had asked him to kiss her? Had she shown herself unworthy of his honour? That she had no honour? She lifted her quill and frowned at the mistake she had just made. Her eyes filled with tears. *I have no honour. No honour. No honour.* She grabbed the tool to scratch out her error and wished she could scratch out that night. She trembled with shame thinking of the way she had kissed him back and melded to his body. No wonder he didn't speak to her. He probably would never speak to her again. Who could blame him?

The days of winter seemed to go on forever. It was so cold that the Thames froze over—an ice so thick and hard that the King journeyed between his river palaces by sleigh, while Aunt Nan, caged by the ill health of her pregnancy, fretted about what he did whilst away from her. But the New Year festivities brought the King back and kept him lingering at Greenwich with his wife and little daughter.

From high to low, all at court exchanged gifts at New Year. Aunt Nan gave the King a gift of a new ornamental clock, and he gifted to her the largest diamond Kate had ever seen. With her royal parents at this time, little Bess did not miss out. Resting in her chamber that afternoon, Aunt Nan gave her daughter a jewelled hornbook with a black alphabet outlined in gold.

Aunt Nan and Kate sat by the fire as Bess played with it on the floor. Aunt Nan smiled. "Look how she prefers the hornbook to the toys others have given her. She may be a little young for it, but soon I will start teaching my Bess her letters."

Bess, hearing her mother's voice, cast aside the hornbook and pulled herself up. Unbalanced by her heavy dress, she swayed for a moment before waddling over to them. Determination all over her face, every few steps she stopped to regain her footing. At last she reached her mother and collapsed against her, grinning in triumph. She held out her arms. "Kiss Bess," she commanded.

Aunt Nan laughed, reaching out her own arms. Thinking her aunt was about to lift Bess, Kate bounded from her chair, picked up the little girl, and placed her onto her mother's lap. When Kate straightened her little cousin's gown, Bess grinned up at her.

"*Ma belle.*" Aunt Nan held her daughter close. She kissed her again and again. Bess laughed, her small, long-fingered hands, perfect miniatures of Aunt Nan's, going to either side of her mother's face.

"Story, Mama." Bess nestled sleepily against her mother's breast.

Aunt Nan shared a smile with Kate. "What story shall I tell you?"

"Fine rooster," the little girl murmured.

"Fine rooster?" Aunt Nan frowned, her face thoughtful while settling her daughter in her arms. At last, leaning back, she smiled, her eyes full of dreams, and began to recite:

> "*A Cock our story tells of,*
> *who high on a dunghill stood and crew.*
> *A Fox, attracted, straight drew nigh,*
> *And spake soft words of flattery.*
> *'Dear Sir!' said he. 'Your look's divine;*
> *I never saw a bird so fine!'*"

Listening, Kate shut her eyes, relishing the warmth of the fire and the melody of her aunt's voice. For the first time at court, she welcomed a sense of peace and homecoming.

The gift giving wasn't ended that day. Kate gave her brother a new cap adorned with an ostrich feather, and he gave her a girdle book with the psalms of King David. Aunt Nan's gift to her was a copy of *The Consolation of Philosophy*.

"You've had mine long enough," she said with a grin. "When our Duchess of Suffolk comes back, I want you to continue your discussion with her about the book's teachings." She then picked up Kate's gift to her. She turned its pages and smiled. "I shall treasure this, knowing the hours you dedicated to the translation. I hope you will do more in the future. How about *The Consolation of Philosophy* next time? From the Latin to English—now that would be a worthy task for you."

To Kate's great astonishment, Francis also gave her a gift. Entering the Queen's chamber, he came to her smiling and bearing a lute, and held it out.

"For you," he said, sitting on the stool beside her.

She took it, and looked at him in confusion. "A lute?" she blurted out. "'Tis too costly a gift." She held it to her like a shield. "And I have nothing to offer you in return. Nothing."

He beamed a wider smile. "As for the cost, it is the lute I had as a boy—I play another now. As for you offering something in return, I would not call your friendship nothing, Kat. I crave pardon for not coming to you sooner and asking for forgiveness. I did not mean for you to suffer at my hand. I acted a villain forgetful of your youth." He leaned closer. "Are we friends again?"

Kate averted her face. She wanted to weep. He spoke as if she was a child. *A child?* But wasn't that better than him thinking her wanton?

She met his gaze and tried to smile. "Aye, friends."

Emotion grabbed her by the throat and rendered her unable to say anything more. She turned to the burning fire, hoping she wouldn't do or say anything foolish. Hoping she hid from him her real feelings. The days of separation had only increased her love of him. With a deep breath, she faced him with another smile—a false smile plastered upon a mask likely to slip at any moment.

He took the lute from her and strummed a few notes of a familiar song.

Kate winkled her brow in thought and the lyrics came to mind:

Pastime with good company
I love and shall unto I die;
Grudge who list, but none deny,
So God be pleased thus live will I.

"'Tis the King's song?" she offered hesitantly.

Francis grinned. "Aye, the King's. I'm glad you recognised it. It will please my father to learn that his coin was well spent with my lute master." He cocked his head towards her. "Is it true you do not play?"

Kate locked her eyes with his, then, as quickly, lowered them. She swallowed hard before she dared to speak again. She couldn't even look at him. "Who told you that?"

"Your brother. I asked him what I should give you as a gift, and he suggested a lute." Francis brushed his fingers against the strings. "He says you spend too much time either reading or writing."

Kate sat straighter in annoyance. "Did he? Did he really say that?"

Francis laughed. "Pray, do not tell him I told you so; he may never speak to me again." He twisted towards Aunt Nan. "I saw the gift you made for the Queen. I don't think your brother has ever pleased the Queen as you did today, even with the jewels he gave to her this morning." Francis grinned. "It is good you are like your aunt and enjoy learning for its own sake. So, I take it that your brother is right and you do not know how to play the lute?"

Kate nodded in confusion.

"That brings me to my next question. Would you like me to teach you?"

Hope flared in her heart. "Would you?"

He nodded. "Aye." He scrutinised her with great seriousness. "For friendship sake—only that."

"For friendship sake," she repeated. Understanding his meaning Kate bowed her head. Could she bear being alone with him as just his friend? Could she bear not seeing him at all? She swallowed. Her whole world seemed to revolve around this man. "For friendship sake," she echoed, praying she hid her tears.

Francis was good as his word. Arranging it with the Queen, he came every day when Kate was with her brother. But Francis also arranged that he would teach Harry. He put her in her place—a child that needed schooling. Francis taught her to play the lute all the while she fought a hard battle with her emotions. When memories surfaced of how he kissed her, it was almost impossible.

Francis never mentioned that night to her. It was as if he wished for her to forget it and remain a child. The only way she could do that was to concentrate on her lessons, ignoring what his closeness did to her insides. Her heart beat faster every time he had reason to touch her hands to show her how to hold the lute or pluck a note.

Almost daily, Kate learnt under Francis's careful hour of tutorage through that long, cold, dark winter. Forced to hide her true feelings from him, he could not know that his efforts to keep her a child made her into a woman.

Not many days after the exchange of gifts, Kate sat sewing next to her aunt's bedchamber, far enough away from the rest of the women for them not to observe her work, but close enough to still savour the sweet, piping voice of the woman singing as they sewed.

Already changed in many ways by her brief time at court, Kate found one thing remained the same—she still hated sewing. Just like at home, she either pricked her fingers, soiling the silk in her hands, or distractedly pulled the thread so she needed to thread her needle yet again. Meg Lee had given her such a simple task, too, edging a square of material with blackwork, but already she had spent precious minutes unpicking the mess she made of it to start again. Her fingers were stiff and painful with cold, too, making her sewing even more clumsy and inept.

She studied the other women and drew a breath of frustration. Serene and unflustered, many chatted quietly together, their needles going in and out with an enviable swiftness and expertise.

Kate pricked her finger again and despaired. Feeling she would go mad before finishing the blackwork, she tossed her sewing in the basket and sucked her sore finger. She fought down the temptation to go to Aunt Nan. But couldn't she beg to be excused or to be given another chore to do? Anything but sewing. Her aunt, though, was so engrossed in the creation of her exquisite handiwork that Kate didn't dare interrupt.

Coughing, she turned her head to the nearby fireplace. Was it smoking? She coughed again. All seemed well with the fire. Its red heat merrily devoured a huge log. She coughed again and again. Her lungs hurting, she struggled to breathe. Near her feet, smoke escaped from underneath the bedroom door. Coughing another time, Kate bounded up, hopping from foot to foot. "My Queen! My Queen!"

Her needle and thread held aloft, Aunt Nan glowered at her with annoyance. "Niece, you forget yourself!"

Kate pointed to the door, at last remembering the right word: "Fire!"

Everything became madness then. Women screamed and scurried around, running for the door to the gallery. Guards and servants rushed in. Apparently unflustered and without hurry, Aunt Nan folded her sewing and leaned down to put it in her basket. Picking that up, she stood. "Come, niece, do not tarry."

Aunt Nan started to follow after her ladies, but then paused at the empty basket by her chair. "Where's Purkoy?" She hunted the room with her eyes, calling, "Purkoy! Purkoy!"

Aunt Nan's bedroom door wide open now, tongues of flames added another red and gold to her bed hangings. *A taper carelessly left alight? How could that be?* Kate took her aunt's arm in reassurance. "He likely found a mouse to chase after. Let's get to the gallery and safety."

Her face white and rigid, Aunt Nan did as Kate bid, joining her ladies to watch the fire take hold. Servants beat at the flames, tossing all the water they could find in the room to douse it.

A loud voice called close by: "The King comes! The King comes!"

Aunt Nan stood apart from her women and waited to greet him. As he neared her, she fell to her knees and all her ladies followed suit. He helped her up and kissed her cheek. Smoke billowed from her bedchamber. "Are you all right, sweetheart? No hurt to you or the child?"

Aunt Nan smiled. "We were in the next room. Kate's quick wits warned us all before there was any true danger. No hurt to me or our strong son." She turned with concern towards her smoke-filled room. "Harry, have you seen Purkoy?"

Glancing again into her chambers, the King shook his head, his mouth grim.

A servant bowed low. "Your Majesties, the fire has been put out. Only the hangings have suffered any damage."

Aunt Nan winced. "Only the hangings? You gave them to me, my Lord. They are irreplaceable, and precious to me." She stepped towards the chambers. "And my dog? My little dog?"

The King pulled her back. "They will find him. And don't worry about your hangings. I will get you new ones. Come with me now, come and play a game of chess while they repair your bedchamber." He smiled. "We haven't played chess together for many a week. Let's see if you can still beat me."

The next day, Kate wrote in her journal:

> My poor aunt. They found little Purkoy
> under her state bed, dead in a pool of its
> own blood. Aunt Nan is inconsolable. She
> believes someone killed Purkoy as a
> warning to her—and even to cause harm
> to her and the child she bears.
>
> No one knows how the fire started, but
> the King acts kindly to my aunt. He acts
> guiltily—like one at fault. Mayhap he is.

Kate re-dipped her quill. Thinking angrily of the King's dalliance with Lady Jane, she scored boldly on the parchment:

> Aye—responsibility is not simply for those
> who do the deed.

She read back her words. It was a good thing she no longer carried her journal in her pocket. Treason seemed to frame her thoughts and poems. She now kept it in a hiding place in her chamber. She just prayed no one would ever find it.

The King was still at Greenwich on the eighth day of January—the day when a messenger knelt before the dais, holding forth his message. The King rose from the throne, took the message, and read. A grim smile tugged at his mouth before he passed the message to the Queen. He stood legs apart, a hand at his dagger, the jewels on his fingers glinting in the light.

"God be praised!" the King cried out. "We are freed at last of the harridan. Katherine of Aragon is dead. No longer do we have to live in fear of war!"

A silence fell—heavy like the shroud that wound around a dead woman far away. Kate turned to her aunt. She sat very still, very pale, all her attention on her husband as he went from courtier to courtier to accept their congratulations. Guarded expressions were everywhere. Aunt Nan read the parchment in her hand and grimaced. She lifted eyes that did not share the smile now sketched upon her face.

"So, I am truly Queen at last," she murmured, not speaking to anyone in particular.

Why did her aunt look so unhappy? Kate remembered the recent conversations amongst her women. There was a rumour that Katherine of Aragon, the dowager princess of Wales, had sent a message to her nephew, Charles, the Holy Roman Emperor, and begged him to do whatever was necessary to protect his cousin Mary's birthright. The spectre of war went hand in hand with a living Katherine. Now she was dead. Surely this should make Aunt Nan happy? But her aunt's face said otherwise.

That same night, the King held a banquet to celebrate the death of Katherine of Aragon. Kate and another woman helped the Queen dress in a gown of yellow silk with a matching cap and delicate caul. The last jewel pinned on, Aunt Nan sat in a chair, waiting to be escorted to her husband. She seemed more despondent than earlier that day. When her aunt sent the other woman for her baby daughter,

Kate took the opportunity to speak to her.

"Why so glum, my aunt?"

Aunt Nan attempted a smile that soon disappeared and left no trace. "Am I? I'd better shake myself out from this doleful mood." She put her hand on the swell of her belly. "I have much to be thankful for, yet I cannot stop thinking that my child here is the only reason they do not get rid of me as they did Katherine." She swallowed. "Blame it on my lonely nights, but I find myself beset by ghosts—too many ghosts— and now Katherine of Aragon joins them."

She sat there with a knuckle to her mouth. "Fool that I am, I could not sleep last night thinking how Thomas More pitied me before his death, saying my head would follow his one day, and dance a like dance. And how the mad Nun of Barton predicted I would meet my death by fire."

Kate gasped. "The fire in your bedchamber?" With all the candles placed a safe distance from the bed, it was still a great mystery how the fire had started.

Aunt Nan nodded. "Aye. I told you, Kate, that I believe it was done deliberately, as was the killing of my little Purkoy. His eyes. I cannot forget them—he died in agony."

"Who would do something so terrible?" How trusting Purkoy had been—save for mice and cats, he had welcomed all with friendliness. Kate shivered.

Aunt Nan lifted her head. "Our uncle Norfolk, Cromwell, one of those who still regard me as the King's concubine— who knows, Kate?"

The piping voice of a child drew their attention to the door. Aunt Nan smiled and stood. Anne Shelton, governess to Princess Elizabeth and aunt to both the Queen and Kate, carried the little princess. The Queen held out her arms.

"Pray, give my child to me."

Lady Shelton considered the Queen so coldly Kate winced. Madge's mother would not—or could not—forgive the Queen for encouraging Madge's dalliance with the King. "The Lady Princess is heavy, Your Grace. I beg of you to sit down before taking her."

Aunt Nan sighed and returned to her vacated seat. "If I must." Grimacing, she smoothed down her dress. "Everyone fusses over me too much." She held out her arms again. "Give my girl to me."

The child on her lap, Aunt Nan bent and kissed her. She was dressed in the same yellow silk as her mother, with her golden red hair held up by a silk cap that matched her gown. Bess pointed to her mother's cap. "Like mine, Mama." She gestured to her dress and her mother's. "'Ellow." She peered behind her mother at the wall tapestry of Amazon women riding into battle. "Sun 'ellow, too."

Aunt Nan hugged her child. "Sweetheart, how right you are! And just wait until you see your Lord Father. He will be just like us, in yellow, too. The sun indeed." She pointed to the tapestry telling the story of Esther. "Can you tell me the name of that Queen, Bess?"

The little girl frowned with deep concentration. "Ethter?" she offered with a lisp.

Aunt Nan grinned. "Close, sweetheart. Her name was Esther. She was a great and good Queen."

Bess patted her mother's face. "Like you, Mama?"

Aunt Nan lowered her head. "I pray to God to help me be so. One day, when you're older, I will tell you the story of Esther."

Bess bolted up straighter in her mother's arms. "Now!"

Aunt Nan's mouth tightened. "Bess, that is not how you speak to your mother. Not now, or ever."

Her daughter crumbled under her mother's stern expression. Hiccupping, tears welling, she nestled her face against her mother's breast. "Bess will be good, Mama."

Patting her daughter's back, Aunt Nan turned to Lady Shelton. "Aunt, how does my daughter? Is she well?"

Lady Shelton gave a brief smile to her charge. "Surely, Your Grace, you see for yourself. My only concern is that the princess is teething, which causes the Lady Princess much distress at night despite rubbing her gums with oil of cloves. As for the child herself, why I have never known a quicker infant for words or understanding." She laughed. "The child heard someone speak Latin the other day and repeated it back to me. Perfect it was, too."

Aunt Nan grinned. "She takes after my father. He has a fine ear and tongue for languages." She stroked her little girl's hair. "I am pleased she starts to learn Latin so early. She will need it when she is older." She lowered her head to her daughter's ear and whispered, "Elisabeth of France? Empress Elizabeth? What throne shall you have, my little Bess? But first you belong to England, and for now—" Aunt Nan kissed her daughter "—you're mine, all mine!"

Aunt Nan and her women walked down to join the King. Together, they entered the banquet hall, and he took the little princess from her governess's arms. Jigging her up and down as if in dance, he took Elizabeth around the room, showing her off to his court and the many ambassadors invited on this night. The King laughed and yanked off her cap. Her hair tumbled free around her face and gleamed fire-bright from the light of many candles.

"Mine once was exactly the same," he said with pride.

The child laughed with her tall father, reaching her hands up to stroke his beard. For a long moment, they regarded each other, their smiles wide and full of love. Aunt Nan's face lit with a happiness that embraced her husband and child from a near distance. She rested a hand on the swell of her belly.

Kate's smile at her aunt's joy disappeared when she noticed Francis talking to a friend. She withdrew into the shadows. He was so animated, so carefree—with no awareness that her heart cried out to him. Brushing away her tears, Kate rushed over to join Madge, now with the princess in her charge.

15

Kate did not know of Catherine Willoughby's return to court until she found her reading in the Queen's apartment. *The Philosophy of Consolation* captured what seemed Catherine's rapt attention, but she lifted her face at Kate's approach.

Putting down her book, Catherine rose to embrace Kate. "I missed you," she whispered.

"I, you, too," Kate replied. Their French hoods touching, she put her cheek against her friend's and hugged her tighter.

They broke apart and sat next to one another. Pale and drawn, Catherine looked older than before, as if she had gone through much during her time away.

"Is all well with your son?" Kate asked.

Worry puckered Catherine's brow. "He is teething, my poor babe. He is not the strong lad that my first born was at the same age." She bent her head and drew a deep breath. "While I am glad to see my friends at court and, of course, the Queen, if my husband hadn't commanded my return to court, I would have chosen to stay with my son." She held the book on her lap tightly. "But my little son is better. I pray and trust in God—that's all we can do. 'Tis in His hands."

"Know that your child is in my prayers, but I cannot lie and say I'm not glad you're back. With you here, I can be merry and enjoy better all the festivities planned to celebrate the death of Katherine of Aragon."

Catherine opened her book to a page. Disturbed by her

silence, Kate moved closer, and the words on the page seized her attention.

> *If then you are master of yourself, you will*
> *be in possession of that which you will never*
> *wish to lose, and which Fortune will never*
> *be able to take from you.*

She rested a hand on Catherine's shoulder. "Why do you not speak?"

The young Duchess shrugged. "I have no reason to take joy in the death of a good woman such as the one who gave me my name." Catherine's fingers cradled one side of her face. "While I do not like being away from my sons, especially when one of my boys is ailing, I know there is another whom I will soon comfort because of the Dowager Princess's death."

She moved her head towards the window. Kate looked, too. The window showed what she already knew—a grey, cold day, but the snow no longer fell as heavily as before.

"I think she will be home soon. I hope so," Catherine murmured.

"Who?"

"My mother." A worried expression on her pale face, Catherine gyrated around, checking the room. Most of the Queen's other women were gathered around the blazing fire, far enough away to make it seem Kate was alone with the Duchess. Even so, Catherine bent closer and whispered in Kate's ear. "Will you vow not to say one word to anyone about what I tell you?"

She nodded at her friend. "I vow. Did you not tell me that silence was the best weapon we have at court?"

The Duchess gave a short laugh. "Yet here am I, about to

speak of matters that may be best left unsaid." She glanced once more towards the other women, then sat back in the chair. "I sent word to my mother that the Princess was dying, and she went to her." Leaning her elbow on the carved armrest of the chair, she cupped the side of her face again. "Even without the King's permission, she managed the Princess's guards somehow. My mother has that way with her. I hear before they knew it, she was with the Queen." Catherine shook her head. "Forgive me, I mean the Dowager Princess of Wales."

Kate remembered that Catherine's mother had come with Katherine of Aragon from Castile. "They were great friends, did you not say?"

Catherine lifted her head. "More than that—they were blood kin. As children, they swore they would always be sisters. My mother went willingly into exile from a country she loved because of her Catalina. When the Duke, my husband, told me the princess was on her deathbed, I had to let my mother know." She visibly swallowed. "I do not think I or anyone else will be able to comfort her on her return."

Two days later she told Kate a messenger had arrived that morning. There was no letter, just a verbal message telling of her mother's homecoming. "Mother is never as brief as that," said Catherine, her brow puckered in apprehension. "I must go to her."

She had still not returned by the time Kate returned to her chamber for the night. She spent the night restless with worry about her friend.

Early the next day, Kate hurried to Catherine's chamber, where a maidservant allowed her in. She found her friend out of bed, but sitting by the fire still in her shift, with a thick shawl slung over her shoulders. At first, her loose, dark hair hid her face from view, but then she raised it. Her pale cheeks splotched red and eyes red-rimmed, Catherine must have wept for hours.

"What is it?" Kate asked in fear. "'Tis not your son?"

Catherine sniffed and reached for her comb on the table beside her, but just as she took hold of it, more tears welled. Lowering her head, she dropped the comb, her hands covering her face. "I do not know how to help her."

Kate picked up the comb and, taking up a lock of her friend's undressed hair, carefully started to untangle it. "So, 'tis your mother you weep for?"

Catherine jerked up. "Aye, my mother. She wants to die. She wants to die so she follows after the Princess"

Kate swallowed her shock while placing a hand on her friend's shoulder. "She does not mean it."

"I wish I could believe that. I have never seen my mother break her heart. I have never thought of her as an old woman, but she is now. When I told her I yet need her, she sighed and said she has lived long enough, and not to beg her to stay if I loved her."

"These are early days," Kate comforted. "Once she has had time to grieve, she will hear you better." Stilling the comb in her hand, she thought of her own mother. "She will not want to leave you."

Catherine turned her head, her lips tight as she fought for control. "You do not know my mother. She is full of hate for the King. Even when I told her that my husband has arranged with the King for us to go to Peterborough and act as chief mourners at the Princess's funeral she still said she would hate him to her last breath." Catherine's shoulders slumped with defeat. "Her Catalina died calling for him—the man who abandoned her, the man who did not care if she died alone, with no kin or friend by her side. You know he would not allow even the Lady Mary to go to her mother?" Catherine bit her bottom lip, her teeth leaving a red mark. "My mother says the Princess thanked her for not letting her die alone like an animal. How can a man be so cruel to a woman he once loved—a woman who bore him child after child?" She rubbed her eyes and sniffed. "I wish now I had never sent word to her. Mayhap, if she hadn't watched her friend die, she would not think the world is a place she would rather not be. She would not say to me she has had enough of living. That she wants it to end—all the pain, all the grief."

Catherine lowered her head, her hands covering her face. Kate stroked her arm, saying the first words to come to mind. "I am your sister, always. I vow that to you."

Catherine wiped her face with one hand, while her other one enclosed Kate's. Her hand was freezing. *No wonder, sitting here in a thin shift.* Her woollen shawl was no protection for a winter morn. "That is what they said to one another, long ago as dawn broke over Granada before they left their home forever." Her hand tightened on Kate's. "Sometimes, with a daughter's main duty given over to her husband and children, the bond between sisters is greater than that of a mother for a daughter. Let it be always that way for us, Kate."

Thoughts of her mother and her stepfather, their arms around each other by the fire at her home, stirred within Kate. Her mother's words to him:

One heart, one flesh, one soul
one soul in bodies twain.

But lovers were not the only ones to sing the words. True friends did, too. More and more life seemed a mountain that must be faced, to be braved, but without friendship, she climbed in the dark, without a hand reaching out to help.

With resolve, Kate straightened. "That I vow freely. Now, sweet Catherine, 'tis time for you to end your melancholy and ready yourself for the new day. Pray sit there quietly, my sweet Gossip, and let me do your hair. Then I'll call the maid to get you dressed."

She combed her friend's hair, all the while yearning for her own mother. She missed her and wished she could speak to her. More than that, she yearned for her mother to hold her—to feel a child again, safe and loved. Now, like it or not, childhood was gone forever.

With Madge called early one morning to attend the Queen, Kate found herself alone with time to write in her journal.

> The preparations for Katherine of Aragon's funeral are now well in hand. I think knowing this has improved the King's temper; most days now, he is tranquil and content.
>
> My aunt is also merry—in public. But I have heard her speak quietly to Meg Lee about her disquiet, her sense of foreboding. I know the reason for it.
>
> Jane Seymour is back at court, again

attending the Queen. Mostly, my aunt is civil to her, but there are times when she fails to hide her jealousy.

I was with her when she discovered Lady Jane on the King's lap. It was terrible. Truly terrible. My aunt yelled at him, yelled at Jane.

If I could have laughed, I would have when Jane scurried away, escaping in the other direction. She most surely deserves her nickname of "White Mouse."

But I couldn't laugh. Not while the King bristled with anger at Aunt Nan. His face was dreadful. Whenever he is angry, his whole body seems to swell up and his cheeks become fiery in their colour. I do not know how else to describe it, other than I think he becomes a demon.

I felt ill at hearing his words. He reminded Aunt Nan again that she was to endure as one better than her had once done. Of course he meant Katherine of Aragon—a woman who loved him, just like my aunt. A woman whose death gave him reason to thank God.

Jane returned to the Queen's chamber wearing a new gold locket.

Understandably so, my aunt's temper was still high after the King's rebuke, and her suspicions aroused. She asked Jane to show the locket to her. When Jane refused, Aunt Nan snatched it from her neck, snapping the thin, gold chain.

Jane ran from the chamber, her hand on her neck, weeping. I wept, too, when I spun around to my poor aunt. She stood there holding open a locket with a portrait of the King. Only the King could have given it her.

I tried my best to comfort Aunt Nan, but I had no words. My poor aunt. She wept and broke her heart, saying over and over, "He promised to be true."

The King's daughter, the Lady Mary, does not help matters. Feeling pity for the grieving girl, my aunt invited her to court. She wrote she would be another mother to her if Mary would only let her.

A letter from the Lady Mary arrived not long afterwards. My aunt hurled it aside in anger. "My friendship conflicts with her honour and conscience," she said.

She paced up and down the room, before she rounded on me as if I was the Lady

Mary. "I wrote to her in charity, and this is the thanks she gives me. What do I care? She can go her own way and be done with it. And if she thinks she will do better with her father, then she will learn otherwise, to her grief."

Rather than make Aunt Nan angry, I wish the Lady Mary had taken her offer of friendship. Aunt Nan meant well by it. But Madge tells me the Lady Mary hates my aunt for what happened to her mother.

Why my aunt and not the King? I do not understand.

There was no abating of the Queen's troubles. Approaching her aunt's chambers with Madge one day, Kate heard raised voices, one a man's, coming from the rooms. They both moved instinctively closer to the wall. The thick, oaken doors made the voices indistinct, difficult to make out, but the anger was real and frightening.

"Who is it?" Kate whispered.

Before Madge had a chance to answer, the door burst open and Norfolk stormed out, his long, thin face red and furious. The guards, startled into fight-ready stances, prepared to barricade the open room, their halberds shifting in their hands.

The Duke of Norfolk turned and shouted one last time, "I warn you, niece."

As if suddenly aware he was in a public place, he whipped around, his gash of a mouth shutting fast, calculating eyes darting from one guard to the other. Thrusting his body forward, he stomped off, passing Kate and Madge without glancing their way.

Madge touched Kate's arm, her fearful eyes following the disappearing figure of the Duke. "Let's go to the Queen."

When Kate passed the guards, both men had resumed their usual pose holding their upright halberds.

Deep within the room, her face hidden from view, the Queen stood holding her belly, leaning against one side of the ornate fireplace. Its marble, carved with Tudor roses, their petals painted red and white, seemed to replicate the rubies and gold of Tudor roses the Queen wore around her neck. Words came unbidden to Kate's mind—a verse Sir Thomas Wyatt had one day scratched out with his pen, as if in pain, in their book of shared poetry.

And graven with diamonds in letters plain,
There is written her fair neck round about,
Noli me tangere, for Caesar's I am.

"Damn him to hell," Aunt Nan said.

Kate rushed over to her and took her arm. Her aunt's skin was milk-white. "Aunt, my Queen, are you ill?"

Aunt Nan offered her an inscrutable face. "Do not concern yourself, Kate. My child is safe, even if it seems our good Uncle wishes otherwise." She lifted and then dropped her frail shoulders. "Perchance I should have known better than to try to have it out with him while I am with child, but his continual ill will towards me is no easy matter. He is the brother of my mother, but that does not stop him from showing his hatred."

"Madam, you should sit and rest." Madge took her arm, leading her to the nearest chair. The Queen sat with visible relief, taking from Madge her proffered drink.

Kate padded over. The strain on her aunt's face dropped her to her knees beside her. "Pray, can you not speak and tell us what happened?"

Aunt Nan grimaced. "What help would that do, child? Would it change anything?" She gave a short, self-mocking laugh. "I wish to speak? 'Tis my desire to do so, my desire to speak my mind, that causes our uncle to hate me. He tells me I forget a woman's proper place and that a good woman is silent. He tells me I owe him obedience because of our kinship." She shook her head, her disbelief plain on her face. "I, the Queen of England, owe him obedience? A man who beats his wife to the ground because she dares to protest about his mistress?"

Putting her goblet on the table beside her, she leaned back in her chair and rubbed her forehead. For a time, she sat there, her fingers trailing back and forth over her mouth. She sighed. "I hoped when he came to see me today that we could call a truce, for the sake of Elizabeth and the son I carry. Now I see he will never forgive me for acting not a Howard. He forgets I am Queen of England and loyalty to my mother's family must come second to that."

January came to its last days and the court continued to celebrate the death of Katherine of Aragon. *Celebrate?* Kate pondered in her journal, trying to make sense of what she observed. *Why do so many celebrate the festivities as if they are counterfeit? An enactment of life rather than real life?* Words in her head darted and played like salmon in a lake waiting to be caught; fishing them up, one by one, she wrote quickly.

> The court is a place for masks
> for illusion
> for trick of hand, hooded eyes
> and carefully considered words.

Is that surprising? She had already learnt that to reveal your real face at court risked death.

Leaning her elbow on the table, she cupped her cheek in her hand and put down her quill. These festivities disturbed her. They seemed frenzied, as if the masked participants wished to put away any thought of the past, any thought of tomorrow, and dance with death. *Seize the day—tomorrow may never come.*

Kate swallowed, sat straighter, pure terror seizing her heart. Every day she had reason to fight down her fears. She picked up her quill and wrote again:

> Death? Why do I think so much of
> death? Is it living here at court that
> makes me think such things? Its
> growing shade darkens my days.

Bar Holy days, Kate continued her lute lessons with Francis. For one hour, she and Harry practiced together while Francis went back and forth between them. He treated them exactly alike, gave them equal time—and finished the lesson as if happy to see his duty done for the day. After he left to search for his friends, Kate fought against tears again. What had she ever done to deserve such torture?

The twentieth day of January arrived, the day before Saint Agnes Day, the day of maidens. Kate had no heart to welcome the planned celebrations with the same merriment as the other unmarried girls. To her surprise, even the usually straight-talking Madge entered into the fun. Now betrothed to Henry Norris, recent days had seen her merry and acting like one confined for months, but now free.

Like a sleepwalker, Kate fasted and prayed with the girls. Their excited chatter in the Queen's chamber drove Kate to distraction, but caught the interest of her aunt. With the King that morning, Aunt Nan looped her arm through his and brought him over to them. "What say you, husband? Shall I fast and eat a boiled egg with my maids so I dream of you tonight?"

He laughed and rested his hand on her stomacher. "None would mistake you for a virgin, Nan, not with your goodly belly. As for fasting, I say nay for my boy." He laughed again. "Praise God, our son makes his presence known more every new day."

Aunt Nan leaned against him. "Have I told you he has quickened already?" She smiled, her hand resting on his over her stomacher. "Last night I felt his first kicks. He will be a strong boy, our son."

The King drew her into half an embrace. Kate smiled

to witness their love, but then a shadow fell. The King broke away from his wife, his confused eyes becoming as hard as flint.

"Nay, no fasting, I command it." Taking away his arm, he bent down to kiss her cheek. "I must be away. Cromwell comes this morning, and there is much work to be done before I meet with Suffolk. He oversees the jousting three days hence." He turned on his heel and strode away, leaving the Queen alone, forlorn, staring after him, her hand still on her belly.

The conversations, the laughter, the wishful thinking about husbands and futures at last became too much for Kate. Suffocated by her misery, she just wanted to be alone. The want grew into a need that dissipated her desire to obey her aunt's command. *With the guards so close by, surely it would be safe in the Queen's own gardens.* She slipped away, grabbed her cloak, escaping down the stairs that led outdoors. The bitter wind and the slush of soft earth under her feet from days of rain and, before that, melting snow, better fitted her mood. *Unloved, unwanted, unloved, unwanted, nothing, nothing, nothing.* The words spun around and around in her head. The world blurred. She drifted down the footpath without any aim or purpose, like a wind-blown autumn leaf.

When she stumbled over her feet, she lifted her head at last. Right in front of her, Mary Shelton sat on a nearby bench, her hood fallen to her shoulders, her eyes closed in a too-white, too-thin face. She looked straight at Kate.

Bitterness shadowed her smile. "Did those silly girls drive you outside, too? What a gaggle of geese they are!"

Kate sat beside her. "I suppose they only wish to be merry."

"Merry? When they talk of dreaming about their husbands? If they had any sense, they would know that no boiled egg or salted herring will bring them what they want." A tear trickled down Mary's wan cheek. "Only the fortunate get that choice. For the likes of you and I, our lives are in other hands."

Kate pulled her cloak tighter around her, her fingers so cold they hurt. During her time at court, Madge had remained silent about her sister's obvious unhappiness. On many occasions the two girls disappeared together. When Madge returned, it was alone, snapping with Boleyn temper. She had stormed so much at Kate the one time she had asked about Mary, she dared not to ask again.

Now, with Mary, Kate found the bravery to ask once more, but this time direct it to the person it concerned. "Why are you always so sad?"

Startled, Mary licked her lovely mouth, and then averted her face from Kate. "Am I?" She attempted a smile. "It must be my bad humours."

Kate took hold of her cousin's arm and felt bone, rather than flesh, through the thick wool of her cloak. Shocked, she let go. "You are ill."

Mary shut her eyes tight before she twisted towards Kate. "Aye, ill—or heartsick. I find it means the same."

"Heartsick?" Kate thought how it had been for her since meeting Francis. "You're in love?"

Mary clasped her hands on her lap before pulling them back under her cloak. "Aye," she answered quietly.

Kate frowned at her cousin. She had never seen Mary with anyone. "Who is he?"

Mary drew in and then exhaled a deep breath, the cold air misting it before them. "You are what—thirteen?"

Kate jerked back. Once again her age seemed to herald the ending of discussion. Tightening her mouth, she controlled her anger before answering. "My birth day has come and gone. I am fourteen now." She winced at how terse her voice sounded.

Shifting, Mary gave a brittle smile. "Fourteen? I wish I was fourteen again—with the wisdom these past years have taught me." She shrugged. "Perchance it would make no difference. When we give our hearts, we rarely listen to wisdom, even when it comes from our own logic. I would likely do it all again, even knowing the suffering it has cost me."

"What would you do again?"

This time, Mary's smile brightened. "Love. Love with all my heart and soul—and my body, too." She tilted her head to the side. "I need not fast, keep my silence, or hope to dream of my husband tonight. I would not wish it. The man I love is wed to another. Even if he wasn't, he is not for the likes of me. I love knowing it is hopeless." She considered Kate. "He is the Earl of Surrey, our cousin, my lover—and—" Mary looked over her shoulder, and then all around "—one with the true-born blood of Edward IV flowing in his veins, not the bastard blood of the Tudors." Tears fell down her face. "I am but a dalliance to him, and it breaks my heart."

That night Kate lay awake for hours, listening to the wind wail and rage, driving the sleet against the windows. Mary had given her heart and body without any hope of a happy outcome. Her aunt loved her husband, knowing he had stopped loving her. Love, Mary had said, she would do all again, for love. The voice was no longer Mary's, but Aunt Nan's. *I would do it all again. I love him, body and soul.*

Opening her eyes to the night, Kate had no need to pray to Saint Agnes to bring her a dream of her husband. There was only one husband she wanted or desired. But he only wanted her friendship. He treated her like a child—a child to be kept her place.

I love him, body and soul, and he has my heart. She drifted into sleep, dreaming of Francis. Dreaming of Francis and her in a bed, naked and locked together. It was a dream that woke her, body stirred, wide-awake and full of strange feelings that burned her cheeks with shame.

16

I write this on the twenty-fourth day of January, 1536, at Greenwich.

After reading back what she had just written, Kate continued.

On this day, at the abbey of Saint Peterborough, the Dowager Princess of Wales will be entombed, while we at court celebrate.

Kate put her quill in the inkpot, not daring for a moment to write any more. Katherine of Aragon's death finally won, for the King, the victory he had sought for years. She went to her grave as his brother's wife, a dowager Princess of Wales, and not a Queen. Kate picked up her quill again.

The King jousts this day at Greenwich, while to my joy I keep the Queen, my aunt, company in her chambers.

The Queen's apartment door opened, drenching the entrance in honey light that gilded a man's shape at the door. Kate blinked, trying to identify the figure. Only when he shouted did she know who it was. The Duke of Norfolk, her uncle, shouted, "Madam! The King is dead."

Like a dagger his words stabbed into her heart. But not only her. She spun around to Aunt Nan's sharp cry.

Everything happened so quickly—a nightmare of confusion and terror. Her aunt rose fast from the chair, her movement entangling her feet in her gown. She stumbled, lost her footing, and fell to the ground. The loud thud of her fall reverberated in the chamber. Silence followed. Curled up, unmoving, Aunt Nan looked like one dead. Kate's world opened to an abyss of disbelief and horror.

Frightened, she cried, "Jesu'! Dear God!" She joined the women rushing to the Queen's aid, reaching her first. Her aunt stirred, and Kate breathed again. Meg Lee now beside her, she did not know what to do next.

Running feet echoed, louder and louder, in the gallery, stopping just outside the door. A familiar voice rose in protest and argument. Yet another shout, a demand for entry, and Wyatt burst into the room. Without time to wonder why, Kate turned back to her aunt.

Aunt Nan spoke through tears, the words babbling out. "The King is dead? The King is dead? I'm done for. My babes, my poor babes..."

Sir Thomas, his face stark with fear, crouched beside her. "Are you hurt? Have you any pain?"

Without waiting for an answer, he took her into his arms. Kate blinked. Wyatt glared at the Duke as if he wished to throttle him—or more. Their eyes fenced and blazed with hate. Kate seemed caught in the middle of a swordfight, a swordfight without blades.

Her uncle broke first, but he kept his hand at the ready to draw his dagger from his belt, all the while backing into the light that flooded the room. The empty doorway framed his dark figure for several heartbeats, then he disappeared into the gallery.

"The King is dead." Aunt Nan clutched Wyatt's doublet like one drowning. She hiccupped, and Wyatt touched her face.

"Anne. Anna. Listen to me. The King's not dead." He swivelled towards the empty doorway. He repeated hoarsely, "The King is not dead."

Not dead? Not dead. Not dead. Not dead. Kate's head hurt with the seemingly unending beat of these two words. Why did her uncle, Aunt Nan's uncle, too, do this? Why did he hate his royal niece so much?

Still enclosed in Wyatt's arms, Aunt Nan convulsed over and over. She whimpered, "Harry's not dead?"

Wyatt shook his head. "Nay, Anna. You know I'd never lie to you. The King's not dead."

"I feel ill, Tom." Her skin so white, Aunt Nan's pupils were enormous and engulfed the irises of her dark eyes. Her breaths fast and ragged, she put a hand against Sir Thomas's chest. Kate trembled as Wyatt gestured for help to get Aunt Nan to her feet.

Carefully, on either side of her, Kate and Meg walked the Queen towards her bedchamber. Before they got there, Aunt Nan swayed. Kate swung to Wyatt in panic. Reflecting back her fear, he scooped up her aunt as if she were the lightest thing in the world. His eyes shifted around the room, as if he, too, felt caught in a dreadful dream where there was no awaking, paying not one jot of attention to the chorus of disapproval coming from some of the Queen's women.

Aunt Nan's head fell back, her gable dropping to the floor. Her white linen cap fell, too, and her plaited hair tumbled free. Tightening his hold on her limp body, Wyatt shouted,

"Someone get help—get the physicians now! Where's the Queen's midwife? In God's name, get her, too." His face wet with tears, he carried her to her bed.

Kate followed, and stood forlornly and helplessly beside Wyatt. Aunt Nan's eyelids fluttered and she opened terrified eyes. Her face grey, she gripped her belly and moaned.

Aunt Nan lost her baby days afterwards. It would have been a son. A prince. The child so wanted by the King that he had turned his Kingdom upside down to reject one marriage to make a new. Like fire catching at kindling, rumours raced around Greenwich. One horrible rumour said the dead child was deformed—a sign of a marriage cursed—a marriage that God did not want.

Still recovering from the injury he received while jousting, his head bruised and swollen, for days King Henry stalked up and down the gallery at Greenwich, with mad, burning eyes in a red-cheeked face. He seemed a firebrand, one that blazed rumour into truth. He seemed a man ready to do murder. Henry Norris, close to the King since boyhood, followed after him, but like a frightened man who expected the King to turn and dagger him. Any forced into the presence of the King at this time put themselves in danger of his abuse and temper.

But Kate cared only about her aunt.

Aunt Nan was still unwell in her chamber when the King called for his sleigh and left his wife in the care of her women. That same day Elizabeth Boleyn arrived at court. Greeting her weary grandmother on her arrival, Kate struggled to hide her shock about how much she had changed since Aunt Nan's coronation. Bowed over, more winkled than ever, all skin and bones, her grandmother had aged to become almost unrecognisable.

Distracted, Elizabeth Boleyn barely acknowledged Kate's greeting before disappearing into her daughter's chamber. Left alone again, Kate reeled from the sound of weeping that was only shut off when the door closed. Even one of the guards paled and lost concentration on his halberd before straightening it up again.

Every morning, Kate either walked or sat on the bench near the brazier outside her aunt's chamber with Madge, hoping to see her grandmother and beg to be allowed in with her aunt, too. On the third morning, she told this to Madge, but her cousin shook her head. "We're unwed and thus forbidden entry," she said.

Kate hid her disbelief. *My kinship is closer to Aunt Nan than Madge's. Surely my blood tie makes a difference.*

Madge passed her the book of shared poetry. "Why not read while you wait. Who knows—it might help you. I always find comfort by reading and writing. Later, you might think of something to add to our pages." She shrugged. "Remember, it doesn't have to be your own words. You can use it to share your favourite songs, poems, or even riddles. This is but a place for your pen, where you do not need fear to bridle your tongue."

Left to wait for Madge's return from visiting her twin, Kate placed the book in her pocket. *Comfort in reading? How could anyone find comfort in reading—especially in times like these, with grief so close by?*

Catherine Willoughby approached without noticing Kate

and slipped into the Queen's chamber. *Will not my friend allow me entry?* She picked up her skirts and raced into her aunt's privy chamber. From the open door of Aunt Nan's bedchamber came the unmistakable, sickening smell of blood. The bedhangings drawn, the slight body of her aunt moved restlessly on her bed and then stilled.

Catherine turned around and opened her eyes wide at Kate before checking on the sleeping Queen. She spoke in barely a whisper. "Kate, you should not be here,"

Coming closer, Kate placed her hand on her friend's arm. "Pray, let me stay."

Catherine shook her head. "I cannot."

She took Kate over to the seats by the fireplace. The fire and candles unlit, the Queen's privy chamber was dark and cold. Shivering, Kate gathered her fur mantle tighter around her and clutched her bare hands underneath. She bit down against the agony of her freezing fingers, trying to ignore how her whole body protested against the bone-hurting cold. Sitting down in one seat, Catherine gestured to Kate to sit in the other, then leaned forward. "I cannot let you stay."

Kate swallowed, leaning forward as well. "Oh why? Why can't I be here, too?"

"You must know why. This is not a place for a girl who has not yet borne a child."

"But—"

"Nay, Kate. It is more than that. The King is displeased with your aunt." Catherine's unhidden fear fuelled Kate's own fear into an inferno. "Displeased is not a strong enough word. He is angry, Kate. He told her, just after she lost her babe, that she would bear him no more sons—now or ever. I will never forget how he slammed the door on the way out

196

as if he ended their life together. He shouted to his men that witchcraft had seduced him into this marriage."

Kate blinked, not believing what she heard. At last she said, "Witchcraft?"

"Aye, witchcraft. Now he sees none but his ministers. For hours, he is closeted with them. I hate to think what they talk about—but it must be about the loss of the King's son."

Kate straightened in the chair. "None of this changes anything. I should be with my aunt, more than ever."

Tension drawn on her white face, Catherine drew a deep breath. "I know you want to be with her, and I promise I will tell her so. But you must realise that by being here you could give the King another reason for anger."

"God's teeth, why?"

Catherine sighed. "Because you are his daughter. You have been at court long enough to know the great store the King puts in royal protocol. If he hears you attend the Queen, he may think the Queen has requested it. You are a maid, Kate. The court rules that there is no place for you here. You do not want to give him any more cause to be angry at her."

Unable to think of any more arguments, Kate wiped away her tears.

Catherine gripped Kate's hand. "Believe me, I find it hard enough to witness your aunt's grief." She sighed. "I was with her when she birthed her dead son. Since then, she speaks little. Most of the time, it is like she doesn't know we are with her. I tell you true, you are fortunate to be a maid and out of it."

Leaving her aunt's chambers to sit again on the bench, Kate found herself wishing she was brave enough to beg to speak to the King, but her fears whipped her into a struck dog with its tail between its legs. *I am a coward. A coward.* She hated herself for it.

Wanting to distract herself, she took the book from her pocket, and became aware that Francis stood close by. He appeared abashed, smiling with uncertainty.

"'Tis the third morning in a row that I have found you here, lurking outside the Queen's chamber. If I did not know better, I would think you've found employment as the Queen's guard."

Kate smiled a little and shook her head in answer. She sighed. "They will not let me see her."

Francis sat beside her. "You are young—"

She rounded on him in fury. "Young! Why is that always the excuse of the world and its dog to leave me out in the cold? Mayhap I am young, but does that mean I am fool—or useless? I could be in there playing to my aunt the songs you have taught me."

"Forgive me. I did not mean to offend you. I commend your loyalty to your aunt, Kate, but you must realise that 'tis not likely they will allow you admittance. Putting aside your youth, you are unwed."

Hearing Francis echo Catherine's words wounded her. She bowed her head, hiding tears of frustration. At home, she had been allowed to visit her mother short hours after childbirth, but a Queen of England lived by different, stricter rules. Once again, it came home that courtly protocol guarded—no, not simply guarded, but imprisoned the Queen, just as much as the two guards who stood outside her doors.

Kate turned to Francis. "Forgive me for my anger. 'Twas wrong to lash you with my tongue when you only spoke the truth." The book blurred in her hand. "I know you offer only kindness, like Madge, who wants me to find other ways to spend my time here." She considered him. "I just wish I did not feel so helpless."

Francis clasped her hand again, but this time did not let it go. "We all feel helpless at times like these. I know it must be hard to know your aunt is ill and you are forbidden her presence."

Kate swallowed. The closed doors of her aunt's chamber seemed to speak of everything in life that shut her out. "'Tis *not knowing* that I find so difficult to bear. For days, I've been closed out in the dark with only my thoughts for company." She shifted closer to Francis. "What if she dies?" she whispered. "What if she dies and I am out here? I should be with her; my place is with her. I belong with her." Tears fell down her face. "I do not want her to think I have forsaken her."

Francis gazed at her with compassion. "You love your aunt. Why?"

Shrugging, Kate tried to collect her thoughts. Memories of Aunt Nan came to mind. The first one was a blur, but it possessed the sheen of sunlight and shimmer of rainbow. In this shimmering light, Aunt Nan stood, a giant adult, carrying Kate in her arms. She put Kate down, then held out her hands to dance with her. They spun around and around until Aunt Nan fell on her knees before Kate, gathering her into her arms. That was not her only treasured memory. Every visit had meant a warm, loving welcome—a sharing of books, songs, and stories. Kate could not remember a time when she did not adore her. She cut the thread of reminiscence, and brushed away her tears, aware of her hand in Francis's.

"She has always loved me," Kate answered. "'Tis easy to

love when you are loved in return."

Francis tightened his grip. "The Queen is fortunate to have your love. In the coming days, she will need not only to know of your love, but also that others love her. It might strengthen her against the tide of hate."

Pity? Why does he seem to be offering me pity? She pulled away, taking her hand from his, shifting into the shadows of the embrasure. Leaning against the wall, she shivered. "Even our uncle of Norfolk hates her. Madge told me that he was almost merry when he heard she lost her son. He said the Queen had miscarried her saviour."

"The Duke and the Queen have long been at loggerheads with one another. The Duke desires a Catholic England. The Queen works against this. She is also a woman who is unafraid to speak her mind, or speak up to the King, the Duke—indeed, all men. Norfolk does not forgive the times she has cut him down with her tongue. He believes she has betrayed him."

Kate sighed. "He is not the only one. The King thinks this, too."

Francis sat back. Half his face was in shadow, half in light. "Because she bore him another dead son?"

Kate nodded. "Aye, because of that. Why else would he act as he does?"

Francis turned to the light. "You're changed, Kate. You're not the young maid I first met two months ago."

"Two months ago—did I only come to court two short months ago? It feels a lifetime." She drew and let out a breath. "I *was* different then. I know now I never had real cause to be heartsore." She swung around to the shut door. "I will never feel so young again."

There was one other who gained admittance to see the Queen. The next day, Kate escaped from Madge's surveillance, hoping to see her grandmother. While her grandmother didn't emerge from Aunt Nan's chamber, another woman came out, the hood of her black cloak drawn over her head. Kate did not recognise her until she moved in her direction.

"Mother!" She ran into her open arms. Mary Stafford hugged and kissed her, while Kate fought back her distaste at the smell of stale milk. She scolded herself. *Am I not a woman now? One day, I, too, will hold my children to my breast and thank God for it.* She took a deep breath and killed the last remnants of her jealousy. Still in her mother's arms, she asked, "Is my little brother with you?"

Her mother sighed. "Nay, we had to get here in all speed, and the little one is safer at home."

Releasing Kate, she smiled. "My girl has grown." She touched the pearl-encrusted gable and sighed. For a breath, Kate returned to the morning she had left home. Then her mother had sighed in exactly the same way, holding her new girdle—regretful, but also resigned.

"My sister cares well for your needs, I see," her mother said.

Kate clasped her hand. "But, Mother, why did no one tell me you were here?" She reached for her mother's other hand. "Do you stay long?"

Shushing her, Mary Stafford looked over her shoulder and then the other way. "Quietly, child." She leaned towards Kate. "Where can we talk in private?"

Without a moment's thought, Kate knew. Still holding on

to her mother's hand, she took her straight to her brother's chambers. Fortune smiled. Harry was alone, quill in hand, mouth and shoulders drooping, with a half-written parchment riddled with corrections before him. At their entry, he paled, but then his eyes lit up to match his wide smile. He stood.

"Mother," he said softly.

Mary stepped closer. Tears fell down her face unchecked. "Oh, Harry. Oh, my beloved boy."

She held out her arms, and he ran into them. They laughed, and cried, turning to Kate to include her, too. Kate's happiness overflowed.

At last, Mary Stafford pulled back, wiping away fresh tears. "My children, I can't stay long. My husband waits in the stables to take me home before the King discovers I am here without his permission." She lowered her head, clasping and unclasping her hands. "I had to come to my poor sister when our mother wrote to me about what had happened."

Kate glanced aside at her brother. She said sadly, "We are refused admittance to her chamber."

Her mother rested a hand on Kate's arm. "Sweetheart, even your grandmother does not know how to help her, and she has lost many babes. Nan is in despair. For the last two hours, she wept and wept in my arms." Her mouth pursed, she drew a breath. "She was better when I left, worrying that the King would find me here. Pray to God this day marks the turning of the tide, and my sister will regain her strength and be ready to fight again. She needs to fight again."

As if determined to change the subject and shake away her worry, Mary stepped over to Harry's desk and picked up the parchment. "And what have we here, Harry?" Her brows furrowed together. "'Tis not Latin or French."

Kate remembered that day not too long ago when Harry seemed so much older than her. Today she resumed her rightful place, content to watch her brother and mother make up a little for all the time they had lost.

Harry stood next to their mother and grinned. "'Tis Greek, Mother." Reddening, he shifted one foot and then the other. "'Tis not likely to please my tutor. I am too slow, he says, and make too many mistakes. But Greek is hard."

Mary beamed at him and put her arm through his. "I know you, my son. You will not give up." Her smile embraced Kate, too. "We are not a family that is easily defeated." Cocking her head, she inspected him. "The last time we were together, I could still put you on my knee. Now you're taller than me by two fingers at least." Mary bit her bottom lip. "Do you forgive your mother that she has missed these last years when you grew from boy to youth?"

Harry hugged her tight. "There's nothing to forgive, Mother. I understand how it has been with you, and that you walked the harder road."

Mary started. "Harder road? Sometimes I wonder if those are the roads where we truly find our lives, especially if we walk roads mapped out by our hearts." She touched his cheek. "Oh, it has cost me—cost me dearly. I did not know when I married William that the King would punish me through you. I have begged him to let me come to you, but always his answer is nay. Methinks he fears I will take you from him—that love will win out in the end." Mary swallowed. "I thank God for your letters. I take them from my writing desk to kiss them over and over. They make you seem close to me, and I know from them your love." She stroked his face and stood on tiptoes to kiss his face. She grinned. "No manly bristles, yet, my boy. Next time we meet, I suspect you will be taller yet and you'll likely call me your little old mother."

She glanced towards the window and frowned. "The day is darkening. I must be away and return to your stepfather."

Harry embraced her again. "Can you not stay, Mother? Just for one night?"

She shook her head, her face lined with grief. "Nay, my Harry." She gestured to her full breasts with a small smile. "Your little brother will be sorely missing me by now, as I am him. Besides that, I must think of the King." She stroked his face again. "He lets you write letters to me. The longer I stay, the more chance I have of being found out. If word comes to him that we have seen one another, he might forbid you to even write to me. I could not bear that." She pulled her hood over her head. "Stay here, my children, but let me bless you before I go."

Kate and Harry knelt at her feet and bent their heads. Kate would never forget the light touch of her mother's hand, and the love that radiated its warmth from the top of her head to her heart.

After farewelling her mother, it became time for another farewell. Kate found Elizabeth Boleyn in her chamber, sitting close to the fireplace. Cloaked, gloved, dressed for travel, she got up and held out her arms when Kate came into the room. After receiving her grandmother's kiss and blessing, Kate sat in the chair across from her. *Grandmother is old.* Even her dark eyes, once bright and lively, seemed dull. Surrounded by wrinkled skin, they sunk deeply into her skull.

"Granddaughter, we have not had much time to speak together in the last sennight or more. And now your grandfather has summoned me home. But I wished to see you before I left."

Kate bent towards her. "How is Aunt Nan?"

Elizabeth Boleyn plucked at her cloak and frowned. "Still weaker than I'd like her to be."

Kate wilted and moved uneasily on her chair.

"Take heart, child." Her grandmother smiled slightly. "I would not be leaving my daughter if she was not improving. The best thing she can do now is to rest."

"And her melancholy, Grandmother? I heard from Mother and others how broken-hearted she is."

Half shutting her eyes, Elizabeth Boleyn pursed her mouth, winkles webbing on either side. "Is that of any surprise? Can you not imagine what it is for a woman to lose her babe—a babe wanted and prayed for as much as your aunt wanted and prayed for this one?" Elizabeth Boleyn sniffed and wiped away tears. "'Tis no wonder it has struck her down soul and heart." She considered Kate. "When she comes out of the birthing chamber, you will find her changed. Help her, Kate."

She stared at her grandmother and licked her dry lips. Days ago, she had told Francis she would never feel young again. Now charged by her grandmother to help her aunt, it came back to her how young she really was. She couldn't even bring herself to ask her grandmother about her brother, the Duke of Norfolk. Life not only weighed down her shoulders, but clearly her grandmother's, too. "Pray,

Grandmother," she said slowly, "how can I help her?"

Her grandmother bowed her head and brought together her gnarled hands on her lap. "By doing what I cannot do. Stay by her side no matter what."

Blinking away tears, Kate squirmed. "I do try, Grandmother. I am but a maid—"

Bitterness pulled down her grandmother's mouth. "You may be but a maid, yet you are of our blood and soon enough will be a woman. You can start acting it in this, Kate. Just be there for your aunt! I wish it could be me, but Grandfather commands me to return to Hever and care again for our estates. If I was strong in body, I would refuse his command, but.... I am too weak and old to withstand his anger." She swallowed. "To my shame, I have always given in to him. God knows I will regret that to my dying day. I lived in fear of his hand and rod, but now find the cost of that fear a far greater one. If only I could have been as strong as my Anne and your mother. Mayhap then I would not now be fearing for my children's safety." Elizabeth Boleyn straightened, then bent over again, as if fighting pain. "Your grandfather, too, will one day regret what he set in action so long ago. Even he can no longer deny that the wind has changed, and not for good."

17

Kate always thought of February as the month of transition, the month that brought her closer to spring. Despite the days of slate-coloured sky, rain came now, not snow. The white shroud of winter melted into the earth, turning the ground soft and soggy. When sunlight burst through the clouds, its light jewelled to emerald green the lush, fast-growing grass. Spring was almost here, but she took no joy in it because her days grew increasingly darker. Winter imprisoned her spirit.

Two days after Elizabeth Boleyn left, Aunt Nan finally left her sick chamber. Followed into her garden by a group of her ladies, she cradled a white terrier puppy. Breaking away from Madge, Kate halted a step or so before her aunt and curtseyed. How she wished to embrace her, but such shows of affection must be kept for moments of privacy.

Aunt Nan smiled. It was a brittle smile, more a distortion on her too-white face. She looked aged, haggard. "I am sorry it has been so long, niece, since we last met." The puppy squirmed in her arms. She firmed her hold, stroking the dog. "Look what Sir Tom has sent to me. She is my Purkoy's granddaughter." She tossed her head and tightened her lips. "'Tis time for Bella to greet the new day, as it is for me. Come, Kate, join us."

Lifting her skirts to free her feet, Aunt Nan strode quickly before her women, so quickly it became almost a race to keep up with her. They arrived at a secluded part of the garden,

Aunt Nan still at last, and out of breath. Meg Lee curtseyed. "My Queen," she said softly, "pray, remember this is your first true day out of sickbed."

"Leave me be, Meg, just leave me," Aunt Nan snapped, waving her away. Gracefully, Aunt Nan sat on a bench underneath an oak tree, putting the puppy on the ground beside her. Her women found their own places close by.

Taking in her aunt's miserable face, Kate decided family ties called for her to be closest of all. Without waiting to ask permission, she sat next to her aunt. The puppy rolled on the grass, then curled itself into a ball of white fluff. Aunt Nan's laugh little resembled her bell-like laughter of old; it sounded shrill and cracked.

"Think you, will Bess like Bella?" Aunt Nan patted the puppy.

Kate petted it; the little dog felt so warm and soft, she couldn't resist picking it up and putting it in her lap. It licked her hand, its rough tongue tickling her.

Aunt Nan laughed again. This time, her laughter rang with brittle gaiety. "I should warn you, Kate. Bella has yet to learn that our garb is not to make water on. I have only just started to teach her." Her shoulders drooped. "Once she has learnt her lessons, I shall give Bella to Bess."

Startled, Kate shifted closer to her aunt. "But Bella was a gift to you."

Aunt Nan frowned and held out her hand for the puppy to lick. "Bella would be better off with Bess." She turned, the spreading oak dappling its shadow on her face. "Bella will be safer with Bess."

Kate's heart beat faster. *Surely I misheard her? Pray she doesn't mean what I think she means.*

Bella, hearing her name, tumbled off Kate's lap to the ground and waddled back to her mistress. Aunt Nan held the dog against her heart. For a long time, she cuddled Bella, her face like one haunted.

Finally, Aunt Nan spoke. "You know Jane Seymour has been placed in one of Cromwell's rooms? One where the King can visit her privately if he so wills?" She smiled cynically and drew a letter from a side pocket in her gown. "I received this from a friend today. My friend writes that our Mistress Jane is also receiving lessons, lessons of behaviour much like my little bitch here." She laughed. "Shame she did not learn behaviour in the past, rather than soil my chamber with her disloyalty and ambition. My friend writes that Jane is being schooled to take my place, and that she tells the King how much his subjects hate his marriage to me. She tells him our marriage is no true marriage. She learns her lessons well, I hear."

The puppy wiggled, and Aunt Nan crooned softly to it before she spoke again. "Jane tells my husband that our marriage is an abomination and adulterous—the same arguments used to rid him of Katherine of Aragon. How it comes around and around." Aunt Nan bent her head. "And I, too, have my dead babies to make it seem our marriage is accursed."

The laughter of the other women caught Kate's attention. The Queen's fool made faces, jigging on one leg and then the other, her arms held above her head.

"My friend also repeats what I have heard already. The King tells many that our love was the result of witchcraft." Aunt Nan turned, her face frightened.

Her aunt's fear caught alight in Kate's stomach and

became a fire that hurt. *Does the King believe that? Does he really think Aunt Nan a witch?* "Methinks," she finally said, "they were but words said in haste and in grief. He cannot believe you are a witch, or would use such methods to win his love."

Aunt Nan pealed with laughter. "Win his love? Did I ask for his love when the King first looked my way? Nay, not with the example of your mother before me." Her mouth trembled, and she stroked the sleeping puppy. "The more I tried to show my disinterest, the more he wanted me." Her lips tightened. "Aye, Jane is well-coached. She also shows her disinterest. He cannot see it is but an act, while with me..." Stroking the dog, she smiled sadly, her face reflective. "The King—your father—was in his glory then—strong and tall, so handsome—a god amongst men.

"We shared so many interests—books, music, the hunt—how we loved to race our horses back to court. When night fell, it was dance after dance. He wrote beautiful letters." Bitterness edged her laughter. "A man who hated writing wrote letters to me; he wrote songs and poetry—all to me. About me. He said I held his heart—he sang I held his heart—that he adored me, that he was mine, forever, forever, forever. I was young. How could I resist him? I believed him when he said he loved me. Can I be blamed for giving him my heart? Now, I find it was only I who spoke true when I vowed I would daily prove my love." She lifted a face wet with tears. "And now he calls me a witch? A witch." She covered her face with her hands. "Oh Harry! Where did love go?"

Where does love go?

On the day the King returned to Greenwich, Kate wrote that question in her journal. She had no answer.

My aunt is desperate—so full of grief.
She feels the King abandons her.

The currents pulled her beyond her strength to fight, and her aunt's desperation fed into her own. She couldn't make sense of life. Was it simply all chaos—the chaos of flux? The chaos that left her helpless because she had no way to control it?

Kate's words poured their ink down the parchment and over the next page. She wrote about watching Aunt Nan watch the King. She snatched at any hope that he still cared for his wife.

Item: He welcomed her back to his side.

She swallowed, her anxiety making it difficult to breathe. It was a simple thing to write that the King welcomed back the Queen, but her love for her aunt made her aware of much more.

Item: He seems to pity her. He seems to
love her. He seems to hate her.

Hate her? At those times, he acted like he thought her a canker—a canker he must cast out. He assessed her every move—unable to hide his confusion when her affection, her gaiety, her bravery, her intelligence made him warm to her once more.

Cromwell watched, too. Every time the King swayed towards his wife, Cromwell moved in and spoke softly in the King's ear. His words made the King flush and fist his hands, as if Cromwell pointed out that she forgot who really ruled. He stayed close by the King's side, stirring up his suspicions and resentments.

Cromwell's message seemed clear: If you want to be free of a canker, you must first rid yourself of it. Day by day, Cromwell, with caution and craft, built a fire in his King, a fire to destroy her aunt.

Kate took up her quill again and wrote what she imagined Cromwell told the King. It was far too easy to imagine when daily the murmurings of so many voices at court reached her ears.

> Item: She lost his prince.
>
> Item: She failed him.
>
> Item: She is the canker in his heart that has weakened him for years—a canker that leaves him less than a man, less than a King.
>
> Item: She wants to be always at his side, his Queen again, murmuring against his most trusted ministers, speaking up about Cromwell and the breaking up of the monasteries; telling him, the King, what course he should take. She refuses

silence. She tells him it is for England's sake. What would she know? He is the King. It is he, not her, who God speaks to. He is the King and he demands, nay, commands, her silence.

Item: Don't forget Jane—Jane, who speaks softly and waits; Jane, who treats him like a King. She does not speak to him as if she dares to be his equal. She does not speak to him forgetting that he is God's mouthpiece—or that his word is law.

Item: Aunt Nan dares to tell the King she knows better than him.

Around and around it went in Kate's mind, her worry making her dizzy and ill. But there was one thing she was certain of. Her quill scored across the parchment.

I will not abandon her. Never.

Kate rarely left her aunt's side now. Without anything being said, she became well and truly a part of the Queen's most trusted circle. There was not much Kate could do other than be with her during the day and long into the night.

With Easter approaching, on Maundy Thursday voices rose in song and announced the Queen's entry into the hall. Kate walked close behind as her aunt headed straight to the long, narrow tables that had everything needed for the ceremony. Poor women waited in a line, waiting for the Queen to wash their feet and give them their purses of alms—a coin for each year of Aunt Nan's life.

The court was not her only audience. Kate swallowed, observing the enthroned King. *His face? His face.* So still. So hard. So bitter. Close to him, Cromwell, his eyes slanted and unreadable, crossed his arms.

She berated herself for being a fool. *Of course, the King does not hate Aunt Nan.* The words she wrote last night came back to her.

> Item: He thinks my aunt a canker in his heart he must destroy.
>
> Item: No wonder God and angels weep.

Kate clasped her hands tightly before her chest, her apprehension cresting into a wave that threatened to pull her out from shore.

Brought by a servant to wait for the royal party, Kate and her brother Harry stood at the entrance of the chapel. When men's voices came close, he paled and pulled her into the dark recess of a nearby embrasure.

"Keep out of sight," he whispered.

"What is it?" Even in the dark, fear illuminated his face.

"Cromwell and Chapuys come."

The slow, considered fall of heavy feet and the tapping of a walking stick echoed another pair of feet. The nearest ones stopped and the walking stick tapped in annoyance.

"Rochford!" The accented voice brought to mind an image of man lit by torchlight, with the trappings of Christmas near. "My lord, he forces me into conversation about his Lutheran beliefs every time I come to court. So what if he is proud of them. What is that to me—a good son of the true Church?"

A muffled sound as if a hand slapped against padded doublet came before Cromwell's voice. "Chapuys, he but plays with you, tests you. Think you—can you not see he really wishes to fish for information?"

"Bah, do I not know this, Lord Cromwell? Big or small, you English Lords come to me to find out what I know! I noted Rochford's pleasure when I hinted to him that my Emperor might be willing to recognise a certain lady. That stopped him in his heretical muttering. He soon left me to tell the concubine."

"That brings me to my next question, my friend," Cromwell said, "What say you to kissing the Lady's hand and show your Emperor's approval of Queen Anne?" He spoke the words as if he spat them out. "You have an invitation to her rooms to do so, if this be your will."

There was a long silence before Chapuys spoke. "The King wants this?"

"So he says, so he says. But he leaves it entirely to your will."

"I have long been the King's slave—and have no other wish than to execute his commands. But I will explain to him that present circumstances make a visit to the Lady..." He paused for a moment. "...inconvenient—and highly so. I beg you, my Lord, make my excuses. Explain to him that such an action, now or in the future, could only be detrimental to our present negotiations."

"Our present negotiations." Cromwell said the words as

if in play. "Aye, we would not wish to put those into jeopardy. I serve first and foremost the King, but the matters before us are also for the good of my country. We cannot let the French overreach for power. That being so, I also wish to serve the Holy Roman Emperor by bringing this issue to fruition. As I have told you before, it would profit you little to pay court to one who is no longer in the King's favour. Ambassador, I must be away to speak to the King. Where will I look for you on my return?"

"On a day in England when it's not raining? I will go out to the garden and find myself a seat to wait for you."

"Until then, sir." Seemingly going in different directions, the echoes of feet and walking stick faded away. Kate moved away from the wall and closer to her brother. Paler than ever, he bit his bottom lip and clutched at his hair, as if a mirror to her own feelings. "'Present negotiations.' Do you know what that all was about?"

Harry shrugged and stepped from the shadows into the light. He popped his head out from the embrasure. "'Tis safe now. We can go."

Kate pulled him back. "Spit it out. What do you know, Harry?"

He leaned a shoulder against the wall and considered her with a cross frown. "I probably know as much as you do. And that it is not good for our aunt if Chapuys and Cromwell are so friendly."

"And the negotiations? What did they mean by that?"

"They spoke about Emperor Charles, Katherine of Aragon's nephew. With his aunt dead, there is talk of the emperor now recognising the marriage of the King and our aunt."

Kate padded into the light. "Do you think we should go

for a stroll in the gardens?"

Harry came to stand beside her. Seemingly pondering the corridor that would take them outside, he scratched his head. "We'll only get in trouble. Besides, Chapuys is not a fool. If we showed ourselves, he would suspect something was afoot." He took Kate's arm. "Sister, would it not be better just to go to Uncle George? He will tell us about these negotiations, if he knows anything. Then we can both avoid Cromwell. He is a man I rather stay clear of."

Kate shivered involuntarily, the thought of a sunlit garden swept aside by fear. She remembered the hurt of Cromwell's grip on her arm and the way his dark eyes bore down on her. She nodded. "Agreed. In any case, the King and the Queen will soon be coming to the chapel. Let's talk to Uncle George afterwards."

They found their uncle in his room tuning his lute. Sir Thomas Wyatt was with him, writing at a desk. He wrote in the same book her cousins passed around, the page before him marked with lines of crossed out words. *Another one of his unfinished poems?* Why couldn't he leave the book to just the circle of women, rather than seemingly compete with them? While many men had made their mark in the book, it was Wyatt who took possession of it more often than not. He had written so many poems in their book there might come a time he could claim it for his own.

When Uncle George's servant announced them, their uncle and Sir Thomas raised surprised faces. Uncle George lifted an eyebrow at Sir Tom.

"I can guess their purpose. They come to talk about Chapuys's kiss."

Kate jumped when Sir Tom swore. He scored out another word with a savagery that Kate recognised from writing in her own journal. "Judas's kiss, more like."

"We don't know that yet." Uncle George's casual shrug could not hide his worry. He gestured with his head toward two stools. "Find yourself a seat. Then you can tell me if I am right."

Clumsy with anxiety, Kate dragged hers closer to Uncle George while Harry demonstrated his strength and carried his to a place next to hers.

Kate sat on the stool as her mind swirled with recent events. A short time ago, to her astonishment, Chapuys had come with her uncle to the royal chapel. He waited until the Queen and King came down from their private gallery to make their offering before the altar. Those in the chapel hushed, anticipating how Chapuys would greet the Queen. He bowed; the Queen smiled and bowed her head to him. He then kissed her hand and gave her two lit candles to take to the altar.

Harry disrupted Kate's thoughts. "Surely this is good? Chapuys and Aunt Nan, I mean."

Uncle George met Sir Tom's eyes. With a brief, sad smile, Wyatt answered, "*Dum Spiro, Spero.*"

"While I live, I hope," Kate said slowly. She pulled at her lip. "That is what you said? But surely we have more than just hope now, Sir Thomas. Chapuys has finally acknowledged our aunt."

"Your uncle and I have debated this, child. I feel what the ambassador really acknowledges is the Queen's support of the Emperor. Surely you've heard her say she will no longer support the French King and his desire for war. Chapuys always does what is in the best interests of his master."

Biting her bottom lip, Kate swung around to her brother. "We heard Chapuys and Cromwell speak together today."

Uncle George's fingers slipped on his lute's strings. A jarring note rang out. He frowned. "And where were you two?"

Harry answered. "In one of the embrasures near the chapel. They didn't see us, Uncle."

"I should hope not." He shook his head. "I have spies enough without calling upon my niece and nephew." He scowled at Harry. "I have told this before—you must stay out of this. I have enough to worry about without concerning myself over your safety, and your sister's, too."

"Uncle, we did not mean to spy." Harry lowered his head and shuffled his feet. "I heard Cromwell's voice and became fearful."

Uncle George turned his head a little and peered through half-hooded eyes. "You're right to feel fearful." He considered his nephew again. "What did you hear?"

Harry put his hands behind his back and half-closed his eyes as if ready to recite. Uncle George and Sir Tom shared a smile while Kate fought her desire to laugh at her brother. "They talked about you." Harry opened his eyes wide. "Chapuys does not like you, Uncle."

While Uncle George grinned, there was a grimness about him that made Kate attend him closely. "Of course not. But this is not a game where liking matters. Is that all, or is there more?"

"They spoke about the invitation to kiss the Queen's hand. Chapuys said no, but Cromwell said..." Harry raised his head.

"Is the Queen truly out of favour with the King?"

Uncle George spun around to Sir Tom. "Out of the mouths of babes." He turned back to his nephew. "I will not tell you falsehoods, Harry. The signs are not good. Cromwell and my sister have fought a war to keep the King in their hand. Sometimes I have hope that your aunt is able to hold her husband. Today gives me hope. But one close to the King tells me our cousin Carew will receive the Order of the Garter on St. George's day—a knighthood promised to me.

"Why knight Carew who daily plots for my sister's removal? We all know he is one of bitch Seymour's tutors—telling her what to do and say to make certain of the King. Her friends spy on my sister and then tell everything to Cromwell. I am not without spies, too, and they tell me that he has sent word to the Lady Mary that the King is tired of my sister, and that he can bear her no longer. She is to keep heart because soon Anne will be gone, and Mary will resume her rightful place. The King has proven himself a fickle man. He swore to love my sister, and now we have this cesspool that creeps upon us more with every new day."

"But what if Chapuys truly acknowledged the Queen today?" Kate asked.

Her uncle rested a hand on her shoulder. "I hope that, too. All who love your aunt do. But we must make ready in case this cesspool becomes a flood."

Sir Thomas picked up his quill. "We will know soon enough. The Queen expects Chapuys to dine with the other ambassadors this evening in her chambers. If he does, we can breathe easy for a time. If not, we have even more cause to fear that the King is taken from the Queen."

Trying to make sense of everything and unable to sleep because of her worry, Kate wrote for a long time in her journal that night.

Judas kiss, that is what Wyatt called the kiss Chapuys gave my aunt. He spoke true, for Chapuys did not come. The King welcomed the last of the ambassadors with the Queen by his side. She asked him, "Where is Chapuys? Why is he not here?" I hated the way he looked at her then. He said, "'Tis not without good reason." He walked away without saying one more word. My aunt seemed so alone I desired to go to her—but I did not dare. Why cannot I be braver? Why am I such a coward? She stood there for such a long time, her eyes following after him. Her white face still, without expression. I did not think she knew what to think or do.

Then her mask fell. While she did not say one word, it seemed like she beseeched him, asking him to come back to her. As if she said, "Look at me, look at me. I beg you, don't walk away."

But the King just kept walking. I hate him; hate him; hate him.

My aunt is so brave. I do not know how she could go to the ambassadors as if nothing had happened. She even shared a joke with the French ambassador and laughed with gaiety. She could not hide from me her breaking heart. I just wanted to weep for her.

Mother is right—all grief is hard to bear—big or small. There is nothing small about the grief my aunt daily bears. 'Tis no wonder the strain of it causes her to lose her temper at times.

Uncle George told her that what happened today was a betrayal—a betrayal by the King. My poor aunt struggled not to weep when Uncle George said that the King had Cromwell invite Chapuys to her chamber for supper with the other ambassadors.

Aunt Nan had been so hopeful and happy about his greeting in the royal chapel. All the court witnessed it—only for it to end with his insult when he did not come to her chamber.

It was an unforgivable insult—all due to the King. Why else would he choose to be blind to it? Why else did he say, "'Tis not without good reason."

The insult was for good reason? The King allowed it to happen, moved for it to happen—so to insult my aunt. Insult my aunt? Why is he so cruel to her? I am of his blood. Pray to God I could never be so cruel.

I want so much to stay hopeful. I know the Queen wants it, too. But daily hope slips away from us. Uncle George told her how the King met Chapuys and

Cromwell in his private chamber to talk together about a matter that seemed very important to my aunt and uncle. They spoke for some time about the King's talks with Chapuys. Uncle George said the King went straight into attack. He called the Emperor cruel and unreasonable for ignoring the rights of France. Chapuys dared to remind the King that the Emperor was the rightful ruler of Milan, not France, and Cromwell dared to remind him his council agreed to this, too. Chapuys is brave, or a fool. Pray to God Cromwell loses favour with the King because of this.

Uncle George told us that when the King swelled up with anger, Chapuys changed the subject to the invasion of Savoy. The King replied that the French invasion was not against the wishes of the Emperor. Chapuys disagreed with great vigour—aye, brave or a fool. For support, the King summoned Cromwell and my Lord Seymour. He told Chapuys to repeat his denial once more. Once they heard him out, Chapuys left with Seymour, while the King and Cromwell talked, quietly at first. Uncle George's spy told him the King lashed Cromwell with his tongue until the man cowered before him. A cowering Cromwell? I wish I had seen that.

The King, furious with Cromwell, returned to Chapuys. He told him they discussed matters far too important and impossible to communicate to his privy council for an answer without Chapuys first writing them down. That stopped Chapuys's tongue, and the King repeated it. My uncle's spy spoke clear that Chapuys did not want to do this. Both Chapuys and Cromwell left the King's chamber very unhappy men. Cromwell was more than unhappy; my uncle's spy believed the King's words left him terrified.

Kate was writing to her mother when Madge burst into the chamber. Pale, her eyes large and frightened, Madge sat on the edge of the bed. Tears trembled on Madge's thick lashes.

"What is it?" Kate asked.

"Oh, Kate, methinks the Queen is losing her wits."

Kate put down her quill and pushed away from the table. She sat beside Madge. "Do not speak so loud!" she whispered close to her cousin's ear. "There are spies everywhere. Now, tell me, quietly."

"I told you; the Queen loses her reason. How else do you explain what just happened?"

Her worry increasing, Kate shook her cousin's arm. "Pray, I do not know of what you speak."

Madge blinked, plucking at her gown. "In front of everyone in her chamber, the Queen went up to my betrothed, my Henry, and asked him why he hasn't yet wed me after all this time. She said I am love sick."

Confused, Kate met her cousin's eyes. "Well, perchance she should have waited for a better moment—"

This time, Madge took her arm. "You have not heard me out. There is more. Henry said—" Madge grimaced. "That fool of a man said his heart was given to another."

Slapped by her cousin's words, Kate jerked back. "What? Why did he say that?"

"Courtly games?" Madge spoke quietly. "He has great affection for the Queen." She shrugged. "Mayhap he just forgot himself and spoke the truth to her." She bounded off the bed, and began walking up and down, wringing her hands.

Kate swallowed. "There is more?"

Madge turned on her heel and came back to stand in front of Kate. "Aye, there is more. By all the saints, if times were not difficult enough without the Queen becoming crazed as if moonstruck!"

Kate stood, her head spinning. "What did my aunt do?"

Madge lifted her chin and her lips trembled. *I never thought Madge could be fearful, but she is now.* "What did she do? She laughed. She laughed like one who has lost her mind. Then she said, 'Harry, you look for dead men's shoes. If anything was to happen to the King, you would have me!'"

"Jesu'," Kate whispered; it became difficult to breathe.

Madge sat on the bed, her shoulders slumping. "Methinks we both know why. Should we be surprised if fear and despair unbridles her tongue?"

Kate sat beside her. "And Norris? How did he reply?"

Madge made a face. "My fool? He realised the danger of his courtly play of words. He denied he meant that and swore to the Queen if he had any thoughts of that kind, he deserved to end his life on the executioner's block. The Queen laughed." Madge clasped Kate's hand. "Coz, I cannot forget her laughter. She laughed like one without hope."

Later, Kate heard the rest of the story. How the fearful Henry Norris went to the Queen's almoner and confessed the conversation. He said it meant naught. The Queen was a good woman, the ill words spoken without thought, without desire for hurt. None was more loyal to the King than his wife, and how could he be thought disloyal, one who had been the King's friend since boyhood. What more could he do?

It didn't help the Queen that this was a time when the King's council swayed fiercely between supporting the French and Imperial factions. With backing for the Queen weakening everywhere, it all seemed part of the same wind blowing at court, a wind that boded no good.

Kate wrote in her journal:

> The King continues his dalliance with Mistress Seymour—his little White Mouse, as we all call her. He sends another purse full of sovereigns and a letter in his own hand. She sends both back to him, but with a kiss. The messenger tells the King that she fell on her knees, entreating the King to remember that she is well-born, the honourable daughter of honourable parents. She would rather die

a thousand deaths than lose her honour—
the one treasure she values above all her
worldly goods. She tells the King he can
send her gold once God sees fit to send
her an advantageous marriage. None doubt
at the court what advantageous marriage
she means.

Aye—she learns her lessons well.

March and the first month of spring drew to a close. One morning, while still in her chamber, Kate received a message from Francis asking her to come back with his servant so he could speak to her alone. *Alone?* The lute lessons still continued but, since the Christmas kiss, the only time she had spoken to Francis alone was when they met outside her aunt's chambers. She damped down the hope that flared in her heart, deciding the only reason he desired privacy must be due to matters concerning her aunt.

It was close to dawn, the gloom just starting to lighten. Madge had already left to attend the Queen, so, leaving a message with their maidservant, Kate snatched her mantle, threw it over her shoulders and followed Francis's servant out the palace and through the Queen's formal gardens.

The air was still with just a hint of breath now and then. Tall, kingly oaks pressed against the lightening sky, their dark forms and branches tinged and outlined by the rising sun. A silken rosy pink coloured the horizon; all around her, birds twittered in excitement, knowing morning began in earnest.

Kate pulled her mantle tighter against the chill. A lark began its song, and then another joined in until it she walked through a chorus of hymns. Several rabbits remained unmoving on the grass, as if waiting to pay homage to the new day. The blushing sky became lighter and lighter with each passing second.

The young sun rose above the trees by the time they reached the wild meadow that grew between the Queen's garden and Friars' Church. Francis leaned against a young oak tree with a hand behind his back. He seemed deep in thought, but then he looked up. Relief apparent on his face, he stood away from the tree and strode towards her. Acknowledging his approaching master, the servant bowed to Kate and said he would wait for her in the Queen's garden.

The wind blew stronger, whipping her gown and skin. With the sunlight behind Francis, she blinked, trying to see his features. Then he came closer; he held a posy of flowers, their gay colours—purples, blues, yellows and reds—blazing bright against the black velvet of his doublet. He must have picked many from the wild flowers growing in the meadow.

At last, he reached her and held out the flowers. He looked shy, younger than his years and vulnerable. Her heart quickening its beat, she smiled, taking the flowers.

"Thank you." Kate lifted them to her nose. "They're beautiful." She tucked the flowers into her girdle. "But why have you asked me here?"

He took her hand. "I thought it time." He hesitated and cleared his throat. "Kate, you once told me you loved me. Have those feelings changed at all?"

Swirling in disbelief and joy, she lifted her face to his. Recent months had taught her hard lessons of caution and restraint, but still she held tightly to his hand. She said, "Why do you ask?"

Francis reddened and bent his head. When he raised his face he wore a wry smile. "Because I love you. I know I called you young months ago. That hasn't changed. I did not know quite what to do when you told me at Christmas you loved me. You being who you are, and you so young. Kate, I thought it safer not to play with fire. But I have come to know you since. You've grown into the woman I want—brave, loyal, intelligent—a woman I love and adore. I want to wed you, Kate. Would you wed me? Pray say yes."

His words tossed all her caution and restraint to the wind. She cried with delight, going into his arms. Violets, daisies, marigolds, purple ragged robin and vetch crushed between them and released their sweet scents. Francis bent down and kissed her, first softly and then with passion. After months apart, she melted into his body with such a sense of belonging, of homecoming. Laughing and crying, she stepped away and clasped his hand.

"Francis, we are hand-fast in the sight of God." Grief swept her. "We live in terrible times; it is possible that the King will not let us wed..."

Francis embraced her. "Nay, sweetheart, I have spoken to my father about you." He grinned. "He is on the hunt for a wife for me and was very amused to hear my tale about how Brutus did the hunting for him." Francis stroked her face. "As soon I met you I knew you were the maid for me. Father is ready to speak to your mother about a proper betrothal. As for the King, Father is certain we need not concern ourselves about him. My lord Father is high in King Harry's favour. All I needed was to know this was what you wanted, too."

Kate swung his hands, wanting to dance in her joy. "Mother will not deny me if I tell her I have already given to you my heart." She considered him gravely. "But it cannot be yet. Not while my aunt has need of me."

His hands tightened on hers. "You are my loyal, brave Katherine, and I love you for it." When Francis took her in his arms again, the wind blew around them the smell of dayspring. "Promise me one thing."

Questioningly, she looked up at him.

"Stay safe, Kate; stay safe for me."

She blinked away tears and leaned her face against his chest. Aware of the warmth of his body, she listened to his strong heart and breathed in his clean scent. The long grass rustled in the wind and stroked back and forth on their bodies. She clutched his doublet as if she never would let go. *No, until to death, I am his.*

Months ago, snow lay at their feet and the moon shone its light as he pointed out the stars to her. Under those stars, he had kissed her, really kissed her, for the first time, a kiss that led her to offer her heart and everything she had to give to him, not thinking or caring about the consequences. The cold of that night was nothing to his rejection when he took her back to the Christmas festivities. She had thought she suffered the worst that life had to offer. Now—knowing the grief suffered by her aunt when she lost her baby and the grief of knowing that her husband no longer loved her—she knew better.

Young. She had heard it so often over the months until it became a refrain. In Francis's arms, she owned the truth of it. She *had* been young, months ago. She was a green girl then, and now she owned herself a woman. A woman older than Francis and weary despite the season of spring and its promise of rebirth. *Rebirth? Something must die to be reborn.* But wasn't life about change? Hadn't she learnt that now?

Coming to court full of resentment and jealousy about being no longer the centre of her mother's world, Kate had wilted at home. Her cares had been petty and brought on by herself. The long winter months had shone a light on hatred, deceit, betrayal. And on how love could die.

She touched Francis's face and tried to smile. "I will do what I can, but you must know as I do, that none of us are ever safe."

18

Kate sat on a cushion on the floor while her aunt paced up and down the room. *Does Aunt Nan think the room a cage—a cage where everything closed in on her? She acts like her life has become a wasteland of hopelessness.* Blind to Kate and everything else in the room, her despair was palpable.

After a public slighting of her brother that morning, Aunt Nan summoned Matthew Parker. She stood by the window, as if deep in thought, when her chamberlain announced him. As the priest bowed low, Kate rose from the cushion at Aunt Nan's feet, preparing to go, when her aunt waved her down. "No—stay. What I say to him I need you to hear, too."

Parker bowed again over the Queen's extended hand. She gestured to the two seats close to the fire. Spring may have come, but winter still fought for and won control over the days.

"Sit, my friend." She sat, too, and gazed at the flickering flames—bright blue, orange and purple. They roared into arresting life when part of the log broke apart with a loud *pop.* Aunt Nan started. Fear swam in her wide eyes before she lowered her face.

Parker bent towards her. "What is it, Your Grace?"

Aunt Nan lifted her head and drew a deep breath. "I have a boon to ask of you."

"If God allows, I'll do whatever you ask." His face puckered with concern despite his smile of reassurance.

She covered her face with her hands. When she removed

them, she swallowed and raised her chin. "Matthew, care for my daughter. I'll die easier if I have your promise that you will watch over her and be as her father in God."

Her hands grabbing the sides of her gown, Kate's breathing quickened to the horror of her aunt's words. Parker's mouth opened and shut before he sputtered and said the words that screamed in Kate's mind. "Die? Die, my Grace? What mean you?"

Aunt Nan held her hands out to the fire before answering. "My friend, the game for me is almost over. Let's not waste time in saying otherwise."

He swallowed. "Madam, the King may cast you off, but I do not understand why you speak of dying."

"I know my enemies. I will not tell you who, but one I trust has told me certain things. The day will soon come when all doors are closed to me, all doors but death."

Tugging his beard, Parker bent forward. "But surely the King will seek an annulment—if only for the sake of the Princess."

"I pray for that—I pray that my husband will not do evil. Even if what I hear of Cromwell's plot is true." She swung around. "He has sent his men to Henry Percy to get from him the confession that we wed so many years ago." Her smile did not match her brooding face. "I wished it, but Hal was too afraid of his father to promise me marriage. He hoped to get his mother to do his work for us, but Wolsey discovered us first. Percy will not lie for Cromwell for the King's satisfaction."

Parker frowned. "But surely, Madam, the King wants truth."

Aunt Nan shook her head. "My husband no longer recognises truth—or mayhap truth is something different to him. He has not been the same man since January, since his head injury. Every day he complains of great pain. He fears death." She firmed her chin, blinking away tears. "He fears dying without a son—so much so it drives him mad. But you know that. 'Tis my daughter I must safeguard now."

"Your daughter, Your Grace?" Parker coughed, his hand going to his mouth. "Pray, why do you think you must safeguard her?"

"Matthew, pray hear me. I do not think I will be here to protect her for many days longer. I need you to vow to me that you will be her father in God. Care for my child. Ensure she has good tutors, knows her duty to God and does not forget the care of her soul." Aunt Nan's mouth became a thin, harsh line. "Do not let the King overlook her. She is his daughter too, after all." Tears falling down her drawn cheeks, she turned to him, including Kate also. "Tell her that she was the one and only true consolation that the world has ever given me."

Parker's face creased in sorrow and he tugged at his beard again. "I vow to you, I will do that. Believe me, I'll not be the only one to keep watch over Bess." Despite eyes darkened by anguish, he chuckled. "She needs watching that one—so like both her parents, and royal to the core. I've heard what happens when she does not get her way."

Aunt Nan wiped her wet face with her handkerchief. "She is very like me, with a temper that comes from both sire and dam." Her eyes glowed from the light of the fire. "A temper to shake the world one day. I would give everything to see it."

Parker leaned forward, his hand on his knee. "But if God allows, there's no reason you shouldn't. Why think of death? You who have done so much for England and the church? Thanks to your good work, we are no longer a dominion of Rome."

Aunt Nan smiled. "I did none of it alone. I do not forget I have the help of good men such as you, Archbishop Cranmer, Latimer—the list goes on and on. And, of course, we must not forget the King. My husband once shared my dream of an England where religion was not a curse and abomination. But rather than build a stronger England on a religion and Bible meant for all men, he stays angry with God. God has only given him dead sons, thus he has decided to put his trust in gold instead."

Kate shifted on the floor, struggling to understand Aunt Nan's words. Was she saying the King had turned away from God? Rejected God? How could that be? Every day, morning and night, the King prayed in chapel. Who did he pray to if it was not God?

Her aunt looked back at the fire, cupped her cheek in her hand and sighed. "My heart tells me that Cromwell will one day discover the error of his way. As King Minos found to his peril, gold always fails in the end; how can it not when it sows the seeds of destruction?" Her shining eyes reflected the flames. "God forgive me, I thought I would do better than Katherine of Aragon. Like her, I could do nothing to save the monasteries that did nothing but good. As God is my witness, I tried to save them." She swung around again. "God help me, Matthew, all I wanted was reform, not destruction, not the breaking up of true men of God who were simply the custodians of our very history—the keepers of England's heart."

She laughed as if mocking herself. "I know I am a vain, sinful woman, but I took an oath when I was crowned

Queen—I have thought of it every day since." She bent, briefly laying a hand on Kate's shoulder. "Listen, this is something I want you to tell Bess when she is older." She held out her hands as if in vow, and then brought them to her chest. "When the sacred oil was placed on my breast, I prayed to be a good Queen. I asked God to help me learn the meaning of true sacrifice, for the good of England and its people. The words I said were not empty, but the charter to map out the rest of my life. I swore then to sacrifice my life for England. I just didn't know I swore a true sacrifice, or the little time I would have to be England's Queen. I believed my husband wanted a true queen. I was mistaken."

Aunt Nan pealed with laughter. "Another one of my sins—arrogance. I should have taken more heed of the woman I supplanted. Until her false marriage came to an end, she was humble with the King, acted with wisdom, and gained her desires through womanly wiles. I, on the other hand, once believed Henry thought me his equal. I was a fool, Matthew—a vain, arrogant fool. I looked down on most women, believing my gifts made me greater than them. I believed God meant for me to be Queen. And now the game is almost over, and I am terrified about what will happen to my daughter. What if he treats Bess the same as Mary?" Her hands rose to hold her temples as if in pain.

Kate licked her dry lips. Her worry for her aunt swelled into a gale that tossed her around like a galleon in a storm. Again, life seemed to leave her rudderless and helpless to withstand the waves threatening to drag her under.

"Dear God—I treated her shamefully, too." Aunt Nan leaned closer to the priest. "She is stubborn like her mother. Mary will never recognise me as her Queen—even with her mother dead. Elizabeth is a bastard in her eyes—the child of the Concubine. What could I do when she refused my hand of friendship time after time, or even my offer to be like another mother to her? She said to agree would conflict against her conscience and honour." Aunt Nan clasped her hands together so tightly her knuckles became white. "Now I pray for her to forgive me; all I want is for her to be a good sister to my child."

Parker reached to clasp her hand. "Shall we pray together, my Queen?"

She gave him an unhappy smile. "Why not? Praying is all I can do now." She swallowed. "I was willing to give my blood when I was crowned, and, if my husband so decides, I am ready to give it now."

The days grow light and warm, yet they remain dark at court. My poor aunt. All know of Cromwell's hold on the King. All know about Lady Jane. She no longer acts the mouse, but a cat making ready to pounce on its prey. Aunt Nan is rarely alone with the King. I suspect that was why my aunt played a desperate hand on Passion Sunday. She asked Skip, her almoner and a man loyal to her, to preach a sermon that none could mistake the meaning of.

For months, I hardly noticed John

Skip amongst the many who served in the Queen's household. But this small, soft-speaking man seemed a lion when he roared out from the pulpit that Sunday: "Which among you accuse me of sin?"

All of once, I became aware of the great discomfort of the chapel's bench, while all around people stilled and hushed, listening to him speak of the injustice of holding up the sins of any single clergyman as if it was the sin of all men of God.

"My Gracious and most noble Majesty," he said. "I call upon you to use wisdom and ignore those evil counsellors who tempt you to go down the road of ignoble actions."

The King flushed then, while nearby, Cromwell's hands became like fists making ready to defend.

I clasped my own hands, digging my nails into my palms as I listened to Skip's words. My aunt sat close by, and very silent, her head bowed in humility, but what he said seemed to come from her own mouth. Many, many times, I have heard her speak of Esther and her husband, the Persian King, Ahasuerus. My aunt prayed often to God to help her be an Esther for England.

In the chapel, Master Skip looked straight at the King and at Cromwell. He spoke of Ahasuerus's sinful counsellors who had led him astray and almost caused the death of his innocent subjects without any just cause. He spoke of ancient customs and how important they were to England. He shouted about the decay of universities and the necessity of learning. Aunt Nan made a movement then, and I knew, without question, this sermon was directed purely at the King. My stomach ached. Master Skip and my aunt are brave, but I began to drown in my own terror. Terror for my aunt. For several heartbeats, it seemed she and I were only people in the chapel when Master Skip began to measure out his words slowly and carefully. He told of Esther, and how she saved the Jews by exposing the evil of the Ahasuerus's counsellors. He told of Haman, who ended up dying the death meant for Esther's protector. He told of Ahasuerus's gratitude to his Queen, and how he recognised her, once and for all, as a woman who not only loved him, but also was ever his friend.

The King, his face red, shifted with anger, a movement echoed by Cromwell when Skip told the court that Solomon lost all nobility at the end of his life by allowing his lust to flourish so that he took to him many wives and concubines.

Skip was summoned to the King's chamber straight after the service, and I heard from my brother of their meeting. "How dare you!" the King had shouted. "How dare you preach seditious doctrines and slander me, my counsellors, my lords and nobles and my whole Parliament?"

The King's fury included my aunt, too. That same day, the King stormed into the Queen's chamber. I guessed she had expected him. For hours, she sat reading, but at times she raised her face with the air of someone who waited. When her chamberlain announced the King, she fell to her knees. Her women and I did likewise. He didn't allow her to speak. He shouted at her to remember her place, his hands opening and shutting as if he wished to strangle her. I felt so frightened for her that I shifted closer to her on my knees, not caring if the King noticed me. My heart only slowed its beat at the King's departure. My aunt wept. No wonder—he left her chamber as if he could not bear to stay in the same room with her.

My aunt's fight became one of desperation. With the fire already an inferno, she added more fuel to keep it so. Knowing their good influence with the King, she pulled out her cards of Latimer and Cranmer.

Latimer preached the next Sunday. His message, too, was easy to understand. If the monasteries must be sold, then let the gold go to a good and worthy cause. Cranmer also sang the same song.

It seems my aunt is determined not to fail in one thing. She may not have given England its Prince, but she will do anything to prevent the wholesale destruction of England's monasteries.

On the twenty-ninth of April, Kate was alone with her aunt in her privy chamber when her chamberlain entered and bowed. "Your Grace, Marc Smeaton begs to speak to you."

Disturbed from her reading, Aunt Nan frowned. "Smeaton? He begs to speak to me?" She swung around to Kate before nodding to her chamberlain. "Let him enter, but pray both of you stay. I wish you to hear whatever he has to say. I hide nothing."

At the door, Smeaton bowed first and then bowed again when closer to the Queen. He was white and drawn, and breathing unsteadily.

Several heartbeats passed before Aunt Nan spoke. "Why do you come here without my command, Marc? I have not asked for you."

"My Queen, Master Cromwell has asked me to come to his house at Stepney to sup with him."

Aunt Nan closed her book and put it aside. She swallowed. "And what of it?"

"Madam, do you not think it strange? He has never paid any notice to me before, and now he invites me to supper at his private dwelling."

Tapping her fingers on the wooden armrest, Aunt Nan's gaze travelled around the room. "Why go then if it disturbs you so?"

"My Queen, I cannot refuse Master Cromwell—not one who is so close to the King. 'Tis like a command for one in the King's service."

Naked of all expression, she averted her face. She murmured, "And when do you sup with Cromwell?"

"Tonight, Your Grace."

"Tonight," repeated Aunt Nan. She pulled her girdle

tighter on her too slender waist. "And you will go?"

"Madam, what choice do I have if I wish to safeguard my position at court?" He swallowed, his Adam's apple going up and down. "Madam, what do I say to him?"

Aunt Nan raised her fingers to her French hood, trailing them down her face and curling them against her cheek. "Say to him? What else but the truth." Her face became stern. "And, Marc, in future do not come here unless I send for you."

"But, my Queen—"

Aunt Nan stood. "Aye—I am your Queen, and I say I do not wish you here unless I send for you." She turned to her chamberlain. "Pray, escort Master Smeaton outside. Now!"

The two men left, and Aunt Nan's eyes flashed with anger. She held on to the back of her chair with shaking hands. "So Master Cromwell questions yet another servant. When will it end, Kate? When will it end?"

When will it end? One thing leads to another—cause and effect.

Still with her aunt, Kate wrote in her journal when a secret message arrived from Uncle George. Aunt Nan read it and lifted a face white with worry. Folding the letter to put in her pocket, she spoke hoarsely. "Cromwell has played his hand, niece. Your uncle writes that Smeaton is in the Tower." She swallowed hard. "There is no reason for it other than what I feared. Cromwell uses Smeaton to get at me." Her hands at either side of her throat, she took a deep breath and let it out. "What am I to do?"

"Could you not speak to the King?" Kate asked. She

tottered on an edge of cliff, ready to fall. This man, her father, seemed fixed on a path to destroy her beloved aunt.

"He has not spoken to me in days. I do not know if he would speak to me now." She whipped around to the door, as if a thought had just come to her. "Come with me, Kate."

"To the King?"

"Aye, but first I will go and get our daughter. Surely he cannot refuse to speak to the mother of his child."

Aunt Nan lifted her skirts then and almost ran to her daughter's nearby nursery. Kate hurried behind her. Once she fetched her daughter, Aunt Nan hurried to the King's chamber. But his guards refused her admittance, telling her the King was closeted with his ministers and must not be disturbed.

"Not be disturbed?" Aunt Nan repeated. In her white face, her pupils engulfed her dark eyes. "Not disturbed?"

She rushed out to the gardens overlooked by the King's chambers.

"Harry, I beg you, listen to me. Don't turn away. I am your wife."

Scared and feeling very ill, Kate stood at Aunt Nan's side. She swayed with dizziness below the lattice window of the council chamber. She still reeled from when the King had looked down at them. It was like a physical blow. Now faced with his immobile back, Kate trembled, uncertain which was worst—scorched by the fire of the King's hatred or feeling the bridge breaking apart beneath her feet. *Why does he refuse to listen to his wife?*

Aunt Nan bowed her head, defeated. Bess, frightened,

reached to touch her mother's cheek. Her aunt lost all control. She straightened to her full height, faced the window, and screamed: "Harry! What have I done?" Her voice broke under the weight of her tears. "I beg you, for the love we once shared, speak to me."

Kate rubbed her wet eyes and lifted her face to the sky. Blue like a robin's egg. Not yet May, the magic of spring pushed back the memory of a dark, oppressive winter. The walled garden was in its full glory, with promise of more to come. Budding roses, sheltering oaks returning to verdancy, the mating songs of birds. With so many beauties of life all around and evidence of life made over, afresh, Kate prayed hard. *Dear God, let the King speak to her. Do not let this be the end.*

Bess sobbed, hiccupping whimpers that went on and on. Aunt Nan clutched her close. "Do not cry, sweetheart. We must be brave." Aunt Nan kissed her face quickly, over and over. "We must not weep. Do not blame your father for believing my enemies. He loves you, *ma belle*, loves you. You're his daughter and precious to him."

The King had vanished from his window. Aunt Nan gave the window a final look and then hurried from the garden, heading to her chamber. Bess still crying, her mother started one of her nonsense stories. Following close behind, Kate seized upon the flow of words, listening, wanting them to take her to another, better place than this. But she could not be like her little cousin, who now laughed as her mother told her about how a rabbit tricked a lion out of his dinner and lived to tell the tale. Nay, Kate could not laugh. *Will I ever laugh again?* Despite the bright, sunlit day, darkness closed in on them.

Nearing the entrance to the palace, Aunt Nan sang softly Bess's favourite lullaby:

Lullay, thou little tiny child, lullay bye, bye,
lully, lullay.
Lullay, thou little tiny child, lullay bye, bye,
lully, lullay

Kate's sight blurred. It was the same lullaby William Carey had once sung. No matter what, the memory of his love meant she would never stop calling him *Father* in her heart. Blinded by tears and falling behind, she cleaved onto her aunt's pure, comforting voice as if she, too, was a little child. But it was not enough. Grief made it difficult to breathe and forced her to find the nearest seat.

Heavy feet tramped near her. She rubbed away her tears, her throat closing in fright. Soothing her little child, Aunt Nan did not notice the men closely following her. Their shadows merged, broke away, and merged again. All the while Aunt Nan sang to her daughter.

19

As was the pattern of her life now, Kate kept close to her aunt. Today, she sat near her in her chamber with a small group of her closest women. The late afternoon had darkened and grown cold, so much so, Meg Lee drew the curtains to help keep the room warmer and lit more candles.

Seated on her favourite chair, Aunt Nan leaned an elbow on the armrest, cupping her cheek in her hand, her eyes turned towards the fire in the hearth. She was quiet, her pale skin taut over the fine bones of her face. Shadows bruised the hollows of temples and cheeks. Through blurry tears, Kate blinked away an image of a fleshless skull, pulled back to months ago when she had come to court to attend her aunt. That first day the ravens had flocked amongst the skulls on the gateway to London Bridge. More than that. They had fought over the flesh of the dead. *Why think that? Why think that?* Feeling helpless, she shifted closer to the warmth of the fire. Orange, red and blue flames licked and ate the huge log.

Aunt Nan sighed and moved. She began to laugh, a hand covering her mouth. "What say you about the King, my husband, today? Was it not strange to see him leave the tournament so early?" This time her laughter cracked. Quiet again, she was all eyes, all emotion.

Trembling, Kate held her hands out to fire, but the warmth it gave to her body did not lessen the anxiety that chilled her heart. With part of the log breaking away, pictures flashed in her mind from the day. A gusty wind flapped the pennant flags. The King and Queen sat together in the royal stands. Around them milled a crowd of courtiers. All boded well—at first.

Small explosions popped in the fire and tall flames shot up. One side of the log crumbled and fell with a *plop* to the blackened brick floor. Aunt Nan had tried to make the King smile. She jested with him about the competitors. She sang softly and then asked if he liked her new song. Answered by his silence, she turned her attention to those competing, calling out to them, encouraging them. When she let fall her handkerchief to Henry Norris, a message from Cromwell arrived for the King. The sun lost its final warmth and the bright day turned black. Without a word, without one last look at his wife, the message still in his hand, King Henry bounded up, snapped a command at his men, and left the stand.

The flames burst again, their *pops* breaking apart Kate's recollections. She swivelled around to Aunt Nan. From the moment the King left her, she had looked like this: abandoned, lost, frightened. A woman of sorrows.

Kate slept the night on the trundle bed in her aunt's bedchamber. Or tried to sleep. Aunt Nan woke several times in nightmare until Kate's deep sleep had been cut asunder by her aunt's terrified scream. Damping down her own terror, she listened to Aunt Nan weep. But not for long. She slipped into her aunt's bed and put her arms around her.

"It will be all right," Kate murmured. "It will be all right."

Her lie left her heart heavy. For what seemed an eternity, she lay awake, unable to sleep.

The next morning came—the second of May. Like the day before, the sky was blue and promised another exquisite spring day. Despite her disturbed night, Aunt Nan arose early and Kate joined the other women to help her to dress.

Her aunt, more picky than usual, changed her mind about several gowns before choosing one of her most costly. She fussed even over her hair, demanding the plaits be pinned decoratively at the back of her head. Then she fussed over the choice of headgear that would cover it. It seemed she wanted to ensure perfection.

For the King. She lives in hope that the King will come to her. Kate, permitted at last to break her fast, found she had no appetite.

Breakfast over and done with, Aunt Nan led her ladies to enjoy the festivities. She was laughing about the victory of her champion and forgetting to put down a wager on him when a servant came with a message from the King. As she read, the colour fled from her cheeks leaving her ashen. When Kate moved towards her in concern, she shook her head.

"I have been summoned to the King's council," she said.

Her women gathered closer together; a few, like Kate, stepped closer to the Queen.

"Let me come." Kate took her aunt's arm. "I beg you."

Aunt Nan shook her head. "In this I need only Meg. If you wish, you may return to my chambers and wait there. Otherwise, stay and make merry." Under her breath, she said, "It may be the last chance today."

With most of the women, Kate hurried to Aunt Nan's chamber. The waiting seemed to go forever before her aunt came through the door. Without speaking, she hurried to the chair by the fireplace. There, she sat and lowered her head between her hands. Her face white and frightened, Meg stood behind her.

Nauseous despite her empty stomach, Kate swallowed back bile. She tried to catch Meg's attention, hoping she might give her an answer to her question. When she didn't look her way, Kate took the question to her aunt, "What happened?"

Aunt Nan raised dazed eyes. "The end has come. The end has come. God help me."

Kate fell to her knees beside her aunt's chair and clasped her cold hands. When Aunt Nan cracked with strained laughter, she tightened her hold. *Do not let go. Do not let go.* Exhausted after a night of little sleep, Kate fought for reality. To let go of her aunt's hands would cast them both adrift, without comfort or help. But it was not Kate who let go; Aunt Nan removed her hands from Kate's and sat back.

"For years they have called me a whore. Now they wish to name me that truly." Aunt Nan's index finger stroked the ruby broach at her breast. "Even the King, my husband."

Kate leaned forward to hold her aunt's free hand. "Whore? Whore? I do not understand."

Her aunt cleared her throat before she spoke. "I am arrested, child."

Kate gasped and a woman burst into noisy tears. Boneless, without substance or strength, Kate crumbled against her aunt's chair.

Releasing Kate's hand, Aunt Nan stood, gesturing angrily. "I do not need weeping women. Stop immediately or leave me." She collapsed back on her chair, holding her head again.

"Norris—can it be true? Have you really confessed to being my lover? I can believe it of Smeaton, but you? You have always been my good friend. A loyal, loving friend—more than I ever deserved—more than your master, the King."

Kate struggled to comprehend her aunt's murmured words through the haze of shock. "Adultery?" she got out at last. "Adultery?"

Aunt Nan turned to her and smiled with bitterness. "Yea, our good uncle of Norfolk spat it out while Cromwell smirked and lapped it up like a cat with cream. It did me no good to deny the charges." Her white face became grave. "If you look out the door, you will see guards from the Tower have replaced the men who were there this morning. I am allowed my dinner, while they wait for the turning of the tide. Then they take me to the Tower."

Her rapid heartbeats drummed loud in her ears. Kate swallowed the fear that threatened to engulf her. "Take me with you. I beseech you."

Aunt Nan shook her head. "Sweetheart, we do not know what waits for me there. I do not wish you to take on a burden that may prove too heavy for you. You're young, Kate. Mayhap too young to companion me on such a journey."

Kate leaned her forehead on her aunt's cold hand, which lay on the carved, wooden armrest. "I cannot see you go alone into imprisonment. You'd break my heart if you left me behind."

Aunt Nan considered her sadly. "I doubt you know about breaking of hearts. Not really."

She opened her mouth to deny this, but her aunt's silent dejection gave her reason to pause. There was no good reason to tell her aunt about Francis and how it had been with her for months. All winter she had broken her heart believing she loved without hope. Now she was at the true beginning of her love story, with the fire burning bright, while for her aunt, the fire was now dead ash.

Aunt Nan stilled and her face became thoughtful. "But you are in my care. I don't think I can leave you here with my enemies ready to destroy all my trappings as Queen. And the King... how can I trust him to care for your safety? His mind will be busy with doing what he wills with me." She considered Kate again. "There's no recourse then; you must come with me. I can rely on my brother to get word to your mother so she can arrange for you to go home in safety."

Kate shook her head. Her temper flared. "I do not wish to go home, Aunt. I want to stay with you."

Aunt Nan averted her face, her hand at her temple, before turning back to Kate. "You can come with me, but only until I work out a better solution for your safety. If my commands are still worth anything, Kate, then do as I say. If that means going home to your mother, so be it."

Kate gathered and tossed clothes into a bag for her journey to the Tower, while Madge sat on the bed "I wish I could come," her cousin said, her fingers at her mouth. "It feels strange that you will be with the Queen while I stay here."

Kate swung around to her cousin. "Do you think Cromwell will want to question you, too?"

Madge paled and visibly swallowed. "God forbid! What do I say if he does?"

Kate returned to packing her bag. How many months ago

had she asked the questions of Madge, not the other way around? How fast everything changed. Her last garment packed, she turned to her cousin. "Speak the truth," she said with firmness. "That's what the Queen would want and expect. We know she is a faithful wife to the King. What more can anyone say?"

Madge drew a long breath. "We know, but that doesn't mean our words cannot be shaped for Cromwell's vile purposes. He is skilled at that."

Kate sat beside her cousin, her shoulders slumping. "Do you think the Queen is right—that they mean to kill her?"

"It seems that way," Madge murmured, averting a face white with grief. She clasped Kate's hand. "I tell myself that no Queen of England has ever been executed. Surely it will not happen to Queen Anne?"

Kate eyed Madge. "Just because it has not happened before does not mean it will not happen now."

Madge reached into the pocket of her gown and drew out the book of shared poetry. "Take this with you."

Kate flicked through its pages before turning back to Madge. "You trust me with this in the Tower?"

"I suspect you will have more need of it than I." Madge smiled. "It hasn't passed my notice that your attempts at poetry have improved in recent weeks. Why not continue your posies in the Tower? It will help to divert you in the days ahead and, I hope, give you means to find some solace."

"Thank you." Kate leaned across and kissed her cousin's cheek. She put the book into the empty pocket of her gown. The other pocket stored her own journal. Now she had another reason for regret. She had shared this chamber with Madge for months and all that time she had never once told her about her private journal. Her cheeks heated as she remembered all the traitorous thoughts that she written down in recent days. "I will look after our book and return it when I see you next."

At the loud knock on the door, both girls started. Alice, their maidservant, entered. "M'ladies, one of the King's servants has come for Lady Katherine. The King commands you to his presence, M'lady."

Her hand at her throat, Kate bounded off the bed. "Why would he want to see me?"

Madge reflected back her own fear and came to stand beside her. "'Tis a command, Kate." She embraced her and then pushed her towards the door. "Go. Pray God, he sends for you because he wants to know the truth."

Grabbing her cloak, Kate joined the King's servant. Refusing to answer any questions, he escorted her down the corridors of the palace, at last leading her through the King's private chambers, taking her to a room she had never seen before. Treasures were everywhere. Clocks whirled away the seconds alongside astrolabes and other gold instruments.

The King was alone, bespectacled, seated and writing at his desk, the curtains closed upon the end of day. A draught played with the lit tapers that cast dancing shadows on his pale skin. The pate of his head was bald like a monk, greying hair encircled the back of his skull from above his ear. His trappings of royalty discarded, he seemed simply an ageing, tired and ill man.

She curtseyed at the door, and he beckoned to her. She treaded closer and curtseyed again, this time staying on her knees.

Taking off his glasses, he squinted at her and gestured

with impatience. "Get up and sit." He pointed to a stool and waited until she perched herself on its edge. "They tell me you go with the Queen to the Tower?" He thrust his face towards her. "Is this true? Speak, Kate."

She stood. She had been at court for five months, and in all that time, he had barely acknowledged her, and only the once had he called her by name. How long ago that seemed. Then she was a different person, an innocent cast into a dark labyrinth. Time had rendered it less dark, but only for the light to reveal fearful paths of hate, jealousy and suspicion. She was no longer the innocent girl who had arrived at court five months ago. How could she remain innocent walking and surmounting paths darkened by hatred? The man before her seemed blinded to the fact that he was responsible for so many of these paths.

He jerked back in annoyance and gestured to the empty stool. "Don't just stand there. Sit down, sit down, I said. And I asked you a question. God's blood, I am your King. Answer me. Now."

She gingerly sat back on the edge of the stool. Her first moment of terror almost rendered her speechless, but she took hold of it and pushed it down. How she had wanted to speak to him after her aunt lost her son. Now, she had that opportunity. Still frightened, she refused to give in to her fears. Not now. "Aye, I go with the Queen. She's my aunt, sire. How can you expect otherwise?"

He glowered at her. "Your aunt? And what of your loyalty to me, your King? What if I told you *your aunt* bedded one hundred men or more—and worse than this, too?"

For a several heartbeats, she seemed looking into her own blue eyes. Her thoughts tumbled in sudden confusion, aware she confronted a suffering man who warred with himself. A man without peace. She swallowed, and gathered back her wits and her courage. "Sire, you are my King, and I owe you my allegiance. But I cannot forget that Aunt Nan is of my blood, and I'm bound to her. My place is with her. As for the hundred men, that is a lie."

His face reddening with fury, he knocked over an inkwell. The black ink spilled over a half-written parchment. "God's oath! See what you made me do!"

She read some of the words on the parchment.

Medicine for the Pestilence

Take one handful of marigolds, a handful of sorel, a handful of burnett, a handful of featherfew, half a handful rue, and a quantity of dragons...

The King folded the parchment over the ink spill to soak it up, and Kate's temper threatened to spill over, too. *How dare he! Aunt Nan's life left in ruins while he writes down recipes? What kind of man is this? Does he not have a heart?*

Her anger lighting a fire under her courage, she lifted her chin. "You cannot blame me for your anger—just as you cannot accuse the Queen of adultery or betrayal." She licked her lips, her mouth suddenly dry.

Pushing away the parchment, he turned to her eyes that seemed to flame. "You dare speak so to your King?"

Kate cast her last remnant of caution to the wind. "I dare speak so to my father."

Yes—he had fathered her. And disowned her. Yet something stirred in her heart. He seemed so ill, with lines of pain etched on his face. Was it pity that tugged at her?

Surely it wasn't pity? Whatever it was, it combated her hatred and left it blunt. "Why is my aunt arrested? You must know her heart, that she would never betray you. She loves you, sire."

The King sat back then as if taking in her measure, his mouth twisting in what seemed an effort to smile. "You're brave." He began to rifle through papers on his desk and moved a sheet next to his seal before raising his face. "Why should I be surprised? Nan and your mother both have stout hearts. And you're my blood, after all." Deep lines scored his brow as he scowled. "Who are you to judge? Do you know how it goes with me? You say my wife has not betrayed me? What of Norris? 'Dead men's shoes,' she said to him. That he waited for dead men's shoes. Aye, my shoes. She has placed England on a road to diminish my power, the power of a crowned King, one placed by God to be his mouthpiece. You say she has not betrayed me or England? You know nothing."

Kate didn't understand how England involved the arrest of her aunt, but Henry Norris was a different matter. "Fie! For shame. Why put weight upon Norris's words to my aunt and hers to him? Do you not know how the last months have been for her? She still grieves for the loss of the babe. Can you not pity her?"

His barren, hopeless eyes seemed to belong to a man on the edge of madness. "Pity her? I cannot afford to pity her. She has failed me, failed England." His hands shaking, he opened one of the drawers to an exquisite wooden writing box and pulled out a thick wad of unused parchment sheets.

Kate looked down at the box, caught by its beauty. Elaborate gold decoration gleamed in candlelight—arrow shafts and *fleurs-de-lys* around an H and K enclosed in a triangle; the small drawer of quills pulled out on one side. Mars and Venus stood side by side, love and hate. Kate fought back tears, listening to the King.

"She failed me like my first wife." He started and dropped the papers. "I thought of Katherine as my wife for many years." He frowned. "I am not a man like any man, yet they both, in the end, tried to make me so. They wanted me a man, not a King."

"But you are a man," Kate blustered in bewilderment.

"Aye a man, but also a King. Kate, God put me here to reign. It is my divine right and sacred duty. None can put that at risk. I cannot risk civil war. If it means doing what I must, I will."

She contemplated him while clock hands moved and marked the passing of time. *Is he sick or simply mad? Perhaps both.* Pity stirred her heart again and left her confused. Quietly she asked, "What are you planning to do?"

He straightened in his chair, a man turned into steel. "What if I command you not to go with the Queen?"

Kate tightened and re-knotted her girdle. She started, her heart swelling. Whenever her aunt was thinking, her beautiful hands would do the exactly the same. Kate had now taken the gesture for her own. "You are my King. My aunt has taught me that I must obey you no matter what you ask." Desperate and afraid, her heart beat so fast that her head swum with dizziness. "But make that command and I will hate you."

The King pointed to the window. A thrush chirped its evening song. "In that direction is the Tower. If you go there, you are likely to hate me in any case." He firmed his mouth.

"Be it on your own head. Do what you wish, but never say I did not warn you."

20

Seeking comfort on her return from seeing the King, Kate wrote in her journal something her mother had once said to her:

All things must come to an end—all things but love.

Her stomach now growling with emptiness, Kate waited for her aunt to finish her dinner so she could ask for release to eat too. But with barely a warning, the Duke of Norfolk entered the Queen's chambers with other members of the council. Hanging back at the door was Cromwell.

Her heart in her throat, Kate moved instinctively towards Aunt Nan when she pushed against the table and stood with her hands holding on for support.

"Good day, Uncle," she said softly. As if ignoring Cromwell, she nodded to the other men. "My Lords. Tell me, is it time?"

The Duke stepped forward, bowed and then straightened again. "My Grace, we come on the King's command to conduct you to the Tower, there to abide during His Highness' pleasure."

Aunt Nan paled and swayed. Swallowing, she lifted her chin. "If that be the King's, my husband's, desire, I am ready to obey."

"Make yourself ready," the Duke said. "The tide waits for no man—or woman." He gestured towards the Queen's women gathered by the window, the ruby on his signet ring flashing in a sudden beam of sunlight "You may choose two of your ladies to accompany you. With them, Lady Boleyn and Mrs. Cosyns will also attend to your needs."

Aunt Nan started. "My Lady Boleyn and Mrs. Cosyns?"

Aunt Boleyn and Mrs. Coysns? Kate shook her head. Jesu', why? They detest Aunt Nan. Aunt Boleyn has never forgiven her about Madge. They must be Cromwell's spies.

Aunt Nan drew a deep breath and bowed her head. "Be it as the King commands."

The bells rang out the second hour when they escorted Aunt Nan to the waiting barge, bare of ceremonial trappings. Kate padded after her aunt in a haze of terror, a terror that made everything seem a dream. A terror that dimmed the bright spring day.

Her aunt stopped, speaking as if to herself. "Not even three years." She took Lady Meg's hand. "Do you remember when we travelled this way? How different it was then. Do you remember, Meg, the dragon on the royal barge? How cleverly it hid the men who caused it look like it was breathing fire. It frightened the barges accompanying us, but not me." She laughed softly, lifted her skirts and stepped down to take her seat. "I had never been so happy as on that day." Sunlight shimmered on the water that glinted and sparkled like diamonds. "I will always remember walking on paths strewn, nay, carpeted, with rose petals and the voices lifted up in song. Now it has come to this."

Aunt Nan's words returned Kate to her last journey on the river. That also had been the day of her aunt's crowning, when she had accompanied her grandparents in the barge belonging to the Boleyns. Now, on another sunlit day, they journeyed the same way—past the majestic Cluniac Abbey, past the Isle of Dogs where the King kept and trained his hunting dogs, past busy wharves and ships being made ready for the sea. They passed an empty gibbet that stood as warning to those who chose piracy as a way of life.

Too soon the foreboding Tower came in sight. Last time, it had marked a happy arrival, but not today. No, not today. This time, the looming Tower threatened death.

Kingston, the Lieutenant of the Tower, waited to greet them at the end of their journey. Leaving the barge behind, Aunt Nan halted in the shadow of the dungeons.

"Am I to go there—to that horrible place?" she asked Kingston as he bowed over her hand. She half-turned one way, then the other, as if seeking escape.

He smiled at her with reassurance. "Nay, your Grace. You will be lodged in the same apartments where you stayed for your coronation."

Aunt Nan stood there as if she struggled to understand, as if reality had lost all meaning and all sense, other than to mock her with its destruction. She fell to her knees and wept.

Kate's heart thumped hard as she wiped her own wet cheeks. A sea of tears. *I am swept out from shore in a sea of tears. Will I ever find my way back again?*

At last, Aunt Nan lifted a white, tear-streaked face. "'Tis too good for me."

Then she laughed and laughed. Kingston, Lady Boleyn, Mrs. Cosyns and some of the guards seemed to pass the same judgment: the Queen had lost her reason.

Cold in body and spirit, Kate gathered her cloak tighter

around her. *My aunt has lost everything else, why not that too?*

Kingston did not lie. Aunt Nan was taken to the apartments built for her in those days of celebration. The first day and night passed. Kate, like the other women attending the Queen, slept on a pallet in Aunt Nan's bedchamber. Or made the attempt to sleep.

Defeating Meg and Kate's earnest attempts to turn the conversation to other matters, all that first night, Lady Boleyn and Mrs. Cosyns had disturbed Aunt Nan's peace by asking her questions. Lady Boleyn seemed to take particular delight in the downfall of her niece.

"I always thought you'd bring shame to your kin," she said with contempt. "I thank God Mary and Madge are free of you at last. You never deserved their loyalty—a mistress who did not protect them. Both my nieces suffered in your service. Mary breaks her heart over a man who can never wed her, and Madge... How could you ask my daughter to put herself in the King's way? You've shown yourself a woman with no honour, niece."

"Bed with her musician, can you believe that?" Mrs. Cosyns asked Lady Boleyn. "Would you and I ever cast as low as that?"

Like one slapped unfairly, Aunt Nan spun around in shock. "I am innocent."

Ignoring her, Lady Boleyn laughed loudly. "He's not the only one. They tell Francis Weston and Henry Norris, Madge's betrothed, are also her paramours."

For hours and hours, they tried to draw from Aunt Nan words she would later regret. Sometimes she did speak—a ramble that often tripped her up.

"Aunt," she said, "I chastised Weston for dallying with

Madge." She was silent for moment. "When I chastised him, he said to me that he and Henry Norris came to my chambers not for my attendants, but because of the high regard they had for me." She laughed then. "Was this what they based their lies on? Something that happened twelve months ago? If they did, then they forget how I defended my honour. Am I fool not to know that my reputation would lie in ashes if rumour spread that I, the Queen of England, acted the wanton with men?

"And Mark Smeaton? Is it my fault that he desired to act above his station? I did not encourage him, but others did, giving him coin as payment for his music and dancing. My brother also favoured him with gifts from his own clothes coffers, but the King was always Mark's greatest benefactor. He thought it amusing whenever Smeaton dressed in the trappings of a lord, because the trappings came from him. Even so, I had to soothe the King's temper when Smeaton began to garb himself and his servants in livery. He grew so overbearing in his pride that he turned his back on his past and disdained his own father. Bourbon was so right about Smeaton; even honey becomes bitter if overused."

Aunt Nan fell silent, clasped her hands in her lap, before rushing on. "I was not amused when Smeaton told me that he was heart-sore over me. I put him in his place and reminded him of his poor degree and that the play of courtly love was only permitted for those of higher station. Smeaton has his talents, but he annoyed me with his artificiality and his constant flattery." She swallowed, her lips moving as if she fought for control. "I am married to the King. Why would a man of that wit, or any wit, tempt me? I am a faithful wife to my Lord King."

She was like a lute string pulled to breaking point. The judgmental silence of Lady Boleyn and Mrs. Cosyns only made her talk go more around in circles.

Lady Boleyn gestured meaningfully at Mrs. Cosyns. She nodded and leaned forward. "Why did Norris swear," she interjected into Aunt Nan's ramble, "that you were a good woman to your almoner?"

Aunt Nan shrugged wearily. "I bade him do so." She turned to Mrs. Cosyns and her aunt. "You both know the story—Norris and I engaged in a foolish conversation. It meant nothing, I swear it, and I swear I only wished to remind Norris that he neglected his duty to Madge."

Lady Boleyn snorted. "You swear! You told Norris he was heart-bound to you and waited for dead men shoes."

Aunt Nan bowed her head and tightly clasped her hands before her. "I spoke without thinking, Aunt. I spoke through the hurt of knowing my husband no longer loves me, or of the times I was left lonely for his company. Or alone in his company. I spoke my foolish words to Norris because I no longer have my Harry. I am unwanted and discarded—so much so I am brought to this place." She turned to both her aunt and Mrs. Cosyns. "But perchance my husband is only testing me. Surely he will soon call me back to him and all will be forgiven?"

Kate wiped away tears. Even Mrs. Cosyns and Lady Boleyn seemed moved at last to compassion, and decision. They got up.

"'It has been a long night," Lady Boleyn said. "Niece, we have talked enough, and you must rest." She reached out a hand. "Come, Nan, come and let me help you to bed."

Reaching for her aunt's hand, Aunt Nan stood and

swayed. Lady Boleyn put her arm around her and turned to Kate and Meg. She snapped, "Help me."

Kate and Meg, together with Lady Boleyn, walked Aunt Nan to the bed.

Aunt Nan, her face etched with despair, sat on its edge, seemingly unaware as they removed her gable and her gown. At last in her shift, she lay in bed. Rolling to face away from them, she curled up, half-hugging her knees to her. Her thin shoulders shook and shook.

Kate met Lady Boleyn's conflicted gaze. Her heart drumming in her ears, Kate sought desperately for words, words with real substance, with real strength—words that would batter down the wall that stood between her two aunts. She wanted Lady Boleyn to realize she judged Aunt Nan too harshly. But like a drawbridge drawn up under attack, Lady Boleyn broke her contact. With a shake of her head and a tightening of her mouth, she hurried away, sitting beside Mrs. Cosyns. Both women turned their heads towards Aunt Nan's bed.

Meg came to stand beside her. "Lady Boleyn is right. The night has been long. Why not you and I try to get some sleep?"

"But the Queen—" Kate's desperation pushed her a step towards her aunt.

Meg grabbed Kate's arm and pulled her back. "Leave her for now." She led Kate away. "We cannot help her if we wear ourselves out by refusing rest when we can get it. Who knows what the morrow will bring? Come, Kate, let's sleep while we may."

Early the next day, they learnt of Uncle George's arrest.

"I am very glad," Aunt Nan said, "that we will both be so nigh together." She paused, averting her face to the shadows. "When I think of our early lives, it was I who always followed after George. Now, at the end, it seems my sweet brother follows me." She reached for Kate's hand. "What do I do with you? I had hoped your uncle would have arranged your safe conduct back to your mother." Her face became tense with thought. "Perchance Parker can make the necessary arrangements."

Kate bolted up. "I will not go, Aunt."

"What mean you? Am I not still your Queen?"

Kate came to her and sank to her knees. "You are my Queen, and I am yours to command, but pray, Aunt, not in this. Do not send me away."

She laid her head on her aunt's lap then, breathing in her scent of rosewater.

Silent, Aunt Nan stroked her hair before letting out a long sigh. "Very well, if you really wish it. I just pray you won't live to regret it." She sighed again. "I do not see any happy end to this."

The fifteenth of May—the day of the trial. The women brought out costly gowns for the Queen to pick from. She selected one, discarded it, selected another, and so it continued until she turned to her women with her finest gown—made for happier times.

Her women robed her—kirtle over smock, gown over kirtle. At last, they finished and stood aside. With her combed hair falling loose and straight down her back, Aunt Nan looked every inch the Queen of England prepared for ceremony. Kate bit down upon her trembling lip. This day witnessed a ceremony in which no other Queen of England had ever played a part.

Kate gathered everything she needed to do her aunt's hair. When she returned, Aunt Nan sat on a chair, waiting for her to begin.

Dividing and plaiting her aunt's long hair, Kate then pinned the plaits tight around her head. Kate finished and wiped the tears from her face. Her aunt's hair looked a crown.

Kate had expected to be left in the chamber to wait for the Queen's return from the trial. But her aunt asked her to come.

"I need you there," Aunt Nan said. "I need you to know the truth of this day to tell my daughter." Her aunt embraced her. "I am proud of you, Kate. You have kept up your courage day by day. But I must warn you. Do not expect justice. 'Tis gone too far for that."

Kingston and his guards took them a huge chamber close to the apartments where they had been placed at the Tower. Despite its size, it was full to overflowing with hundreds and hundreds of men sitting in high stands all around the room, the judges at one end. Norfolk and Suffolk, both known enemies of the Queen, sat amongst the judges. Encircled by men and close to the Queen, Kate shuddered. *Is this how an animal feels? An animal cast in a pit and baited for entertainment?*

Norfolk sat right above them. Ignoring Aunt Nan's efforts

to catch his eye, he kept his face stony, like one belonging to a statue and not a man. Kate's heart swelled, squeezing her throat until she could barely breathe. *Why does our uncle Norfolk hate my aunt?* An image came to mind of him at the door to the Queen's chamber, and it seemed she heard him again cry out, "The King is dead." Even if he believed his words, the way he brought the news to her aunt was vile and cruel. Had he meant for Aunt Nan to miscarry her son?

The Royal lion rampant hung from rafters at the end of the chamber. Now and then, the banner flapped and fluttered in a draught—just one of the many reasons for Kate to shiver.

Yet another thing caught Kate's attention: a man in the stands, his face stark and white, and haunted. Kate turned to Meg Lee in question, giving a slight gesture in his direction. "The Earl of Northumberland," Meg whispered.

Kate knew the story from her mother. Aunt Nan had once hoped to wed him, before the wooing of the King.

The trial began with the reading of the charges. Treason. Adultery. Incest. Each word made Kate tremble; her chest hurt from holding her breath. But Aunt Nan remained stoic and calm. She just straightened her shoulders and lifted her chin—a woman ready to make battle against ludicrous charges. Her courage strengthened Kate. And her pride in her aunt; it became like a shield to withstand the day.

The claims became even more preposterous. Kate bit back her own denial when they claimed Aunt Nan had committed adultery during the months of her last pregnancy. *How could that be? How could she have been unfaithful then?* With her aunt often ill because of pregnancy, Kate was amongst the group of her women who had rarely left her side during that time.

Aunt Nan's mouth opened as if to laugh when the court official read out that her women had hidden Smeaton in a closet in her bedchamber, bringing him to her when she asked for her nightly marmalade.

Kate swayed, as if tottering on the edge of a sticky jar of the stuff. She seemed to fall, fall, fall. Like a helpless insect, she, too, would not be able to escape. More and more, the trial became a congealing mess of deceit and lies and plots.

Aunt Nan stayed calm and rebutted the accusations, one by one. She told them the men had never been her lovers, and that she was the loyal and loving wife of the King. Her voice carried strong in the chamber as she said that she never plotted the King's death, or promised Norris she would marry him if free to do so.

"Of course," Aunt Nan said, "my brother Rochford visits me in my chamber. We speak together every day, but I swear to God, there is no evil in our relationship, just the bond of brother and sister."

Around the chamber, many stern, pitiless faces altered to admiration—few men seemed untouched by Aunt Nan's words.

But the time arrived for the jury to come to its decision. Short minutes passed before Norfolk stood up to call out the guilty verdict. The ground opened at Kate's feet, at his words "...to be either burnt or beheaded—to be decided at the discretion of our merciful King." Again she fell. And fell and fell into an abyss.

Aunt Nan stirred and straightened. Kate padded closer to her. "God," her aunt said softly, as if simply in prayer, "you know if I have merited this death."

Men watched her, as if they waited to see what she would

do next.

A loud thud echoed in the chamber and started a commotion amongst the judges. The Earl of Northumberland was carried out, his body limp and senseless. Aunt Nan inhaled a sharp breath, her face struggling with composure. As they removed the Earl in silence, she clasped her hands before her.

The Duke of Norfolk stamped his staff to return the room to order. "Do you have any more to say?" he asked Aunt Nan.

She met his eyes and shook her head. "I am ready for death," she said. "I only regret that innocent persons must lose their lives because of me. I am a faithful wife to the King. My only sin against the King has been my jealousy and lack of humility. I think you know well the reason why you have condemned me to be other than that which led you to this judgement."

She bent her head and cleared her throat, shifting in her seat. "I willingly give up my titles to the King who gave them."

The abyss was without end. Seeking a handhold, Kate balled her hands. She feared the moment she lost her last remnant of control. She wouldn't be able to stop crying. Meg came to her then. She clasped her hand and shook her head.

Her aunt stood, curtsied to the judges. Without another word, she made her way out of the chamber. The Constable of the Tower followed close behind her and, behind him, the royal executioner. He held the sharp edge of his axe towards Aunt Nan.

Kate's heart drummed, a beat that seemed to count out his heavy steps. She followed with the other women. She trembled, feeling so cold, so despairing. All her fear had become a reality. Death. It had come to death.

Death. It had come to death.

Kate wrote in her journal that night. Her tears spilled over, spattering the parchment. Aunt Nan condemned—and now Uncle George.

> Father Parker came and told us. My good and most beloved uncle defied the King in speaking up for his defense. Uncle George so impressed his judges that there had been some hope that he would be acquitted. Father Parker thought the judges wanted to be merciful after bringing down the sentence upon Aunt Nan.
>
> That foul dog Cromwell put an end to that hope. He had a letter signed by my uncle's wife. The lies she told! How could she say she had witnessed the incestuous relationship of my uncle and aunt? She also wrote that she heard them speak of the King's lack of virility in the bedchamber. I have never heard my aunt and uncle speak of such matters.
>
> I weep. I cannot stop weeping. But what use are my tears? Uncle George! He is condemned to a traitor's death, to be

hanged, drawn and quartered. My aunt has not stopped crying since hearing the news. I must go to her now so we can pray together that the King will allow my good uncle the mercy of the axe.

21

Kate dreamt. She dreamt of Cranmer.

"I am a good man," he said. "Good, but imperfect." He smiled sadly at her. "We are all imperfect."

"But are you not a man of God?" she asked.

He shook his head a little and rumbled out a deep laugh. "Do you think men of God are perfect? They are men like other men. I know my sins."

The dream changed, and he wept in a beautiful garden. All around him, roses bloomed. He gestured to them. "Kate, another archbishop, a man who served men rather than the God he vowed his life to, planted the red and white roses in celebration, in tribute—to honour and mark the joining of two noble houses, Lancaster and Tudor. He had much to do with their joining. Look at them now. So many roses. See how the wind blows?"

All around them, red and white petals swirled.

Cranmer laughed a laugh that seemed more like a sob. "See how the white and red marry? So gently, so tenderly." He rubbed at his face. "None of this belonged to that marriage of long ago; none belongs to this marriage I weep for now."

The old man stood there, looking left and right, seeming uncaring of the tears running down his face. "See the petals, Kate. See the blood."

The petals became droplets of blood that showered on them. They dropped on her face and hands, and soiled her clothes. Her stomach heaved.

A canon boomed above her head—a crack like thunder that belied the sunlit day. Cranmer raised his head, and then bowed it again in prayer.

"What does it mean?" she asked.

"What does it mean? It means the same for you as it does for me. Death has come for someone we love."

She began to cry.

He looked at her with eyes of a man who hates himself. "Say it, Kate."

"Say what, my Lord?"

"Say I am traitor, a traitor in my compliance; a traitor in my silence; nay, worse, a Judas—nay, far worse, a Judas sheep."

"I do not understand." Kate twisted towards the garden path, wanting to run away, wanting to wake up. But the dream kept her in its grip.

"You will understand soon. Pray, do not hate me." He fell to his knees, his hands coming together in prayer. "I could not help but give her hope. I hoped, too. Oh why, God, oh why? Is my inaction that of the devil? I am only a man, an imperfect man. I must stay on to continue our work. That is what she wants, and for that, I must live."

In the dream garden, Kate smelled her aunt's perfume, and Cranmer looked around in confusion, blinking at the bright sun. A breeze stirred the roses into a gentle dance.

What does he see? What is it? There, near the roses. A shadow? An apparition? Kate hears the laughter of one she knows so well—and the gaiety of one going home.

Kate woke, her pillow soaked with her own tears. Yet—while she could make no sense of it—comfort stirred in her heart.

Confusing fragments of the dream remained with Kate all morning: red and white roses, petals that turned into blood, a weeping Cranmer. She wanted to talk about it to someone, but Aunt Nan and Lady Meg were the only two people close enough for conversation. Strain and worry marked both women. So she kept silent while her thoughts continued to circle around what could have caused her dream. Was it because the Archbishop had stayed away from her aunt? He had even been absent during the trial. Remembering all the times Cranmer and her aunt spent together, heads close, utterly engrossed over a new book recently brought to the Queen by Latimer or discussing church reform, day by day Kate had expected him to come, out of friendship, or in his role as her priest. But later that day, her dream seemed a herald of his visit.

Kate was with her aunt when Cranmer entered the apartment at the Tower as if a cowering, whipped dog, searching the chamber until he located the Queen. Even after he bowed, he still seemed unable to stand to his full height. He blinked, straightened and then quickened his pace as he came closer.

Aunt Nan put aside her book and rose from her chair. She smiled and offered her hand. Cranmer clasped it and bowed, keeping his forehand on her hand before he stood. His shoulders shook. He seemed to Kate like a man holding himself up by just a thread.

Releasing his hand, Aunt Nan gestured to a nearby empty seat. "Sit down, Tom." She returned to hers, cocked her head and considered him with a laugh. "What to do—another long face. What is it, Tom? Have you more bad news for me." She laughed again. "Besides the old news of yesterday?"

Easing his aged body into the chair, he lifted bleak, red-rimmed eyes. "Pray, could I be alone with you, Your Grace? The King has sent me to hear your confession."

Kate rose on her knees, preparing to go, but her aunt waved her down.

"Confession, Tom?" Aunt Nan laughed with a note of hysteria. She covered her mouth and turned towards the lattice window. Its shadow cast a criss-cross pattern on her face and form. She gripped the armrests of her chair. "I have nothing to hide from my niece. I have asked her to be by my side until the end, so she can tell my daughter how I died."

Kate sat straighter, ready to do as her aunt desired. Duty and responsibility seemed so heavy for a heartbeat, but she thanked God she could do this for Aunt Nan. There was much she would one day tell Bess.

Aunt Nan spoke again. "Thomas, do you wish to hear again the sins I spoke of last time we met? I swear on my soul, what I confessed to you last time remains exactly the same to what I would confess to you now. Nay—there is one thing I must add. I have committed the sin of despair since coming to this place, and it has broken me—" She paused for a moment, her fingers at her mouth. "Despair that my husband, the King, desires to have me dead and branded a whore."

Cranmer shifted towards her. "My Queen, you must believe as I do that the King is convinced of your guilt. He is full of deep sorrow—inflicted in adversity like Job in his grief."

Aunt Nan's eyes widened. "Do you really believe that, Tom? That the King in his heart believes I was ever unfaithful to him? More importantly, do you believe it—you who has listened to my heart and soul? What say you? Am I wanton in thought, word or deed, a woman who would bed with her own brother in her lust?"

He shook and bent his head. He raised such a dismayed, tragic face that Kate started. "Madam, I wrote to the King what I believe. I have never had a better opinion of a woman than of you. I know the love you bear to God and His Gospel. My Queen, I believe in your innocence and come here bound to you, as I have been for always."

She smiled. "I thank you for your faithfulness. It takes great courage to speak the truth to my husband. So how did he reply? What did he say when you told him you believe I am innocent of the charges that have brought me here?"

"Your Grace—" Cranmer squirmed in his seat and lowered his head again. "I spoke only briefly to the King. Cromwell was close by. Forgive me, I did not dare ask the King to speak to him alone. I do not think it would have mattered in any case. I have never seen the King like this. He brooks no argument, no discussion and no attempt to gainsay his determination to see this matter ended. Forgive me, Your Grace, but I need to tread carefully if I am to be of any help to you." His Adam's apple going up and down in his long neck, Cranmer licked his lips. "Madam, the case they built against you none dare knock down."

Aunt Nan sighed. "Aye, 'tis the case Cromwell built. He knows his work well and has had long to conspire against me."

Her aunt's hand rested on her shoulder. "He used so many of my friends against me, but at least he left you alone, Kate."

Putting her hand over her aunt's, she remembered that night—it seemed so long ago—when Cromwell had tested her loyalty, threatening to tell her aunt what Kate wanted him to believe—that she had met with a man. As if that, or anything, would make her disloyal to Aunt Nan.

Taking her hand away from Kate's shoulder, Aunt Nan sat back in her chair. "I find it hard to forgive how they used a death bed confession that none now can refute, or twisted the words of Lady Elizabeth. She could not have said what they claimed—that she heard a man's voice in my bedchamber."

Kate started. "Aunt Nan, it must have been that day when Lady Margaret and Lord Howard were in your chamber! Lady Elizabeth heard them laughing together."

Aunt Nan's eyes glowed with sudden tears. "So she told them that, did she, without even asking me for an explanation? I would have vouched for my friend's loyalty."

Cranmer leaned forward. "You must not doubt my loyalty, my Queen! I swear to you I am your servant."

Aunt Nan considered him. "Thomas, I do not doubt if matters were different, that would be the case. But this time, my friend, we must face how the world must be. If you are loyal to me, you commit treason against the King. I am a dead woman; I know this. My only hope is to be soon with Jesus." She looked away. "Five innocent men, one my own brother, die soon because of me. 'Tis my heart's great desire that you are not one of them. We have long worked together in God's service. Now you must work alone and continue what we began."

Cranmer swallowed again. "When I spoke to the King, he promised to consider another solution. Madam, if you agree to an annulment of your marriage, the King said he would think of allowing you to live out your life in a nunnery."

Aunt Nan stared. "Annul my marriage?" Now it was she who swallowed hard. "But what of my child? What of Elizabeth?"

"You must remember, my Queen—you who will always be my Queen—of the arguments used to persuade the Princess of Wales to take this road. Your marriage was made in good faith. I promise you I will ensure your daughter's rights are protected."

Aunt Nan sucked in her bottom lip. She turned her face away before she spoke slowly. "If my marriage is annulled, would this not mean that my brother and friends are saved from the executioner? I cannot be an adulterous wife if I am not a wife at all."

Cranmer lowered his head; he plucked anxiously at his robes.

Aunt Nan rounded on him. "Why are you silent, Thomas? You are not only my chaplain, but also the King's. Surely you must know the answer."

He stirred, leaning closer. "Dear Madam, I wish I could tell you what you want to hear. Alas, I cannot. All I can say is the King has given me some hope that by annulling your marriage you may yet live."

Aunt Nan lifted her fine eyebrows. "In a nunnery, did you say?" She laughed. "No doubt Cromwell is busy ensuring that there is no nunnery left in England for the King to put me in."

"My Queen, the King would not have said this unless it was in his mind to act on it."

Aunt Nan nodded and toyed with her marriage ring. "Aye, you're right. If he spoke of it, there is hope he spoke true." She lifted her face. "And what are the grounds for this annulment?"

He reddened. "The King's relationship with your sister."

All colour fled from her aunt's cheeks. "My sister?"

"Madam, as the head of the English church, the King

disregards the dispensation given to him by the Pope to marry you. His prior relationship with your sister makes your relationship with the King a sin and against the teachings of the Bible."

Aunt Nan laughed and laughed until she held her stomach. "So my husband uses Leviticus again. And you, Tom, what did you say to this?"

Cranmer bowed head and slumped his shoulders. "Madam, without a dispensation, the King's marriage to you must be deemed invalid." He raised a white face, his eyes blinking. "But it was made in good faith, thus your daughter is legitimate."

"Around and around we go, and life twirls us in its dance." Aunt Nan sighed. "As long as my daughter's rights are protected, I care not if my marriage to the King is annulled. But pray, Thomas, make him realise he cannot bring men to face the executioner's axe without just cause. If the marriage is annulled, there is no adultery."

"I vow I will talk to the King. And you, madam, would you want life for yourself if offered, even if it meant you were never free again?"

She smiled. "You said I'd live out my days in a nunnery? After the last months, I would be content to take the veil. God has never forsaken me. What does it matter where I dedicate my life to Him, as long as I can have a chance to be a mother to my daughter? The King may one day regain his kind, generous heart and allow me to write her letters." She turned her head, her eyes filling with dreams. "Perchance when she is grown, she will come and see her old mother— and bring her own children, too."

Cranmer smiled. "That is what I pray for also. I know you

may find a life of prayer and contemplation difficult, but I know you well enough to think such a life would only deepen your already deep commitment with God." He leaned forward, his hand on his knee. "I vow to you that the nunnery will never be short of books for you to read, and I, as your shepherd, will not leave you to languish alone."

Outside, a church bell tolled. Cranmer turned, listening, his mouth drooping down again. Gingerly, he stood and bowed low. "Madam, I'm afraid my time has run its course. I must depart before they come for me and anger the King with news of his disobedient priest. One thing we do not need now is an angry King who refuses to listen to me."

Aunt Nan arose, too. Walking over to him, she took his arm and stood on tiptoes to kiss his winkled cheek. Cranmer blushed and smiled shyly at her.

"Let me walk you to the door, my friend." She threaded her arm through his.

Arm in arm, they walked together slowly. It seemed to Kate that they wanted to hold on to this moment forever. At the door, Aunt Nan embraced and kissed Cranmer again. "Farewell, Thomas. Farewell."

His mouth moved, then he swallowed. Abruptly, he turned on his heel and left the chamber without another word.

Cranmer wasn't the only the man of God who came to support the Queen. Kate grew to love Mathew Parker in these days. He not only comforted her aunt, but always made time to speak to her, too. He also brought them news of what happened outside the Tower. Often, it was news that left

Kate sick at heart and utterly defeated.

Parker told them how the family of Francis Weston, one of the five men accused of adultery with the Queen, offered the King a ransom of 100,000 marks that would likely beggar the family if only he would be merciful and allow Weston to live and go free. When Parker told them about the loud mutterings of high to low, and that few believed in the Queen's guilt, only that the King wished to rid himself of one wife to get himself another, Kate wanted to find somewhere to curl up and close her eyes and ears. Pretend that none of this was happening. This man, her father, seemed determined to murder her beloved aunt. Her stomach just ached and ached.

After hearing Parker out, Aunt Nan raised a hand as if protecting herself, and Kate leaned closer to her. Her aunt said quietly, "My husband has always been good at believing in what he wishes to believe."

Parker scowled. "How can he believe when only Mark Smeaton has admitted any guilt? The rumour is rife that Cromwell had him tortured, and even now I hear he is in chains. None can see him, even I, a man of God. He is a broken man without comfort."

Aunt Nan clasped her hands, her knuckles becoming white. "I pity him. No doubt Cromwell has promised him an easy death for his grave falsehood." She laughed a little. "Always Smeaton's great desire was to find his place amongst his betters. Now he has his wish—in death." She sighed, her hand at her throat. "What news of my father and mother?"

Parker pulled at his upper lip. "Your mother has spoken to me. She has no doubt about your innocence and prays every day for your release."

Kate brushed tears away. An image of her grandmother flashed in her mind—so aged, so worn with worry—and she heard her grandmother's voice, her desperate, hopeless prayer.

With a deep breath, Aunt Nan rubbed her eyes, too. "Oh my poor mother. How will she cope? She will die for sorrow, her loving heart broken over George and I. Tell her I pray to God to keep her safe, and I am honoured to call myself her daughter." She raised her head. "You say nothing of my lord father."

Parker brought his hands together as if in prayer. "His loyalty is with the King."

Aunt Nan sat unmoving, silent. Then she shrugged. "I knew that when you told me he offered himself as one of my jurors. I could expect none other from him." Her gaze alighted on Kate and she seemed to speak only to her. "What else can he do? All is lost for George and me. If he aligned himself with me, he, too, would be in this place. I do not blame my father for choosing survival."

Parker nodded. "No doubt, but knowing that is one thing, living it is another. It must hurt you to see your father care so for his own skin when it betrays his own children. I, for one, am shocked at his heartlessness."

Aunt Nan reached for his hand. "Your tender heart is one turned to God, Matthew. My husband would likely not agree, but serving God is different to serving the crown." She rubbed her temple, her fingers slipping for a moment under her headdress. "That calls for ambition and to be pragmatic. Even at the cost of your closest kin." She blinked away tears. "Since my arrest I have had time to think and pray for forgiveness of all my sins." Aunt Nan smiled slightly. "I have sinned much in my life. But I cannot blame my father when I also shared his sins of arrogance and ambition. He is in the world, while I will soon be out of it."

22

A man stood as if straddling the world, legs apart like rooted tree trunks, his broad hand planted on padded, tilted hip. Rubies, diamonds, polished gold glinted on his thick, long fingers and flexed thumb. Impassive slanted eyes—too small for such a wide, heavy face—stared out from a puffy, unsmiling, bearded mask, the mask of a tyrant king.

The wind blew a trumpet call and thunder boomed a cannon roar. Lightning blazed bright across the night sky. In the pulsating light, shadows fluttered about like windblown autumn leaves. In a purple haze, one by one, the fragments gathered shape and substance. A movement. A breath. A sigh.

Uncovered, two bowed heads brushed against each other, mingling together hair of raven black and fiery red. The lovers kissed, then drew away—the man beardless, handsome, in his prime. The woman, much younger, looked at him with love, and in surrender. A surrender surmounting fear.

No matter what happened now, she was committed to the end.

A small white terrier whined and jumped, trying to get onto the woman's lap. Defeated, the dog whimpered again, pawing at her black velvet gown. The woman laughed suddenly. "You forget yourself, young sir," she said. "Show your respect for the King."

The man guffawed. Seizing her, he kissed her again, releasing her lips with a groan. Cheek against cheek, he murmured into her hair, "Nan, Nan, Nan. I could ask the same of you." He kissed her again, tightening his hold.

Pushing him away in play, Nan whispered, "Harry, not now. Not yet." She touched his cheek and smiled. "Soon we shall be wed. Soon we will always be together, and I'll be your wife, your helpmeet till death. I vow this to you."

Leaning against him, she picked up her lute, plucked its string, and sang. An exquisite, haunting voice—pitched to touch the heart. He watched her, silent and proud. She smiled, her hand resting on the lute, stilling its strings. "Sing with me."

He laughed at her command and inhaled a breath. Two melodic voices dipped and

soared, dipped and soared again, blending in
harmony, perfection. Eden before the fall.

Kate bolted up wide-awake in her trundle bed. Around her everyone slept—even her aunt. Trembling, she lay down again, but without any hope of sleep.

The next evening, Kate nestled against Aunt Nan's knee. Flickering fire and candlelight netted them in amber glow. Shifting on her cushion in discomfort, Kate bent her head and lowered her gaze, trying not to think about the night and how it walled her in. How it gave her dreams that frightened her. The days were upsetting enough without fearing to sleep. She twisted towards her aunt. For a long time now—too long—Aunt Nan had sat on her stool without moving, without speaking.

Since the great outpouring of grief when her brother went to the block, she had been like this. Even the news following shortly afterwards of the annulment of her marriage to the King had not stirred her.

Cold fingers of air poked Kate's back, her bladder tingled and twinged. Shivering, she gathered her shawl over her shift and turned towards the darkness that hid the bed and the clothes coffer. Should she get her woollen cloak? Within the circle of light was Aunt Nan's workbasket. Draped over one side was the sleeve of a child's night shift. Aunt Nan had finished it tonight, putting the last touches to the beautiful needlework that embroidered the edges of sleeves, neck and hem with scarlet thread. Reminded of her little cousin, Kate murmured without thinking, "Do you think they'll tell Bess?"

Aunt Nan jerked and then cried out in agony—a primeval cry that caused Kate's heart to thump harder against her chest. Men forced to watch their entrails burnt before their eyes—did they cry out like her aunt? Cry out so the very stones would hear and remember forever?

Aunt Nan bent over and pressed her white handkerchief to her mouth in her efforts to regain control. She turned to Kate, tears rolling down her cheeks. Once more, Kate nestled against her. She swallowed and licked away her own tears from her mouth

Over and over, Aunt Nan twisted her handkerchief until it tore. The ripping sound made Kate start and wince. Her aunt straightened. "Bess is not even three."

Kate strained to hear her soft words.

"How will she remember me? God help me, will she remember me at all?"

The heartsore misery of Aunt Nan sliced asunder Kate's fragile control. She leant her wet cheek on her aunt's limp hand. "Aunt—"

What can I say to comfort her? Was it possible to give her solace at all?

The slow tread of footsteps crunched outside the chamber. Meg, returning from the privy, froze, seemingly aware of her aunt's despair. She tossed back her head, like a horse smelling the approach of storm or blood. Smoothing down the sides of her gown, Meg walked forward again, grim and determined. "Pray tell," she said, in a voice forced, cheerful, "whatever is this? Didn't we agree to cast aside melancholy tonight?"

Candlelight struck Aunt Nan's face. Black hair combed

back from her forehead, her eyes glowed as she attempted a smile. "Kate asked about Bess. Forgive me, but it undid me."

Wiping away new tears, Kate could barely breathe. "I promise you, your kin will not let Bess forget you. I vow I'll tell my cousin all she needs to know about her mother."

Aunt Nan touched her cheek. "Kate." Her laughter belled and cracked. "Almost six months at court and still innocent. Still thinking life gives us what we want."

Meg dragged her stool closer, bent forward, spreading out plump fingers over her thighs. "Now, Nan, Kate may be young, but she means what she says."

Aunt Nan bounded up and half swirled one way, then the other. Her wide eyes wild, haunted, she seemed like a doe hunted beyond endurance now facing the dogs and her doom. Kate swallowed, shifting on her knees. *Does she think she has nowhere else to run?*

As if in pain, arms tight across her breasts, her aunt spoke fast, forcing out the words. "Harry will strip my child of all that reminds him of me."

Meg's stool toppled to the floor with a resounding thud. Gripping Aunt Nan's shoulders, Meg turned her around. "For that to happen he would need to destroy his Kingdom and build it over. England is made anew because of you. We're no longer puppets to the papacy. It was you who set us free."

Aunt Nan broke away, brushing away more tears. "Politics? Do you think I care one jot about politics on this night of nights? Politics is what cast me in this cesspool." She wrung her hands. "But Bess—what of her? My child will be motherless, without my protection."

She wrapped her arms around her body and dropped to her knees. She laughed and laughed. Her raw, ugly hysteria made Kate wish to curl up and hide. *Anywhere. Anywhere but here.* Shadows fluttered in the dark recesses of the chamber. They took on demon shapes, reaching for her, for Aunt Nan, for the others, seeking souls.

Aunt Nan hiccupped, and began speaking again. "I'll be well and truly dead before the sun sets on the morrow. I'll never see another daybreak." Standing like a sleepwalker, she returned to her stool, taking Kate's hand, and then Meg's. Feeling her aunt's cold hand tremble, Kate tightened her hold.

"Forgive me. I have much to be grateful for; I do not deserve you both. Thank you for wanting to be with me ... and not letting me face death alone." Aunt Nan's trembling fingers lifted Kate's chin. "You're young, Kate. So young. Do you truly desire to remain with me to the very end, to witness a bloody death? I would not blame you if you changed your mind."

Aunt Nan's eyes and teeth glittered from the light of the nearby candle. "Meg and I have shared the good and bad since girlhood. I love her almost as much as I love your mother." She gave a little laugh, and tightened her grip on Kate's hand. "Tell my sister she had the right of it. Don't concern yourself over a King's love; just bed with him, wait until his passion is spent, and bow off the stage for a freer life." Letting Kate loose, she stared at her shaking hands. "Mary did not sink in the quicksand of ambition and pride, or cause our sweet brother to be put so horribly to death." She inhaled and exhaled a ragged breath. "I digress. But you, niece, you've seen enough heartache because of me. 'Tis enough Meg sees me to the end."

Kate sat straighter and shook her head with such fervency it hurt. "You'll not make me change my mind. I'm of your blood. I'll not fail you or make you ashamed."

Her heart stopped, frozen by the thought of the coming day. She tried to laugh, like her brave-hearted aunt, who often laughed at the whims of fate. Even in the Tower, she laughed, waiting for death. Kate knotted her hands together. "I cannot lie and say I'll not weep on the scaffold. But I pray to God I will be brave and do what needs to be done."

Drawn back to the darkness, Kate told herself there were no demons there, only shifting shadows. Why fear fleeting shadows when the darkness lay within, darkness that could seed a harvest of evil?

On a nearby stool sat the book Madge had given to her. Before the sun set on another day, Kate had flicked through the pages, wondering if she should write. But no words had come. Now they did. She wanted to write that vigilance was not only for the night, but also for the day. She wanted to write that during the day, it was too easy to slide into stagnation, rather than face hard truths or the light and dark within ourselves. She rubbed at her face. She had learnt so much in her months with her aunt. But the most important lesson was this: to not let her own darkness flourish and overwhelm her by refusing to look in the mirror at her true self and recognise when she did evil.

Kate swallowed back bile. *Evil like the King's... her father. God forgive him.* He believed the lies because it was easier for him than to make do with two daughters as his heirs. He killed the man within him who loved her aunt and sacrificed his soul for the sake of his crown. He told himself it was for England and that God desired it, not him. Taking a deep breath, she turned to her aunt and vowed, "I pray God to honour you and to be a good witness to your unjust death."

Aunt Nan smiled with bitterness and put her hands around her neck. "My neck is so little, my husband's well paid headsman will have an easy job of it. Think you what history will call me in years to come: Queen Anne lack-a-head."

She pealed with uncontrolled laughter, laughing until she held her stomach. Meg stood, poured water into a goblet, and then put her hand on Aunt Nan's thin shoulder. Kate shivered. The days of imprisonment had stripped more flesh from her aunt's bones.

"Drink, dear fool." Meg's voice shook with emotion. She cleared her throat. "Stop this fuss before you make yourself ill."

With exhausted obedience, Aunt Nan sipped and then wiped her mouth. She swished the goblet's contents. "I lost my courage when they told me my execution was postponed until tomorrow. Meg, I was tempted to beg you to bring me the escape of poison, rather than risk breaking down on the scaffold."

"Nan!" Meg stood there, her mouth open.

Aunt Nan smiled. "Like our Kate here, I'll speak no falsehoods, not so close to meeting my maker. While I own to many sins, none but my pride, jealousy and lack of humility bring me here. God knows I am innocent of the evil they charge me with." She clasped Meg's hand. "Aye, I thought of poison, but only for a moment. The last thing I can give my daughter is the knowledge her mother made a good death. As long as I remember that, I'll have no trouble dying well." Aunt Nan chuckled softly. "The King, my *dearly beloved* husband, has been ever constant in his career of advancing me. From private gentlewoman he made me Marchioness, from Marchioness a Queen, and now he honours me by giving my innocence the crown of martyrdom. No other Queen of England could say the same."

Kate averted her face, struggling not to weep. Her aunt's lute leaned forlornly and forgotten against a footstool. She got up and brought it to her. "Will you not play?"

Aunt Nan stared at the instrument. "Do you really wish it?" she whispered. She twined her hands in her lap, as she didn't dare touch it.

Kate swam in grief, but refused to drown. "I love it when you play." Ignoring the smart of fresh tears, she swallowed hard. "Pray, could you not sing for us tonight?"

With a sigh, Aunt Nan took the lute. She swallowed and spoke hoarsely. "My beloved husband once said my voice belonged to an angel. Little did I realise he believed it so well that he would ensure a place for me in the Heavenly choir."

Meg enclosed Aunt Nan's hand in hers. "Don't think of the King. My brother Tom and you played so many songs together. Why not play and sing one of those tonight?"

"You told the truth before? Tom's safe?"

"I heard the news from Father's own lips. He worked every day to secure Tom's release." Meg laughed. "You know my brother; all he has to do is write a poem for the world to love him. Even Cromwell cares for him too well to feed his fine head to the ravens."

"I'm glad of it." Aunt Nan shifted the lute in hands. "Tom shared enough of my woes without sharing my enemies too. He warned me I'd find myself bailed up by the dogs one day." She smiled slightly. "I always thought I could dance myself out of any trap set for me. But this year.... When I lost my babe, my son, I lost all heart to dance. By the time I looked around, the time for dancing was over." Her tears welled again and she lowered her head. "I wish my brother had never taken it upon himself to dance this dance with me, nor the four good men who died bravely because they were my friends."

"Cromwell knew their loyalty to you." Meg's face stilled. "Leave any of them alive with you dead and Cromwell would have been murdered in his bed before the month was out. My brother could have easily drawn the same short straw. Father said he had a bad time convincing Tom not to seek out his own death, or vengeance. Father reminded him that his son is the same age as our Kate—old enough to wield a sword, old enough to dance at the end of the rope. The Wyatts have long served the Tudors well. Brother mouthed the words of gratitude that Cromwell wanted to hear." Meg returned her attention to Aunt Nan. "He'll be released, Nan ... soon. Father tells me that Tom is heartbroken."

Her head still lowered, Aunt Nan brushed gentle fingers against the lute's strings, rustling its notes. "I've always made your brother heartsore. Pray, when you give Tom my *Book of Hours*, make certain he reads my message straight away. I know he will grieve for me, but I pray my words will comfort him. And, my child.... Don't let her cry. Tell her she was my greatest consolation and joy. Nothing else matters but her. I'd do it all again—aye, even face another dawn break knowing death waits for me before the new day is old—for my daughter. Oh, if only I could hold my Bess one more time."

Church bells tolled. Without saying one word, they huddled in closer. Utterly still, an unsung dirge of silence wound a knot of comfort around them. The twelfth hour struck.

Aunt Nan moved first, going back to her stool. "So it

comes to this—the last day of my life. I should not leave you afraid, my Kate. Death comes for us all. I spoke the truth that I am not unhappy to die." She smiled with grimness. "I took the crown life offered me only to find it came at a hefty cost. Do I regret it now?" She paused for a moment, her thin face tensed in thought. "I regret what it cost others, but for myself, I cannot see what other choice I had but to follow this road that has brought me here."

She turned to Meg. "It means much to me that you believe my life did more good than bad. And how can I regret my daughter?" Aunt Nan shook her head. "At the end, I cannot even regret Harry. He loved me once, and I will go to my death loving him, his true wife. How many women can boast of a love like ours once was—a love that shook the world?" She turned to Kate. "I tell you truly, child, that is the love that counts in the end. And I have loved, really, truly loved. Tell my daughter that."

Aunt Nan straightened her shoulders. "I've my courage back. I will face my death with a good heart. What have I to be afraid of, after all? God knows my sins, my great imperfections, but He also knows my heart. These last years I tried to do right by England and its people, even if they hated me and believed me arrogant." She laughed grimly. "And I was. I thought I could be like Esther, but I did not save my people from the evil of Cromwell's plans. Esther was wiser than I—she knew the rules and how to play them to win." She smiled. "But at least I have learnt humility at the end. I have even stopped hating Cromwell. He will overplay his hand and find himself in this place before too long. I suspect he will have more regrets than me."

Aunt Nan brought her hand up to her head and shifted

in her seat. "Geoffrey Chaucer once wrote:

Tragedy means a certain kind of story,
As old books tell, of those who fell from glory,
People that stood in great prosperity
And were cast down from their high degree
Into calamity, and so they die."

She sighed. "So they die." She bent her head. "I always prided myself on my intelligence, yet this is the reward for my vainglory." She smiled tenderly at Kate. "When you're young, you think yourself immortal—life is forever. You can do anything, and do it again and again without hurt. Now I'm at the end of my road. I'm wiser now. I know life is uncertain and that we can never take anything for granted.

"Nay, I tell you true, I'm ready for death. The worst of it is to die at the hand of someone I love so dearly; to know the fire that burnt between my husband and I is but ash to him. It must be ash if I am here. Mayhap, the fire was too powerful after all and, by its heat, burnt itself out. I also told you the truth when I said I have no regrets. To regret would be to regret living, and I cannot do that. The choices we make are the threads we weave in life's tapestry—for good or ill, it is useless to bemoan the threads once woven. All we can do is learn and pick out the right colours while we live." She stared at her lute. "Kate has asked for a song, but I am afraid I've lost my heart to play tonight." Her sad smile embraced both Kate and Meg. "Forgive me."

Kate came over and took the lute from her aunt's hands. "Let me, then." With effort, she grinned. "You haven't heard my skill with the lute, Aunt Nan. Francis has been a good teacher, and he taught me a song about a lost heart." She smiled at her aunt and Meg. "I believe it is by Sir Thomas."

Aunt Nan and Meg shared a look of amusement.

"I know it well," Aunt Nan said. "Play it for me, Kate. I would like to hear you sing; just to see you make music with my lute will restore my spirits."

At first hesitant, but growing in confidence, Kate plucked the notes of her aunt's lute and sang.

> *Help me to seek!*
> *For I lost it there;*
> *And, if that ye have found it,*
> *ye that be here,*
> *And seek to convey it secretly,*
> *Handle it soft and treat it tenderly,*
> *Or else it will 'plain, and then appear.*
> *But pray restore it mannerly,*
> *Since that I do ask it thus honestly;*
> *For to lose it, it sitteth me near;*
> *Help me to seek!*
> *Alas, and is there no remedy?*
> *But have I thus lost it wilfully?*
> *I twist, it was a thing all too dear*
> *To be bestowed, and wist not where!*
> *It was mine heart! I pray you heartily*
> *Help me to seek!*

23

The final night and no one slept. There was no way to hide from the coming day. Outside, men shouted and tortured wood with saw, hammer and nail. Banging and hammering punctuated and pounded the slow hours to morning. All night long the sounds told Kate they built the scaffold for her aunt's execution.

The other women tried to rest in the antechamber while Kate and Meg stayed with Aunt Nan in her bedchamber. Sitting close together, they talked of small things, but avoided what they would soon face.

When conversation lulled, Aunt Nan at last picked up her lute and played, strumming loved songs for hours. As dawn approached, she lifted her head. "I have a new song, if you would like to hear it." She brushed her fingers against the strings. "I wrote it on the other night I thought my last." Her mouth trembled. "Mayhap, this night, too, will prove not to be my last."

She sang her song, for the first and final time:

> *Oh death rock me asleep,*
> *Bring me on my quiet rest,*
> *Let pass my very guiltless ghost*

Out of my careful breast.
Ring out the doleful knell,
Let its sound my death tell;
For I must die,
There is no remedy,
For now I die...
Defiled is my name full sore
Through cruel spite and false report,
That I may say for evermore,
Farewell to joy, adieu comfort.
For wrongfully you judge of me
Unto my fame a mortal wound,
Say what ye list, it may not be,
Ye seek for that shall not be found.

Aunt Nan always sang beautifully, but never as beautifully as that dark, dreadful night. Like an angel, she sang, pure and heart touching, like one who had already left life behind. Her narrow face tense with thought, she seemed a sprite or spirit flame not of this world.

She still played her lute when Master Kingston and Mathew Parker came with guards lighting the way with torches, their footsteps advancing closer and closer, the bell tolling out the hour for Matins. With the last toll of the bell, a group of men gathered at the open door. Very still, they listened for a time. One guard and then another watched the Queen with faces alight with pity, but also admiration. Usually so stern, even Master Kingston seemed moved. He murmured to Parker, loud enough for Kate to hear.

"I have seen many men and also women executed, and they have been in great sorrow. This lady has much joy in death."

Not answering Kingston, Parker came into the chamber and shook his head. The hopelessness of the good father twisted a knife into Kate's heart. She covered her face, everything in her desiring to scream out, *No!* She should have known. The death of George Boleyn had snapped the last straw of hope for reprieve.

Her courage retreating in a tidal wave of emotion, Kate reminded herself that women in her family faced their fears with bravery. She would swim and not drown. She would survive this awful day. She would survive for her aunt, for her mother, and for Bess, who would soon have no living mother.

Aunt Nan stopped playing and straightened on her stool. The silent men approached. Master Kingston bowed, followed by the priest. "Madam," Kingston said, "your chaplain has come as requested."

Laying down her lute beside her, Aunt Nan rose with a welcoming smile. "That I see, Master Kingston." She held out her hands for Parker to take. "My heart is glad to see you, Matthew. We've much to speak of." She turned back to Kingston. "How many more hours do you make it, good sir?"

He shook his head and straightened his shoulders. "We're been told to make ready by the ninth hour." He swallowed. "Forgive me, I cannot even vouch for that."

Aunt Nan sighed. "It cannot be helped. The good Father will give us solace as we wait." She frowned. "Is Cranmer still coming to give me the Host?"

"Aye, Madam."

"I request a boon of you, Master Kingston. When I receive the Host, pray remain here, too. I wish you to witness my confession so you'll possess no doubt about my innocence and the manner of my death."

He seemed to shutter away his thoughts, but even so, Kingston nodded and bowed. "As you wish, Madam. I leave you now with the good Father. Expect my return at daybreak." He bowed again, exiting from the chamber with the guards.

As if her legs refused to hold her up any longer, Aunt Nan collapsed onto the window-seat. Father Parker stepped towards her. "Your Grace, have you not slept?"

She knotted her hands together on her lap. "Sleep, Matthew? I'll soon have eternity to sleep." She gestured beside her. "Pray, sit. I wish to speak to you."

For all that, she bowed her head and remained silent. He sat, folding his hands in his lap, and waited. As he waited, he turned and smiled at Kate with compassion.

At last, Aunt Nan lifted her head. Wavering candlelight danced shadows upon her hollowed face. "Shall I speak now of my sins, Matthew?"

He stirred uneasily. "Your Grace—"

She smiled slightly. "You have come to see me every day of my imprisonment, and we've been too long friends for you not to call me by my given name on this night of nights. Pray, put away the title. 'Tis worthless now. Call me Anne, or Nan, if you wish; I care not. Do not forget that the King, my husband, has taken back everything." Grief carved into her pale face. "What did George say before his death? 'Trust in God, and not in the vanities of the world.' If only had I done so, I would not be here waiting to die." She licked at the tears running over her trembling mouth. "I brought this on myself, on my brother, on my friends. Too many heads now rot on the gates of London because of me." She bent her head and repeated, "Because of me."

Kate shivered, and not with cold. Five months before, she had arrived in London—it seemed a lifetime ago—a lifetime since she first paid true attention to those very gates, and saw the ravens flocking amongst skulls, gore and blood. She imagined them feasting now on fresh skulls, one the head of her uncle. Already, his beautiful eyes would be gone, gorged out and eaten by scavenging birds.

"Katie. Our Katie. How dare you grow," Uncle George had said to her, welcoming her that first day at court. He had laughed, lifted her in his arms and kissed her. "You make me feel old. Not so long ago, a child, and now—look at you; you're a young woman."

She had made him feel old. She clenched her jaw, fearing any moment her teeth would chatter, and shifted around to Aunt Nan. Her ebony hair fell long and loose, undressed around her shoulders; blue lights gleamed in her tresses whenever she moved. The candlelight showed her clear eyes, wide mouth and firm chin. The last few months had drained her of youth, but these days in the Tower, when the battle for survival finally approached a brutal end and there was nothing left to lose, had seen a return of her moments of true beauty. In the candlelight, she could be mistaken for a girl. Uncle George would never be old, and neither, it seemed, would his sister.

Kate listened as Aunt Nan spoke to her chaplain. She spoke first of the Princess Mary. "On my knees, I begged Lady Kingston to go to her and do as I did to her and beg Mary for her forgiveness of what I brought upon her and her mother." She confessed to ambition and jealousy, the many, many angry words spoken in haste and now regretted. "I brought this on myself," she repeated again to her chaplain.

"But to die the death of a traitor? Do I deserve such a death, my name blackened by lies? Adulteress, foiled murderess, witch they call me. My name is defiled, cruelly and falsely." She licked her lips. "And to die knowing I have brought those I love also to death? To die knowing my daughter will be left motherless before the day is old."

Parker took her hands. "Your sins are shared by many, but none give reason for this end."

Aunt Nan turned towards the window, and Kate turned, too. While still dark, the hour had come when all remained hushed and waited for dawn. She sighed. The last dawn for her aunt.

Her aunt moved restlessly. Shoulders hunched, mouth trembling, she gripped either side of the stone seat. "Can love disappear like this—utterly and without trace?" She rubbed the side of her face. "I did not love the King at first. I refused to listen to his promises. Believe me, Matthew, I sent his gifts back. But then he promised me marriage, a crown..." Staring out into space, she swirled a finger in her loose hair. "I did not know my ambition until then. Six years... six years to be ruled by ambition. Strange, by the time we did marry, I found another passion ruling me." She sighed. "I love Harry. I will die loving him. I cannot believe he has stopped loving me. He swore to love me to his dying day." Pain darkened her face. She whispered, "Perchance my Harry is dead."

Parker leaned back, hands palm-to-palm, fingers steepled under his chin. "Mayhap he is. Since he came close to death earlier this year, I, too, have thought the King a different man. His desire for a son has become all to him. I believe he would do anything to begat his true born prince." He leaned closer to Aunt Nan. "Even murder."

"Even murder," she repeated. Her lips twisted as if she tasted something vile. "Kings do not murder. All that they do is right in God's eyes; my husband told me so."

Parker shook his head. "I would beg to differ, madam."

Aunt Nan rounded on him. "Then you dispute with your King and commit treason." Her face pale with fear, she bent forward. "Be careful of what you say, Matthew. I need you to be careful. Very, very careful. Remember your vow to me: to keep Elizabeth safe and guide her. Help her make not the mistakes of her mother."

"If the good God permits, Nan, I vow I will keep Bess under my watch." He blinked at the window. Moment by moment, the dark sky lightened. "Cranmer will be here soon. Do you wish for time alone in prayer before then?"

Aunt Nan shook her head and picked up her lute. She took his hand, smiling in reassurance. "Nay. I think God will forgive me if I just allow myself the pleasure of staying with those I love these last hours. I shall play and sing a little while I wait for Cranmer to bring the Host."

She played and sang. Dawn broke behind her, its light engulfing her in a net of gold. Birds chirped and twittered their joy and welcome to another day's awakening. Too soon, approaching footsteps echoed outside the chamber. The heavy fall of thudding feet became louder and louder, like the beat of a drum, like the drub of frightened hearts. A march that trampled upon all songs.

24

The scaffold was not yet finished. Aunt Nan received the message that the execution was delayed once more and she would need to wait longer to meet her doom. Master Kingston followed the news. He bowed as she rose from her seat. Rising from the floor, Kate stood beside her aunt, wanting to support her in whatever way she could.

"Mr. Kingston, I hear I shall not die afore noon and I am very sorry therefore, for I thought to be dead by this time and past my pain."

Kingston paled. His mouth moved, but no words came at first. "It should be no pain, or but a little," he blustered, as if she somehow accused him.

Aunt Nan answered with a peal of laughter, bending a little, her hand to her side. "The executioner is very good, I hear..." she put her hands around her throat "...and I have but a little neck."

Kingston bowed and made a hasty retreat.

Kate gathered the garments her aunt had chosen for her execution. A loose robe of dark grey damask with a wide collar of white ermine, a red underskirt—the colour of blood—a small gable, and a white coif to cover her hair. Kate first picked up the coif. Her heart in her throat, Kate stilled and tried to swallow. Only one hour ago, she had combed and plaited her aunt's hair for the last time. For the last time ever.

"Kate," her aunt called. "'Tis time for me to dress."

Kate straightened her shoulders. Picking up everything, she walked back to her aunt, determined to serve her well until the end.

By close to ten, the muted sounds of building ceased and a strange quiet settled outside. Inside, it was time for the last prayers, the last words of comfort, the last farewells. Aunt Nan kissed her ladies, even Lady Boleyn and Mistress Cosyns. Last of all, she took Kate in her arms. "God bless you. I rely on you; do not let Bess forget me." Gently, Aunt Nan lifted her chin with a finger. "I have another boon to ask of you." She took from the top of her clothes chest a large white handkerchief and handed it to Kate. "I beg you, don't let them see my face after ... after I'm dead. Kate, pray use this...." She turned to the nearby altar for a moment. "Do not give my enemies time to gloat and mock, Kate—or point out how I look in death."

The Tower bell tolled out the twelfth hour when they walked into the spring day. Escorted by Father Parker and Master Kingston, Aunt Nan was also guarded front and back. Kate swallowed and raised her face. The sky was blue silk, laced here and there with white cloud. The deep, sweet perfume of flowering red roses wafted in the warm breeze, coming before the rich, heady odour of horse droppings. Flies swarmed and buzzed around. This month of May had given them many days of feasting.

At first, the Queen's apartments hid the scaffold from them, but then it came into view. Aunt Nan stood still, glancing behind her. Kate's heart thumped harder. There could be no turning back, no escape, for her aunt.

Aunt Nan straightened her shoulders and walked forward, every inch the Queen. Assisted by Master Kingston, she made her slow, careful way up the high platform. She paused, turning again to murmur something to Meg, her eyes scanning the huge crowd watching her every movement.

Kate swallowed down her tears. Beauty was always something that came and went for Aunt Nan. She was like the sea. Happy, she shone with bright sunlight. Sad, she could not hide the darkness of her melancholy, and light became night. On this day of all days, she was all beauty, as if she held all the essence of life in her hand.

Coming up behind her, Kate became aware of her heart beating loud in her ears. All of it felt dreamlike. Her desperation made it more and more difficult to breathe. *Mayhap it is...?* She stepped up another step. *Let it be a dream*, she begged God. *Pray, let it be a dream. Let me wake up and find this a dream.*

Grief strangled her almost to suffocation. Each step swirled and crested within her a tide of fear. What if she broke down? What if she failed Aunt Nan? Her courage felt as flimsy as butterfly wings. One touch could break it into nothingness. She licked her dry lips, deafened by the drubbing of her heart.

The French swordsman greeted her aunt. Kate winced. Masked, all in black, he reminded her of a raven, of death soon to come. She clasped her clammy hands together before wiping them on her dress, and steeled herself for what lay ahead.

On the scaffold, Aunt Nan raised her face heavenward, inhaling and exhaling a deep breath. With shining eyes, she smiled at her women. "I am ready. Pray, help me," she said softly.

Meg removed Aunt Nan's damask cloak, revealing the underdress of crimson.

The executioner fell to his knees. "I crave Your Majesty's pardon," he said in French, his voice hinting at his emotion.

The King took from her that title only for death to give it back. Rattled, Kate almost broke down. *God help me. How am I to bear this? How can I?*

"Willingly." Aunt Nan gave him a purse of gold as his payment to ensure a swift and easy death. She looked beyond the crowd. Kate's heart fluttered. Aunt Nan wanted so much to live for her daughter's sake. Even now, pacing over to the rails to make her final speech, she hoped for reprieve.

Aunt Nan leaned towards the crowd and began speaking. At first, her voice was thin and trembling, but soon her words reverberated for all to hear.

"Good Christian people, I come hither to die, for according to the law, and by law, I am judged to die, and therefore will speak nothing against it. I come hither to accuse no man, nor speak anything of that whereof I am accused and condemned to die. But I pray God to save the King and send him long to reign over you, for a gentler nor merciful prince there was never; and to me he was ever a good, a gentle and sovereign lord. If any person will meddle with my cause, I require them to judge the best. And thus I take my leave of the world, and of you all, and I heartily desire you all to pray for me."

As if in answer, the crowd come to witness the death of a woman crowned England's Queen fell to their knees before the scaffold. What remained of her aunt's life could be measured in breaths.

Kate brushed away her tears. Straightening her shoulders, she reminded herself that she was of Aunt Nan's blood. If her aunt could be brave knowing death was seconds away, she could too. As if guessing her thought, Aunt Nan moved closer, touched her arm and tried to smile. Meg smothered a sob, and Aunt Nan's slight smile faltered. She shook her head.

"Pray, just a short time to go," she whispered. "Help me now." She passed to Meg her scarf and the tiny prayer book from her girdle. "Tell Tom," she said quietly, "'tis for remembrance. Pray, make sure he reads my message."

Kate took from Meg a white linen cap and gave it to her aunt. For several heartbeats, Aunt Nan held it in her hands before taking off her coif. Black and glossy, her hair shone with blue lights in the sunlight. There was not one grey hair to be seen. Her aunt covered her hair with the cap.

Meg came over to tie the scarf. Robbed of sight, Aunt Nan raised her arms for balance, straight out in front of her. Kate swallowed at the memory of her doing the same during the Christmas festivities. Then she played a game for laughter. *Now?* She hardly bore to think about now—she only knew it was no game she played. She went to her aunt and took her hand.

"I'm here," Kate said softly. "I'm here." *Dear God—please do not let her know I am weeping.*

The executioner stepped forward, his shadow casting Kate in dimmed light before it fell and shrouded her aunt.

"Madame," he said, "I beg you now to kneel and say your prayers."

Kate and Margaret helped Aunt Nan to the block, holding onto her until she knelt before it. Blindly, fretfully, Aunt Nan straightened her gown and then lifted her arms to the heavens, crying out, "To Jesus Christ I commit my soul! Oh, Lord, have mercy on me. To Christ I commend my soul. Jesus, receive my soul!"

She felt for the block and gripped it tightly. Her beautiful hands held it as if she didn't dare let go.

The French executioner murmured something to his assistant. He reached behind the bale of straw on the stage and passed to the executioner his sword. Kate took in its shine, its beauty—it looked what it was, a perfect instrument of death.

One breath. One breath was all it took. The executioner swung back his sword in one mighty movement. The sword swished through the air, gathering momentum, power, churning up air into a gust of wind. *Whoosh*. The sword sliced through Aunt Nan's slender neck, an awful *crunch* sounding as it rent through flesh and bone. Aunt Nan had been so right. Cutting off her head gave the executioner little trouble. One breath—one breath, the threshold between life and death.

Other sounds, muffled by straw, followed, ones that would wake Kate in the cold sweat of nightmare for the rest of her life. Aunt Nan's head thudded on the scaffold, bounced, rolled. At the same moment, the headless body, spurting blood from the severed neck, fell like a cut down sapling and toppled to the platform.

Blood. Bright red blood everywhere.

Cannons boomed and cracked like thunder. Kate fell to her knees, the straw shifting underneath her. Before her was Aunt Nan's body. She turned the other way and put her hand to her mouth in horror. Her aunt's eyelids and mouth moved as if still alive, trying to say something, the eyes looked straight at Kate. Terror shone from Aunt Nan's eyes before death dulled them forever. Kate's empty stomach heaved.

Close by, Meg tottered like one decrepit. Her control about to snap, Kate lowered her head and prayed. Meg shook her arm. Turning to her, it seemed to Kate she saw her own shock and terror.

"We have work to do," Meg said, swallowing, seemingly unaware of the tears falling down her face. "Pray, pull yourself together." She spoke automatically, as if speaking also to herself. She hurried over to rally the other weeping women.

Time stood still. Kate's world had constricted to the dimensions of this wooden scaffold, this terrible place of living nightmare, soaked in blood. Already, flies buzzed around Aunt Nan's body and head. The other women on the scaffold wailed and wept, but did what was necessary.

The handkerchief. Kate untied it from her girdle. *Do this for me,* her aunt had said. *Do not give my enemies time to gloat and mock.*

Kate knelt, still praying, waving away flies, and gently closed her aunt's eyes. With great care, Kate draped the handkerchief to completely cover her face. Then, her hands on her knees, she bowed her head. *No one can hurt her again. God has her in His care, and she is with her brother now. Love will wash away her last memory of when she was so viciously murdered.*

Aunt Nan's last words came back to her, words of forgiveness. Kate's tears dripped like spots of rain upon the handkerchief. Soaked by blood, it was red and no longer white. Blood seeped into her gown, too.

Meg came back. "No time for prayer, not yet. We must be quick and get Nan to the church. I and the others will carry her body. Do you think you can take her head?" Grey with exhaustion, Meg held out her cloak. "Use this, Kate."

Everything blurred. Kate nodded, taking Meg's cloak. Minute by minute, reality slipped away as she securely wrapped up her aunt's head, her hands becoming wet and bloodied. She stood gingerly, cradling the head as if an infant. Her knees shook, and the world swirled around her. She took one step and then another, refusing to give in. All she could do, she would; she would make certain all was done right by Aunt Nan, her Queen. That she was buried with respect, with dignity.

She glared at the guards and the crowd. If any of the men approached her or dared to lay a hand on Aunt Nan, she would go mad. Turn animal. Snarl at them. Use her teeth to rip out their throats and nails to gore their faces. She wanted to scream, she wanted to weep, but not now, not yet. Not until she was away from this place of death.

Someone moved in the crowd towards the scaffold. *Francis.* Just like her aunt's mouth had moved in death, her mouth was moving now, but no words came. She gathered the bloodied cloak-swaddled head firmer in her arms, and then turned back to him. He tried to mouth something at her, his hand lifted up towards her before gesturing in the direction of the chapel of St. Peter. Realising he wanted to join her there, she shook her head with vehemence, suddenly terrified. *What if he, too, falls foul of this awful day by giving away his allegiance to my aunt? What if the King kills him, too? How could I live then?* She stood there, with her bloody burden, her mouth shaping the words, *Tomorrow. Come to me tomorrow.* Turning away, she tightened the grip on her aunt's head and joined Meg.

The fragrance of bruised, heady rosemary announced the arrival of a hooded woman, followed by another, more bowed than the first, carrying bundles of herbs. A sudden ray of daylight revealed them both.

"Mother! Grandmother!" Kate ran into the arms of her mother. Once there, she wept. Her sobs rent the silence of the chapel, scarring time itself.

A hand rested on her shoulder. Kate wiped her face and half turned in her mother's arms to see her stepfather. He kissed her with compassion. "'Our Kate—now 'tis time for you to come home."

But first there were duties to do. Father Thirlwall, another one of her aunt's loyal chaplains, led the prayers for Aunt Nan's soul. They buried her close to her brother. There had been no true coffin for her mangled remains, rather an arrow chest found for that purpose. The rosemary bought by Mary Stafford and her mother now blanketed under and over the body.

Aunt Nan safely interred, Kate sat with her sorrowing mother and grandmother while her stepfather spoke quietly to the priest. The cresting tide of grief made her yearn for her brother, and then gave her another reason for deep pain. *Poor Harry! How hard it must be for him, forced to remain with the King and his court. Pray God, Madge comforts him.*

She plucked at her gown. Much of it was stiff with drying blood—the smell left her nauseous. But she felt no urge to change her clothes. She wore a banner of accusation. Did her mother and grandmother feel the same? Like her dead aunt, they were women who insisted on cleanliness, but both had said nothing about changing out of her bloody clothes.

Her grandmother stirred beside her and wiped her tear-wet face. "'Tis wrong that I must leave them here when they should be at rest with their kin."

Mary put her arm around her mother. "Perchance in the future, the King will soften his heart and give us permission to do so." She smiled slightly. "When he has a right-born son, I will write to Cromwell and beg him to speak on our behalf."

Grandmother Boleyn sighed again. "Jane Seymour may be more fortunate than my daughters, but my heart tells me she, too, will regret her ambition to be our King's new Queen."

"Aye. What's made in blood ends in blood, more often than not. My poor sister found that out in the end."

Kate found her mother's eyes upon her. "Can you make ready to come back with us by the morrow? Our horses are at an inn not too far from here. I do not think I could bear to stay in this place more than one night, and even that is too long for me."

Kate swallowed. "Aye, mother, I can make ready. But I will not be home for long."

Her mother frowned. "You speak of Knollys child? I have written to his father and given my approval of a betrothal, but have told him I do not wish for your marriage to take place until you are sixteen. Believe me, fourteen is too young for a girl to wed."

Kate smiled sadly at her mother. The news that she was now truly betrothed to Francis should have been reason for celebration, but it had come on this day of days. Once again, she tasted the bittersweet of life. "I am content, Mother, to wait for marriage." She swallowed. "I believe Francis will be, too. He was loyal to Aunt Nan and will understand what I must do now."

"Do now?" Her mother blinked with confusion. "What must you do now?"

Kate straightened and lifted her chin. "I have another promise to keep. I'll come home for a time, but only for as long as it takes for me to get the King's permission to be with Elizabeth."

Not only did her mother turn to her, but her grandmother, too. Her grandmother reached for Kate's hand and held it.

Mary Stafford half-hooded her eyes, and Kate's grief surged up, choking her. Aunt Nan had always done likewise when she thought deeply or wanted to hide her thoughts. *Did she do this, too?* She hoped so.

"Do you think he will?" her mother asked at last.

A short time ago, when she had spoken to him, he could not hide his guilt and torment. He seemed a man going under, drowning—a man now a wisp, a ghost, closing his heart to what he once loved, choosing kingship for once and for all. But there was also in his eyes the panic of one who begged to be saved, and to be forgiven. She nodded. "He will give me permission. 'Tis a debt he must pay to the dead."

With her mother's help, Kate packed her clothes chests. They were almost finished when Lady Shelton rushed into the chamber. Kate remembered how Lady Shelton disliked the Queen. Kate's first instinct was to greet her angrily, but then something crumbled inside. *Do I want this burden of hate?* If she did not let it go now, she would carry it all the days of her life. She shut her eyes and swallowed before she spoke. "My lady, I thought you were at Hatfield with the Princess Elizabeth."

Lady Shelton started. "You must call her the Lady Elizabeth now, Kate. I brought the child back to gather all her belongings. I could not leave her at Hatfield, not at this time. I could trust none not to blab out about her mother."

Too tired to make sense of Lady Shelton's apparent distress, Kate stood by her mother and gazed aside at her. Mary Stafford shrugged, clearly bemused, too. Something— or someone—had shaken Shelton out of her usual calm composure. Mary Stafford searched around Lady Shelton. "Then where is the child? Where's my niece?"

Lady Shelton raised her hand to her ashen face. "I am a fool. I thought she was safe with Blanche Parry, but the girl let her get away from her. I could not help it, Mary, that she followed me."

"Followed you? Followed you where?" Mary Stafford frowned in confusion.

"Aye, she followed me." Lady Shelton put her hand to her face, as if ready to weep. "Even Blanche is no help. The child screams every time we try to pick her up. It was like a prayer answered when Madge told me your daughter was back." She turned to Kate. "Pray help me. The King will never forgive me if he knows I brought Bess to Greenwich without his permission."

Kate didn't have to hear any more. She didn't even have to ask where Bess was. She lifted her skirts and raced past her mother and Lady Shelton, heading straight to her aunt's unguarded, open chamber. Inside, Bess sat enthroned in her mother's chair as Blanche, her nurse, begged her to come with her.

317

Forcing herself not to hurry, Kate stepped nearer to her little cousin. She dropped to her knees by the chair. "Bess, what do you do here?"

She could have bitten off her tongue. Miserable and scolding herself for her stupidity, she felt no surprise when Bess answered, "Waiting for Mama."

Over Bess's head, Kate met Blanche's shining eyes. With a muffled cry, the nursemaid brought her hands to her face before hurrying away from the room.

Now alone with Bess, Kate blinked and swallowed. She took deep breaths, regaining her composure.

Bess tugged at her. "Katie, where's my mama?"

Kate stood and gestured to the chair. "Pray, may I sit next to you, Bess? I'm very tired."

Bess moved to make space. "Is Katie sick?"

Shaking her head, Kate sat and put her arm around Bess. "No, just tired." Kate swallowed. "Bess, you know I will never tell you lies."

Bess nodded and rested against Kate's shoulder. "Mama told me Katie does not lie."

Controlling her sudden surge of grief, she took yet another deep breath. "Bess, I cannot tell you where your mama is. The King, your father, would be very angry if I did that." She tightened her hold on her cousin. "You know we must never disobey the King."

Her face white and serious, Bess nodded. "Mama told me, too."

Kate raised her face, hoping Bess didn't notice her tears. "Your mama asked me to take care of you. Is that all right with you? After I go home to see my little brother and sister, may I come and stay with you?"

Wiggling beside her in excitement, Bess grinned. "Katie will play with me?"

With effort, she smiled back at her cousin. "Aye, I will be yours to command."

What else could she safely say to her cousin? She gazed around the room until her eyes came to the Queen Esther tapestry. Likely, it would soon be taken down. She pulled Bess closer to her. "Before we go and find Lady Shelton, shall I tell you a story?"

"Like Mama?"

Kate tried another smile. *God, pray help me! One more word may push me over the edge.* But then, like an answer to her prayer, she remembered her aunt. She could not fail, not in this, her last duty to Aunt Nan. For the rest of her life, she would have her aunt's example to help her, guide her and remind her how to live.

"I'll try—I'll try my best," she said at last, feeling she spoke not only to Bess, but also to a woman who would never be dead to her. A woman who had shown her how to live, and how to die.

Kate pointed to the tapestry. "Do you remember the name of that Queen?"

"Mama told me. She's Esther. Mama said I wasn't old enough for her story. Am I old enough now, Katie?"

"Aye, I think so."

"Mama said she was a good Queen."

"Aye, a good Queen."

"Like my mama?"

"Just like your mama."

THE END

Historical personages in
The Light in the Labyrinth.

Henry VIII—Born 28 June, 1491, died 28 January, 1547. The second son of Henry VII, he ascended the throne in 1509.

Katherine of Aragon—Born 16 December, 1485, died 7 January, 1536. She was Henry VIII's first Queen and mother of Mary, his eldest daughter. In many hearts, Anne Boleyn could never replace Katherine as England's Queen.

Anne Boleyn—Birth year is unknown, but put forward as early as 1501 and as late as 1507. Henry VIII's second wife and mother of Elizabeth Tudor. Anne was executed 19 May, 1536.

Mary Boleyn—Birth year also unknown. I believe she was older than her sister Anne, perhaps born 1501. Married first to William Carey and then to William Stafford. Mary died 19 July, 1543.

Margaret Douglas—Born 8 October, 1515, died 7 March, 1578. The daughter of Margaret Tudor, elder sister of Henry VIII.

Mary Rose Tudor—Born 18 March, 1496, died 25 June, 1533. She was married to Louis XII at eighteen and danced him to the grave. After the King's death, she secretly married Charles Brandon, a close friend of Henry VIII. The King, having lost a bargaining pawn by his sister's marriage to Brandon, punished them by fining them heavily for marrying without his approval. But the King's displeasure was felt only in money terms. Not long after Mary's marriage, the King created Brandon, Duke of Suffolk. A widow of a French King, Mary was known at her brother's court as The White Queen.

Mary Tudor—Born 18 February, 1516, died 17 November, 1558. The only surviving child of Henry VIII and Katherine of Aragon, she became Queen in 1553.

Elizabeth Tudor—Born 7 September, 1533, died 24 March, 1603. Ascended England's throne 17 November, 1558 and was Queen of England for over forty-four years. She gave her name to an age.

C/Katherine Carey—Birth year unknown, died 15 January, 1568. Daughter of Mary Boleyn and supposedly William Carey. But was she the illegitimate daughter of Henry VIII? My research makes me think so and led to the writing of this novel.

Henry Carey—Born c. 1524, died in 1596. The son of Mary Boleyn and supposedly William Carey. I also believe him to be the illegitimate son of Henry VIII.

Katherine Willoughby—Born 22 March, 1519, died 19 September, 1580. Wed to Charles Brandon at fourteen after the death of Mary Tudor, and thus Duchess of Suffolk. She was renowned for her intelligence, sharp wit and strong religious beliefs.

Francis Knollys—Born c. 1514, died 1596. Husband of Catherine Carey.

Thomas Cromwell—Born c. 1485, executed 28 July, 1540. A brilliant, self-made man, Cromwell was a ruthless politician who worked tirelessly for Henry VIII. Charming and generous to his friends, to his enemies he would do whatever was necessary to bring them down.

Thomas Cramner— Born 2 July, 1489, died 21 March, 1556. A religious leader who loyally served both Henry VIII and Anne Boleyn. Instrumental in helping the King achieve the annulment of his first marriage to Katherine of Aragon, he was also one of the prime movers behind the English reformation. A man of true faith working tirelessly for his church and beliefs, yet he also had feet of clay. His finest moment was his martyrdom, which saw him first try to save his life, but then chose to die for his beliefs.

Mary Howard, Duchess of Richmond—Born 1519, died 7 December, 1557. The wife of Henry VIII's bastard son Henry Fitzroy and a very strong personality in her own right. Was she a poet like her brother Henry, Earl of Surrey? I would like to think so.

Margaret (Madge) and Mary Shelton—Born 1510/15, died 1570/71. There is a lot of confusion about these two women, and it is possible that they are one and the same. But I wonder if these two women were not only sisters, but also twins? That might explain the confusion. Madge has been identified as a mistress of Henry VIII and it is possible this relationship came about as part of the faction war between the Boleyns and Seymours.

ENTERING THE LABYRINTH:
Writing *The Light in the Labyrinth*

"The frontiers of a book are never clear-cut: beyond the title, the first lines, and the last full-stop, beyond its internal configuration and its autonomous form, it is caught up in a system of references to other books, other texts, other sentences: it is a node within a network."
— Foucault, quoted in Hutcheon, 1989

All novels begin with an idea, a response to living life. The idea for my first published novel was seeded when, as a teenager, I first read one of Sir Thomas Wyatt's poems, the poem I will always think of as *Dear Heart, How Like You This?* Many years went by before I was brave enough to marry this poem with my heart and mind to discover it enabled me to tell Anne Boleyn's story through the voice of Sir Thomas Wyatt, which ended up becoming my first Tudor novel.

The idea for *The Light in the Labyrinth*, my first young adult Tudor novel, arrived close to a decade after the publication of that novel. In late December 2008, one of my writing friends asked me to accompany her to the Melbourne *Short and Sweet Festival*, a ten-minute play competition. We spent an inspiring afternoon watching the performances of the ten finalists, so inspired that we challenged ourselves to write our own ten-minute plays and see if we could write something good enough to enter into the 2009 *Short and Sweet Festival*. I wanted to do it because I hadn't written a play since high school—too long ago to count. *Smile*. Since taking up the calling of a serious writer, I am very prepared to push myself out of my comfort zone because I want to grow as a writer. *Sigh*. Signing up for a PhD in Writing provides a perfect example of how willing I am to suffer for my craft.

But back to my story. Weeks went by and I realised my first idea for a funny play was proving not funny at all, and I had to face the fact that writing comedy is something I still needed to conquer. My summer holidays fast disappearing on me, I tried to think of another idea for a play; I picked up a copy of my novel *Dear Heart, How Like You This?* and pondered once more the beautiful painting used as its cover. Edouard Cibot's *Anne Boleyn in the Tower* (painted in 1835) helped to inspire my first novel; now it inspired me anew.

I feel absolutely certain that the weeping woman in the background is the artist's depiction of Anne Boleyn. But who was the girl in the foreground—the girl so desolate, so still with despair, that she can only hold the hand of the older woman?

That summer day, my years of research ignited my imagination and I asked myself the question asked by all fiction writers: What if? What if, I asked myself, the girl depicted Anne Boleyn's teenage niece, Katherine Carey?

I mulled over what I knew about Katherine Carey. During my research about Anne Boleyn, I had also been tantalised by tidbits of information regarding Kate. A number of historians suggest she may have accompanied her aunt to the Tower. They also suggested she stayed with her during the long nineteen days of her imprisonment and witnessed her death. But most historians generally put forward the year 1524 for Katherine's birth, some even claim as late as 1527. If one accepted 1524, that means she was no more than twelve at the time of Anne Boleyn's execution.

In the past I asked myself: would Anne ask an untried twelve-year-old to support her on this dreadful day? A girl she would have to trust to keep calm on the scaffold and help deal with her decapitated body afterwards? I could not give it credence. Even sixty-seven years in the future, a thirteen-year-old was *"held too young"* to sit by the body of Elizabeth I during the nights and days of *Watching over the Dead* (Cressy 1997, p. 428).

I also asked myself one further question: Would this be Anne Boleyn's desire, that her twelve-year-old niece accompany her to the scaffold and witness her death? No, I thought. Anne Boleyn would have chosen only witnesses of proven maturity; witnesses who were not only capable of speaking of her end but also understood their duty to bear witness to her "good death."

I have no doubt that Anne would have been utterly determined to make *a good death*. Her culture believed the innocent died well, not the guilty. By achieving *a good death*, she left behind a legacy of doubt about her guilt. Considering how important these witnesses were to her, choosing a twelve-year-old to number amongst them, a girl who might break under the strain of watching her aunt's final moments and also possibly undermine Anne's fortitude to achieve a good death, made no sense to me.

Then I read Varlow's "Sir Francis Knollys's Latin

dictionary: New evidence for Katherine Carey." This article added more weight to the uncertainty of Katherine's birth year. An argument for a fourteen-year-old Kate, a girl mature enough to be with her aunt on the last day of her life, strengthened—enough for me to imagine her with her aunt on Anne's final night in my play *Before Dawn Breaks*.

My play first gave Kate a voice, but she wouldn't leave my imagination. Further tugged by what I already knew, I wanted to know more. I asked myself, could she be a good subject for my next historical novel? A character I could construct through novel writing and, by doing so, would also help me understand and gain meaning about life? For writing has always been one of the ways I achieve growth as a human being. I want to build a bridge of empathy between my text and my reader, but more than that; my own empathy grows by building that bridge.

My next step was to study the portraits of Katherine Carey. Kate's friendly face made it easy to imagine why Anne would have wanted her with her in the Tower, and until the very end.

Until the end.... I thought about that. Anne Boleyn's witnesses also had the duty to oversee proper burial of her remains. Religion narrates the context of the Tudor period; the majority of men and women whole-heartedly believed in the resurrection of *bodies* on Judgement Day. Thus, it was very important to them that all body parts be buried together, for the "bodies of the faithful shall be 'quickened and raised up, their souls restored to them again'" (Cressy 1997, p. 385).

Who took up these final duties of caring for Anne Boleyn's body? While history does not tell us their names, we can easily guess their gender. Women, just as they gathered together to bring life into the world, prepared the dead for burial. As also in childbirth, the women who took on these duties were, in most cases, kin or close friends of the dead. If Kate had been there for her aunt's death, then it follows she was also one of those committed to care for Anne's body afterwards.

My research for my first published novel, *Dear Heart, How Like You This?*, concentrated only on what was necessary for the point of view of my character Sir Thomas Wyatt. Now, thinking about Kate, I could not remember reading a detailed account of what happened to Anne Boleyn's body afterwards—besides noting the fact that they were forced to use an empty arrow box for her interment because no one had readied a proper coffin. *Did they expect the King to send a last minute reprieve?* Wondering about that, I also reminded myself that their lack of preparation could be easily explained: no one had ever written before the script for the execution of a crowned queen of England.

I also wondered who provided the necessary burial winding cloth. Man or woman, in this time and place, to be buried *unclothed* was to be treated like a beast (Cressy 1997, p. 430). I rechecked two biographies about Anne Boleyn: Denny (2007, p. 315) and Ives (2004, p. 359); both provided identical accounts. One of her ladies covered and then carried her head while the other women wrapped her body. Unaided, they carried her remains to St Peter ad Vincula. Once in the chapel, they removed Anne's blood-soaked clothes and placed her in an emptied arrow box. More and more, my imagination placed my Kate in the chapel. My imagination painted her as a grief stricken young girl who now helped ready her aunt for burial.

Hoping to find out more, I soon added another book to my Tudor library: Geoffrey Abbott's *Severed Heads, British Beheadings through Ages*. Abbot (p. 42) includes the account of the historian Crispin, who lived during these times. Crispin describes the understandable anguish of Anne's women, bracing themselves for the duty of carrying her body from the scaffold for burial. One of Anne Boleyn's chaplains, Father Thirlwall, blessed Anne's makeshift coffin before it was interred in the vault near the altar. Already in this vault lay the remains of Anne Boleyn's brother, George (Abbot 2003, p. 43).

They interred her with the brother she supposedly committed incest with? Why? The more I thought about that, the more it felt an act of appeasement.

Katherine Carey presented, I thought, the perfect voice for the Young Adult historical novel I wanted to write, a vehicle I also hoped, as a writer, would help me reach a better understanding as to why Henry VIII chose to bloody his hands with the death of Anne Boleyn through revisiting the last months of her life. But of course it is more than this. My concerns about Kate Carey's age were at last put to rest through thorough research, *The Light in the Labyrinth*, also my PhD artefact, became a story of a young girl forced to grow up fast in the adult world ruled over by Henry VIII.

This essay was first published at THE HISTORICAL NOVEL SOCIETY Blog (Sydney Chapter):

http://hnssydney.blogspot.com.au/2013/12/entering-labyrinth-writing-light-in.html?spref=fb

References

Abbott, G. 2003 *Severed Heads: British Beheadings through the Ages.* London, Carlton Publishing Group.

Cressy, D. 1997. *Birth, Marriage, And Death: Ritual, Religion, and the Life-Cycle in Tudor and Stuart England.* Oxford [Eng.]; New York, Oxford University Press.

Denny, J. 2007. *Anne Boleyn: A New Life of England's Tragic Queen.* Cambridge, MA, Da Capo Press.

Dunn, W. J. 2002. *Dear Heart, How Like You This?* Yarnell, AZ, Metropolis Ink.

Hutcheon, L. 1989. *Historiographic Metafiction.* https://tspace.library.utoronto.ca/bitstream/1807/10252/1/TSpace0167.pdf (accessed 29/07/09).

Ives, E. W. 2004. *The Life and Death of Anne Boleyn: "The Most Happy".* Malden, MA, Blackwell Pub.

Varlow, S. 2007. "Sir Francis Knollys's Latin dictionary: New evidence for Katherine Carey." Historical Research 80 (209): 315–323.

Bibliography

Abbott, G. 2003. *Severed Heads: British Beheadings Through the Ages*. London, Carlton Publishing Group.

Bailey, K. 1998. *The Coronation of Anne Boleyn*. British Heritage; **19**(1): 4.

Baron, H. 1994. *Mary (Howard) Fitzroy's Hand in the Devonshire Manuscript*. Review of English Studies: A Quarterly Journal of English Literature and the English Language. 45 p. 332.

Bell, S. G. 2004. *The Lost Tapestries of the City of Ladies: Christine de Pizan's Renaissance Legacy*. University of California Press.

Bruce, M. L. 1972. *Anne Boleyn*. London, Collins.

Boethius and Watts, V.E. 1999. *The Consolation of Philosophy*. London; New York, Penguin Books

Carley, J. P. 2004. *The Books of King Henry VIII and His Wives*. London, British Library.

Chapman, H. W. 1974. *Anne Boleyn*. London, J. Cape.

Cressy, D. 1997. *Birth, marriage, and death: ritual, religion, and the life-cycle in Tudor and Stuart England*. Oxford [Eng.]; New York, Oxford University Press.

De Lorris, G. 1962. *Romance of the Rose*. Plume.

Acknowledgments

I love writing acknowledgment pages because they give me the opportunity to thank all people important in my writing journey. This novel gives me reason to thank many people—and I really don't know where to start, except to say that every person mentioned deserves my sincere and deepest gratitude.

My first thanks must go not to a person, but an institution. I will always be indebted to Swinburne University for giving me the opportunity to devote more of my life to the calling that comes from my heart. Swinburne University provided me with two wonderful and generous supervisors, Professor Josie Arnold and Dr. Martin Andrew, to act as my critical friends, as well as a third supervisor to keep me on track in my last year: Dr. Julian Novitz. Dr. Carolyn Beasley also encouraged and supported me every step of the way to completing my novel and PhD. Thank you all.

Whilst a scholarship-supported PhD by artefact and exegesis entails a lot of academic study, it also provided the financial support necessary for the writing of this novel. This included financing a mentor-supported week at Varuna, The Writers' House. My mentor was author Stephen Measday. He arrived on my first full day at Varuna with the folder of my manuscript under his arm, shook my hand, and said, "I like this work."

Of course, it is never as simple as that when it comes to critical friendship. When we sat down at the table, he opened the folder. Seeing all the yellow stickers on pages and pages of my work, I gulped back an "Oh, my!" But it was an "Oh, my" in a very, very good way. His feedback was just what I needed to move forward with my new novel. Thank you, Stephen.

Writers need people to believe in their writing. I'm so fortunate there, too. My dear mate Glenice Whitting, author of the award winning *Pickle to Pie*, has *always* believed in this book. She has seen it rough and unpolished, yet knew exactly the right words to keep me at it.

Nerina Jones and Lydia Fuscko also read this work in its early life. Nerina offered her usual brilliant insights. She encouraged, gently steered and nurtured me as only the best editors can do, as well as acting as my driver many times and accompanying me on annual writing retreats.

Lydia, understanding I have a hobbit love of little gifts, sent me soft toys, jewelled golden frogs, polished stones, good luck charms—the list goes on and go. My sister Karen asked, watching me open yet another package from Lydia, "Aren't you the one supposed to be sending gifts when someone takes the time to read an early draft of your work?" Yes, I believe so. No wonder then I was so overcome by Lydia's thoughtfulness and generosity.

Another generous soul and important, talented member of this very special fellowship is Rachel Le Rossignol. Rachel was always there to listen to me moan and groan about the difficulty of climbing my PhD mountain, but also, after Metropolis Ink accepted it for publication, acted as one of the important editors of this work. Thank you, Rachel! Any mistakes are now purely my own responsibility.

Then there are my other great mates—Sandra Worth and Cindy Vallar. All wonderful historical authors in their own right, yet always so generous with the time and encouragement they gave in my quest to finish this novel.

My long time friend Cindy Vallar once again gave my work the benefit of her red pen and her talents as a gifted editor. She lifted it to a point I just wanted to polish the novel more and more.

I thank Karina Machado and her sister Natalie Grueninger for their treasured friendship, wonderful support and encouragement. Karina deserves a special *thank you* for her honesty as one of my critical friends for this work.

My friend Valerie is owed my immense gratitude for her London hospitality, not forgetting taking me on extraordinary Tudor adventures.

Authors Barbara Kyle, Kristie Dean Davis and Pauline Montagna I also wish to thank for their support and encouragement.

And thank you Paula Armstrong for not only believing in me but also for producing the Eltham Little Theatre Quickie competition. This competition gave me one of my greatest writing thrills when I saw my first ten-minute play performed as one the ten finalists, the play that initially gave me Kate's voice and set my feet upon the road to writing this novel.

I thank Kurt Florman for his precious friendship, as well as being the publisher who has always believed in me, and David Major who always does a wonderful job with novel layout and cover design.

How I treasure all these friends. I feel a lump in my throat just thinking of how each of you always believed in me. One new friend I must mention: Dr. Flavia Adriana Andrade— who not only gave me the joy of hosting a fellow Anne Boleyn devotee during Christmas 2013, but the thrill of knowing my first novel spoke loud enough to a reader to be included in her PhD.

I also wish to express my deepest gratitude to Tony Thomas and Maurice Drage for their delightful company and hospitality, which included a private tour of St. Andrew, Rochford's Parish Church, a church once well-known to the Boleyn family.

Of course, I thank my family. They put up with a great deal because of my writing obsession. I just want them to know they are everything to me. While writing gives me a voice to speak to others, my family is the core of my existence.

Talking of family—I must give overdue thanks to my cousin Donna, her husband, Christopher, and their children, Brittany and Charlie. Donna and crew hosted my son and me for ten days in England. They took us for a Tudor tour—and they don't even share my Tudor obsession.

Alan Dunn also treated us by organising, through his generous friend *Beefeater Tom*, a special tour of the Tower of London. Thank you all.

I also thank David Foley, my school principal at Eltham North Primary, who kindly allowed me to take months of leave from my regular teacher duties, although I couldn't stay away from my writing extension class. My students' passion and desire to learn gives me hope for the future and inspiration for every day of my life.

I am a fortunate woman.

Wendy J. Dunn